Their friendship was bitterly shattered years ago.
Now they're brought together again—
by murder. . . .

UNTIL PROVEN GUILTY

Praise for the most riveting
courtroom drama of the year . . .

"STREAM HAS . . . DELIVERED A SMASHING COURT-
ROOM NOVEL . . .
illuminating the perils of taking on the defense of one to
whom counsel has an emotional relationship. The
novel's plot will keep the reader riveted, ever looking for
a 'break' point to freshen the drink and never finding one.
A must!"   —F. LEE BAILEY

"FASCINATING AND DRAMATIC!"   —*Macon Beacon*

"ENTERTAINING . . . IMPRESSIVE . . . Arnold C. Stream
handles his complex plot so dexterously that he may be
tempted to have two careers in the future.
Read his book!"
—*John Barkham Reviews*

"AN ENTERTAINING NOVEL, one that explicates the
contradictory bonds of friendship and love."
—*Deltona Enterprise*

"A COURTROOM DRAMA IN THE GENRE OF
PRESUMED INNOCENT . . .
The court case is brilliantly delineated."
—*Glen Cove Record-Post*

UNTIL PROVEN GUILTY

Arnold C. Stream

BERKLEY BOOKS, NEW YORK

"It is no great wonder in long
process of time, while fortune
takes her course hither and
thither, numerous coincidences
should spontaneously occur."

Plutarch said it a couple of thousand years ago. Thus, while Florida is real, all else is fiction. The people who march across the pages—Tommy and Felix most of all—never existed. And none of the events ever occurred in my experience. Any perceived resemblance to persons or events is a "spontaneous occurrence."

This Berkley book contains the complete text
of the original hardcover edition. It has been
completely reset in a typeface designed for easy
reading and was printed from new film.

UNTIL PROVEN GUILTY

A Berkley Book / published by arrangement with
Scarborough House, Publishers

PRINTING HISTORY
Scarborough House edition published 1991
Berkley edition / August 1992

ISBN: 0-425-13373-7

A BERKLEY BOOK® TM 757,375
Berkley Books are published by The Berkley Publishing Group,
200 Madison Avenue, New York, New York 10016.
The name "Berkley" and the "B" logo
are trademarks belonging to Berkley Publishing Corporation.

PRINTED IN THE UNITED STATES OF AMERICA

10 9 8 7 6 5 4 3 2 1

To Jane and Abigail,
or *vice versa*

And again and always,
to my wife, Barbara

Acknowledgments

Thanks are due to a doctor who prefers to remain nameless for guiding me along the wondrous paths of forensic medicine to some understanding of blood and its detection. If there are errors, they are mine. The indefatiguable efforts of Deborah L. Kircher, who typed draft after draft during the gestation period, call for a special salute.

"We are apt to shut our eyes against a painful truth, and listen to the song of that siren till she transforms us into beasts."

—PATRICK HENRY

UNTIL PROVEN GUILTY

Tommy

1

When I first caught sight of it through the morning haze, I thought maybe it was a big white bird skimming over the surface of the sea. But as the motor launch I was riding in got closer, I recognized that it was the yacht, and a big one at that. I glanced over at my pilot, a dark-skinned South American with an angular face running to fat. He grinned at me through his great mustache, authentic Fu Manchu, and pointed a hairy arm at the distant object. I couldn't make out what he was saying because his voice was drowned in the engine's roar.

I put aside thinking about the explanation I would have to give when I got back to my law office in New York as to why I had walked out yesterday afternoon without even telling my partner, Amos Stern, where I was going, and why the next morning at seven o'clock I was cutting through the waters off of Marathon, and heading toward a boat with its sea anchor dropped three miles out in the Atlantic. I could not fully understand why I had so readily responded to a telephone call from a girl—now a woman—whom I hadn't seen or spoken to in fifteen years, when she asked me—begged me, really—to come down because Felix was in trouble. Again.

I had been able to catch an afternoon flight to Miami. When I got there, too tired to drive, I hired someone to take me down to Key West. I arrived just as night was falling and checked into a small hotel where I had stayed before, when I was on a fishing junket. The next morning I took a taxi back to Marathon to make my rendezvous out in the ocean.

In a few minutes I could read the name on the prow: PEGASUS, a 45-foot ChrisCraft cruiser. A Jacob's ladder had been thrown over the side by a blond Venus wearing nothing but the lower part of a bikini, and who leaned as far over the edge of the deck as she dared.

As I clambered onto the deck, I tried to keep my eyes on her face but they had a will of their own. Her body was an even brown, unmarked except for a tiny cicatrix on her left shoulder, which could have been caused by the nick of an épée in a duel, but probably had a more commonplace explanation, such as falling off a bike when she was a kid. Unmindful of her state, she spoke to me in strident tones.

"Tommy, darling! My God, am I glad to see you! You haven't changed at all! How absolutely wonderful of you to come down! I can't tell you how much I appreciate it."

And then she leaned over and kissed me on the mouth. All I could manage was a weak smile with wonderment in my eyes.

"Don't you recognize me? Silly, I'm Chris. Christine! Say something!"

I found my voice somewhere on the deck. "For Crissake, Chris, I haven't seen you in over fifteen years. You were a sixteen-year-old kid then." That was all I could manage as she stood back, her arms crossed beneath her breasts.

Then I heard feet on the steps from the hold, and onto the deck came two men and two women. The men wore swimming trunks, the women had on robes. One of the women, the older of the two, frowned at Christine.

"Chris, please go downstairs and put something on."

"Sun cream?" asked Venus sweetly.

"Christine!" The voice of piqued authority. Venus rose and padded off.

The woman who had spoken walked over to me. She was tall, taller even than the men, who lingered behind her.

I took a step toward her and extended my hand, which she accepted as though it had been an obeisance. I nearly curtsied. "My name is Tom Attleboro. Chris—Christine—asked me to come down. I don't know whether she told you why. I don't really know too much myself yet." I smiled politely, but it was a waste of time.

"I'm Rose Crystal," she said, tugging at the belt to her purple robe. Pointing to a slim, middle-aged man with a receding hairline and a puckered expression that suggested a lemon habit, she said, "That's my husband Harry." Harry considered the distant horizon.

Nodding her head at the other couple, "Fred and Ellen Bannock." The couple managed a faint smile.

"This is my boat," she said distinctly, lest I think it was mine. Then with sudden graciousness: "Come inside and let me get you something cool to drink."

The room was furnished in satin-soft tan leather. The walls were paneled. Instead of the usual wall decorations of stuffed fish and second-rate pictures of ships and sailboats, the Crystals had hung handsome oils. I spotted what looked like a Kandinsky and a Utrillo.

As Rose Crystal stalked into the room, she called out a name in a low voice which nonetheless carried across the room. A curly-headed boy leaned out of the galley at the far end. Rose asked him to bring some iced tea. Hers was a trained voice—and in that moment I knew who Rose Crystal was.

My hostess had launched a promising career on the American stage. Her stage name had been Flora Cristal. Her career had come to an abrupt halt when she became the subject of a bruising series of newspaper articles concerning a bizarre death.

Two or three years back, she and her husband had been hosting a party on a yacht such as this one—maybe, in fact, this very one. Early on Sunday morning, one of their guests was spotted in the water by a Coast Guard cutter that had been circling around the yacht, moored outside the two-mile limit. He was dead when he was fished out of the sea. The autopsy report certified that death was due to drowning; but so much cocaine had been found in his system that he should have gone up, not down. In fact, he may have tried to do exactly that, for colleagues confirmed that he couldn't swim.

Flora Cristal's career was irreversibly tainted. She retired to the couple's home in Carmel, diverting her energies to art collecting and running a very posh gallery.

The party settled into seats in the cabin. The windows were wide open and the fresh sea breeze swept with refreshing coolness in the port side and out the starboard. Rose Crystal sat in a fan-backed chair, her purple robe draped theatrically over its rounded sides. Harry Crystal sat near her in a club chair. The Bannocks were wedged side by side on a two-seater couch edged with brass studs.

There was tension in the air. Conversation lagged, and the cabin boy walked in with the iced tea and a tray of cookies. Ellen Bannock kept glancing nervously at Rose Crystal. Mr.

Bannock drummed a silent tattoo on a bulging stomach with two of his interlaced fingers. It was clear that I was interfering with *something*. I finally figured it out. The upholstery in the cabin gave off a faint but unmistakable scent of sweet corn silk. In short, *cannabis* was making its presence known. Rose was at it again, I decided.

Christine chose that moment to make her reappearance, wearing a pair of white silk slacks and a matching silk blouse. She had arranged her hair in a golden braid, and she wore a long chain from which hung an oriental ivory espalier of a ruby-eyed cat.

Rose Crystal's nostrils flared. No love lost there, I thought. Harry was sitting bolt upright, his lips sucking in and out, his eyes riveted on the thing of beauty, which, it occurred to me, might already have begun to be his joy forever.

I turned toward Rose Crystal. "Is there somewhere I can speak privately with Chris?" She led us forward to an ash wood cocktail lounge with curving picture windows on three sides allowing an unfettered view over the prow of the yacht and to both sides. We sat down facing each other at a small table. Chris's eyes were round with apprehension.

Chris had still been a gawky teenager the last time I saw her. Now, suddenly age somehow didn't matter. She was a beautiful woman. I watched the tell-tale flicker of her pulse in the triangular niche below her throat. The Book of Revelations was about to open.

2

Christine took a moment to collect her thoughts, fussing with the corner of a painted fingernail. I decided to lead off.

"When you called me yesterday from this boat, you said that Felix was in big trouble but that you couldn't give me details over a radiophone. I'll tell the truth right off, Chris. If you hadn't mentioned that Lorna was missing, I wouldn't have come down, and you know it. Felix is part of my past, not my present."

Chris ignored my speech. I don't believe she even listened. She clasped her hands on the table and began to speak.

"My answering service in West Palm Beach got a call early—very early—yesterday morning. The caller said it was urgent, so the service radioed me here on board, and I called the number given to me. It turned out to be the Sheriff's Office in Everglades City. That's just below Fort Myers on the west coast."

"Spare me the geography lesson, Chris. I know Florida."

"Anyhow, I spoke to a deputy. I think his name was Charlson. Something like that. Wait, I scribbled it down as we spoke." She stood up and fetched a slip of paper from a pocket in her slacks. "His name is Carelton; I never got the first name."

Sitting down, she clasped her hands again, this time so tightly that the knuckles turned white. I dug into my slacks for a cigarette before I remembered that I had been smoke-free for nearly six months; I still got the occasional urge.

"This deputy told me that my sister and Felix had rented an outboard motorboat from some motel near Everglades City where they had been staying, and that there seemed to have been some kind of accident. I was too upset to ask questions, so I don't know whether they had a collision with another boat or just ran aground somewhere. The deputy told me that Felix had had to swim for help."

"And your sister?"

Christine's eyes got lost in shimmering pools of tears that spilled down her cheeks. "That's just it," she said, her voice trembling, "I understand that Lorna tried to swim for it, too. But she hasn't turned up. She just hasn't turned up yet."

I gave her a minute, and then handed her a packet of Kleenex. I needed to get myself under tight control, too.

"Are they holding Felix?" I asked.

"The deputy told me that Felix had been sedated; that he said he'd been swimming most of the night, and that the last time he saw Lorna she had been holding flotation cushions. He told me that Felix had given him my name and number."

"I asked you whether they're holding Felix."

"They said they intended to *keep* him, at least long enough for him to give them a statement. That's all I know. I called you right after that."

Chris walked over to the window and gazed off into the distance. I went to her and led her back to a couch in the middle of the room. It was my turn.

"Tell me something, Chris. After all the years that have passed since I last saw the three of you—Lorna and Felix and you—why the hell did Felix ask you to call me? I'm a stranger by now."

"That's not so; you've always been close to us. We keep reading about you in the papers. Dinner with this one, at the track with that one. This trial, that trial. My God, you're a celebrity, don't you know that? Lorna and I would have called you a half a dozen times if Felix hadn't bared his fangs."

Suddenly she stood up and brushed her slacks smooth against her thighs. Resting her fingertips lightly on my shoulders, she said: "Tommy, we have to get back to shore and do something. Both of us. Right now."

She had made up her mind, but I hadn't. I sniffed the air in the lounge. It had that tell-tale scent, burned or raw I couldn't tell.

"What about your pleasure jaunt?" I asked with not a little irony in my voice. "You seem to be doing more than fishing— and sun bathing," I added as an afterthought. I had always been very unhappy with pot smokers, and for that matter with users of any of the other fashionable powders and pills. I would never defend a drug dealer.

Chris took a long, wondering look at me, but I kept my face neutral. "I don't know where your mind is heading, my dear—"

"It's not my mind, it's my nose."

She continued as though I had been speaking silently to myself. "The trouble is I'm only along for the ride, just to freshen up my tan—as you may have noticed." She smiled with a coyness that was out of place in the circumstances.

"If you say so," I answered.

I had a trunk full of questions about Felix and Lorna, but not at this time or place. I also was more than a little interested in learning more about Christine, who had only a slight resemblance to the young girl I had known, and whose greatest pleasure then was sketching faces and figures on scrap paper, even on brown shopping bags, which she tore up and threw away almost immediately.

We walked back into the cabin. The occupants fell silent. All eyes focused on Christine waiting for an explanation. She gave it quietly and succinctly. She asked that we be allowed to go ashore as quickly as possible so that we could find out what had really happened. I noticed from her choice of pronouns that I had already been drafted into service, but I said nothing before the assembled group.

We got into the tender, aided by the young cabin boy *cum* assistant pilot, and headed toward shore. It was a good time for us to continue to talk.

"Look," I said to her, placing my hand on her knee for a moment to catch her attention. I had to speak loudly over the roar of the engine. "Remember, I haven't decided whether I want to get involved."

"But—"

"No buts, please. Just listen to me. Sure, there was a time when Lorna was a part of my life. And there was a time when Felix and I were like brothers. But that was long ago and far away. I no longer like his peculiar brand of loyalty. So the best I'll do is promise to think about it carefully and give you my answer in the morning."

I touched Christine's lips with a finger to silence the plea I saw welling up, and took a detour.

"Let's catch up a little. It may help me decide."

Her face lit up and she tried to hug me, but I denied myself the painful pleasure. "First of all, tell me about Felix and Lorna. What are they up to these days?"

Christine sat back and gathered her thoughts. "Well," she said, "Felix still works for Daddy, as he has since Lorna and he married."

"Doing what?"

"He's in charge of the Miami office of the company. Daddy divides his time between there and the home office in New York. You remember my parents, don't you?"

Mervyn and Sophia Ward had always worn their considerable wealth with grace and dignity. If they had a flaw at all, it was their overindulgence of Lorna. They always doted on her. Mervyn Ward was a founding partner of Ward and Stenrod, a private investment banking firm which kept a low profile in the financial community. Its name rarely appeared in the newspapers, but it was known in the right circles to be holding substantial equity positions in an array of high-tech risk ventures that had become huge successes.

Christine continued: "Daddy and Mother have a condo apartment in West Palm Beach. They split their time between New York and West Palm."

"And Lorna?"

The answer came evasively. "Well, she keeps busy."

"Children?"

"No."

"Is the marriage working?" I asked with very mixed emotions.

"I guess so, Tommy. It has its ups and downs, but I haven't heard any big trouble between them. So, don't you want to know about me?" Christine wanted to change the subject badly. I tucked that observation in a drawer for later consideration.

"Of course I do. So what's up in your life?"

"Well, I do a lot of painting. I always loved to draw, and now I'm into oils. I spend a lot of time in France, but I also have a place out on the tip of Long Island. And I also stay a lot in Florida, visiting with Lorna and Felix, and my parents, of course. They have an extra room for me."

I knew more about Christine Ward's career as an artist than I had disclosed. There had been a recent article about her work in one of the New York papers. As I remembered it, she was described as a "neo-impressionist," whatever that term was meant to denote. Her name had caught my eye and I had read the article from beginning to end. The paper had a black-and-white photograph of one of her paintings depicting a wild and abandoned scene, a kind of Walpurgis Night. Much frenzy and outflung arms by writhing groups of people.

As I had been watching Christine, it had been difficult at first to see the sensitive artist. Then I began to notice her hands. She had a habit of moving her slender fingers, which quivered slightly, the way fan coral sways in the translucent currents of the Caribbean.

She told me that she had a house in Angers, in southern France, and said that when matters were "straightened out"— she refused to accept the tragedy that loomed before her as fact—perhaps sometime I might like to visit her.

And so the conversation went, with the accident kept in the background until the ride ended.

We were dropped off at a small fishing dock at Coral Gables. We exchanged phone numbers. I told her I'd call in the morning. It took me a couple of hours to get back to Key West in a battered old taxi driven by a battered old lady wearing a battered blue hat, who kept feeding me morsels from the New Testament.

3

It was dark by the time I reached my hotel. The phone was ringing as I opened the door to my suite.

It was Chris. She sounded terrible. "My parents found out before I called them. The radio and TV people are climbing all over the story. They're reporting it as a probable drowning. Felix gave some kind of a statement, and then they released him. But he's not back at his place in Miami . . . their place," she added quickly, unwilling to look facts in the face.

"How did you find all this out?"

"Dad had his company lawyer call up."

I took a deep breath and looked at myself in the mirror behind the phone table.

"I've been thinking about all this," I said, "and I still can't see how I can help. Your parents have lawyers. Felix must have them, too, if he works in the firm down here. I don't even understand why he called me. After all, fifteen years. . . ."

Chris cut me off. "Forget the fifteen years, Tommy. You've never been out of our minds. I told you that already. Felix *always* turned to you when he was in big trouble as a kid. He knows you're the best. And you've been friends your whole life."

Minus fifteen years, I remarked to myself, but I said nothing, refusing to break the silence when she paused. So she continued.

"Anyhow, he did ask for your help, and you just can't let us down. Actually," she added after a slight pause, "I don't think he really wants you to help *him*; he's not in any trouble. He wants you to help find Lorna."

"Quit kidding me, Chris. Felix has never had an unselfish thought in his life. He called you from the Sheriff's Office to get me. Remember?"

"Then *you* think of Lorna. And think about my Mom and Dad. For God's sake, what are you, some kind of elephant? I guess I know how you feel about Felix, but that was years ago."

"I told you before. Fifteen years." My voice seemed to have a crack in it. "I'll think about it and call you back in a couple of hours," I said.

I knew all the time, of course, that I was going to help out, if I could. Maybe it was because he was part of my youth— our youth. Our uncomplicated days. A time when I basked in the love and pride of my parents. No juries or courtroom wins or losses then. The old habit of helping Felix was powerful. It was more than that. It was nearly unbreakable. Then, too, Chris was right: there was Lorna.

Ten minutes after our conversation ended I called New York and spoke to my partner, Amos Stern. I asked him to get in touch right away with Ben Abbott, our staff investigator, and have him meet me in the morning at the Sheriff's Office in Everglades City. Then I called the Sheriff's Office and told the deputy in charge that I was a New York lawyer on vacation, but that I would be acting for Felix and his wife as best I could, and would he please ask Felix to stay where he was till I got there tomorrow. The deputy agreed to pass on the word, saying that Felix had mentioned that he was going to stay overnight at the Seaboard Motel, where Lorna and he had checked in the day before, and that he was returning to the Sheriff's Office in the morning.

Of course, I could have called Felix directly, but I wasn't ready to speak to him. However, I did call Chris to tell her my plans. I felt strangely elated, I suppose because I was going to the aid of Felix once again. His protagonist and protector. He needed me again.

I sat in the dark for a long time, sipping at Mr. Jack Daniel. I hadn't eaten all day, but I was not hungry. I kept thinking about our early years. I knew such thoughts were unproductive. I tried to whip my recollections back into place in the dimness of the subconscious past. They usually sat there on their haunches like creatures ringed around me. A few of them leaped out at me, out of the darkness.

4

Felix Evans and I grew up together in New York City. We attended the same public school at 109th Street, east of Broadway, and we lived in the same apartment building on 112th Street. From our corner, we could see the growing Cathedral of St. John the Divine. It was a good neighborhood then. It may still be; I have never gone back to see. It's like paying to see a movie a second time: you already know the ending.

Columbia University was a few blocks north at 116th Street. Felix and I often walked over to its paved campus and stared at the college students. More often, we would walk over to the cathedral, perennially under construction, and watch the stone cutters whacking away at big granite cubes that split at just the right places as if by magic. The workers spoke a foreign language.

My mother, a quiet woman, had a large book entitled *Cathedrals of Europe*. She liked to show me black-and-white plates of some of the churches she and my father had visited on their honeymoon trip to Europe. She took pride in her ability to explain to me the architectural features of each church, her spidery fingers trembling with excitement as she spoke in quiet, almost reverent tones, pointing out naves and apses and flying buttresses to illustrate her comments. It had been their only trip abroad. We were not poor, but there was no money to spare. My father was a ranking official in the Postal System, but civil servants—honest ones, that is—never get rich.

We were a close-knit family. Each of my parents was an only child and, as it turned out, so was I. My birth had been difficult, and I retained a twinge of guilt over the bad manners I had shown on my arrival, which put an end to my mother's hopes for a larger family. They were very ambitious for me, and I made up my mind as a young man that I would not let them down.

Shortly after I became a lawyer, my father retired on a well-earned pension supplemented by an inheritance which took all of us by surprise. An unmarried uncle of his, my Grand Uncle Tobias, left my father a home in Smithtown, Long Island, mortgage free, together with enough money to maintain it. He opened a small office as a security consultant, and my mother kept busy with the house and her garden.

These days, I see them whenever I can, but never, of course, enough to satisfy them.

Felix and I were a study in contrasts; as though we were the opposite sides of the moon. Felix was the dark side, withdrawn and often moody. He was short and very thin. His large head, with dark, liquid eyes, seemed to be balanced precariously on his narrow shoulders. I used to think that if he stopped the habitual hunching of his shoulders as he walked, it might roll off. His face was long, and the end of his nose curved slightly toward his mouth. He had worn glasses for as long as I could remember.

He also had a temper which flared up unpredictably. I remembered a day when one of our more venomous classmates took Felix's glasses from his locker while he was showering after a gym session. The boy was a big, dark-skinned Armenian who always carried a knife that he used to skin stray cats. *Live* stray cats. We used to peer at the knife with fascination, looking for bloodstains. That day, when Felix reached for his glasses and discovered they were gone, he became enraged. Shouting, he took a bottle of ink from his gym bag, opened it, and flung the contents into the shocked face of his tormentor. Despite the fact that the Armenian boy was a head taller and twenty pounds heavier, Felix went after him, fingers curled like claws, reaching for the face he could barely make out without his glasses. I raced over to separate them.

It was days before the last signs of the permanent ink were gone from the face of the Armenian boy. Felix was lucky that within weeks the boy's family had to move, and he disappeared from the class. But I always remembered the way Felix forgot the knife and the skinned cats, and attacked the Armenian kid. Even then, I think I knew that there was a large reserve of ready violence in Felix. Maybe I even sensed that frustration over his physical inadequacies had something to do with it.

Still, I loved Felix then, partly because I had to protect him and because he always turned to me. It always made me feel good to be needed. Although our birthdays were only five months apart, I regarded him as I would a younger brother. Yet, there was more to it than that: Felix fascinated me. I suppose it was his eyes. They seemed so deep and mysterious, hiding secrets never to be revealed. When he looked at me, his eyes would seem not to stop at my face but rather to penetrate my very brain, pinion my most private thoughts. That gave him a power over me which I had trouble deciphering.

My father once took me along to visit a friend, a retired Jesuit priest who lived in an apartment in a residential hotel on 79th Street. It was only a two-room apartment but I was dazzled by its furnishings. My small feet sunk to the ankles in lush maroon carpeting. The furniture was heavy and large, upholstered in a dark velveteen. The room was lighted by many small sconces whose bulbs resembled candles and cast a flickering light. Father Paul answered the door wearing a black cassock that reached the floor, and nodded gravely at me as I entered, pushed forward by my father. His eyes skewered me. Even though I knew this was a holy man, Father Paul's eyes made me think of Hell. When Felix looked at me in the strange way he had, my mind immediately summoned up the image of Father Paul.

The years rolled by quickly. Both of us went to DeWitt Clinton High School. Then I headed for New York University, and Felix began at City College. It was less expensive. We double-dated now and then, but it was clear that we were beginning to drift apart. I worked at keeping things as they had been but Felix made no effort to meet me halfway, which upset me more than I was willing to admit to myself at the time. Our interests began to diverge. I liked school and let it be known that I wanted to go to law school. Felix lacked that kind of ambition. He stayed home a great deal. His father had died, and his mother's demands upon him increased.

Then, one Saturday morning in my junior year, while I was in the Public Library at 100th Street and Broadway gathering books for the week ahead, I met Lorna Ward.

5

Ben Abbott was just the man. He had been a police detective, first class, in the Midwest. Unfortunately for Ben, he followed a lead in a vice investigation that eventually tied together a city councilman and the proprietress of the leading brothel, which bore the tongue-in-cheek name Always Inn. He busted the councilman. The Inn was closed. But there were suggestions that the mayor received favored treatment at Always Inn. Periodically. Ben found himself assigned to checking for expired inspection stickers on the windshields of automobiles parked in garages. The message was clear. He quit the force and came East.

He had been working for me for two years. He was short but perfectly proportioned; a symmetrical man, balanced in person and mind, a kind of flywheel that kept me from running too fast or too slow. His methodical, deliberate approach to his assignments had a salutary—almost inertial—effect upon my fluctuating speeds. He made me pause on occasions when I was about to leap prematurely; and he pushed me toward decisions when I became over-reflective. He was worth his weight in gold to me. Indeed, much more. He didn't weigh enough.

I met with him the morning after my boat visit. Ben had taken a late night flight, and by the time he reached Everglades City, the sky was lightening. He had rented an Avis at Fort Myers and checked into a Ramada Inn. Our plan was to meet outside the Sheriff's Office at eight.

He was sitting behind the wheel, munching on a greasy cheese Danish and sipping lukewarm gray coffee. I had started out long before dawn from Key West, traveled north until I reached the Tamiami Trail, and ran it west to the Gulf.

I eased myself into Ben's car, and listened to his report.

He had called the number I had given him, and spoken with Jeffrey Baker, the assistant state's attorney for the area. Yes, he, Baker, had been up at Everglades City the day before. Yes, a statement had been taken from a Felix Evans. No, the office had not reached any conclusions. No, Evans was not there, he had been released, but had been told to return to the Sheriff's Office to sign his statement.

Of the actual incident Ben had learned precious little more than he had gotten out of my telephone briefing the night before. The boating incident—he noted that Jeffrey Baker did not say "accident"—had taken place toward sundown two days before. Lorna and Felix had rented an outboard motorboat around two o'clock at the inland dock facility of the Seaboard Motel. The boat had apparently drifted out into the Gulf after the engine somehow had conked out while they were navigating the inland waterways. So said Felix. He had turned up at daybreak yesterday on a small key a mile from shore, when a couple who lived on a neighboring isle caught sight of something white being waved in the early rays of the sun. And, finally, in response to Ben's question, Baker had said that Lorna's "body"—not Lorna—had not been found. Neither had the outboard motorboat.

The whole thing had a peculiar odor; not exactly putrid, but something definitely smelled, something you wouldn't want to keep in a bureau drawer.

On the flight down, Ben had studied a map he had taken from his extraordinary collection. He had one book for each state, scaled at one inch for ten miles. Using his detailed maps, he could find potholes, he would joke. Moreover, from junketing golf trips to that southernmost peninsula he had a familiarity with Florida, and particularly with the Gulf, which he knew to be unpredictable. With a glassine sheet taped over the pertinent map, he highlighted the coastal area from Fort Myers Beach to Whitewater Bay off Cape Sable in yellow. He paid particular attention to Cape Romano and the Ten Thousand Islands, a euphemistic description of a desolate, craterlike archipelago of stunted pine and cypress and mangrove swamplands. He pictured these islands as a packet of unassembled pieces from a jigsaw puzzle, scattered randomly over the waters, forming an apron to the western mainland. Some of nature's most delightful creatures lived there:

mosquitoes, sand fleas, crabs, raccoons, certainly alligators. He restored the book to his map carrier, and dozed briefly before he was awakened as the plane made a sharp, bouncing landing.

I tried to take a corner from Ben's Danish. He growled and bared his teeth. The digital clock in the car flashed a pallid green eight-thirty as I shrugged and, opening the car door, said, "I'm hungry for *something*. Let's get moving."

6

If Everglades City could speak, it would have to admit that calling itself a city was a hyperbole. It lies quietly in sight of the Gulf of Mexico, a gently undulating expanse that artfully conceals its true nature. For beneath its placid surface, currents and cross-currents constantly battle, a trap for the unwary navigator; and storms reveal its true nature when they transfigure the waters into white-capped furies.

Although the city had not suffered from the growing pains that had become the plight of the coastal areas on the other side of the peninsula, where developers had transformed raw natural beauty into mile after mile of windowed condominiums, it still had seen enough of growth. The crime rate had risen to a point where the staff of the local Sheriff's Office developed a tendency to disregard, or at least to place on a back burner, complaints of criminal activities that were not readily provable by clear, direct evidence. In short, the Sheriff's Office was not out drumming up business.

This essentially was the explanation we got during our visit with Deputy Sheriff Harry Carelton in the one-story granite building near the edge of the city. Sitting in his small cubicle, I felt smothered by heat and nearness. Carelton was big. I estimated that he stood six feet three inches tall and weighed a muscular two hundred twenty-plus pounds. He could have tucked a motorcycle under his arm. Yet his smooth-skinned face would have seemed almost cherubic, but for his mustache which curled around a firm mouth. His speech was mild, belying a tenacious devotion to his duties: homicide investigations and the supervision of the Missing Persons Bureau. I allowed my Benno to take over. We described ourselves as friends of the Evans family rather than as attorney and investigator. It didn't work. He knew of me.

The deputy gave me a dour look. "You're the attorney who returned Tony Savino to society here last year, aren't you?"

"You had a bad case. No pistol. No motive."

"No provable motive, Mr. Attleboro."

"Tommy, please."

"Why not?" He smiled a smile that could be measured in millimeters, which said first names changed nothing.

He was right, too. From the start, Tony Savino had me call him Tony, and I did. I had another private name for his kind, but then I didn't have to like him to represent him. I had been retained to represent him on a murder charge. Tony had no known occupation, at least none that he could list on his income tax returns. But a Rolls Royce and expensive tastes in clothes, women, and restaurants bespoke his success in something. He had been found talking over a telephone as he lay in his king-size, round bed at home, not ten yards from the body of a Bahamian gambler, with whom he shared a common hobby—more likely a vocation: high-stakes poker. An anonymous call had brought patrol cars to the Savino residence where the body was found in the pool just outside the bedroom, one clean bullet in the forehead.

A search without a warrant turned up some Bahamian correspondence with heavy-handed threats and two firearms: a Baretta and a Magnum. Tony was talking to his lawyer on the telephone when the law-enforcement people broke in. The bullet in the head of the victim had come from the Magnum. The warrantless search, however, led to a court order suppressing any reference to either gun, both of which were otherwise covered by proper permits. No gun, no case. No need to argue self-defense. The victory thus achieved left me with mixed feelings. The price of true liberty is often high. But still, worth it.

Deputy Carelton addressed his remarks to Ben. "We got a missing person report—it was actually the report of a missing boat—from the Seaboard Motel's manager around eight o'clock in the evening of June 2nd. We notified the Coast Guard right after that. Nothing developed that night. But the next morning we learned that the Coast Guard Station had received a telephone call from a couple who lived off-shore. There were no details at that time other than that the couple was bringing in a man they had found stranded on a nearby key."

"Can you tell me who reported the woman missing?" Ben asked.

Harry Carelton rubbed his chin as he recollected the facts.

"Yes, sir. A man named Melville. Lester Melville. He and his wife have a small cabin on one of the keys outside the inland waterways. Actually it's in the Gulf. Anyway, he called the Coast Guard Station and told them he had picked up a man who identified himself as Felix Evans—it came to us misspelled as E-v-e-r-t—at about seven A.M. When Evans and Melville got here, Melville told us that he'd found Evans wading naked in the waters off of Round Key, a small reef slightly further in the Gulf than the one the Melvilles were on. Melville had seen a white rag—it turned out to be his shorts— that Evans was waving to catch his attention. Otherwise he wouldn't have noticed the man at all. He took his outboard and ran over to pick the man up. After he got him back to his cabin, he learned that Evans and his wife had evidently foundered in their boat during a storm the afternoon before, and had tried to swim for it. Evans said he thought his wife had drowned."

"Did you get a statement from Mr. Melville?" I asked.

"The rest of the file is confidential. I won't say yes, and I won't say no. You can visit him, if you want to."

"Have you got his phone number?"

"Yes. We can locate him, if we need him. So can you." The deputy scribbled a number on a slip of paper and handed it to Ben. "He and his wife have lived in the cabin for years and the local fishermen and guides know them pretty well. They're both into booze, and get pretty sozzled on most weekends. It's a standing joke among the locals that they don't *catch* the fish. The fish get their brains beat out on booze bottles floating off their key." Carelton's mustache quivered over a small smile.

"Did your office conduct a search?" Ben asked.

"That was a Coast Guard function, Mr. Abbott."

"Ben."

"Ben, then. The boat was reported missing in coastal waters. We have no jurisdiction." Carelton leaned forward confidentially. "However, I took a police launch out after my eight-to-four shift." An unlit cigar jutted out under his mustache. "After all, what I do with my own time is my business, and the police launch does go out into Gullivan Bay in pursuit situations. Anyway, I ran a course for six miles on either side of the point where the inland waterways empty into the Gulf of Mexico, and then tacked out for nearly three miles. I couldn't find a single sign of the boat or the girl."

"Did the Coast Guard turn anything up?" asked Ben.

"Not a thing. No sign of any kind. But that's not surprising."

"Why not?"

"Because the waters of the Gulf at that point are a mess of currents that can pull a boat around like it was on a string. And if that's not bad enough, there are schools of barracuda that can cut any fish into ribbons in less time than it takes you to tie your shoelace."

"But not people."

"No, not people. But they sure can make you bleed a lot. And then, sharks are seen from time to time. And you know what blood does to *them*."

Christ, I thought, what a way to go. To see them circling, fins cutting the surface like periscopes. The waiting. And then the jaws biting into human flesh. Bit by bit. I snapped the door shut, refusing access to further images.

Harry Carelton lit a cigar. Ben wrinkled his nose. "I know somebody who just died of emphysema. She choked to death from the fluid in her own lungs. She smoked herself to death."

"Yeah, well, I'm going to Smoke Enders school one of these days when I have the time."

"It's worth making the time."

"Yeah, I suppose so." The officer put the cigar on the window ledge.

"Did you get a full story from Felix Evans?" I asked.

"Yes, we did, but I don't think there's a case, if that's what you're leading up to."

"I'm not leading up to anything. I'm just trying to find out what happened. Anyhow, can you tell me whether you had his statement taken down by a stenographer?"

"Nope." The answer was abrupt but the deputy's eyes twinkled.

"Did I miss something?"

"You sure did."

"Can you tell me what?"

"Yep."

"What?"

"We taped him." Carelton chuckled, and then added seriously, "Evans is not a target of a criminal investigation. At least not yet. And no egghead court forbids us from taping a witness's statement. It's cheaper and more accurate."

Funny thing, I thought, how law enforcement people everywhere always think the courts and lawyers are ganging up on them, making their job tougher just to protect the killers and the rapists. They can't see that they only *apprehend* people charged with crime—who may be innocent. Only juries can make them killers and rapists, not cops or sheriffs or even prosecutors.

Ben walked over to Harry Carelton's desk and rested a thigh on the edge. He had a talent for developing an easy, relaxed relationship with people from whom he wanted facts or a favor. I waited curiously to see whether Carelton was susceptible to Ben's particular kind of easy charm.

Ben, perched on the corner of the desk, arms folded, was speaking confidentially to the deputy. Knowing the routine, I wandered over to the window where I appeared to be inspecting a moribund philodendron.

"I know regulations," Ben said, "but I'd sure like to hear that tape."

"We're typing a transcription, and although that's a police document, since the two of you're here as Evans's representatives, I don't see why we can't let you read it. It'll be ready in—say ten or fifteen minutes more at the most."

"Thanks, Harry. By the way, where's Evans now?"

"Over at the Seaboard Motel, I guess, having breakfast and packing up his things. And his wife's, I suppose. He's due back here in a while to sign the transcript. Then he's all yours."

"What about Mrs. Evans?" I asked, walking back toward them. "You've given up on her already?"

"Counselor," said Carelton with a softness that took me by surprise, "we aren't staffed to do more than one day on an MP case like this. The Coast Guard will stay with it, though. They're good friends of ours. We work well together."

Well, I had an old friend, too, and I decided it was time to look him up. So I left Ben at the Sheriff's Office, and I headed for the Seaboard Motel to get the story straight from Felix. Fifteen years, I thought, is a very long time.

7

The last time I had seen Felix was the day I left for law school. Now, all these years later, years in which I had crafted a life in which there seemingly was no place for Felix, I looked forward to meeting him with almost the same impatience that I had felt as a youth. It was as though I had succeeded in turning back the clock. My old anger at him seemed to have dissolved.

As I drove up the curving driveway of the Seaboard Motel, I saw Felix standing near the entrance. He seemed out of place among the blooming hibiscus and pink oleander. His large, frameless glasses caught the glint of the sun. He was wearing a batiste shirt with pale blue pinstripes and white linen slacks.

I pulled up next to him and got out. His eyes widened, but he didn't speak. I cracked the frozen moment.

"Yes, it's me, Felix." I walked over to him but kept my hands in my pocket.

"Tom. Tommy. So you're here. I wasn't sure you'd answer my S.O.S. Thanks, old buddy." He stuck out his hand. Rudeness does not come naturally to me, but at that moment, the past clashed with the present and a wave of anger swept over me. It had evidently not dissolved, it had just been slumbering. So I disregarded his offered hand, doubly resentful because a part of me that had no connection with etiquette still wanted to grab it.

"Let's go into the lobby and grab a cup of coffee," I said, trying, if nothing else, to be civil. I started up the wide stone steps.

"Can't," came the terse reply. "My car's been ordered and I have to get back to Miami. I checked out." He indicated two valises near the pillars.

He sounded a lot like the Felix I remembered; physically he had not changed much either. He looked a little older, slightly shopworn. But he was no longer tentative and shy. To the contrary, it didn't seem as though he needed me any more at all. His casual offhandedness left me speechless for a moment.

"Aren't you supposed to be going over to the Sheriff's Office to sign your statement?" I knew I sounded exasperated, but I didn't care. I watched Felix rub his smooth jaw with one hand, a gesture which gave him a flippant, perhaps disdainful look.

"I was told that no charges were going to be filed against me, so what's the big deal about signing a statement?" And he waved a hand dismissively.

"You should go over and sign it because you were directed by law enforcement here to do so, and you said you would," I said to him, trying for a professional calm.

Felix shrugged so nonchalantly that I told myself to hell with professional detachment.

"Aren't those good enough reasons for you? Or are you a law unto yourself now? How about the search for Lorna? Are you washing your hands of that too? What the hell's the hurry to get back to Miami? Your wife's missing, God dammit."

Felix cast me a patronizing smile. "Still playing big brother, eh, Tommy? Abel's keeper? Since no charges have been filed against me, I don't need you. Send me a bill. Thanks, old buddy."

It occurred to me that Christine had had it wrong. The marriage apparently had not just had its ups and downs; it looked as though it had been all downhill. Felix started down the steps toward an approaching Lincoln convertible driven by a car jockey in a white jump suit. I grabbed him by the shoulder and swung him around. He reeled into one of the pillars that lined both sides of the entranceway steps, and bounced off into his two valises. My heart punched me as I realized that one of them must have contained Lorna's clothing.

"Damn you, Felix! Yesterday morning, you were begging Chris to call me. What the hell had you so scared that you needed to dig me up? What's going on? Tell me!" As if my shouting were not enough, I grabbed him by the shoulders and shook him.

A crowd of guests had begun to gather. The doorman emerged from the lobby ready to play referee. I glared at him and told him to butt out of a private matter. Felix wriggled out of my grasp and walked a short distance down the curved walk alongside the driveway; the jockey stood impatiently next to the open car door. I chased after Felix, wiping my sweaty palms on my hips.

"Leave me alone, Tom, go away. Please?" Felix's voice had become a whiny falsetto. He had a glassy look in his eyes, and his hands were extended, palms flexed up as though to ward me off. But I got the feeling that he didn't even see me.

"I did nothing, nothing at all. What happened was an accident. A pure accident. They suggested at first it might have been my *fault*. What did I do wrong? They frightened me. So I asked Chris to get you because you were the only person I could think of. I knew you wouldn't let them hurt me. They were going to hurt me, make me say I did something wrong to her. Make me confess. But it was an accident. I swear to God! I loved Lorna. You knew that. So I called Chris. I wanted *you*, Tom. My buddy."

Then, just as suddenly as the storm in his head had started, it ended, and he resumed normal speech as though some sinister force had fled from his body.

"Hours later, they told me that they were not going to hold me. That meant they believed me." His look was direct now, his voice calm. "I was not in trouble. They told me the Coast Guard would continue the search and would call me immediately if there were any developments. So I'm going home. I can be back here any time in a couple of hours."

He paused, smiled, and hugged me around my shoulders. "I'm sorry I troubled you. I really am. And I really am glad to see you. You look great. I read that you're knocking them dead." He walked over to the car door. As he got in, he shook my hand and shot his last line at me. "As I said, send me a bill." And drove off, leaving me—a sophisticated big-city lawyer—standing in the driveway with my mouth open. Felix had simply decided to close the book.

Even then, though, part of my brain went on red alert. It was unnatural that he had shown no remorse, uttered no grief at the loss of Lorna.

There was a telephone room off the whitewashed lobby. I called Ben at the Sheriff's Office and told him that I wasn't coming back, and that neither was Felix. I asked him to tell the deputy sheriff, assuring Ben that apart from annoyance there was nothing the sheriff could do over Felix's refusal to sign his statement. I might have given him that advice anyhow. But I said that I still was uncomfortable with the situation and I wanted him to poke around a little and report to me at Key West as he progressed. When he asked me how the visit had gone, I snorted my disgust. I didn't trust words. Ben didn't ask me any questions. He rarely did.

As I drove back across the peninsula, I forced encroaching thoughts of Lorna out of my mind, and tried to focus on Christine. But despite my efforts, I couldn't hold back the memories; my personal demons crept out of the darkness. I thought about Lorna and her foreshortened life. But life is always an unfinished story, I told myself. No matter how long it lasts, it's cut off in midsentence.

8

The 100th Street Branch of the New York Public Library had been my Mecca. I used to head there every Saturday morning. Now at nineteen, in my junior year at N.Y.U., I still made the weekly trek there to renew my book supply for the week ahead. That was where I first met Lorna.

I liked to wander through the aisles, feeding on snippets and snatches from books on either side until I had collected four titles, the maximum, to sign out. My library card was my most precious possession.

We collided in the fiction section; both of us were reaching for *Buddenbrooks* by Thomas Mann. I gave her my sunniest smile, which had served me in good stead before. It worked. She smiled back and offered me first choice. I returned the grace. Real Alfonse and Gaston. We resolved the impasse with my suggestion that we toss a coin, the winner required to buy the loser an ice cream cone. The coin flipped, and bounced and jangled on the tiling, making a particularly loud noise in the library silence. Heads, I won. I got the book, and happily bought the ice cream.

We walked uptown together, chattering away, our cones melting, discovering common interests and enthusiasms.

By the time I found out that Lorna lived only a block from me, I had a new interest—and enthusiasm aplenty. We had arranged to meet the following Saturday so that she could claim the book before it was placed back on the shelf. After I left her, I realized that we hadn't exchanged last names. No matter; a technicality. As I wafted up to my apartment, I nursed a vision of a head of dark hair framing a quietly beautiful face, and a trim figure in what seemed to me to be a very expensive skirt, blouse, and sweater set. Most of all I remembered a bright smile.

That afternoon, I told Felix about her. He listened quietly, said very little. I supposed him to be having a silent attack of hysteria. I suspected that Felix was afraid that she might break us up. That day had to come, of course. Felix had begun to criticize my friends, refusing to make them his as well. He had great difficulty in finding good in anybody. He scrutinized everything I did, like a skeptical scientist testing a hypothesis, putting everything under a microscope. So while I still treated him as my dearest friend, my feelings for him had begun to change into a mixture of affection and pity. He had dropped out of college after his sophomore year. He used to exasperate me by saying he'd rather have stock certificates in his safe than parchment on the wall.

Punctually at eleven the next Saturday, Lorna and I met in front of the library door. I had put on a bright red sweater. And I had replaced the irreplaceable: my white, scuffed sneakers had been cast aside for a pair of polished brown loafers. Lorna had also added an item to her wardrobe. She had a violet ribbon tied in her hair. I thought it matched her eyes. Clearly, signals were on.

Lorna was going to Barnard. She was toying with the idea of going into fashion. I could almost understand why. I don't remember her ever wearing the same outfit twice. Her wardrobe seemed to be limitless. I sensed that her parents must have been rich, which in a way made her even more attractive to me.

Lorna and I started going out regularly on Saturday nights. We usually went to a movie and then headed for Greenwich Village, where we would either spend a couple of hours walking or listening to a small combo at one of the cafes that dotted the neighborhood. I generally sipped beer. It was cheap. Lorna preferred vermouth cassis. Which was not cheap. But she contributed to the expenses in such a quiet and offhand way that I was never embarrassed. The "lib" movement had very much arrived. If I referred to a female over the age of eighteen as a "girl," Lorna was sure to reprimand me by saying: "Woman, Tommy. Boy-girl, man-woman."

Once in a while we would invite Felix along and become a happy threesome. And once in a while, when I saw her drooping and doleful at being left out, I invited Lorna's kid sister along, too. On those occasions, she kept Felix busy, chattering away, which left Lorna and me to ourselves. Lorna never objected to my including Felix. She seemed to like him. She used to tease him about his large, brown eyes and solemn, pouting expression, telling him that if he learned how to use those eyes and smile, he could have any woman he wanted.

But Felix remained a loner. It was a rare occasion when he brought a date along. When he did, it was easy to see that they were sharing an uncomfortably quiet time of it. He would walk along, his hands stuffed in his pockets, his narrow shoulders hunched, looking like a little man carrying about the worries of the world.

By the time I reached my senior year in college, my feelings for Lorna had deepened. I couldn't say I loved her, but I liked her very much; enough so that I stopped dating other *women*. She was nice to be with. Nevertheless, she made me uncomfortable because she began to take her clothes so seriously. I couldn't afford to dress up to her expensive style. It seemed to me that our dates were becoming occasions for her to model new outfits, attractive to be sure, but all very costly. There were Saturdays when she pleaded off seeing me. And while I trusted her, I had vagrant misgivings that perhaps— just perhaps—she was not as single-minded over me as I was over her.

I used to tell her how I planned to become a great lawyer and have my own firm someday. I would fantasize out loud about how, each morning, I would visit the rooms occupied by my staff and review their work, throwing out brilliant ideas.

What I didn't know was that all through our last year in college Lorna and Felix had been spending evenings togeth-er while I was enslaved to my homework, and that their pleasures in each other's company had passed rapidly beyond handholding. Felix the introvert, Felix the shy one with the melting eyes, had with Lorna's help wriggled out of his chrysa-lis.

After I left for law school, I wrote to her regularly, but I took dead aim at finishing high in my class. I was consumed with ambition not merely to be a lawyer but to be the best. Lorna figured in my long-range plans, but first I had to get my feet firmly planted in the law. No encumbrances until then. I was confident Lorna would wait.

When I came home at the end of the first semester, I knew immediately that something was wrong. Lorna vehemently denied it, saying that a persistent cold made her spiritless. I did not see Felix at all. Apparently the illness of a relative I had never heard of had taken him to Dallas for the week.

A month after I returned to school, I received two letters, one from Lorna and the other from Felix. They arrived in the same mail. Each announced their engagement to the other; each hoped I would understand. Each declared that there was no reason the three of us could not remain friends. But there it was. It was real love. They had to marry, of course, and planned the ceremony for the coming month. Just a private affair. They would like me to attend. I didn't.

Instead, I immersed myself in my studies. My trips to New York became short. I would visit my parents for a few days and return to school. At least my academic ambitions were fulfilled. I was graduated from Michigan *summa cum laude*. I wrote a valedictory address that was a tribute to my parents, whose sacrifices had made my education possible. As I think back now, my speech was old-fashioned in viewpoint and style, but then I was not yet fully seated in my own generation.

When I returned to New York, I got a job in a large Wall Street firm and was assigned to the litigation department. I worked hard; I had no outside pleasures to distract me. Hard work became my pleasure. In two years, I headed a work team. In another year I was trying substantial cases, and winning them.

I took a chance: I declined a junior partnership and I went out on my own. I did not want my success, if I achieved it, to be due to anybody's contributions but my own. My practice thrived, and I prospered. I used to visit my staff of one each morning to review his work. From time to time, I felt the bitterness of losing Lorna. Oh how I hated to lose!

I never completely forgot Lorna. And I never forgave Felix for his treachery.

9

Ben Abbott had stayed at the Sheriff's Office on that Friday morning. Harry Carelton came back into his office with a thin file under his arm, along with a large rolled-up map. Ben had been staring out the window into the middle distance, trying to fathom a man he had never met. As the deputy unrolled the map across his desk, Ben exposed his thinking. "Harry, don't you think Evans should have notified his wife's parents right off?"

Carelton shrugged his massive shoulders. "He probably didn't know how to tell them what happened. It's a hell of a thing to tell parents their child's drowned—is missing even."

"Did you get the impression that Evans was in shock when you saw him?"

The deputy smiled. "What's shock? How do I know? We're policemen, not doctors. Do you know how many MP's we get here now each month? Twenty-five on average. That's nearly one a day." Carelton stuck out a giant hand and began counting out on his splayed fingers. "We get calls for children lost in town while their mothers are traipsing around the mall. Parents call from midnight to six in the morning convinced their kids are in a hospital or the morgue. We have to cope with runaways, hide-aways, sleep-aways, lovers, elopers, dope users. Name 'em, we got 'em all here." Back and forth on his fingers, he ticked off the groups.

"I joined this staff nine years ago," he said, "and for the last four of them I've had the MP Department in addition to my regular duties and tours. Can you figure out how many people I've interviewed?" He glared as he pulled out a fresh cigar from a packet in the breast pocket of his shirt and bit off the end.

Abbott gave him the answer he thought Carelton wanted.

"Keep cool, I'm on your side. I got the impression at first that you fellows might have felt there was something special, something a little different about this case."

"Why should we? A couple of dumb people come over from Miami, get into a boat they don't know the first damn thing about, and it joyrides one of them to kingdom come. I call that stupid, not special."

Carelton fiddled with the holster holding the Smith and Wesson which lay on his desk. Then, looking directly into his visitor's eyes, he said soberly, "Ben, we have an enormous workload here. We have serious crime problems here, just like you do up north. We have our crimes of violence, our dope problems, just like you do. And we're short-staffed as hell. The fact is, we simply don't give a high priority rating to a missing person report except, of course, to send out a deputy or a car to chase around for a missing child. And also where the circumstances are suspicious."

"And if I find they're suspicious here?" Abbott asked.

"Come back to me with something you base your suspicions on, with something that's got a handle, and I'll take it from there. Just keep yourself straight about us," he added with convincing intensity. "We're busy, not lazy. And never indifferent."

Abbott walked behind the deputy's desk and leaned over his shoulder. What Deputy Carelton had spread out was an official map of the coastal waters in the area. In a corner, it said it had been prepared by the United States Coast Geodetic Survey Department. The map reflected depths at mean low tide; it showed reefs, sand bars and other subsurface irregularities and obstructions by means of subtle differences in map coloring and shading techniques. Finally, it showed land formations and adjacencies without, however, attempting to define or describe those areas, as might be done on a topographical map.

"Are you familiar with maps like this?" Carelton asked politely.

"To tell the truth, I've been a landlubber all my life. The only use I have for water is drinking."

"And washing."

"Are you trying to tell me something?" asked Abbott, taking a step backwards with mock embarrassment. They both laughed. Their initial strangeness and regional differences had narrowed: basically, they were both cops.

"Let me explain how this map works." The deputy hitched on his belt and cleared his throat importantly. Obviously he was pleased to assume the role of a pedagogue. "First of all, you are familiar with markers, water course markers?" He picked up two desk ornaments, miniature triangular pennants made of metal attached to thin staffs which in turn were mounted in heavy, square wooden bases. One pennant was painted in dark green-black with the numeral 1 superimposed in a white circle. The other, painted red, showed a number 2. He handed them to Abbott.

"In all inland waterways which are navigable, and in all tidal waterways which serve as water passages for ships and other craft to and from inland waterways, the state and federal governments cooperate so as to give the operators of those crafts markers identifying safe water channels. They're usually called 'navigable channels.' "

He pointed to the miniature versions in Ben Abbott's hands. "Operators departing from any inland base must always navigate so as to keep the red markers to their left and the green-black ones to their right. This means they must stay inside those boundary markers at all times. If they don't, they're likely to be in big trouble. They'll either ground, or collide with an underwater reef or other obstruction, or get hooked by a dangerous current, or find themselves some other disaster. D'you see?"

Abbott nodded.

"Good," the deputy said. "The markers are all numbered. The red ones all carry even numbers. The green-black flags carry odd numbers. Down in these waters, the numbers end inland somewhere in the thirties, and they run down to 1 and 2. Those are out in the Gulf and mark the entrance point into the inland water channel. Got it?"

Abbott nodded. "Got it, chief—deputy."

Carelton smiled. "Harry."

Harry pulled an accordion map from a stack of papers on his desk and handed it to Abbott, who noted that it was a simplified version of the larger geodetic survey map. Moreover, it was limited to the channel from the Seaboard Motel to the Gulf.

"You can keep this. It was prepared by the motel as a

giveaway to guests who rent outboards from them. It matches up with the survey map without as much detail. No currents, contours, depth soundings, and so forth, but the markers are shown. By the way, a revised map is being made up based on a new survey. This here's ten years old, and underwater conditions are constantly changing. Sands shift, depths change, and so forth. It's a big job, but it's due out soon. Some of the markers have been changed since the old map came out—the motel's too—but the channel's the same."

Carelton pointed to the file on the corner of the desk. "Evidence, even in missing persons cases, is kept in a case file. You never know."

He handed the file to Abbott. "Evans's statement is in here. You can read it. But don't leave the room with it. Make notes if you want. Do you have a camera?" Abbott shook his head. "Okay, no pictures. Everything clear?"

Abbott nodded, smiling inwardly at the deputy's sudden show of authority.

"Okay, then. If I were you, I'd skip forward to the part of the transcript where Evans relates the actual accident. Use either map to help yourself get oriented. Then call me and I'll answer whatever questions you've got, if I can. I'm taking the car out for about an hour. We've got a brush fire burning up the road and I want to see where it's turning."

Abbott sat down at Carelton's desk, and picked up the Seaboard Motel map. He opened the file to Felix Evans's statement and began reading. It took him nearly twenty minutes to get to the boating accident. Working with his own homemade brand of shorthand, Ben recorded what he thought were the essential parts, taking special care when he reached the description of the accident.

—*Knows water marking system . . . red-right-return . . . headed due West from Seaboard dock.*

—*First marker he saw was 26. Boat running fine.*

Abbott located the marker on the Seaboard map. Then he turned to the geodetic survey map and found the marker there. On both, it was shown by a red triangle.

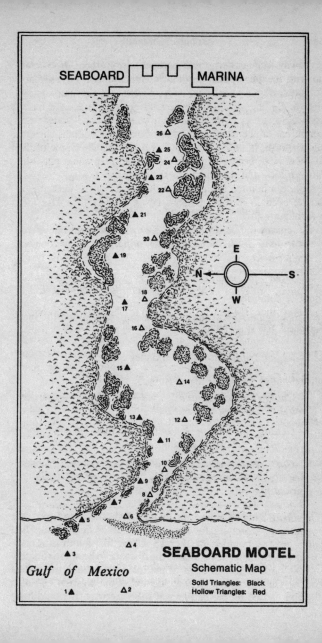

SEABOARD MARINA

26 △

▲ 25
24 △

▲ 23
22 △

▲ 21

20 △

▲ 19

E
N ← ◉ — S
W

18 △
▲ 17

16 △

15 ▲

△ 14

13 ▲
12 △

▲ 11

10 △

▲ 9
8 △
▲ 7
△ 6
▲ 5

△ 4

▲ 3

SEABOARD MOTEL

Schematic Map

Gulf of Mexico

1 ▲   △ 2

Solid Triangles: Black
Hollow Triangles: Red

—We had gotten to a lagoon, very wide, about half-way to the mouth of the channel . . . water beginning to ripple. . . .

—Lorna wanted to go back . . . out long enough . . . not 4:00 p.m. yet. . . .

—It was getting very cloudy . . . wind stronger . . . decided to go back. . . .

—Began making big circle [in lagoon] . . . an arc. . . .

—All of a sudden throttle [handle] whipped out of my hand . . . hadn't hit anything . . . just making wide turn. . . .

—Saw two clamps holding motor plate to rear end of boat had come loose . . . motor had stopped . . . prop dragging under boat. . . .

—Tried to paddle . . . couldn't (?) . . . seemed ridiculous . . . so close to Marker 13 could have touched it. . . .

Once again Abbott turned to the maps and found the black triangle denoting Marker 13.

—Began drifting down the channel. . . .

—In Gulf 30 minutes . . . waves building up. . . .

—Couldn't touch bottom . . . got to 6 p.m. . . . water very rough . . . drifting way out. . . .

—Getting dark when L. and F. decided to swim for it (8 p.m.? 9?) . . . used flotation cushions. . . .

—Got separated . . . reached a key . . . can't remember . . . woke up . . . signaled . . . Professor Melville (?) picked him up. . . .

Abbott laid the transcript on the desk and stood over the open map, searching for the second marker Felix Evans had identified by number: Marker 13. Using his thumb as a measuring instrument, he estimated the distance to be approximately 1,000 yards to the junction of the inland canal and the waters of the Gulf. The marker was located at the western end of a lagoon caused by the bellying of the waterway. It would have been due north of a boat passing it—to the right as Felix Evans navigated toward the Gulf. Markers Number 11 and 9 were shown next to black triangles. At the end of the waterway where it entered the Gulf he saw a "5" and a black triangle, and a counterbalancing "6" with a red triangle. Further west in the Gulf he found Markers 4, 3, 2 and 1. Tracing the water course back east toward the Seaboard Motel, he located all the markers up to black 25 and red 26.

Ben walked over to the window and stood there, arms folded, staring at the scene in the yard below, a parking area for the Sheriff's Office. Something wasn't quite right. The course charted by the markers was irregular. It twisted and curled around countless small isles. If he had so much trouble following the channel markers on the map, Abbott wondered, how could anyone not completely familiar with the actual terrain avoid getting lost?

"How's about some lunch?"

Abbott jumped. Deputy Carelton stood in the door, an unlighted cigar stump clamped in his jaws. Then he moved behind his desk and looked down at the geodetic survey. "Have you finished reading the statement?"

"Most of it. He sure had a lot to say about his past. I thought he'd never get to the accident. Almost as if he was shocked out of his head."

"Have you gotten what you came for?" Carelton asked.

"I came down to find out what really happened. All I have so far is Felix Evans's story."

"Who else can give you the story?"

"You tell me." Abbott sat down and flung a leg over the arm of the chair.

"Do you have any reason to doubt Evans's story?" asked the deputy.

Abbott shook his head. "No. Absolutely no reason at all. But what's got me is how did you find the time to let Evans tell such a long story?"

"We try to give the people as much time as they want. Part of our public image." He grinned. "But the real answer is that the report was not just an MP. It was an apparent death under unknown circumstances. And although we didn't, and still don't, find anything suspicious about it—dumb, yes, but not suspicious—we had to take a statement."

He looked at Abbott somberly, stroking his cheek as though testing whether he needed a shave. "But then who the hell thought the guy was going to tell the story of his life? He must have had a shitty youth."

Abbott leaned over and, rapping the corner of the desk for emphasis, said, "That's the point. That's exactly it. Evans's wife is drowned, and instead of his being desperate to search for her, he's recapping his life."

"Do you think he done her in, like in the dime novels?" This time the deputy's smile was entirely mirthless.

"I can't say that I do, Harry, but I can't prove that he didn't."

"Who says you have to prove he didn't? Your lawyer boss would tell you Evans doesn't have to do that. Remember he is Simon-pure until proven guilty. Unless you know something we don't." He moved his face into Abbott's. "And if you do, you owe it to us to put it on the table."

"I don't have a damn thing except now I'm getting the gut feeling that Evans is a rat. Maybe I only want to prove he's a coward. I can't seem to shake this nagging feeling that he deserted his wife in the water. I think he chose to save his own skin, and swam off on her."

Abbott could tell he had the deputy's attention. He took his time, thinking out loud. "I know the law doesn't require anybody to save anybody else, especially at the risk of his own life. But at the very least, the family has a right to learn all the facts. If all the facts there can be are in this file," he said, motioning toward the deputy's desk, "then that's that. But even so, I'm puzzled by a couple of things."

"Like what?"

"Well, like this. I said this a couple times before, but this transcript is the damnedest thing of its kind I've ever read. Here's a man hauled in after a fantastic ordeal and he's so busy telling you about his life, he takes forever to get to the drowning."

"People do strange things, Ben," the deputy repeated, studying the backs of his hands. "I run into them every day. I had a man in here last month who reported his wife as missing. We learned later she had run off with his business associate. But there he sat, worried to death over her, and when we asked him for a description, he pulled out a picture of his mother, who had died when he was nineteen."

"Okay, but here's another thing," Abbott persisted. "What ever happened to the boat and the body?"

"They haven't turned up. Yet. But that's not too surprising. I told you there've been shark sightings from time to time. That could account for the girl. As for the boat, once it's caught in the Gulf Stream it can be carried a hundred miles out in twenty-four hours. It could turn up in Louisiana as easily as Key West."

"Well if you can account for her absence by supposing the sharks . . ." He had to leave the sentence unfinished. "Anyhow, if the waters were so dangerous, how do you explain Felix Evans's swimming in them?"

The deputy shrugged off the question. "I can't. But I don't have to."

Abbott stared stonily at the deputy, whose face flushed.

"I'm sorry. I really am sorry."

"Was the boat sinkable?"

"I don't know." Impatiently. "I told you before, these questions of yours don't lead anywhere. By your own admission there's no reason to believe that the accident didn't happen just as Evans said. And I doubt you'll be able to find out much more."

"We'll see," Abbott mumbled.

The deputy stood. "If you want lunch, come with me," he said. "If you don't, then I'm going alone." He picked up his broad-brimmed felt hat from the top of the low metal filing cabinet next to his desk. Abbott retrieved his from the floor next to him.

He read that as an invitation. "Okay, lunch it is. My treat. I'm grateful for what you've done, I want you to know that." As the two of them left the office, he reached up and touched the deputy's shoulder. I wonder, he thought, if Harry really likes this job.

10

I wasn't really hell bent to get back to New York. So I had planned to charter a boat Sunday morning and casually fish my way northeast toward Bimini. If I got lucky, I would continue on to the Bahamas and spend a day there playing blackjack and maybe even take a couple of rolls at the tables. As a rule I shy away from gambling. I felt that my life contained enough risks and perils, the endless win-lose syndrome that enmeshes all trial lawyers. More to the point, I'm a bad loser. Whether with a jury or in a gambling casino, I soon forget the times I've won, but I can instantly summon up from an ineradicable ledger in my mind each painful loss.

But once in a while I develop a tinnitus in my right ear. The ringing usually means that the tides of my fortune are running full. Right then my right ear was clanging. Sunday morning augured to be the start of great conquests, first with the deep sea rod, then with cards and cubes.

When the telephone rang at six o'clock that morning, I expected it to be my charter captain. But it was my Benno, with a report. I sighed and told him to drive on over. He'd find me on the beach. Back into the deep flashed the marlin that had escaped my relentless pursuit, and into the pockets of others clinked the silver dollars that were to have been mine.

Around noon, Ben Abbott came scuffing through the sand toward my encampment near the water. Groups of sun worshippers nearby frowned as he passed. Small wonder. He was wearing a business suit, brown shoes and a snap-brim felt hat. I nodded at him as he approached and pointed to the empty chair beside mine. He sat down heavily, his head shaded by the oversized red-and-white striped umbrella-table I had also had the forethought to provide.

"Get comfortable, Ben," I said.

He took off his hat.

I laughed. "Want a drink, a sandwich?"

"No thanks, Tommy. The sooner I get away from all this—" He swept his arm across the scene, glancing in the direction of topless women baking their well-oiled bodies in the high sun.

Ben's parents were Mennonites. To his everlasting chagrin, he had been born and raised in Intercourse, Pennsylvania. While he had separated himself from most of the Amish ways, some were too deeply ingrained for him to cast aside. Wearing a hat even in this weather was such a retained custom. Nudity disturbed him, even in paintings. It disturbed me, too, but I liked being disturbed by it.

"Frankly, the sooner I get away from this—this depravity," Abbott was saying, "the better I'll like it."

I had learned not to challenge his beliefs. He was entitled to them, free from interference. First Amendment. I insisted, however, that in return he spare me any efforts to convert me from godlessness. Still, I noticed that as his body swiveled toward the unthreatening ocean, Abbott's head seemed to lag a bit. It occurred to me that maybe his attitudes were beginning to fall prey to the pressure of normal impulses.

I pointed to a frosted drink on the umbrella table and some sweet rolls in a covered bowl. He refused the drink lest it contain a noxious substance like rum, which it did. But he moved to the bench around the table, and wolfed down three sweet rolls as though he hadn't eaten for two days. Then he asked me how my visit with Felix had turned out, and what the game plan was. I told him that Felix had told me to send him a bill, that so far as he was concerned my services were no longer needed.

"So?" asked Abbott.

"He's probably right. My services may or may not be needed, depending upon what you have to tell me. So tell me."

Ben explained the ground rules that Carelton had imposed. No photographing of the report, but notes were permissible. He grinned and showed me some squiggles in his notebook, which to my eyes were definitely not cipherable. "Let's see how he started off his statement, Tommy. Here's his first comments."

Questioning by Harry Carelton, *Deputy Sheriff*
Q. First tell us who you are?

A. Do I need a lawyer?
Q. Well, do you?
A. I'd like to call one.

Abbott looked up. "That's when he called for you, Tommy." He pushed his glasses back up the bridge of his nose.

LATER
Q. O.K.?
A. I didn't reach him, but I see no reason not to speak. For God's sake, I want to find my wife.
Carelton: You're the one who wanted to call your lawyer.
Evans: Where do you want me to start?
Q. First tell us who you are.
A. My name is Felix Evans. I'm 37. I live in Miami. I work for my wife's father, Mervyn Ward. He's an investment banker in New York. I run the Miami branch. My wife's name is Lorna.
Q. What brought you down here?

Ben stopped reading from his notes. "Evans began to meander all over the lot," he said. "Made me wonder how he could put off talking about the accident, or asking about a search party."

"Maybe it was shock," I replied. "Shock makes people do crazy things."

"You may be right. But the next thirty pages of the transcript consisted of rambling about his childhood. He mentioned you by name."

My face flooded with a sudden anger I didn't understand.

Then Ben did a wild thing: he took off his jacket. "After that, Felix spoke about his work, saying how he found it boring, unfulfilling."

"Maybe you should have become a lifeguard," I said, my eyes following the route of Ben's to a girl a few yards away.

He looked puzzled. He never did have a sense of humor. Worse, he didn't even realize he couldn't take his eyes off the hateful sights. "Then he took a pot shot at his father-in-law," he was saying. "Called him an organization man and ungenerous. After fifteen or twenty minutes of that kind of rambling, he suddenly stopped and asked Baker to repeat his last question.

Carelton threw the question back at him: 'What brought you down here?' "

"Felix," Ben said, "explained that he was thinking of recommending to Mervyn Ward, his father-in-law, that the branch office of Ward and Stenrod which Felix managed in Miami be moved either to St. Petersburg or Fort Myers to follow the migration of venture projects. Capital interests were growing uneasy in Miami with its mounting social problems. He and Lorna had driven over and up to St. Petersburg, and then doubled back toward Fort Myers, looking over the areas for a possible removal site. Late in the afternoon, motoring south toward the Tamiami Trail back to Miami, Lorna had said she was too tired to make the trip east. So they decided to spend the rest of the day being lazy at a beach motel."

I interrupted the recital. "Did he ever say why he wanted an attorney—me—first thing?"

"I didn't see anything in the transcript."

"Doesn't that seem strange to you?"

"Darn right it does, mighty strange. But you told me that shock makes people do funny things."

"I also told you that a guilty conscience never feels secure."

"*What's that?*" asked Abbott.

"Publilius Syrus."

"What are you talking about?"

"Skip it, Ben." I was showing off, mainly to bolster my sagging spirits. But there was no avoiding the dark thoughts that had started gathering in my head. "How about Lorna, what are they doing about her?"

"The Coast Guard will continue to make regular sweeps with a plane, probably a helicopter, for a while. Then I guess. . . ." He spread his arms in a gesture of helplessness.

I left Ben sitting under the umbrella and walked down to the water's edge. I was wearing swimming trunks and a sport shirt. The chilly fingers of the incoming tide tickled my toes as I stood there staring vacantly at a small boat towing a bumbling water skier. Absent any charges against Felix, there really was nothing that required my skills and arts. Yet the situation was like a dangling participle. I hate loose ends. They're sloppy. And if you trip over them, you can hurt yourself.

My inclination was to turn Abbott loose and let him finish his investigation at my personal expense. But before that, there

were a few questions I had to answer for myself. Where was
I heading? What was my objective? What was I going to
do, what might I have to do, with the information and facts
Abbott uncovered? Suppose they showed . . . I did not dare to
complete that particular question. I certainly could not conceal
evidence of a crime, if I found any. Nobody has that right.
And that meant neither could Abbott. Hence, the question of
questions: Did I *really* want Abbott to do any more fishing?

There was a tiny, little man with an oversized shiny bald
head who used to turn up, perched on my shoulder, unan-
nounced and uninvited, whenever I faced a personal crisis.
Nobody ever saw him there but me; but then, I never claimed
that eye witnesses were infallible.

The little man was back on my shoulder, damn him,
whispering Thomas Gray's pettifogging advice in my ear.
"Where ignorance is bliss, 'tis folly to be wise." I squatted
on the sand to think it through.

When I walked back, I noticed that Ben had twisted his
body around, and was staring with a deep frown at a blond
nymph who was relubricating her upper chassis. Her fingers
and palms slipped sensuously over her dark brown skin as she
stared disdainfully over and around the heads that had twisted
toward her like sunflowers following the sun. I began to sense
that his frown was a cover, a kind of shield. Maybe he wasn't
as different from me as I had always believed. Somehow that
disappointed me.

Ben caught me watching him and came dangerously close to
blushing. I shrugged dismissively, as if to say that I wouldn't
tease him later.

In any case, I had decided on full speed ahead, Gridley. I
directed Ben to finish the job; go visit the man who rescued
Felix, and take a run over to the marina where he had rented
the boat. I wasn't clear as to what I expected him to learn, but
those seemed to be the proper steps to take. Telling me he
would keep in touch, he stumbled away as quickly as the street
shoes on sand allowed, leaving me to Sodom and Gomorrah,
and the beauty of it all.

11

The west and east coasts of the peninsula of Florida are governed by the same laws; their citizens send representatives to the same legislative bodies. But in attitudes and tempo they are very different. The Gulf side is unhurried, relaxed, interests generally localized and uncomplicated. The ocean side is another matter. It's like an older brother. Most of its communities reflect a sense of urgency and the sophistication which marks a more highly developed, older society. But even more significant is the population density of the east coast cities, which creates social unrest, tension, and an escalation of crime. Serious crime.

East coast readers glanced at the news story about the water accident in the Gulf near Everglades City, and then turned the page. It was no concern of theirs. They had their own problems. If people didn't know how to navigate they should stay out of boats. Any trouble they got into, they brought on themselves. The residents at the lower end of the Atlantic side had bigger, more immediate problems, in Miami most of all.

A brazen sun drew shimmering heat waves off the corrugated roof of the hut next to the entrance to the Miami Car Auction Center. It stood at the western outskirts of the city, where the tinsel and show of ocean-front properties were replaced by scarred lots and commercial structures. These places now doubled as residences for squatters, illegal aliens from Mexico and Central and South America hoping for something other than squalor.

The shrill voices of young boys fragmented the oppressive air as they played soccer with bare feet in the glass-sprinkled street, using a tin can for their ball. A chain-link fence mounted with coils of barbed wire traced the outline of the auto lot

which covered a square block. A dark green tarpaulin lined
the inner side of the fence, lending a sense of mystery to the
activities that took place within. At regular intervals along the
sides, air flaps had been introduced to prevent ripping; and
when the boys of the neighborhood were at loose ends over
what to do during long, stagnant summer evenings, they would
peer through the flap holes. They would hoot and whistle until
the guard dogs, made vicious by trainers, slavered and hurled
themselves into the fence in impotent fury, to the delight of
their tormentors, some of whose parents had fled from just
such conditions.

Inside the hut, as the sun towered almost directly overhead,
Manuel Cruz released a gargantuan belch as he rose from a
wooden table and wiped the beer foam from his mouth and
off the mustache that curled down and around its corners.
His wife glanced up from her seat at the far end of the
table and wrinkled her brow. A lovely woman, her olive skin
was taut over prominent cheekbones. Shadows under her dark,
luminous eyes and faint vertical lines forming along the sides
of her nose had begun to attack her natural beauty. But she
was still well formed, and when she walked, men still looked
at her carefully.

As Manuel stalked out the door, he aimed the beer can,
which he had crushed ostentatiously in one fist, at the trash
basket. And missed.

He always misses, his wife muttered safely under her breath.
Maybe on purpose to irritate me, she thought. She sighed,
walked over to retrieve the can, and dropped it into the basket.
The Persian cat in the crook of her arm switched its tail in
annoyance as she inadvertently squeezed him. She glanced out
the window toward the metal arch that framed the entrance to
the lot. She saw her husband stop purposefully next to the sign
on the steel grating that read, "Miami Car Auction Center,
Manuel Cruz, Manager."

The morning sun caught her in the eyes, making them water.
She walked over to a smoky, fly-specked mirror that hung on
the wall next to the window, sensuously pressing the sleek
fur in her arms against her breasts. But the movement was
reflexive; her mind was elsewhere, far from the hut and its
baking heat, far from Manuel, who lolled indolently beside
his sign with a cigarette drooping from his lips. When she

recognized herself in the mirror, she was momentarily taken aback by what she saw. If only life stood still, she thought.

She had been a reigning beauty, the only daughter of the third largest coffee grower in Colombia. Hemmed in by luxuries, she and her large family lived in a rambling hacienda in Santanda Province, which lay in the shadow of the great Andes chain, a daunting barrier to the Pacific Ocean 200 miles to the west. Manuel Cruz was her father's field boss, the absolute despot over one hundred hands who planted, pruned, cared for, harvested, and packed the precious bean crop over ten square miles of rolling hills, and of course stole as much as they picked.

Maria used to linger around the house, finding some pretext to burst into the study on the days Manuel made his regular reports to her father. She was captivated by this man, tall, lean, with fierce mustachios, who would stride restlessly around the room, his tooled leather boots pounding the gnarled wood floor. He personified the freedom for which Maria yearned. Men were afraid of him, and he was ambitious. She dreamed of this handsome hidalgo, who some day would ride away with her from this prison of wealth. And dreamed, too, of course, of the ineffable delights she would share with her Manuelito under the star-studded skies of a summer night.

One day at the height of a blistering hot spell, when tempers were short and irritations greatly magnified, Manuel shot and killed one of his *labriegos* whom he had surprised loading bags of coffee beans into a small pick-up truck he had stolen from one of the stations scattered around the plantation. Manuel later claimed that he had aimed above the man's head—a warning shot, he called it—but that his horse had shied at the instant he fired, and the bullet had penetrated the brain of the hapless worker. The truckload had a wholesale value of $175. The dead man left a wife and four hungry children.

Maria's father was furious, and directed Manuel to remain in his quarters until he summoned the police. Maria, her heart thumping in her chest, stood dry-mouthed outside the door, listening to the explosive words that passed between the two men.

Manuel had not waited, of course. He had packed his belongings and driven off in his station wagon, heading south toward Bogota where his family lived. Maria sat beside him,

trying to imagine the shabby car as a proud horse. Her chin
didn't quiver; her eyes were dry. Manuel had talents beyond
boss man. Maria was pregnant, the consequence of one of a
series of secret encounters on a cot in the empty dispensary
at station headquarters a mile from her home.

He stopped on his hegira long enough to marry Maria in
a burst of morality which was an admixture of his Catholic
upbringing and a certain amount of ambivalent respect for his
newfound treasure. After a short stay with his family, the two
of them drove off to the heartland of Colombian gold, where
Manuel planned to strike it rich, having heard that there were
jobs for the asking and that the wealth from cocaine production was generously shared. So much for a man's daydreams,
thought Maria many years later.

In due course Manuel became a regional boss. The local
police chief under whom he served attributed his rapid rise
to the fact that the owner of the establishment, a 50-year-old
virago with stringy gray hair and an insatiable lust for young
men, found Manuel not wanting. Whether that was the case or
his advancement simply the product of attrition—internecine
war among these lawless men was endless—Manuel's financial needs were still not adequately met. And, as he quickly
learned to his chagrin, wealth-sharing was a relative term.
It turned out that the Señora Duena distributed largesse on
a rotating basis among her local regional bosses, pit bosses,
security bosses, police bosses, and last but not least, American
drug enforcement agents who regularly turned up with noble
intentions. They were invited by the national police authorities
to aid them in stemming the relentless proliferation of local
drug centers, but not infrequently stayed to share the spoils.
The weather was ideal.

One evening Manuel packed Maria, of whom he was still
genuinely fond, and the two children she had by then given
him, whom he genuinely detested, into a gutted surplus U.S.
Army transport filled with bales of marijuana, and landed in
a remote corner of the Hoosawatchie Swamp at the coastal
tip of South Carolina. Maria and he carried only two valises
with the clothing of farm people. Under her cape Maria wore
a cache of jewels, all that remained of her glittering days as
heiress presumptive to a coffee empire. The security forces
that were trained to protect the workers from incursions also

had had secret instructions from the Señora Duena to stop them from making excursions. It had taken a substantial portion of their family savings and a sixteen-inch strand of ten-millimeter pearls to buy their way out of the camp and onto a plane.

Manuel brought something else with him of inestimable value: entrée to a source of custom quality marijuana, and, like the star twins Castor and Pollux, its inseparable sibling, cocaine.

He quickly embraced his unsuspecting foster land, melting into the vast army of illegal aliens who comprise a substantial segment of the population of southern Florida. Both Maria and Manuel had mastered rudimentary English, having had lessons for years from the American agents resident in Santanda Province. They eventually found an apartment of sorts in a ramshackle building on the outskirts of Miami. Across the street they watched the clearing of a lot and ultimately the hoisting of a metal archway. A metal sign was affixed to the gate. It read: Miami Car Auction Center.

12

Manuel Cruz sometimes had trouble sleeping. After three or four hours he would wake up wide-eyed. He got into the habit of finding his way into the front room of the apartment, a pillow tucked under his arm. He would station himself at the window overlooking the broad, littered avenue, resting his arms on the cushioned sill. There he would gaze at the deserted street scene, which occasionally was enlivened by a passing car or a small gray form streaking to the nearest sewer. Sometimes he would return to Maria's side; more often, he would open his eyes at dawn to find his head on his arms, resting on the pillow.

One night several months after the Miami Car Auction Center opened, Manuel happened to focus his eyes on the tin-plated roof of the hut which was located just inside the entrance gate. What he saw there ended his temporary career as a handyman at the Hotel Fountainbleau, and Maria's as a cashier at Wolfie's.

What he saw was this: a truck with its headlights turned off emerging from the darkness that enveloped the rear of the lot, and coming to a halt at the side of the hut. He suddenly realized that the night lights in the car lot were turned off also, and that the dobermans were nowhere to be seen. The truck had evidently come into the lot through a back entrance. Distance and darkness impaired his vision, but he saw enough.

Two men jumped down from either side of the cabin of the truck and, approaching the side of the hut, began moving to the side a pile of lumber stacked on the ground. Another man parted the dropped tarpaulin that covered the back of the truck, and the three of them proceeded to unload from it square bales wrapped in dark burlap. As they were lowered to the ground, they seemed to disappear from sight. Two of the men then reached up into the passenger side of the cabin of the truck and hauled out an oblong chest which they carried over to the edge of the lumber pile. It, too, seemed to be swallowed up in the ground. The planks of wood were then moved back, and the three workers climbed into the truck. It melted away in the veil of darkness.

The whole episode had taken twenty-two minutes. Manuel timed everything with his stop watch. It was an obsession. Sometimes it made Maria very self-conscious.

The following evening the two of them had a long talk. Maria displayed anger at what her husband proposed to do. But Manuel had made up his mind.

When he returned the next day from his six-to-two shift at the Fountainbleau, he walked over to the Auction Center and asked one of the men washing cars for the person in charge. He was directed to the hut. A young man in camouflage fatigues and old sneakers stood leaning against the open door. His face was scarred from still-festering acne, and one leg dragged under the weight of a steel brace.

Manuel approached him, receiving in response to his smiled greeting only an insolent glance. The man held a cigarette in his teeth like a cigar.

"Por favor, where is the boss, amigo?" Manuel spoke with forced deference.

"Nobody meets the boss. You wanna car, go look around." Glancing at Manuel's work clothes, he added contemptuously, "You gotta buy for cash. You got cash, greaseball?"

Manuel came close enough to him to smell his fetid breath, drew a deep, restraining breath of his own, and took one step backward.

"Watch yourself, amigo. I can't hit you . . ." he glanced at the boy's steel encased leg, "but I can kill you."

The last words were a whisper, but Manuel's eyes bored a hole in the boy's face like a laser beam. The boy blanched and ran the back of his hand across his mouth forgetful of the cigarette, which tumbled to the ground. He made no move to pick it up.

"What's your name, amigo?" Apparent cordiality crept back into Manuel's voice.

"Frank. Frank Donnelly. I'm in charge."

"My name's Manuel Cruz, and I have a business proposition for your patron. How do I reach him?"

"Who?"

"The patron. The boss, borrico."

"The boss what?"

"The boss, donkey."

Frank clenched his fists, but took no other overt measure.

"You know where I can find the boss?"

"Maybe yes, maybe no." Frank's eyes shifted to a point above Manuel's head. Manuel leaned forward, brushing his hand down the boy's shoulder. Suddenly his fingers snapped shut around Frank's skinny arm.

"Maybe yes, muchacho. No more shit from you. Maybe quick, sí?" Manuel's face was grim and foreboding. The question was a command.

Frank, staring through rheumy eyes, tried to wrench free from the bear trap of Manuel's hand, failed, and surrendered.

"Are you the law or somethin'? I don't know nothin'. I'm just watching this place. Are you maybe a government man?" Insolence had given way to dark fear. Manuel could feel the boy's body begin to tremble. He released his arm.

Frank rubbed it gingerly with his other hand. "Jesus, you're strong. Am I in trouble?"

"Shit, no. I live cross the street. Fifth floor. Front." Spoken proudly. "My woman, you see her in the window?" Maria's white clad figure stood in clear sight. Manuel waved. Maria waved back.

"Why you wanna see the boss, sir?" asked Frank with new respect.

"You call the boss and tell him I can triple his money from car sales, pronto. Tell him I know where he can find gold. You tell him we have the same kind of friends, but my friends are better. And bigger. I can help. You tell him that?"

Manuel laughed broadly. Then, still smiling, he slapped the boy sharply across the face. "I'll be back one hour, maybe two. Adios." He strode off across the street.

Maria, watching, saw the Manuel who used to swagger across her father's wooden floors. When he got upstairs, he settled in front of the window and watched. She waited with him, her hands massaging his neck.

In less than an hour, a Lincoln drew up outside the hut. Manuel went down, not hurrying. Still not hurrying, he entered the lot, then the back of the car.

He had a talk with the passenger in the Lincoln behind smoked window panes, while Frank walked off with the chauffeur, whose jacket clearly outlined a firearm at the hip line. Maria, a step back from the window, kept her eyes riveted on the car, her hands pressed against her breasts, holding her heart in place. The meeting lasted close to an hour. She was just about to go downstairs and, at the risk of Manuel's ire, make certain that he was safe, when she saw the chauffeur hurry back to the car and open the rear door on the driver's side. Manuel came out. Frank Donnelly stepped in. He stayed inside less than five minutes.

As the car backed out and sped away, Manuel read its license plate: the letter B, nothing more. He waited beside Frank until it disappeared from view. But when Frank offered his hand, Manuel ignored him and strode back proudly across the street.

Two days later, after several telephone calls between Miami and Bogota, a second conference took place in the back of the Lincoln. Cordiality reigned. Small vodka glasses were tapped, toasts were exchanged.

The following Monday, Manuel attached a new sign to the gate, as Maria watched from the window in the front room, her face tense. Manuel went into the hut. Frank Donnelly was gone. Manuel Cruz had a new job.

Evidently it paid well, for in no time he moved Maria into a garden apartment on Collins Avenue, and bought her a pedigreed Persian with long, silky hair. Stubborn woman, she insisted on keeping the other cat, too. Manuel also bought a second-hand Pontiac convertible, fire engine red.

Life had taken a wondrous turn for Manuel, and for Maria, too, whether she liked it or not, all because Manuel had insomnia.

And very good friends in Colombia.

13

The only distinguishing mark on No Name Key, which served as the land mass for the Melville cottage, was the dirty white-and-black structure itself, whose aluminum stovepipe chimney periodically became a beacon as it reflected the sun's rays. The key itself was one of thousands of islets that dot the Gulf, stretching from Naples south to Key West. Although there are other cottages in the Ten Thousand Islands region, most of the islets are impenetrable tangles of mangroves and scrub pines growing from stagnant pools of water discolored by rotted vegetation and dissolved minerals. Large snapping turtles, crabs, and raccoons call the islands home. And, of course, millions of voracious little sand fleas hop around the sand. From the air, the area appears to be a gigantic jigsaw puzzle, the irregular pieces of which are scattered without plan or design on the water's surface.

It took Ben Abbott fifteen minutes to reach the Melville cottage by motor launch, courtesy of the U.S. Coast Guard. He was escorted by an ensign, one Peggoty Shea, who, despite the heat, wore her uniform and insignia in a tidy display of dress-parade neatness. He appreciated her attire. A pigtail trailing behind her regulation cap took the edge off the toy soldier look she assumed.

She moored the launch alone. Ben was impressed. He noted she seemed slightly captivated by her prowess. They climbed the steps to the cottage, a small, dilapidated affair from the outside. Standing in the open doorway was a wisp of a man who peered at them through thick lenses, his watery blue eyes beaming with pleasure.

"Come in, come in. Peg, I haven't seen you since Richard Crookback snuffed out his nephews under the stairs."

"He's a professor, Mr. Abbott," Ensign Shea explained.

"Likes to show off his knowledge of English history. I hardly ever know what he's talking about. Professor, this is Mr. Ben Abbott from New York. Mr. Abbott, Professor Lester Melville."

"My pleasure. Please come in. Mrs. Melville will join us shortly. You must excuse the condition of our summer home, Mr. Abbott." Then his glance went from Ben Abbott's business attire, including hat and tie, to his own yellow slippers and dingy white and gray bathrobe, and he smiled ingratiatingly. "We see so few people we tend to get sloppy, the two of us."

But Ben noted, the teacher's hands were carefully kept, his nails manicured and polished. Not a simple straightforward man, he thought. But then very few men were.

The room they entered was in flagrant disarray. Dirty dishes of varying vintage were strewn on tables and ledges. In one corner stood a pile of yellowing newspapers. A stack of books capped by a dirty coffee cup stood on a Victorian table in the middle of the room. It had been used as an ash tray. Several undistinguished prints hung on the walls, and on a bridge table next to the window, which was held open by a half-empty soda bottle, a mass of pages was piled haphazardly.

Motioning his guests to a battered couch, Professor Melville pulled up an easy chair for himself, casually tossing a dirty beach towel that had been draped over its back onto the stack of newspapers. He seemed oblivious to the impact of the room. Ben wondered what kind of wife would allow this to accumulate.

Beckoning toward the bridge table, Lester Melville began to speak in a voice that had lost only part of its resonance. "Peg calls me professor but of course she's teasing. I haven't taught for five years come next December." He uttered the words wistfully. "However, I don't believe retirement should mark the end of a man's productivity. No human being should go down life's tracks on a single rail."

His slightly stilted speech had a certain charm for the investigator. "As for me," Melville was saying, "when I stopped teaching, I decided to write a comprehensive history of the Plantagenets and the Tudors, emphasizing the influence on the course of history of the women who were married to or otherwise allied with those sovereigns. Agnes Strickland tried to do it, but I fear she saw the wives of the English kings more as generating forces than as active participants themselves in the affairs of state. Eleanor of Aquitaine, of course, was an example of such a woman. Despite Henry, indeed in spite of him. And Elizabeth was at the end of the line. After her—" He pulled up short and stood, a rueful smile playing across his face. "Oh dear, I'm talking too much about matters which have no interest for you. I'm sorry. I've even forgotten my manners. Would you like some coffee or tea? Or maybe something else?" he added hopefully.

Ensign Shea opted for coffee, black. She sat perfectly straight in a rickety chair, her knees clamped and hands clasped. She seemed painfully self-conscious of her uniform and her rank. Ben had already surmised the latter was newly achieved.

Repelled by his surroundings, Ben elected to skip a second breakfast. Melville excused himself and shuffled to the back of the house in his yellow slippers, which Ben recognized as the *babouches* worn throughout the Middle East.

The professor reappeared a few minutes later. "Mrs. Melville will be out in a minute," he said in a reverent tone. "She will bring along the coffee service." The two guests sat quietly, waiting for him to settle down.

His heralded spouse appeared in short order with a battered silver tray and a Spode china coffee service which had clearly weathered many a storm. Placing it on the wooden coffee table in front of the couch, she extended a hand to Ben. "Howdy do. I'm Pat Melville." The investigator stood; he found her handshake surprisingly strong. Ensign Shea stretched out her hand, but in mock annoyance Mrs. Melville refused to take it. "You promised us stone crabs last week, Peg, and then went and forgot all about us. I'm not forgetting that. Probably lying around some saloon drinking." She was a tiny person, an inch or two short of five feet. Built very slight, she had few physical attractions and a tremulous way of moving her fingers. An overindulgence in alcohol, Ben said to himself. She continually brushed back wisps of straw-colored hair from her cheek.

The ensign smiled. "A bar, Pat, not a saloon. A bar. Saloons went out with prohibition and cowboys. And officers in the Coast Guard couldn't frequent them anyhow."

Mrs. Melville returned the smile. "Only teasing, Peg. Congratulations on your promotion. I knew it was coming, but it's nice to see you in your uniform."

"I, also, offer my congratulations," chimed in Professor Melville. "It's not that I didn't notice. It was simply . . ." he hesitated, glancing at Ben. "I didn't want to embarrass you before a stranger."

Pat Melville served the coffee, but skipped her cup, which seemed to be filled with steaming tea. Then she turned her attention to Ben. "So you're from New York? Professor Melville used to teach Medieval History at Columbia University. We lived on Riverside Drive overlooking the Hudson River. Near Grant's Tomb. You know the neighborhood, of course."

Ben nodded, but Mrs. Melville moved ahead without waiting for confirmation. "We live in Fort Myers now. Our children are grown and married and have no real interest in us. The professor and I spend a few days a week here, and the rest of the time in our apartment in Fort Myers. The professor does his writing here, and I give astrological readings in our apartment."

Her husband shifted uneasily in his chair, apparently embarrassed by the disclosure of his wife's dabblings in the occult. "Now Pat, these folks have some questions to ask and I think it would be best to let them get on with it. Mr. Abbott, can you tell us what your interest is in the matter that brought you down here? Does your presence signify an official investigation?"

The ensign jumped in quickly. "We have an open file on an unexplained disappearance. It will stay open for the time being."

"Unexplained?" interjected Ben.

"Any disappearance not finally accounted for is unexplained. The statement, we understand, that was given by . . ."

"Felix Evans." Ben supplied the name.

"By Felix Evans. That's a version, not an explanation. Until there are established facts beyond a mere disappearance, his statement is nothing more than that. Mr. Abbott is a family representative just trying to learn the facts. He has no official standing." Ensign Shea matched Professor Melville for pedantry. She must have been one mean noncom, the investigator thought. Too smug, too self-assured. He understood why Professor Melville had hesitated to flatter her in the presence of a stranger.

Turning to his hosts, he smiled reassuringly and said: "Professor Melville, you asked me before what my interest is in this matter. That's a fair question." He watched the professor fill a briar pipe and light it. Mrs. Melville went inside to pour herself another cup of tea. "Felix Evans is—was—a childhood friend of my boss. That's Tom Attleboro."

"I've heard the name," said Professor Melville.

"I'm not surprised," Ben said, proudly clasping his hands over a folded knee and rocking gently backward and forward. "Anyway, the loss—disappearance, if you will—" glancing at Ensign Shea, "of his wife, is a great shock to Mr. Evans, of course, and to her parents, who spend a lot of time in West Palm Beach. Felix Evans and the Wards—Lorna Evans's parents—have asked us merely to learn as much about the matter as possible."

"Isn't that a little morbid on their part?" wondered Mrs. Melville out loud. "Let the dead deal with the dead, I always say." Spoken with an air of mystery. She set her lips firmly around the edge of her cup.

"Not at all, Mrs. Melville," he replied. "There's no real way of knowing at this time whether Lorna Evans *is* dead. For all we know, she reached shore somewhere. Maybe she's suffering from amnesia. Or maybe she's in hiding for one reason or another. It's only been a couple of days. She doesn't have to be dead, you know."

Professor Melville leaned over to nudge the investigator. "Come now, you don't believe that, do you?"

"It really doesn't matter what I believe. My job is simply to gather as much information as I can, and that's why I'm here."

"How can we help?" asked the professor. "We witnessed nothing. All we know is what young Evans told us in the morning hours. You already have his story, I suppose. We only have more of the same."

"Perhaps so. But stories are what they are. Merely stories. Maybe true, maybe false. Maybe confused. I think that's what Ensign Shea wanted to say." The ensign bobbed her head. "Besides you saw him before the police did. You picked him up, I understand. He was closer to the accident then and his recollection may have been clearer. Or different. All I would like to have you do is to tell me what you've told the deputy sheriff. You did speak to him, didn't you?" The Melvilles glanced at each other. Pat nodded her head slightly, and Lester Melville picked up the thread.

"Yes. I spoke to a deputy named Carelton."

"Harry Carelton?"

"Yes. How do you know his name?"

"We've met."

"Nice man," Pat Melville said. "But very big."

"All right," her husband said. "We'll tell you what we know for what it's worth but we want your word that you will not use it for any kind of newspaper story or the like. We like our privacy."

Ben Abbott assured them both that he would not leak the interview to anybody but his boss.

"As you know," the teacher began, "this key is just past the delta of an inland waterway. Beyond us is the Gulf of Mexico. To either side and in front of us are the Ten Thousand Islands, Fakhahatchee Bay and the mainland. I forget the date—we pay no attention at all to calendars out here—but I can remember clearly the night before we found young Evans. We'd had a little dinner party but it broke up early." He glanced at his wife as though seeking her corroboration, but she was busy nursing her teacup. So he continued. "I had been anxious to finish the section of my work on Eleanor's activities in England while her beautiful son Richard was off on his crusade against the Saracens." He paused for a moment. He gave the impression that Richard had left just the other day.

"By the way, did you know that Queen Berengaria of Navarre, who was married to Richard the First, never set foot on English soil during their entire reign? Think about that some time. The importance of Eleanor's role—Richard's mother—in the light of that fact. Some state of affairs, that. Eh?" The professor puffed furiously at his pipe.

Ben had some difficulty concealing his impatience but replied politely. "Very interesting, sir. But could we stay with the Evanses for the present, and perhaps at some other time we can get into English history."

Professor Melville chuckled. "All right, sir, away from the Plantagenets and back to the Evanses. Rather to young Felix, to be precise. I never did meet his wife. Chances are, I won't get the opportunity now."

He puffed away as he told his story, slowly and carefully. Ben sat back, his hat next to him, his vest buttoned, as though he were in a lecture hall instead of a cottage on a tiny islet called No Name Key in the Gulf of Mexico. Occasionally, he made a note on a small pocket pad. Mainly, he just listened. Later on, he would report it all to Tom Attleboro with almost perfect recall. Professor Melville started with his first sighting of Felix in the morning sun on the nearby key.

14

The sun had climbed high by the time the professor finished his narrative, occasionally interrupted by his wife. She sat at his side sipping tea that to Ben Abbott's sharp sense smelled remarkably like a buttered rum toddy. She kept the china teapot covered with a greasy chintz cozy, which from its burn marks must have doubled as a potholder. As Melville spoke, Ensign Shea had moved about the room, picking up curios and inspecting them. But Ben was certain that she was stuffing her mental pigeonholes with morsels for Harry Carelton to pick out later. When the professor finished, she asked a question that Ben pinched himself for not having thought of on his own.

"Did Evans ask to make any telephone calls?"

Pat Melville answered her. "Funny your asking that, Peg. Matter of fact he did. He tried some number, but there was no answer Then he called the Miami operator and asked for the number of somebody in that city, but she couldn't find a listing."

"What was the party's name?"

"I don't know. He spoke quite low."

Ben turned to Professor Melville.

"I wasn't listening either, Mr. Abbott," he said. "Didn't seem to be polite."

"Did he ask you to call anybody else?"

"No. The only other thing he asked for was to borrow some clothing, a shirt and slacks. He said he'd pay me for them when he got home. I told him not to be silly, to concentrate on his bigger worry. His missing wife."

"How did Evans get back to shore?"

"We took him back in our boat. Pat and I had to do some shopping." He paused to clear his throat, and he shot a look at the ensign. He seemed to have hit a snag in his narrative. When he continued, he was on a different tack. "I wondered why the place where he rented the boat hadn't sent out a search party. After all, they must have known there was a boat of theirs missing."

"They did," said Ben. "The Coast Guard made a sweep the night the two of them disappeared, after the motel notified them that a boat of theirs was missing with two guests. But they had to give up because of the dark. The motel didn't make the call until early evening."

Pat Melville had chosen this unlikely time to make a desultory attempt at cleaning up the room, gathering glasses and cups from under the sofa. She paused, shaking a cup in her hand for emphasis. "People ought no more to be allowed to drive off in a motor boat without a pilot's permit than they can in a car. They're a menace to themselves and others."

Ben walked over to the window. It was a habit of his; taking his focus off close objects enhanced his concentration. In the distance, caught in the sun, lay Round Key, the island on which Felix had turned up, resting quietly like a giant porpoise in the flashing waters of the Gulf. Turning back to Professor Melville, who had relighted his pipe and was trying to send one smoke ring through another, he ran his finger along the inside of his collar and then hooked both hands into his vest pockets. "Did you find anything odd about Evans's behavior or in what he said?"

The professor did not respond for a minute. Then he walked over to the investigator and reached up to place a hand on each of his shoulders. "Young man, if you wish for trouble, you can will it. What do you wish for?"

"I don't wish for anything," said Ben, stepping back in annoyance. This made the second time, he thought, that he had been criticized. The deputy sheriff had hinted at witch hunts, and now here he was being called a trouble seeker. Well, perhaps he was. But the more he thought about it, the stronger his disposition was to label Felix Evans a coward. He did not want him to walk away a bereaved husband with the world believing that his loss had been an act of God. Another thing. Ben had the feeling that the professor was holding something back. If he were a betting man, he'd lay odds the man had noticed something awry in Felix's behavior.

Now he spoke quietly to Lester Melville. "Excuse my rudeness. I'm sorry I was impatient. What I'm looking for is something more than the explanation the deputy sheriff and the state's attorney got from Evans himself."

"You didn't tell me this was a police matter," said Professor Melville sharply.

"It isn't. All they did was follow routine procedure and take a statement."

"Are they going to bother us?" Anxiousness triggered a twitch at the corner of his mouth. "We really cherish our privacy."

In order to drink and carouse with impunity, Ben Abbott said to himself.

"I doubt they'll bother you." He looked at Ensign Shea for reassurance, but she simply sat with lips pressed together, hands unmoving in her lap. "It's just that the Wards want to get as close to what happened as they can. To them missing doesn't have to mean dead. Is there any chance that she was saved? And if she did die, *how* did she? I'm here to get answers or at least leads, if I can. Surely that's understandable."

"If that's what you're looking to find out," said Mrs. Melville from the door to the kitchen, "you'd best speak to Peg. She'll tell you about these waters. They're horrible. I have never overcome my fear of them, even after all our years here."

Ben looked at the ensign, who uttered one word. "Sharks."

Lester Melville began to fidget. The welcome mat clearly was being withdrawn. Ben stood up and advanced his hand to his host. Peggoty Shea also caught the signal and walked toward Pat Melville, who kissed her lightly on the cheek.

"Don't be so scarce here, Peg, now that you've become an officer. We love you just as much as before." Mrs. Melville smiled as she spoke the words, brushing away a stray strand with the back of her fingers.

The ensign grinned back at her. "I won't," she said, "I promise you that. It's just that all this is so new—" she caressed the shiny gold stripe on the cuffs of her jacket— "and I want to get the feel. . . ." Her voice drifted off, and, blushing, she glanced sheepishly at Ben as though she had been caught disclosing a state secret. The investigator, aware of her embarrassment, busied himself with the strap on his wristwatch, which suddenly was either too tight or too loose.

"I'll see you both soon," she said awkwardly, and they left.

During the return trip to the mainland, Ben's companion retrieved some folded sheets from a drawer in the cabinet beneath the throttle board. As she read them, he could see a signature at the bottom of each sheet. So Melville *did* give a statement, he thought, and she's checking for matching parts or inconsistencies. What he had heard had not satisfied him, but he had kept his doubts to himself. If the Sheriff's Office was treating this matter as a routine M.P. case, why had they given the Coast Guard copies of the Melville statement? And why, he asked himself further, hadn't Carelton shown it to him? He had no answer.

What the heck, he thought, I'm a fact finder, not a diviner. He sat back and enjoyed the ride.

Peggoty Shea dropped him off at the Coast Guard station. He waited until she moored, and then he thanked her again. She said goodbye stiffly; her shoulder twitched as though she were about to structure a salute. Just like a little toy soldier, he thought. But watching her walk toward the station office, he changed his mind. Her pigtail twitched jauntily—and so did her derrière. The latter observation was as close as he had ever come to defying his Amish training.

15

A series of horn blasts awakened Maria from her reveries in the hut on the premises of the Auction Center. It was precisely one o'clock. A buffed white Mercedes 400 drew up to the curb. The front and back doors opened and two men emerged. The driver stayed behind the wheel. She watched them approach Manuel, who stood next to the opened iron gate.

His arms folded across his chest, he looked with distrust at the pair. "So?" Not a question so much as a challenge.

The older of the two, silver hair parted neatly on the left, fingered a jagged scar on his left cheek.

"Are you Manuel?" His voice was soft.

"Who wants to know?"

"Ralph Twilling wants to know. I'm Twilling. Are you Manuel?" This time the voice had authority.

"I'm Señor Cruz. I'm manager here." He nodded his head at the gold lettering behind him.

"We're interested in the 1980 Chevy, the black and tan."

"For who? You got a car. Muy grande."

Twilling looked at the other man hesitatingly, still touching his scar tenderly as though it hurt. "We want another car," he said, "so show us the Chevy. Pronto."

Manuel looked at his watch with a bored expression. "This is Thursday. Auction day is Saturday. You look at cars Saturday morning. Sí? Not today, not mañana. You come back Saturday, early. Okay?"

The younger man nudged Twilling to the side. He was dapper in a summer silk with Gucci belt, Gucci shoes and a snap-brim Panama emboldened by a floral band. He lowered his head until his eyes stared stonily over narrow, black sunglasses. He reached with his right hand into the side pocket of his jacket. Manuel clawed reactively at his hip pocket beneath his white sport shirt, but before he could reach his small-caliber pistol, the other's hand emerged from his jacket pocket cupping a small yellow parchment card. Manuel took it, keeping his eyes fixed on Mr. Panama Hat. He flicked his eyes down at the card. It showed no name, no company. Just the solitary figure of a black horse with wings. He turned the card over. It bore the number 163 in black ink.

Manuel relaxed, dropping his arms to his sides. "Next time, show me quick, right away. Sabe? How I know who you are?" He shook his head in disgust. Panama Hat shrugged unconcernedly.

"Next time you know us."

"Who you, por favor?"

"Joe Scotto. Joseph Caruso Scotto. Show us. Now." The last word was a command.

Manuel led the two men toward the rear, catching a glimpse of his wife ducking back from the window. They passed through aisles of cars neatly arranged by vintage and condition. The fierce heat waves from the sun shimmered off the metal and attacked the three of them. The lot was otherwise empty. Manuel often thought of the lot as though it were a cemetery. Some cars were entombed after a full life, some in the flush of midlife, and a few shiny models were evidently accident victims at a young age. Only a few of them would be auctioned that Saturday. Others would be held for sale to junk metal dealers. Three would be auctioned at controlled floor bids or "reserve" prices that assured special customers they would capture the cars they wanted. Those were the special cars. The Chevrolet was one of the three.

A visitor to the monthly car fairs conducted by Miami Car Auction Center, "Manuel Cruz, Manager," who gained entrance by flashing a small yellow card purchased more than a secondhand car. He also bought the car's contents. And to the initiate, the cardholders, the cars and contents were worth their weight in gold. Often more.

As Manuel approached the Chevrolet he drew a set of keys from his pocket. Panama Hat snatched them rudely and beckoned Manuel to walk over to the covered fence some distance away. Maybe three names, he thought with bruised feelings, but definitely not Caballero. Not like my Maria's father. Some day for me fat pockets, a casa de campo like the old times.

Some day. He took a deep breath and hitched up his trousers as though he were wearing a gun belt.

Joe Scotto got into the car. It seemed to be in good condition. The motor turned over and caught instantly at the pressure of the key in the ignition. The two strangers then walked around to the trunk, which Scotto opened with the second key. He pulled up the floor board exposing a spare tire. He punched it with a clenched fist. It was soft, unresisting.

Twilling watched meditatively, still fingering his scar. When Scotto was done, he whispered to Twilling, "Well?"

"Maybe they want proof first."

"Maybe. Should I show him?"

At a nod from Scotto, Twilling stepped back and motioned to Manuel, who was watching out of the corner of his eye. When Manuel reached them, Scotto pointed to Twilling over his shoulder with a deprecating glance.

"He'll take care of the financial arrangements on Saturday. I'm quality control. Comprende?"

"Comprende, señor. And mia esposa, she is Jefe de Rente."

"What are you talking about. Speak English, dammit."

"Our chief of finance, you say. Money matters. Me, I'm manager." Manuel stood tall.

Ralph Twilling ventured a few words, diffidently, softly. "When will the car be ready for delivery to us?" Again the unconscious touching of the scar on his cheek.

"When Maria—my esposa—sees the payment. All cash, por favor."

They walked back to the hut. Manuel went into it; Twilling and Scotto headed for the white Mercedes, where they stood and waited.

Maria Cruz, cradling the Persian in her arm, came out of the hut followed by her husband. She glided languorously toward the car with eyelids lowered over slitted eyes that missed nothing. Her large breasts moved beneath her blouse. Both men stared unabashedly. Manuel pushed her roughly from behind, and she hunched her shoulders forward. The cat twitched his tail nervously and dug his claws gently into Maria's bare arm.

She and Twilling slipped into the back seat. At a word from Twilling, the driver handed back a metal attaché case. Manuel and Scotto stationed themselves at either side of the car. Maria opened the case while Twilling sat back and watched with his arms folded. The case was filled with neatly stacked hundreds. She sample-counted one packet from each stack, counted the total number of packets, and closed the case. Not a word had passed between them. Ralph Twilling reached out a tremulous hand and touched Maria's shoulder. A darting look put an end to that venture. A slut's put-down, he thought. He'd try again some other time with a handful of pesos, when Manuel was off fishing. And Scotto was away, too, he said to himself.

The two of them emerged from the car, and Maria nodded at Manuel, and murmured "Correcto, caro." Then she glided back to the hut, fully aware of two sets of gimlet eyes fixed upon her hips.

Manuel then turned and led the two men to a pile of lumber stacked behind the hut. He moved some planks to the side, disclosing a trap door. He and Scotto descended into a cement-walled tomb lit by a hanging light bulb. Twilling drew a cigarette with compressed lips from a pack of unfiltereds, and lit it with a wooden match that he scraped to a flame with his thumbnail. He tilted his Stetson forward over his eyes like a cowboy in a Camel ad and stalked over to the side of the car at the curb. He could play at macho while Scotto was out of the way. He caught Maria watching him from the window in the hut and, leaning against the car, he savored the waiting time.

It took ten minutes before Scotto and Manuel came back up the steps. Manuel lowered the trap door, piled the lumber back on its cover, and returned to the hut without further conversation. Scotto and Twilling drove off.

Inside the hut, Manuel walked over to Maria and cupped her breasts from behind. "Call the Rider, carita. Tell him the third horse is in the stable." He turned her around and kissed her on the mouth. She accepted the kiss submissively. When he walked away, she wiped her mouth.

Maria reached for the phone, dialed and waited. A familiar voice answered. She conveyed the message and hung up. There was nothing left to do until Saturday.

16

George Feeley would not have admitted to daydreams, but he had them. Now, standing in the shade of a plane tree, one of a line which bordered the approach to the Seaboard Motel off to his right, he dreamed of a girl in a red dress with even redder lips. She was smiling at him in a way the local girls didn't. Behind him were the marina and mooring stalls, all empty save one which held a boat, down for repairs.

Suddenly Feeley stirred as his eye caught a dust cloud moving steadily closer between the rows of plane trees. In a moment, a car came to a halt in front of him, and a man stepped from it. He looked about, his felt hat tilted to shield his eyes from the sun. Despite the heat, he wore a tie and jacket. Feeley remained where he was, changing his position only enough to extract a plastic toothpick from his shirt pocket and place it between his thin lips. The man spoke first.

"Are you George Feeley?"

"That's right."

"We spoke on the telephone about an hour ago. I'm Ben Abbott."

"I guess we did," Feeley said, glancing over Abbott's shoulder toward the office.

Abbott immediately sensed that extracting information from him was not going to be easy. Earlier, over the telephone, he had merely asked whether he had been the one in charge of the marina docks when the drowning had occurred. Feeley's answer was yes, but he sounded as though that was every bit of what he had to say about the matter. When Abbott told him he wanted to come by and take a boat out, Feeley said there were no boats available. The investigator said he would take his chances.

"Still no boat available for me?" he asked now.

"I told you that on the phone," the boy answered sullenly.

"Look here," said Abbott. "I really want to talk to you a bit, and I'm willing to pay you for your time." He put his hand meaningfully in the pocket of his trousers, and pushed his felt hat up on his forehead with his thumb. "I don't know what you're worried about, but I can tell you that I can keep a confidence. All I want are a couple of facts which you may or may not have." Handing him a twenty dollar bill, he said, "I'll double this, if you have answers for me."

The boat boy hesitated, again glancing toward the marina office. "I could lose my job if I got caught talking about that. The manager is one tough bastard and I ain't about to take him on."

"When do you get off duty?"

"Five."

"Will you meet me at the bar of the Ramada Inn at five-thirty? It'll only take us twenty minutes."

Feeley still hung back, avoiding eye contact.

"I'll tell you what. If you show up, there's twenty for you first for showing. If you have answers, there's twenty more. How's that sound?"

"Maybe yes, maybe no. I gotta think about it." Again he glanced toward the office.

Ben followed his glance and saw a curtain at the office window move slightly. Now he was sure there was something wrong here. Somebody was pulling Feeley's strings like a puppet. Ben's eye caught a glint of metal to the side of the building. He backed off from Feeley a few steps as though he wanted to scuff a stone. And then he saw it. A sheriff's car was parked on the blind side. Glare on the windshield made it impossible to see into the vehicle, but a tendril of cigarette smoke drifted out of the window on the driver's side.

Not a good sign, thought Ben. Case not closed. Case wide open. The twenty dollar bill he had handed to Feeley was not likely to be matched and rematched. He'd play out the hand, however. Drawing to an inside straight was foolhardy but not impossible.

"Okay, now, George. I'll be at the bar of the Ramada Inn at five-thirty. I'll even wait for you till six. Try to make it. Fair enough?" He attempted to clap Feeley on the shoulder, but the boy sidestepped him and headed toward the broken boat.

Ben sauntered over to the office and helped himself to the last copy of a waterway map in the rack next to the door. As he closed the door behind him, he twisted around the corner of the small office building and waved to whoever sat behind the sun-blinding window of the sheriff's car.

Ben waited at the bar at the Ramada Inn until close to seven. He was disappointed that George Feeley did not come, but he was not surprised. As for having wasted the past hour, he just added that with philosophical resignation to the long, long list of hours he had spent in his professional life waiting for people who didn't show.

17

On Saturday, the auction at the Miami Car Auction Center went off without incident. The three special cars, fully readied for sale and delivery, had been sold and delivered. It had started at one o'clock under a canopy opposite the hut, and it was well attended. Maria presided over the financial side in the hut. Manuel was not to be seen. A burly guard wearing sidearms stood outside the door, which was locked for the occasion. Only one customer at a time was allowed in the hut.

Long after the auction had ended, the visitors had departed, and darkness had descended, a station wagon pulled up in front of the hut. A dark-paned Lincoln tailed behind. In the dark, Manuel transferred a couple of valises from the hut to the station wagon. When he finished, it drove off, followed at a respectable distance by the Lincoln. Maria and Manuel shook hands with the guard, who helped them free the dogs, turn on the night lights, and lock the gates. Then the three of them drove off in their two cars.

Monday would bring fresh produce, as from any fertile field.

18

Ben Abbott and I returned to New York several days after his unsuccessful visit to George Feeley. Before leaving, we had both gone over to West Palm Beach to visit Lorna's parents. Christine was there, too, this time dressed in a one-piece jumper zippered decorously above her clavicle. The Wards' beachfront condo was decorated in high-grade Art Deco. Statuettes with shimmering brass curves; nymphs on agate bases shaded by ivory silk lampshades disguised as umbrellas; groups of porcelain children hovering over the edges of Lalique candy trays; and enough Tiffany glass to send ten worthy candidates through Princeton. On each table was a cluster of family pictures in gold baroque frames. My heart stopped for an instant when I saw one of Lorna taken when she was in college, books under her arm, a smile lighting her face. The basic furniture, however, was relentlessly modern, all white leather, built for comfort, but undersized. All a very confusing anachronism to me. I felt as though I were looking simultaneously backward and forward in a schizophrenic time warp.

Sophie and Mervyn Ward sat side by side, diminutive figures on a leather loveseat, a low brass and glass coffee table in front of them. A tea service was set up but had not been touched. They watched expressionlessly as we came into the room and sat down opposite them on matching white club chairs. Sophie Ward gestured politely toward the tea set. I leaned forward, but Chris came over and poured out cups. She squeezed a thin wheel of lemon into her mother's and left it floating on top. A few words passed between us, but you couldn't really call it conversation. Finally—mercifully—Mervyn Ward croaked a single, dry-mouthed direction. "Report, please."

Ben told what he had learned: his interview at the Sheriff's Office; his visit to the Melvilles; his talk with George Feeley; and, last of all, his almost photographic recollection of the statement Felix had given to the authorities. When he finished, Mervyn Ward swiveled his head toward me and glowered a query. I shrugged my shoulders haplessly. There was nothing I could add. I had decided earlier not to report my conversation with Felix outside the Seaboard Motel in Everglades City.

"What do you think, son?" If voicing his question was an act of persistence, the words themselves still were soft, almost wistful.

"I don't know, sir. I can't see the picture yet. There just aren't enough pieces."

"Tom, I didn't ask what you knew, I asked you what you think."

From her perch on the edge of the sofa on which her parents sat, her hand resting lightly on her mother's wrist, Chris interjected, "Daddy, that's not fair. You can't ask him to make a judgment call on the little he knows. Not yet, at least." She looked at me for approval. I avoided her green eyes, which were clearly a threat to my pulse.

"I can, and I have," said the old man. Now there was a grimness in his voice. "Did Felix do it?"

Sophie Ward moved slowly, like an automated mannequin, wheeling forward from the waist and raising a thin arm. She pointed her index finger at me. "You knew I loved you. And you knew Lorna idolized you. How could you have deserted her? How could you have given up without a fight? This should never have happened. It's all your fault, Tommy, all your fault. You let her down. I never liked Felix. There was always a way about him that made me think he was hiding something. I never felt I knew him. And I don't think Lorna did, either. And now she's gone. And it's all your fault." Her finger folded into a fist and dropped into her lap.

I cringed momentarily like a kid, forgetting that Mrs. Ward had dropped fifteen years somewhere, maybe in the same time warp that had snared me when I first arrived. Ben made no attempt to disguise his incomprehension.

"Mrs. Ward. . . ." But that was all I could manage.

Grabbing control of myself with difficulty, I faced Mervyn Ward. "Mr. Ward, as I said, I don't have much of a picture yet.

But my hunch is that Felix did a stupid thing, not a criminal act. He evidently went out in bad weather and got into unfamiliar waters—tricky currents that he just wasn't able to handle. He says the outboard engine snapped loose from its moorings and he lost control. Ben told you the rest." I didn't want to get into the hard part.

But Sophie Ward did. Evidently I had underestimated her inner strength. "And then what? What did he do after that? Leave her in the boat?"

I saw then that I had no choice. There was no avoiding the hard part. I asked Ben to describe what followed—briefly. I hoped he would understand I meant vaguely, to spare both of them the anguish of an explicit word picture.

Ben got the message. He told them how Lorna and Felix had used the boat cushions as flotation aids and tried to swim to safety, but "had gotten separated." Silently, I blessed Ben for the euphemism and cursed Felix for his desertion.

By the time he finished, Mrs. Ward was in no condition to ask any more questions. But clearly she remained unsatisfied. She kept whispering, "It's his fault. My daughter, my flesh and blood. It's his fault, my daughter, my flesh and blood." I didn't know whether she meant Felix or me, or perhaps both of us. Mr. Ward could find no way to comfort her, or himself for that matter.

Chris tried to lessen her mother's anguish by sharing it. "Mom, I'm sorry, so sorry. I feel absolutely awful about this whole thing. For God's sake, she's . . . was my sister . . ."

"She was my daughter, my flesh and blood," whispered Mrs. Ward once again. "It's his fault."

"I know, I know, darling," Chris said soothingly. But she didn't come close. "Stop and think what you're suggesting. Felix is your son-in-law. You can't point a finger at the poor guy unless you are on solid ground. Think for a minute. They were a happy couple. No problems. . . ."

"That we knew of," interjected Mrs. Ward.

"Okay. No problems we knew of. If something was wrong, Lorna would have told you, right?"

There was no answer. Chris stood up and walked over to the coffee table. She picked up an early St. Louis paperweight and rolled it between her palms. Mrs. Ward beckoned her to put it down. Chris complied obediently.

Then she asserted herself. "I don't think there's anything to be done. And I think you both should see Felix." She stood before the group with arms folded. Then she added softly, "Believe me, my dears, he's suffering too. He needs to see you. He needs you."

Chris might as well have been addressing the air in the room. Neither of her parents showed the slightest reaction. I began to feel that my presence was superfluous, almost an irritant to the couple. Nodding to Ben, we stood, preparing to leave. We shook hands, expressed meaningless and unappreciated words of sympathy to the stricken couple, and walked to the door with Christine. I looked back as we left. Sophie and Mervyn Ward were still sitting motionless on the loveseat, holding hands. They looked as if they might disintegrate into ashes at the slightest puff. It occurred to me that they were casting aside any feelings for Christine. It was as though they had lost an only child. But then, no child is ever loved as much as one who has died.

Chris went down to the car to see us off. She thanked us, shaking Ben's hand with her other one cupped over the clasp as a gesture of friendliness. Then she kissed me goodbye. Her darting tongue again caught me unawares. Maybe forced to face the reality of death at close range, she felt the need to reaffirm life—somehow.

Or did she really like me?

19

I was glad to be home again. I had especially missed my rocking chair. I had missed coming home in the evening and sitting in that sanctuary of a chair, holding a glass of Jack Daniel's next to my heart. I rocked slowly, contentedly, enjoying the certain, comforting motion. The infrequent visitors who secured visas to come up to play with me sometimes made silly jokes about my chair, and would ask me what a man in his mid-30's was doing in a rocking chair. But it had lived with my family for over a hundred years, rocking my grandfather, my father, and now me through countless hours. All it required was an occasional rubdown with lemon oil to keep its skin moist and fragrant, and a restuffed seat cushion every year or two to give its occupant a comfortable ride. I had solved many problems rocking away on it, and had no intentions of heeding the advice of my friends to replace it with a chair more in keeping with the ambience of my masculine surroundings.

Yes, I was back in my rocking chair, away from Florida. For good. Enough of the sun and sand and broiling Atlantic. Next trip I'd try the Alaskan inland waterways. As I rocked away, I listened to Mozart on a station my radio liked, and sitting there, revisited some years gone by.

I had advertised to secure someone to share my increasing office load. I wanted a young lawyer with plenty of enthusiasm, plenty of capability, and a willingness to work without a clock in his room or a watch on his wrist. Like me. The responses were sparse because the salary was unattractive. But one candidate showed a lively interest and seemed to have a compatible disposition. We made a deal over a sandwich and a soft drink at a delicatessen on Second Avenue.

Terry Henderson and I became friends as well as office mates. We shared many common interests. Both of us were Mozart freaks, and we both enjoyed chamber music concerts. Most of all we enjoyed opera. Terry also had a fine athletic body built on a five-foot-three-inch frame, and topped with light brown hair and a snub nose. We were married a year later on her birthday.

I rocked a little faster as I relived the following years. We decided against taking a honeymoon trip because we wanted to keep the law office open, and we couldn't figure out how to stagger our honeymoon. Our priorities were ordered. Seven lean years, then seven fat years.

Music was as important to Terry as her daily slices of whole wheat. It energized her in the morning while she dressed; and it soothed both of us during our cocktail hour, an inviolate get-together each evening before dinner, with the telephone off the hook, during which we chased around all manner of topics and subjects, excluding only law. I didn't try to be clever in those tranquil and unruffled days. Terry in gentle reproof used to tell me that stupidity comes in many forms, and cleverness was one of the worst.

Man makes plans, and God sits back and laughs. On a dreary, rain-drenched day in July, four years, seven months and eleven days after we were married, Terry was admitted into New York Hospital suffering from acute headaches and intermittent memory lapses. She died the following Christmas Eve at home while I decorated a tree in the bedroom so she could watch. She lay there wearing a flimsy, beribboned white cap with ruffles to hide her hairless scalp, the product of chemotherapy and radiation treatments. About midnight, her eyes closed and she stopped breathing. I nearly did, too. Much later the doctor told me she had been in her third month of pregnancy. She had never mentioned it.

To my mind they had not been four years, seven months and eleven days. Then and still, they seemed like a short lifetime in paradise, pleasures given selflessly and received gratefully. Since then, I often think how astonished others would be if they knew of my vulnerable underside; that there was more to my life than doing battle in hard armor.

20

Ten days after Ben and I returned to New York, I got a call from West Palm Beach. It had been a perfect Sunday afternoon. I had spent it wandering through Central Park, feeding peanuts to pigeons and myself, share and share alike.

It was Christine Ward.

I immediately sensed trouble. Her voice was pitched high, trembling on the edge of hysteria. The Coast Guard, she said, had found Lorna's boat not far from Everglades City. In the Gulf of Mexico, on a small island. But not Lorna. There was no sign of her yet. Then Christine dropped the bombshell. Felix had been indicted for murder and was being held at the county jail. Would I help—again? she asked.

I listened with feigned impassivity, pretending that I needed time to think it through.

"Tom," she said, "nothing will bring Lorna back. Okay?"

"Not okay. Who says she's dead?"

"She'd have shown up by now, if she were still alive."

"Unless she's hiding."

"Hiding from what? Her husband? Her parents? Me? Don't talk nonsense. Her loss is a horror we'll all have to live with. My parents still have each other, thank God, and they have me. I have them, too, of course—and I've got my painting. But Felix has nothing. Nothing at all. No children, no parents—"

"What happened to his mother?" I knew his father had died when Felix was a kid.

"She died a few years ago from a heart attack. Anyhow," she continued, "no parents and no brothers or sisters. And now no work. Daddy wouldn't have him back. He's pathetic. All alone and helpless."

I privately disagreed. Felix had been far from a pitiable object, I told myself, when he had walked off from me. "I hate him," I said to her. I had never said that even to myself.

"No, I don't think so," she replied. "I really don't think you hate him. I don't believe you know how to hate. Tom, believe me, he's asking for you. If you don't want to do it for him, then take it on for my sake. He's my one and only brother-in-law."

That last touch was pure theatrics. It deserved the mocking laugh I gave it. But Christine didn't flinch. "Tom," she said, "here we are. Just the three of us now. You and Felix and me—"

"I." My interruption was silly pedantry, and out of order, but I did it to pretend that the entire matter was unimportant to me. I could feel Christine's exasperation. "Stop playing games with me. Please. This is no joking matter. For God's sake, your friend has been arrested, he's in jail. This is your business, what you're trained to do, and so wonderfully well. You just can't let Felix down. He needs you. Desperately."

Damn the unerring accuracy of her last shot, I said to myself. The cleverness, the easy mockery suddenly fled. I didn't like the naked feeling of vulnerability left in their wake. For the real truth was that I was not as angry with Felix as I was with myself, because Felix exposed my weakness— my vulnerability. It could be summed up in a single word: NEED. I had always yearned to be needed. Not by clients, who simply bought my talents and experience on a short-term basis, and when my work was done, went their way while I went mine. I wanted to be needed as part of a relationship that did not start and end with a handshake and a payment. My parents had never needed me; they needed each other. Terry had needed me, but not in the quiet, grassy nook where she now lay slumbering.

But there was Felix, damn him. I had fought his battles, chased away his fears, and had given him the only rays of sunshine that could penetrate his dark soul. He *had* needed me, and I was always there. Now he was turning to me again, and a long-forgotten feeling surged within me.

"All right, Chris, all right!" I finally said to her. She had continued to talk to me, plead with me. "But I won't do it for you. You don't really have a stake in Felix. He's not even your brother-in-law any more." I paused so long that she finally asked if I was still there. I had reached a decision.

It was the only one I could make; and deep down I had known that from the outset. "I will take the case on, but for Felix. Not you or anybody else." And abruptly—almost rudely, to hide my weakness—I hung up the receiver. Still, I felt honest with myself, and disturbingly pleased.

There he was again, the little man with the big, shiny, bald head, perched on my shoulder, just waiting for me to finish my long talk with Christine, uninvited as usual, leering at me, whispering in my ear. "You're a damn fool!" he said. Twice.

The gold hands on the clock pointed close to seven. I canceled my dinner plans and went to the comfort cabinet in my study. I fetched a bottle of my friend, Mr. D. The little man growled fiercely and vanished. He knew when he was beaten.

21

Amos Stern, my stalwart partner, was dead set against it.

The day after Chris called, Amos and I thrashed out our differences. It started off by my telling him over the intercom that I was going to take on the defense of Felix. Amos was speechless—but only for the instant before he exploded. My door was open and I could hear him stalking hard-heeled toward my room.

As he crossed the entrance area from his wing on the side opposite mine, our receptionist tapped out my secretary's extension number. Forgetting my door was open, Rebecca took it on her squawk box. "Take cover, Becky doll, it looks like rough seas ahead."

I could picture Rebecca smiling at the storm warnings. She had been on my ship for twelve years. She no longer got seasick.

Amos closed the door behind him. He might be angry, but he was never rude. The only sign of his outrage was a characteristic pulse in his jaw. I seized the initiative.

"Before you start, Amos, let me tell you what's behind my decision."

"Money is my guess. Doesn't it always come down to money?"

"Not this time. This has nothing to do with money. It may sound strange to you but, growing up, Felix and I were very close, almost like brothers. More, twins—fraternal twins. That close, but also very different. The point is I have been his protector, his protagonist, at least until . . ." I faltered.

"Until he became your antagonist. Until he married Lorna."

Amos knew the whole story. One night after losing a case, Amos had dragged me out to Long Island to forget the pain at Abel Conklin, one of our favorite restaurants. It looked like a colonial cottage with a picket fence. When you walked in, you expected to be greeted by an elderly couple wearing wire frame spectacles. Instead, it was a luxurious steakhouse with a thoughtfully filled wine cellar and a comfortable, friendly ambience. Dana, one of the owners, greeted us at the door and took us quickly to a corner table. A few minutes later John, the other owner, came to the table with martinis for both of us. On the house. I never failed to get a laugh out of him by saying, "Good evening, Mr. Chief Justice." His full name was John Marshall.

Amos and I talked more personally than usual that night. I told him about Lorna and me. He was a good listener.

Pacing around my office, Amos continued relentlessly. "Some friend! Some brother! It seems to me Felix never knew the first thing about loyalty. If I were you, I'd kick his bottom over the moon."

So much for second-hand understanding. Amos didn't understand. He knew the facts about Lorna and me—and Felix—but he had not lived my life, he could not feel the impress of my early years, or the unbreakable ties—chains—that bound Felix and me.

I elected not to respond to him.

So he took aim again—and, oh, Amos does have good aim when it counts. "Have you stopped to think about the ethics of accepting this job? I'll bet Lorna's parents don't want you. Right?"

I ducked a direct answer. I hadn't asked Christine about them, but Amos was most likely right. "They've tried and convicted him. But we're sworn to defend just such people."

"That's pompous bullcrackers, and you know it."

I had to chuckle. That was about as close as Amos could come to vulgarity. Once in a great while, when he got really angry, he would resort to "horsetoads." But only when he was truly white-lipped.

"So, partner mine, instruct me in ethics."

Amos disregarded my archness. "You, yourself," he said, "have more of a motive to hurt Evans than to help him."

"Nobody knows that."

"I know it. Lorna's parents know it. Christine knows it, too."

"She's the one who talked me into accepting the engagement." I wasn't able to come closer to the truth than that.

Amos tossed me his most scoffing laugh, and put away the cigarette he had drawn from his pocket, remembering my office was now off-limits to smokers. Even clients had to refrain. "But what if you lose?"

"What if we win?"

"It's the loss that can sink you on ethical grounds. Just think about it. You take on a case for a guy who stole and married your girl. What sweet revenge! You crap up the trial, and justice triumphs! Tom, you and your client are in square conflict. He wins, you lose; he loses, you win. And I have to go out looking for another partner!"

Amos had a point, but it wasn't that cut and dried. "I know that Felix trusts me, and he can. And so can you, Amos my friend, so can you. No evidence, no motive, no body. Not guilty. Depend on it."

"How can I help?"

The capitulation, when it came after a long hour of verbal badminton, with Felix the shuttlecock, was abrupt and unreserved. One of Amos's most likable traits was his ability to put differences to the side once a decision had been reached, and to work toward a common goal. He assured me that he would take care of the shop.

And so I went south, this time knowing it could not be for pleasure. So much for my recent rocking-chair decision to declare Florida off limits.

Felix

22

I hate to start a trial in July, even the last day in July. If it weren't for the Fourth, I would vote the month out of the Union.

It's a great month for kids. School is out, vacations are in. Camp counselors salivate sadistically in anticipation, and parents secretly make plans to reawaken connubial practices which have lain dormant during the school year under the watchful eyes and pricked up ears of children who never sleep.

But the month never worked for me.

July. The month I had left home. And Lorna. It was in July that I went off to find an apartment close to Michigan Law School. And it was on a rainy day in July when my mother announced that Dad had discovered a strange lump in his neck, which signaled his terminal illness too young, too soon.

I set up my command station in the offices of Harvey Woodstock, the attorney who had worked with me on the Tony Savino pool murder case. It wasn't the luxurious space Amos and I had high up in the steel and marble flanks we called home in New York, but it was certainly adequate. And Harvey's arranging for me to have a temporary secretary helped to put me at my ease.

Until I met her.

He must have found her in Central Casting under "Pipe Dreams." She walked in, a slender willow, flashed me a smile that would have made a blind man blink, and stood there with her legs parted just enough for the salacious sun, streaming through the window behind her, to filter through her white skirt. I forced my eyes upward, only to be dazzled by her violet eyes and soft blond hair piled up on the top of her head. I bet myself it would reach the small of her back.

"Good morning," I said, recalling too late that gaping dried the throat. My words came out like the croaking call of a swamp frog.

"I'm Ida Greenstein. I'm supposed to help you while you're here."

Pure silver droplets of sound that could have showered over me forever. Ida, sweet as apple cider. My instincts, bolstered by my will, told me that I was not to suffer from all work and no play.

Work first. I dictated a letter for hand-delivery to Jeffrey Baker, the Assistant State Attorney, who I learned had secured the indictment and was going to try the case. I let him know he would have me to contend with in the courtroom and I asked him to give a copy of the indictment to Ida when she dropped off the letter.

Ida called me from his office. No copy until I signed a formal appearance on behalf of the accused. So I high-tailed down and took Ida in with me to visit Baker.

As I proceeded to the matter at hand, Baker tried to fasten his eyes on me. But they repeatedly skipped off dead center as Ida kept crossing her legs, left over right, right over left. I could almost hear Baker asking, if she was only my secretary temporarily, was she available for a longer term. He had an affable manner. He smiled politely when he said yes, and grinned broadly when he said no. He was a little younger than I, sandy haired, of middling height. Probably appealing to middle-aged women. I made a mental note to remember that during the jury-selection process.

I signed in as attorney of record for Felix Evans, after which Baker handed me a copy of the indictment. It contained no surprises, and nothing in the way of helpful facts. It charged Felix with the intentional, willful, deliberate, and premeditated killing of Lorna Ward Evans within the jurisdiction of the State of Florida, to wit, in the environs of the inland waterways of the State "by the application of force to her body resulting in her death." That meant that the State wasn't sure yet how she had died. *If* she had died, I added to myself. To me it looked as though the State would have a problem proving that Felix killed her.

But then I was not privy to the State's case. Despite a wide-spread doctrinaire belief in the modernity of the law—how in the words of the extraordinary Justice Oliver Wendell Holmes, the law is a living organism that responds to the felt necessities of the times—in too many criminal cases prosecutor and defense counsel still play a cat-and-mouse game. The state is not required to inform defense counsel of its evidence in advance of trial. Indeed, defense counsel are forced to cope with proof disclosures as they pop up—surprise!—like cardboard dummies from behind rocks and trees in a combat training course. The hard, cold truth is that the criminal-justice system feeds on the element of surprise.

I arranged again with Harvey Woodstock to secure permission for me to try the case—I had no Florida license—which presented no problem. I then arranged for Felix to plead not guilty a few days later amidst a battery of cameras from local newspapers and TV stations. Bail, however, was another matter. With no hope of help from the Wards, it looked as if Felix would have to stay in jail until his case was tried. He claimed to be without enough funds to support a $500,000 bail bond.

Then a curious thing happened. Amos called to say that a man had walked into the office in New York, identifying himself as Charles Santiago of Mexico City. He presented a business card with his name, but no address, no telephone number. It described him as the Mexican agent of Banque de Resources Commerciales, Geneva, Switzerland. He told Amos that his principals operated a small private banking institution in Geneva which had benefited recently from an investment opportunity offered by Felix through Ward and Stenrod. The bank had heard of his difficulty and wanted to assist Felix. He produced a cashier's check for $750,000.

When Amos asked him what the terms were, Señor Santiago proclaimed sanctimoniously that the check paid off a debt of honor, and stalked out of the office. Amos took the check to the International Department of Chase Manhattan Bank in Rockefeller Center, and was told that the bank signatures corresponded with those registered in the volume of international banking services and, after a call, that the Swiss bank had the highest rating. Amos sent the check down to me by Federal Express.

I took it in to Felix for an explanation. He told me vaguely that it involved his share of arbitrage profits in connection with the operations of a midwestern grain company. No, he didn't know Señor Santiago, but the Geneva group changed agents frequently to avoid business espionage. If they stayed too long, they learned too much.

Felix's explanation sounded impromptu, and certainly at variance with Señor Santiago's story; but since only $500,000 was needed for bail, and the balance, he told me, was toward our fees, I resisted checking any further. Felix was free within forty-eight hours. He enjoined us to reimburse Chris for the funds she had advanced as a retainer. I got the money to Chris immediately, explaining my windfall. I expected a box full of questions, but I got none at all. Which left me with a few questions of my own that I resolved to ask about at another time.

As the trial approached, I took on two jobs. First, I reread all of Ben's notes on his various interviews. I had brought him down to handle any matters that might come up unexpectedly. I also valued his judgment on tactical calls I would have to make during the trial.

After I finished my reading sessions, Ben and Felix and I holed up in my motel room, just the three of us with plenty of sandwiches and water and coffee. No beer, no alcohol, no telephone calls. We went over and over Felix's story. No decision was made as to whether we would call him as a witness in his own defense. That decision could be made at the last minute, depending upon the State's case.

The trial was scheduled to start on a Friday, which seemed an unusual date. But I was not in a position to ask any questions. It was early to bed the Thursday night before. I suffered the usual pre-opening day jitters. I never escaped them. Agonizing indigestion, periodic palpitations, unyielding insomnia, and a host of hobgoblins lurking wickedly offstage. The jurors, however, would never know that I would be jump-started in the morning by jolting fears of my inadequacy.

23

Ben Abbott and I walked up the courthouse steps together at nine o'clock. Felix had called and said he would go straight to the courthouse himself. The sky was cloudless, the temperature high and climbing. It was a good day for golf or a picnic or a wedding. It was a terrible day to start a trial. All first days of trials are terrible.

The courtroom was on the second floor of the old building which served as the county courthouse, centered between the two curved marble staircases that began in the lobby. This courtroom looked like most, except smaller and without architectural grace, the builders' sense of grandeur having ended at the top of the stairs. At the front, the judge's bench, the so-called seat of justice, was actually a capacious, well-stuffed, high-back armchair designed to allow His Honor to listen and meditate, head comfortably cushioned, eyes closed perhaps, all the better to concentrate or cat-nap.

The jurors would sit in a long box below and along the side wall, their carefully constructed wooden expressions obliterating any conception that they felt surprise, amusement, interest, incredulity, or any other emotion in response to the testimony offered by fellow humans. The court clerk was in his corner, an old wizened figure with his head stretched like a crane over a massive tome that contained the daily, longhand minutes of the judicial proceedings in his courtroom.

The witnesses would sit next to but lower than the judge, usually in isostatic rigidity like a kind of open jack-in-the-box, while the court reporter was positioned near at hand, the easier for her to seize every uttered sound and pinion it in a stenotype machine, a device which transforms spoken words into cabalistic symbols.

The lawyers and their clients are always stationed in the

central area directly in front of the spectators, separated from them by a wooden rail and gate, called the bar. In an elemental sense, trial lawyers are gladiators in gray pinstripes. One will win. The other will fall.

As Ben and I walked down the aisle, which was covered with a threadbare strip of red carpet, the clerk looked up and cast us a bored glance. Despite such encouragement, I introduced myself to him before settling down at our counsel table, which was identified by a wooden plaque nailed to the front edge that read Defendant. Into the courtroom, which was already populated by countless families of flies noisily beating their frustration against tightly shut dirty windows, came some eighty or ninety solemn men and women who, at the direction of the court clerk, took seats at random. These were the veniremen, the prospective jurors from whom we would select twelve individuals good and true, we hoped, and a few alternates as potential substitutes should any of the regular jurors have to be excused.

The eye game began. It would not end until the jury announced a verdict. It would take place in the courtroom, in the corridors and in the street if we confronted one another. The game takes the form of a contest in which juror and lawyer try to watch each other without being caught. The juror watches the lawyer out of curiosity; the lawyer watches the juror to detect his attitude or to affect it, the idea being that friendliness developed in a juror may ultimately evoke sympathy for one's client. My view of all that, to borrow one of Amos Stern's expletives, is: bullcrackers. I have undiluted contempt for lawyers and psychologists and behavior experts who claim to be able to read the proclivities and instinctual reactions of a prospective juror from his or her occupation, or answers to a few questions, or the shape of a head.

I once selected a lady juror because she had a sunny smile that I was certain saw good in everything. And in everybody, I hoped. Eventually she returned to the courtroom with her fellow members to announce their verdict in a grand theft case. As she sat down, she showered the sunniest of smiles upon me. I whispered into my client's ear, "We're home." The foreman stood up and announced a unanimous verdict of guilt on all fourteen counts. Whereupon the same lady cast upon me yet another sunny smile. I felt I was getting a sunburn and heartburn at the same time.

I patted my client on the back, commiserated with him because he wasn't home after all, told him tough luck, and saw him led off dejectedly to the dungeons to await sentencing at a later date. In the corridor I spotted Sunny Jane and caught up with her as she reached the elevators. She smiled.

I gave her a cold reciprocating grimace. "May I ask you a question, ma'am?"

"Sure."

"As part of my course in continuing education in human behavior and nonclinical psychology, will you tell my why you kept smiling at me?"

"Sure."

"Well?"

"I'm a sucker for men with arched eyebrows."

I blinked. "That's it?"

"They make me tingle," she said as the elevator door opened and she got in.

I watched it close on her smile.

Nevertheless, human nature being relentlessly persistent, as I sat idly awaiting the arrival of the State's team I tried to read some of the potential jurors from whose ranks the clerk would call twelve by lot from cards drawn from a revolving drum. Something like Lotto, but no game. Little conversation took place among them, strangers thrown together by chance. Some sat reading a newspaper, others a magazine or a book. Still others showed an amorphous resentment, perhaps physical discomfort, but more likely displeasure over having their own fascinating lives interrupted by jury duty. I made a mental note of the most conspicuous grouches.

Out of the corner of my eye I saw Jeffrey Baker walk into the room through a door behind the clerk's desk. He was accompanied by a young woman who wore her blond hair short, her bangs parted with knifelike precision dead center. They stopped at our table.

"Gentlemen, this is Susan Harwick. Sue, meet Mr. Attleboro, Tom Attleboro, and . . ." He fumbled over Ben's name. After I completed the introduction, Jeffrey tugged me by the sleeve to a side conference, leaving Susan Harwick and Ben to fend for themselves with small talk.

"Last chance, Tom. Deal time is about to end. I can offer

you culpable negligence with seven year max, until the jury gets sworn. Then it'll be too late."

"Shouldn't you be the one looking for a deal, Jeff?"

"Quit your kidding, old boy. I have the case, you've got the empty bag."

"So fill my bag, junior. Give me some goodies to take over to my client to entice him to spare you from the embarrassment of not guilty." Faking a move away from the prosecutor, as though I were ready to head back to my counsel table, I saw Felix coming down the aisle, his characteristically hunched shoulders sagging even in his well-tailored dark gray suit. Walking through the wooden gate, which instantly let out a screeching protest, he shook hands with Ben, then nodded at me.

I turned my attention back to Jeff Baker; we moved over to the jury rail for privacy.

"What have you got, Jeff? Where's the case? No evidence, no motive, no body. You're the one holding an empty bag. What mirrors did you use before the Grand Jury?"

"You're a nice guy, Tommy, so I'll feed you a little something to chew on—or choke on. Boat, shovel, hatchet, sand fleas, sand bar." He paused, and then added, "And eyewitness."

"What's all that supposed to mean?" I asked.

"Wait and see. The grab bag doesn't have a book of instructions." Jeff Baker's mouth twitched a smile. "And guess what else?"

"I give up."

"Bloodstains. Human."

My heart lurched. I shoved it back in place.

"Whose?"

"Wait and see, counselor."

As my stomach heaved, I pretended to belch politely into my fist. "What boat? Where is it?"

Jeff Baker looked away as though he had not heard my admirably cool, clinical question.

"Well, where is it? Where did you get it? From the manufacturer?" My humor sat on me heavily.

Baker ignored it altogether. "All in good time, my friend, all in good time. Well, do you want to deal or not?"

"Do you have a story line, Jeff, or are all those tidbits like a tin box of cheap assorted cookies? Do you have a motive? Do you have a body? Can you prove a death?"

"Sharks." Baker gave me one of his sunniest smiles.

"I still think you used mirrors before the Grand Jury," I said, and returned to my table. The three of us conferred briefly. Felix said he could make no sense out of the disclosed information; he sat back in his chair with a bland expression, rolling his lips in and out of his mouth. Ben asked if we could see the boat. I told him I had no right to attend a preview. "Anyhow," I said, "what would we gain?" He shrugged. In my mind, I shrugged, too.

So I walked over to Baker. He was riffling through a looseleaf notebook with a zippered cover. "Let's pick a jury," I said. I went back to my seat, posture perfect. In truth I wasn't so steady on the horse's back. Still, I was riding it, and I didn't intend to allow it to throw me. Not this accomplished equestrian.

Judge Brian Sperry came out of his robing room behind the court clerk's station and sauntered casually to his seat. We all started to stand up, but a hand signal from him returned us to our seats. The judge was wearing a business suit and a striped tie. His robe would be donned when the jury was ready to be sworn in, signaling the real commencement of the trial. I took Brian Sperry's measure carefully. He was of average height and white haired, with startlingly blue eyes and a ruddy complexion. He showed a wide smile behind a bushy, white mustache.

He beckoned, and we stepped up before him. Jeff Baker knew him, and introduced me as a learned attorney from New York who, with the court's permission, was going to represent Felix Evans.

"Did Mr. Baker tell you how we do things here, young fella?" A booming voice. It seemed too large for his body.

"No, sir, no previews at all." I gave him one of the ingratiating smiles I reserved for judges, traffic cops and box office clerks.

"Well, son, we try 'em quick and we try 'em fair. No high jinks, no grandstanding, and no smart ass cracks. . . ."

I gave him a look with raised eyebrows and a pouting mouth: who, me? it said.

"From either of you," he continued. "And most of all no disrespect. To each other or to the court. So go pick yourselves a jury plus three alternates. I'll work in the back. If you need me for rulings, tell Sol," nodding at the court clerk. Then he gave me a knowing wink as though he had decided to let me in on a state secret. "Jeff told you, didn't he, why I like to start jury trials on Friday?"

I looked at Jeff Baker, who looked at me but said nothing. "Well?"

"No, Your Honor," said the prosecutor.

"Well, it's very simple, sir. I like to encourage counsel to move the jury selection process along expeditiously. That means quickly—consistent, of course, with due process under our Constitooshen." Said with a grave nod of respect for that noble document. "Hence, therefore and consequently, if we can't pick twelve judges of the facts and a couple of bullpen subs in one day, we'll just finish tomorrer. Or Sunday. Got it, boys?"

I smiled. The judge beamed. Jeff Baker joined in dutifully.

Then His Honor pursed his lips through the underbrush of his mustache. I thought he was aiming at me. An impish grin spread across his face. "Today's my birthday. I don't plan to start a murder trial on so auspicious an occasion. I suspect a little surprise party. I caught Mrs. Sperry polishing the sterling this morning, and yesterday I noticed her peeking into the liquor closet. That's my domain, usually. Sumpin's up. So I'd better get home early. I know you fellers are going to try and oblige me—consistent with due process, mind you!" Another grave nod followed.

Jeff and I wished him a happy birthday and walked back to our tables. Judge Sperry went off to the robing room, and the crane in the corner twisted a look at us and snapped his beak peevishly. Jeff and I nodded our state of readiness. Around and around went the drum, the name cards within tumbling noisily against the tin sides. Jury selection had begun. The bell had rung for Round One.

24

We selected a jury and three alternates by late afternoon, spending much time excusing people who had read about the case in the papers and developed a slant. Other than for excluding them, I had no particular jury pattern in mind. However, I make it an invariable practice to seek one juror with high marks for brains. His or her education or work is my clue. I have always believed that when push comes to shove during jury deliberations, the pooled mental resources of the panel rise to the level of the most intelligent juror. I had a winner on that score tucked neatly among the others selected. Reginald Archer was going to be my emissary into the jury room. He held a B.S. and a doctorate in chemistry. He taught at Miami University, but lived in Naples, which made him subject to the jury draft call of this court.

I looked over the array of twelve, reading them from left to right in the front row and in the opposite direction along the back row. There was precious little I had learned about most of them. Four—three women and one man—were unmarried, or divorced. Another was a widow. There was a computer programmer, a drugstore clerk, and, surprisingly, we had selected two telephone linemen. Most of the others were small business people. One white-haired lady was a librarian. And then there was Reggie, who probably was a pipe smoker and would wear the same kind of unstylish, wrinkled suits that probably graced his narrow frame in his classrooms. I hoped he would not come across to his compatriots as an academic snob. Nobody likes to be lectured. What the hell, I thought, they were what they were, chosen by us to be a cross section of the community. They had their likes and dislikes, their preferences and their attitudes. Five of them were women, and four were black.

I looked inquiringly at Ben seated to my right. Although he had not gone to college, he was a trained observer, and I welcomed his comments. One slip he had passed to me read "nail biter." He had scrawled on another, "She's reading *The Magic Mountain*." That had been Kathryn Adelaide, my white-haired librarian. I had fallen in love with her already. She sat on the edge of the seat, back straight, tiny manicured hands folded at rest in her lap. Maybe she had lived a sheltered life, but she had to be well-read, and I imagined that she had endured her share of life's slings and arrows. I wanted her compassion and understanding. Clearly she was well endowed in those areas. And she didn't smile at me.

Ben gave me a discreet thumbs up sign. Felix was seated to my left, furthest from the jury to my right, so that if he reacted to a telling blow during the trial, by leaning forward I could shield him from their view. I asked for his approval in a whisper. After all, he alone would have to stand up and face their judgment. It was his life that was placed in jeopardy when the jury was sworn in. His eyes relayed his uncertainty, but he expressed no real dislike for any of the panel. So I sauntered over to Jeff Baker and Susan Harwick, with just a suggestion of confident satisfaction as I glanced at the lucky twelve.

"They're great, Jeff," I told him in a voice just loud enough to allow the jurors to hear. Who doesn't like to be liked?

Baker was not in a bantering mood. Perhaps he had noted this first skillful thespian performance before the jury, because now he stood up stiffly and addressed Judge Sperry, who, having been apprised that jury selection was complete, had just entered wearing his judicial robes.

"Jury is satisfactory, Your Honor," he said.

Judge Sperry waited expectantly for my response. I paused, touched each juror with my eyes, and allowed a smile to flit across my face.

"Each of the jurors is eminently satisfactory to me, if the court pleases."

The court definitely did not please. I earned my first glower, which I accepted blandly. Judge Sperry rubbed his chin, which had a small cleft, and recovered his good humor. After all, it was his birthday. I guessed it to be around his sixty-fifth.

"Ladies and gentlemen," he said in a conversational tone, "Mr. Hobson, the clerk, will administer the oath to you in a moment. We will then recess until ten o'clock Monday morning, when you must return to the jury room right behind the courtroom. Mr. Hobson will show it to you before you leave. Please be prompt. If we start late because of one of you, the time will be subtracted from your luncheon recess." A deft touch, I thought.

He stood up and leaned against the wall with arms folded inside the capacious sleeves of his black, pleated robe. The jurors watched him intently as though he were about to serve match point.

"From now on until you are discharged, you are the judges of this accused person, Felix Evans. Keep that heavy responsibility in mind. That means, keep yourselves impartial. You must hear the case only and exclusively on the evidence presented to you in this courtroom. Do not read newspaper accounts of it, as sorely as you may be tempted to do so. And of course you must not watch television news dealing with the case. We do not want to—indeed we cannot—deny the press access to these proceedings. But you must not allow their reporting and observations to affect your judgment in any way. That's why I ask you to turn off or tune out TV news of the trial."

Judge Sperry paused and wrapped his robe about him. "Finally, and most important of all. Do not discuss this case with your family or friends, or among yourselves. You must not reach any conclusions or make any judgments until all the evidence is before you and I have instructed you on how to weigh it. Is that clear?"

Heads nodded in unison. One voice piped out "Of course!" That was Kathryn Adelaide, whose face colored when she realized that she had vocalized her response. The judge beamed. The jurors smiled. Even a murder trial, I said to myself, will have its light moments.

I hoped I'd find something to laugh about when the trial was over.

25

Monday morning was another gala day for the sun. It splashed all over the courtroom. Jeffrey Baker and his stone maiden, Susan Harwick, strode in lockstep to their table. The swinging gate again scraped and screeched in decreasing tempo behind them, until it finally ground to a stop. Maybe a little graphite or oil, I thought. I had spent the early morning hours achieving a single modest goal: living through them. My nerves jangled, my stomach was knotted, my head a bell tower, and ringing. I was in sorry shape. There was no way, I had thought, that I would even make it to court.

Yet here I was, in my lion's disguise, my roar in readiness.

Jeff was wearing a tan suit, a blue shirt and a patterned tie, all set for a television interview. I had to admit he looked very pretty. The women jurors unconsciously preened, fingering their hair and adjusting the necklines of their dresses. Not my librarian, however, my Kathryn Adelaide. She sat quietly in her seat, still on her own time, reading *The Magic Mountain*. The temperature was already pushing eighty. Reginald Archer's suit was more crumpled than ever. He was looking at the sports pages. I was pleased. But then I thought, he's probably a Yankee fan. Unforgivable.

Felix came in with Ben after having had breakfast together, an invitation I had passed on, partly because it's more polite to be terminal by oneself. Felix was dressed expensively, too expensively, I thought. He wore dark linen slacks and a patterned tan sports jacket, doubtless by some Italian superstar designer. His shoes were unmistakable Gucci. Thank God he was not flaunting a boutonnière. I made a note to tell him to dress down.

Judge Sperry, busy in chambers with paperwork, did not

come down until nearly eleven o'clock, by which time everyone in the courtroom had begun to show impatience. Finally, there was a stirring as the door opened behind the dais, and in came His Honor, trailing clouds of glory.

"Hear ye, hear ye, hear ye, all persons having business in this Criminal Term of the Superior Court of the State of Florida for the County of Lee, draw near, give your attention, and ye shall be heard."

The stentorian voice of the uniformed, red-haired bailiff brought the filled room to a hush. So he continued into his second manifesto in plainer English. "Put all newspapers away, no talking, and pay attention to the proceedings in this court, the Honorable Brian Sperry presiding."

The honorable one nodded at the prosecutor's table, and Jeff Baker walked over to the jury box. His opening address to the jury was brief and to the point. It was also somewhat unusual, like this case. There was no getting away from the fact that there was no *corpus delicti*; no body, nothing evidencing the commission of any crime, much less a murder. And no motive that at least I had uncovered.

"Ladies and gentlemen," he started. "The case we propose to present to you has two principal components. One is the oral statement of this man." He pointed at Felix.

"The defendant or Mr. Evans, please." I stood and made the point quietly. The judge looked up, nodded his approval, but said nothing. Good, I thought, at least he's not going to be a drill sergeant.

"All right, sir," continued Baker with an ingratiating smile that did not sit comfortably on his face, "the statement of the defendant. The other component is evidence. Now I tell you at the outset that much of the evidence is circumstantial. But it is nonetheless compelling.

"Let me give you an example of circumstantial evidence." Jeff assumed a tutorial posture, index finger touching the palm of his other hand, his words emerging slowly. Reginald Archer permitted himself a gossamer smile but looked bored. He evidently didn't need the lesson.

"If when you go to sleep at night you notice the grounds outside your apartment or home are clean and dry, and when you awaken they are covered with snow, you may safely conclude that snow fell during the night even though you did not witness its falling. That is circumstantial evidence. And if you see the tracks of an animal in the snow, you—"

Enough, I thought. School's out. I stood. "Your Honor, perhaps you will give instructions to the jury, if they ever get the case to decide, rather than the state's attorney. I suggest that he present his case rather than deliver a lecture."

"Your point is well taken, Mr. Attleboro, but a *leetle* long in its statement. Get to the case, Mr. Baker." It began to look as though the learned judge liked to be a leetle regional to show he was a regular guy.

Baker set back his shoulders and moved on. "We shall play a tape for you which records the free and voluntary statement of this . . . of the defendant following what *he* regarded as his *rescue*." The emphasis and irony were a bit heavy-handed, I thought.

"I shall not dwell on it at length now," he was saying. "It is best that you hear it in full at the right time. It's enough for you to know now that the defendant *claims* that he and his wife had rented an outboard motor boat at the Seaboard Motel out of Everglades City, had motored through the everglades and inland waterways, and drifted—drifted, mind you—into the Gulf of Mexico. He *claims* that the motor broke down. That's one of the issues you'll have to decide. He *says* the two of them eventually tried to swim to safety, that he got separated from his wife, and that she simply vanished from his sight. He says he made it to No Name Key, a small land mass in the Gulf, from which he was rescued in the morning. The boat was gone and so was his wife. Whom he somehow got separated from. *He says*."

A long, dense pause. And then: "She couldn't swim." Pause. "We'll prove that to you." The jury snapped that tidbit up like a seal going for a morsel of fish thrown on the fly.

"And finally we shall show you that his story was and is a total, unmitigated tissue of lies meant to cover up his brutal, gruesome, and deliberate killing of Lorna Ward Evans. His wife."

He definitely had the jury's attention. No pushover, that man, I thought ruefully. Baker walked over to his table where Suzie Q handed him a sheet of paper. I was glad to see she had something to do.

"You will hear the testimony of the man who brought Felix

Evans back to the mainland in the morning from that small key in the Gulf where we contend he arranged to be found. He will tear the first corner off that tissue of lies when he describes to you the defendant's physical condition. And what he—Felix Evans—said to him."

I flicked through Ben's notes of his visit to the Melvilles with Ensign Shea. There was nothing in them about a statement that Felix had made to either of them. I whispered a question to Felix, and he shook his head from side to side. I picked up Jeff Baker's opening.

" . . . and then you'll hear the testimony of the dockmaster at the Seaboard Motel who, on the afternoon of June 2nd last, rented the outboard motor boat to Felix and Lorna Evans. What he said to them and what they said to him will, I submit to you, lead you to conclude that the defendant forced his wife to take that ride, that she was frightened and told the defendant so. You will hear how the dockmaster tried to discourage the defendant from renting a boat because of the weather, but how Evans . . ."

"Mister," I corrected his manners again, quietly.

" . . . *Mr.* Evans insisted, irrationally . . ."

"Objection, Your Honor."

Judge Sperry frowned. Repeated interruptions please no jurist. But he said, "Mr. Baker, stick to facts. State of mind ain't a fact; it's a conclusion that falls within the jurors' province. You know that. Please." Then to the jurors: "Disregard the conclusion expressed by the state's attorney."

"Anyhow, you'll hear how the dockmaster insisted to Mr. Evans . . . I mean how Mr. Evans insisted on going out anyhow."

My objection had had the effect that I hoped it would: to rupture Baker's narration and dilute the attention of the jurors. It seems I had also reaped a bonus. Baker's concentration had been cracked.

"The dockmaster," he was saying, "will tell you how he gave the defendant a map of the inland waterways and warned him not to venture into the Gulf. And how the defendant nevertheless did just that. Deliberately."

He then told them they would hear from a Coast Guard officer who had found the boat, *what* he found in the boat, and its condition. I felt a frisson to which no pleasure was attached.

And then Baker moved on to introduce the name of a fishing captain who, according to some vague allusions of the prosecutor, would describe "weather, water, drift, and ground conditions," which he assured the jurors they would find "most interesting." The captain would tell the jurors, he added somberly, something even more significant. "This seasoned boat captain will tell you where she observed the defendant—Felix Evans—in the Gulf—in the boat—alone." The pauses were deadly. He looked over at Felix at each juncture.

"And finally, we shall call a forensic pathologist who will identify certain stains found in the boat. He will testify that they were bloodstains. And will further testify that the bloodstains were of human blood, probably from the body of—"

I rose, slamming the table top. The rest of the sentence jammed in Jeff's throat. The eyes of the jurors widened. Damn him and the horse he was riding.

"I respectfully suggest that that was a highly improper comment, and deeply prejudicial to my client."

The judge cut me off with a hand gesture. "Yes, Mr. Attleboro, your objection is well taken." He turned to the jurors, leaning his elbows on the table in front of him while Jeff stood wide-eyed pretending to be mystified. "Ladies and gentlemen, no doctor—and a forensic pathologist really isn't anything more than a medical doctor who inquires into the causes of death when it takes place under unexplained circumstances—ain't that so, Mr. Baker?"

Baker gave a misery-ridden, "Yes, sir."

"The point is, ladies and gentlemen," continued Judge Sperry in an even more sober tone, "no doctor can do any more than give his *opinion* in the area of his specialty. What Mr. Baker meant to tell you was that the doctor he intends to call as a witness may state it to be his *opinion* that a certain stain he examined was human blood. And nothing more than that. Probabilities don't count in this court. Do I have that right, sir?"

"Yes, sir." Bravely but still misery ridden.

The judge stood up. "You are to erase entirely from your minds Mr. Baker's statement of a fact conclusion on that topic. He should not have said that. Fact conclusions are in your exclusive province. Now and forever more. Got it clear, ladies and gentlemen?"

Mixed nods and yesses from the jurors.

"Counselors, please getcherselves up to the bench."

We huddled in the corner furthest from the jury box. His Honor was quite unhappy.

"Jeff, that was wrong, and you know it. I know you know it. You're too damn good a lawyer to plead innocent mistake. If that doctor had testified the way you spoke, I'd have honored a motion for a mistrial. I told both of you before, no high jinks. I meant it. If you pull that kind of a stunt again, you'll pay a nasty price. Wanna stay friends with me?" The loaded question was followed by a characteristic pursing of the judge's lips. I instinctively ducked again. Jeff Baker said, "I do" in a voice laden with relief. We returned to our respective tables.

Jeff Baker wound up quickly after that. The spell had been broken. He had paid a heavy price for the high-risk shot he had taken.

When he sat down, Judge Sperry gave me the floor. I silently vowed to avoid any high-risk shots.

26

As I walked over to the jury box, fingering my tie to be sure it was perpendicular, I glanced over at the gold-leaf lettering on the wall behind the judge's chair. IN GOD WE TRUST. It always troubled me in a vague way to read that commonplace inscription in courtrooms. I wondered how it made a person feel, who expected justice to be meted out by a judge and jury on the record made before them, to be thrown back on divine intervention. Was the system so flawed it needed that extra lift?

Some years earlier I was trying a civil case on behalf of a young woman charged with having exercised undue influence on her recently departed dearly beloved to alter his will so as to exclude the children of his previous marriage. They relied on his eighty years, contrasted with the defendant's thirty-seven, as evidence of his impaired senses. I was arguing that the old gentleman may have lost some of them, but God had been good to him, so that he had retained sufficient mental agility to recognize a caring and loving wife, and distinguish her from greedy and uncaring children. In the middle of my persuasive oration, the first T in a similar wall inscription fell from the wall and bounced off His Honor's head. The comic relief was enhanced by the wall legend in its revised version.

I suddenly became aware that Judge Sperry was waiting, and that Miss Kathryn Adelaide was taking my measure as though I were a new acquisition it was her responsibility to catalogue as drama, history—or fiction. Her bright blue eyes bored into me, her head cocked slightly to the side.

I cleared my throat and gave the impression I was holding four aces and a king. "Your Honor, ladies and gentlemen, you have just listened to a speech. Nothing more than that. Not one word spoken by Mr. Baker can be accepted by you as a fact.

"What, then, are the facts? You will find them to be precious few, at least so far as the matter before us is concerned!"

I focused my eyes alternately upon Reginald Archer and Kathryn Adelaide, both of whom were paying the kind of attention litigators pine for. From time to time, I glanced at the others. The Number One juror, Molly Schneider, the widow, was elegantly dressed, slender, almost anorectic in appearance. She had to be climbing past fifty, but a skilled hand at makeup had covered over a good ten years. At the moment, she was having a cuticle problem with her left pinky which she was trying to solve discreetly with her teeth. But she was listening. And so were most of the others. I had my doubts, however, about a couple of them. Alex Raymond, the drugstore clerk, was whispering to the neighbor on his left. I felt like rapping my pencil on the rail for attention.

"All of you, along with me, will surely wait with great interest for the prosecutor's witnesses, not to learn about weather and tides and ground conditions, and surely not rescue operations and water searches. For remember, ladies and gentlemen, Felix Evans is on trial for murder, not merely the mysterious disappearance of his wife. You must therefore listen for evidence, hard evidence, I say, and not some flimsy reeds of circumstantial possibilities. You must decide whether there is hard and certain evidence of the death of Lorna Evans. Not merely her disappearance, *but her death*."

I let that sink in, taking a slow swallow of water.

"And I await with special interest, as I expect you will, too, the way the State of Florida proposes to convince you beyond a reasonable doubt that my client killed his wife—without even a body to show that she is indeed dead. Let alone how she died."

I ticked off the problems as I saw them, using my fingers as counting sticks. "No body. No evidence of foul play. No motive. No death. No murder."

I sat down.

The jurors looked around blankly. They had probably expected fireworks from my mouth. Not this time, I said to myself. Best to leave this a mystery story.

Judge Sperry glanced at the clock and announced a recess

until two o'clock. The spectators buzzed as they left the court-room. Act One, Scene One was about to begin. I took a deep breath, pushing out of my mind the thought that I hadn't the foggiest idea how the play was going to end.

27

Jeffrey Baker stood up and faced the audience behind the bar as though he were the master of ceremonies, which at that moment he happened to be. "The State calls George Feeley as its first witness."

George Feeley slouched up to the jury box. He had an odd walk, almost sideways, as though he wanted to keep his back against an invisible wall. His hands were stuffed in the pockets of khaki trousers; a cigarette box squared out the breast pocket of his checkered shirt. His eyes flickered with momentary recognition as he caught sight of Ben Abbott. A real prince of a guy, I thought.

I looked around the courtroom and caught Sophie Ward glaring at me, lips set. Mervyn sat quietly next to her. She was unforgiving, and I could understand why. Chris was also there, wearing a straight-line suit and a gray-green silk shirt. When I caught her eye, she gave me a big smile and a thumbs-up sign which I pretended not to see.

". . . so help you God?" Peter Hobson, bony hand upraised, finished administering the oath.

"I do," said George Feeley through barely open lips. He perched on the edge of the witness chair, his hands tucked under his thighs. Jeff Baker lounged against the far end of the jury box. Feeley gave his educational history, which began with kindergarten and ended with his dropping out of high school during the first year. When he left school, he got a job at a machine shop. A couple of years later he changed his career goals. He went to work at the Seaboard Motel, first as a busboy, and later, when he showed some rudimentary mechanical aptitude, as a handyman. He had been moved over to the boats about six months before the Evans episode.

Jeff Baker moved quickly to the business at hand.

"Can you remember renting an outboard motor boat to Felix and Lorna Evans on June 2 last?"

"My log says I did."

"Objection, move to strike the answer. Not responsive."

"Sustained," intoned His Honor through his bushy mustache. "Yur gonna have trouble, young man, unless yuh listen to th' question." Sometimes the judge overdid his slurring of the King's English, I mused, but he was sharp enough. "The answer is stricken. Donna, read back the question."

Donna Redmond, the court reporter, her white linen skirt stretched tightly, and a little too far above her knees, tucked her chewing gum in one cheek, and read the question back primly.

"Yep, I remember."

"Do you remember what they looked like?"

"Do I remember what they looked like? Aren't ever likely to forget her. She was great looking."

I restrained myself. Even though he kept slipping off the edge of the question, I didn't want the jurors to get the feeling I was being a pest.

"Yeah, I remember them both." Pointing in the direction of our table, he said, "There's the Mister sitting at the lawyer table."

I stood up with a "who-me?" look.

"Not him," said George Feeley. "The guy next to him."

Ben Abbott stood up.

"Not him neither. The other one, the other one," said George Feeley impatiently.

I placed my hand on Felix's arm to keep him seated.

"Do you remember when they reached the boat dock?"

"When they reached the boat? Yeah. Around two or so. Two, two-thirty. They signed out at two-forty. I wondered what they wanted. Nobody had been down all morning, and I was getting ready to shut down the marina. The weather was lousy."

"What do you mean, 'lousy'? Was it raining?"

"No, not raining. But it was a plain lousy day. Skies overcast. Small craft warnings up along the Gulf front. Wind up and growing."

"What did they want?" Baker asked as if he really wanted to know.

"What did they want? Okay. A boat, of course." George's opinion of the prosecutor plummeted.

"What were they wearing?"

"Like I said, him and the girl was the only ones down that day. He had on a white shirt and white pants. He looked like a medic from an ambulance. She—his wife—I think she had on something red, like a kind of sweater, that reached down to her knees. She was carrying a blanket from the room. I was gonna tell her she couldn't take it with her. But she gave me a big smile—she was real cute, well-made, if you know what I mean—and I made like I didn't see her slip the blanket into the boat."

"What kind of boat was it, George?"

"What kind of boat? Okay. All our boats are the same. Well, they're all fiberglass, reinforced hulls with nine horsepower outboards."

"How big are they?"

"How big? About twelve feet."

Feeley made me feel as though I were in an echo chamber.

"You said they were fiberglass?" Baker asked.

"That's right. Unsinkable. They float like a canoe. Even when they're full up with water, you can sit in 'em and you'll still stay above the water from the waist up."

"What did the boats carry? How were they fitted out?"

"Okay. The equipment. I gotcha. Each boat has two seat cushions, a five-gallon can of gas, an anchor, a small G.I. spade, and an oar. If you ask for a flashlight, we lend you one. Oh, and a hatchet—an ax."

Jeff Baker paused for effect I supposed. Then: "Why a hatchet?"

"Why a hatchet!" He repeated the question as if the answer were obvious. " 'Cause some people stray out of the markers in the channel and get the prop caught in roots and branches. Gotta chop 'emselves free. The spade's for the same reason."

"All right. Now George, tell me what happened when they came down for the boat."

"Okay. When they came down for the boat. Like I said, when they come down for the boat, it wuz a real lousy day."

The day he first saw the couple, George Feeley thought to himself, why couldn't he meet a girl like that one? Probably rich. With a girl like that, a fellow could go places. Maybe buy a small restaurant and get the hell out of the damn sun once and for all. Maybe even open a good restaurant with liquor and the works. All it took was a little luck. A nice and rich, nifty girl ready for anything in exchange for a gold ring. A big bed, some great music. . . .

"Can you tell us how we can arrange to take out a boat?" The question turned off his daydream.

He stopped pulling a plastic weather sheet over one of the outboards and looked skeptically at the couple standing before him. "On a day like this, Mister? You gotta be kidding. The flags are going up all along the coast and it's gonna get worse."

"We don't want to go out in the Gulf. Just around the inland waterways," said the man. He pulled a folded map from his pocket, which he said he had found in the book rack in the rental office, marked "Compliments of the Chamber of Commerce and Seaboard Motel."

"Can't we just take a boat along the marked course?" He indicated the course leading from the marina across the Bay and into the everglades.

"Suit yourself. If you wanna go, you go. I wouldn't." He led the way back to the office to sign them up for a boat. The girl hung back.

"Felix, darling," she said, "why don't we just hang around, and leave later for Miami? If the young man—" she pointed to Feeley—"thinks the weather is too bad, we really should listen to him, shouldn't we?"

"Come on, honey," he replied, "we'll stay in the channel where it's completely safe. I've got a map and we'll turn around whenever you say so."

The three of them entered the office where the formalities were quickly completed. Feeley glanced at the register and noted their names: "Mr. and Mrs. Felix Evans." Leading them back to one of the boat stalls, he turned to the man and asked him whether he knew how to operate the boat. He said he did. Still, when it came time to step in the boat, the girl hung back again. Feeley had the distinct impression that she was very reluctant about going out. He got into the boat with both of them and spread the map across his knees. He pointed out the markers and the water course. "Remember, both of you, stay inside them markers. Don't go beyond this lagoon here." He put his finger next to a belly in the canal depicted on the map well inside the narrows to the Gulf of Mexico. "And don't get outside the boundaries or you'll sure as hell get lost. I don't want to have to send out a search party on this kind of a shitty day—excuse me, ma'am."

The woman smiled faintly. Feeley stepped out of the boat and cast the lines free. As the man cranked up the engine, Feeley called to him. "When do you expect to be back?"

"Before dark," came the reply.

"In about an hour or so," called his wife in a strained voice, "look for us in about an hour."

The boat's motor coughed, grabbed, coughed again. Then it caught its fuel and began to purr quietly. As they drew away from the docks, Feeley called out to the couple. "If you return after five, secure the boat and put the keys through the slot in the office door. I close up at five sharp. The boss comes down later to check the place out and pick up the late keys."

"That was the first and last time I saw them," Feeley said.

Jeff Baker sat down. But, then, as I started to get up, he stood again. "I forgot one thing," he said, a trifle apologetically.

"Forgot like hell," I muttered to Ben Abbott, as I lowered myself reluctantly back into the chair.

Baker walked up to George Feeley and stood in front of him with his arms folded, his head stuck forward and his legs spread. He looked like a short giraffe getting set to take a sip of water.

"One last thing, George. I should have asked you before," Jeff Baker said, his embarrassment transparently false—to me. You never knew what a jury saw through till after they brought in their verdict. And even then only if they felt like talking. "Did the couple look like they had had a fight, an argument?" Baker asked.

"Yes, sir, they sure did." Feeley's answer popped out before I could stop him.

"C'mon now!" I felt the blood rushing to my head. "Your Honor, he knows better than that. They wouldn't even try that on a TV show. Look like! A fight! Some motive! Objection!"

Judge Sperry stared at me. I stood staring at the prosecutor. The jurors stared at the judge. The only sounds were my teeth gnashing for not having spoken up fast enough.

Finally Judge Sperry broke the silence.

"Mr. Attleboro, the only proper word in that explosion of yours was 'Objection.' We have a long way to go, and at this rate we'll be here until each of the jurors there celebrates his and her birthday. You fellahs got to control yourselves. Be respectful, speak quietly." Then with a roar that jolted everyone in the courtroom: *"Do you understand me?"*

Even Peter Hobson, the permanent fixture, in his corner, dropped his pen and craned around to look at the judge.

"Yes, sir," I said deferentially.

The judge was not finished. He swiveled around and transfixed Jeff Baker with a lethal look. "And you, sir, the State's representative. I'm sustaining the objection, of course. The question was improper. *And you know it.*" The silence that followed was so profound that had a glove fallen to the floor, it would have sounded like a tree crashing to earth.

Benevolent in his triumph, Judge Sperry stood up, and walking to the edge of the dais nearer to the jury box, leaned over and bestowed a beatific smile upon the chosen few. His mustache quivered and his blue eyes twinkled. A regular dapper Summer Santa.

"These men," he said nodding at Baker and me alternately, "are fine perfessionals. They're a leetle tense, like fighters in the first round. But don't hold my reprimand against 'em. I like 'em both, even if I gotta step in from time to time, like a referee. That's really my job, to see to it that rules are followed that allow you to hear and see only proper evidence, and to keep you free from prejudicial matter that can improperly affect your ultimate judgment as the triers of the fact issues." He paused, then smiled again.

"If I sounded like a perfessor, it was an important lesson. You *must* disregard the last answer. The witness may only testify to what he saw and heard, and not to his opinions or conclusions. That's *your* responsibility." Returning to his chair, he sat down and looked up at the ceiling.

"All right, proceed, Mr. Baker. And both of you, try to mind yer manners."

I felt more comfortable. But I had learned a *leetle* lesson. Don't play around with a buzz saw. It may start running unexpectedly.

"No further questions," Baker said quietly.

This time when he sat down he stayed down. His aide-de-camp, Susan Harwick, traced the sharp part in her blond hair with a fingernail and glowed at him as though he had just passed the Bar exam on the first try. Mollie Schneider, the Number One juror, watched their interplay with evident distaste, possibly aware that the two were playacting. Most of the others looked expectantly at me, awaiting fireworks, I suppose. I wanted to tell them Perry Mason was in the fiction section, but restrained myself.

I stood behind my table, which meant I could make George Feeley speak louder than he had been. Experience had taught me that a witness finds it harder to lie when he is shouting his answers.

I tossed a smile at George Feeley. He hadn't hurt Felix. He had only been a curtain-raiser, setting the stage for things to come. Nevertheless, the scene he had set held a certain foreboding. Some revision was needed. But first I had to sweep away the debris left by the judge's explosion. It's one thing to be told to disregard a statement. It's an entirely different matter to do it. The mind can be infuriatingly retentive.

"Speaking about fights, did Lorna Evans have a black eye?"

"A what?"

"A black eye, a shiner."

"I didn't notice one."

"Didn't you now! Was her face bruised or discolored?"

George Feeley glanced at Jeff Baker. No help there.

"Was her face what?"

"Please pay attention to me, not to the prosecutor. Was Lorna Evans's face bruised or discolored?"

"Not that I could see."

"Really! Did you see *any* visible signs that she had been abused?"

George Feeley shook his head.

"Please answer the question. The court reporter can't record a head shake."

"What do you mean 'visible signs,' sir?"

I had forgotten. I had to keep the questions very simple.

"Did you see *anything* that showed that anybody had hit Mrs. Evans. Anything at all?"

"Anything at all? Okay. She seemed frightened—okay, okay. No hitting. Nothing like that. Nothing I could see."

"Did Mr. Evans in your presence shout at his wife or push her around?"

"Shout at her? She were scared."

I threw him another smile, allowing him a moment to nibble at his nail like a mouse chewing at a piece of cheese.

"Scared of what?"

"Scared of what? Well, she kept looking around at her husband as we stood at the boat. And when she got in . . ."

"Did he push her in?"

"Push her? Not exactly."

"And when she got in, what then?"

"What then? Well, she asked me to look for her after about an hour. To send out a search party, like she were expecting trouble."

"From her husband *or the weather?*"

"She didn't say."

"She took along a blanket, didn't she? To protect herself from her husband or the weather?"

"I guess the weather."

I waited a beat. The point had been made. Trial lawyers who sought to polish to perfection, more often than not rubbed away the patina. I had cast the issue in doubt. Time to move along.

"Are you aware of any law that requires your motel guests to follow your orders?" A little brow-beating is good for the soul.

"Whaddya mean?"

"You told the state's attorney that in effect you ordered Mr. and Mrs. Evans not to venture past a certain lagoon in the inland waterway, didn't you?"

"Yup."

"Well, did you tell them that your order had the force and effect of law?"

"Of what? Of law? Of course not." He jutted out his chin pugnaciously as if daring me to take a punch.

I didn't have to do that. "The point is," I said, "it wasn't against the law for them to disobey your direction, if they chose to do so; isn't that a fact?"

"I'm responsible for them boats," he mumbled.

"I asked you whether it was against the law for them to disobey you. Do you understand the question?"

"I suppose so."

"Well, it wasn't against the law, was it? Answer the question, please."

"Nope. It weren't."

I walked closer to him before continuing. Professor Archer was fiddling with the ends of his bow tie but his attention was on the witness. All the members were similarly focused.

"There are times, however, when weather conditions are such that the Coast Guard forbids any boats from venturing into the Gulf, right?"

"Right? You betcha they are. They's times when the water is whipped up something fearful. Gale force, that is."

"On June second?"

"On June second? Well, not exactly. Not on June second."

"The Coast Guard had not closed the Gulf to small craft on that day, had it?"

"Closed it? Not that I can remember. But it were a bad day. That it were."

I moved over toward the prosecution table before asking my next question. Baker and Ms. Harwick looked up at me as if they'd like to chisel my features just a bit more.

"Where is the map you said Mr. Evans had with him?"

"How do I know?" Defiantly and with a slight sneer.

My mistake. The dumb question deserved the dumb answer. I had asked Felix what had happened to his map. He said he'd left it in the boat with his clothes when Lorna and he swam for it.

"Does the state's attorney have a copy of the Chamber of Commerce map?" I knew there were a couple around. Deputy Sheriff Harry Carelton had shown one to Ben Abbott when we were down at his office before the Missing Persons case had become Murder One, and Ben had picked one up when he went to see Feeley. But I wanted them to produce it, as though they had been keeping it from the jurors.

Jeff conferred with Susan Harwick, who fussed around in a box under the table. She came up with the map and handed it to her boss, who handed it to me.

I handed it to George Feeley. But first Ben and I peered at it to make certain it matched our copies. "Can you tell us, Mr. Feeley, whether this is a facsimile—the same as, that is—of the map Mr. and Mrs. Evans picked up in the office at your dock station?"

"Looks like."

"It's the same, isn't it?"

"I guess."

"It's the same, *isn't it?*" I tried my own version of the Sperry growl.

"It's the same."

"Thank you. Please, may it be marked Defendant's Exhibit A in evidence, Your Honor?"

"Any objection, Mr. Baker?"

"No, sir."

"Received in evidence."

Donna Redmond put a yellow sticker on the back of the map, wrote in a large A, dated and initialed it, and handed it back to me with a Grade A smile. To the visible disappointment of the jurors, I put the map to the side. It was of no immediate use to me. Had I been Jeff Baker, however, I would have had Feeley point out the markers and the lagoon on the map.

My thoughts must have traveled telepathically across to the prosecution table. For as soon as I sat down, Baker hopped up, grabbed the map and shoved it in front of George Feeley. He had the witness draw a red X in the middle of the so-called lagoon which he said he had told Felix to stay within.

The map was printed vertically on the long accordion sheet. The top was east, the bottom west. Seaboard Motel was at the top, and the Gulf of Mexico was at the bottom. The marked-out channel proceeded in a generally western direction from the motel until it reached the Gulf of Mexico. Markers delimited safe navigational waters. The channel had been partially cleared but the sides were dotted with islets and land clumps which became swamps and cragged land formations covered with mangroves, dwarfed evergreens, and roots that I knew writhed and contorted like creatures out of Dante's Inferno.

George Feeley had placed his red mark two-thirds of the way down the course, but still a good distance from the entrance to the Gulf of Mexico. Marker No. 13, shown as a solid black triangle, lay at the northwestern corner of the lagoon, which was to the starboard side of an outgoing boat. On the opposite side of the lagoon there was a triangle depicting Marker No. 12. Beyond the lagoon, the channel became a bottleneck until it emptied into the Gulf waters.

The bailiff gave the map to Mollie Schneider, our Number One. She handled it carefully, obviously concerned about chipping her long red nails. The jurors proceeded to huddle briefly over the map in groups of two and three as it was passed along. When they were through, the last juror in the back row returned it to the court officer. Jeff Baker motioned him off and sat down. So did I.

As George Feeley left the witness stand and passed our counsel table, he leaned over and whispered something to my Benno which I did not hear. I was enjoying a wave of relief. The court day was over. Nobody hurt, not even a bloody nose. Sufficient unto the day is the evil thereof.

As Ben, Felix and I left the courtroom, I asked Ben what George had whispered to him.

"He said to me, 'I owe you twenty bucks.' "

An honorable man, I thought. Maybe an honest one, too?

28

Felix and I had not had a heart-to-heart talk. We had barely had what could be called a friendly conversation. It had been lawyer and client between us. Sometimes I had been abusive on the pretext that I was preparing him for cross-examination, if he took the stand, although we had made no decision on that yet. The truth was that my tangled feelings about him kept getting in the way; which only proved that the insight shown by Amos Stern, when we were sparring over my engagement as counsel, had been right on target. Yet, I should have familiarized myself with his background. And Lorna's too. So I invited Christine out to dinner, which only proved how tangled my feelings *really* were.

I caught up with her at the close of the session that day as she and her parents were walking down the corridor outside the courtroom. I gave her a come-hither wave. She whispered something to her mother. The Wards kept walking without so much as a glance in my direction. I told her the reason I wanted to have dinner with her, and when she asked why I hadn't invited Felix instead of her, I told her there were good and sufficient reasons I'd make clear to her later.

We arranged to meet at a French restaurant in Naples at eight. That gave me a chance to get some mail off to New York with Ida's help. It also gave me time to think of the reason I invited Christine instead of Felix to a cozy dinner for two.

We were given a corner table dressed with a posy of flowers. The maitre d', who must have fancied himself a modern Houdini, stood at our tableside and snapped his fingers; and presto! warm French bread in a napkin, butter balls nestled in green leaves, bottled water, and a wine list. He gave me a triumphant smile. I refrained from applauding. He lit a pink candle and stood awaiting our pleasure, which was two martinis with olives. Very cold and very dry. Sahara martinis, if you please. He whisked off in his low-cut patent leather pumps.

Christine had pulled her hair back in a pony tail, drawn tightly across her temples, which set off the smooth contours of her face. She was tantalizingly beautiful, and she knew it. For a while we sat quietly, sipping our martinis from frosted glasses that were eggshell thin, which somehow enhanced the drinks. Both of us gazed out over the Gulf, placid and glowing in the sunset. Conversation came haltingly: Christine seemed lost in her thoughts, and I was finding it difficult to strike a proper note. I had to balance my wish to treat her impersonally as a kind of research bureau and my awareness of her sensuality. The flickering flame of the candle played tricks with the soft contours of her face.

As we ordered another round of drinks, I explained that I wanted to get her perception of Lorna and Felix, some sense of how they had spent the past fifteen years. First, however, out of a mixture of politeness and genuine concern I also wanted to know how her parents were handling the situation.

Christine answered my question somberly. "Not well. Not too well at all. They're isolating themselves from all their friends. Daddy hasn't gone back to New York to his office. I spend a great deal of time with them in the evenings and on weekends. And during the days—well, you know. I'm in court."

"Do they see Felix?"

"Are you serious? He doesn't exist as far as they are concerned. Daddy has barred him from the Miami office."

"Have they accepted Lorna's death?"

Christine shook her head. "Daddy has. He wants to have a funeral service, but Mother refuses. She keeps telling him that Lorna is alive, that she's in hiding for some good reason, and that she'll get a letter one of these days. The trouble is, Tommy," Christine added after a long sip and a pause, "who's to say Mother is hallucinating? Stranger things have happened."

I steered away slightly. "What about you? What do you think?"

She stopped trying to spear the olive, and looked directly at me. "Me? I think she's gone. Dead. I'm sure of it." She anticipated the question that I was about to ask. "And I don't

hold Felix responsible in any way. I'm convinced the whole
thing was an accident. A horrible accident."

"Has he talked to you about it?"

The question made her visibly uncomfortable. She finished
the drink, olive and all, before answering me. "No, not really."

"So you've been seeing him. Do your parents know?"

"I haven't been *seeing* him, Tommy. At least not in the sense
you mean. I've called him to ask whether there's anything I can
do for him. For Chrissake, he's all alone now. I don't think
he even knows where to go to buy a loaf of bread. He's so
helpless. Damn it, you're just like Mother and Daddy! He's
my brother-in-law!"

I tried to quiet her down. I was going to say former brother-
in-law, as I had done when she first called me, but that wasn't
fair. After all, who was to say that her mother was wrong? My
defense itself rested partly upon Lorna's unexplained absence,
and no solid proof that she was indeed dead.

I caught the attention of a waitress. We placed an order for
cold medium-size lobsters and a bottle of Margaux Pavillion
Blanc, and another round of drinks while we waited. Then I
picked up the subject.

"When we first met—I guess it was as we were heading
back to shore in the tender—you told me a few things about
Felix and Lorna. But the truth is, not all of it registered."

"It didn't?" she asked with a mischievous smile.

A naked Venus flashed on my inward eye. "Well, some of
it did. You know it did!" We laughed together as I touched
her fingers. "Chris, tell me first about Lorna. Did you tell me
that she had no children?"

"She couldn't. That was a big blow to her. It was something
organic. It couldn't be corrected. She wanted to adopt a child
but Felix was against it. I tried to talk him into it too, but it
was no good. He refused to consent. He had odd notions about
bringing up somebody else's child."

"So what did she do with herself? I think she once said she
wanted to be a clothes designer or a fashion consultant."

"She did for a little while. Then she got into decorating. She
took a whole bunch of courses. Their apartment was filled with
books on styles of furniture and furnishing—European, early
American, Oriental, you name it. She even studied woods,

wood finishes, waxes, even a little painting. And she was doing great. Then, after about four or five years, she learned that she would be childless. We thought it would increase her intensity for her decorating career. It worked the opposite way. She simply stopped cold. All she would say was that it had begun to bore her. After that she sat around a lot. And she did a lot of shopping. Felix was doing very well, and she bought a lot of clothes. It became a sort of hobby. And that's about all."

The lobsters arrived and the wine was poured. We made a silent toast and touched glasses. I turned to the main event. "What about Felix? How was he doing in your Dad's business?"

Christine showed signs of evasiveness, almost as if I were asking her to play Peeping Tom into the private life of a stranger. But she answered me.

"Well, very well financially. After all he's running—at least he *was* running—a large branch office, and was on salary plus a percentage. But I had the feeling he was not thrilled with his work. Too much desk duty, I suppose."

"And the marriage?"

"I told you before. The usual barnyard pecking. Apart from that, they seemed to get along fine when we were together. Except when we read something about you," she added with a light giggle. "Felix got very uncomfortable. I think there was a little jealousy there. But that's human. I think he is a little jealous of me, too. Envious might be a better way to put it. He calls me a free spirit, which I am. I have my art, and there's little more than that to my life. I like to make money from it, and I do. I need a lot to keep my house going. It cost me an arm and a leg to buy it. But my painting—my art—is my consuming passion—it really is!" she added a little self-consciously when she saw my lifted eyebrows.

She talked about her house, which was in Angers. "It's a very old house," she said, "even by European standards, but remarkably well-preserved." Her face lit up as she told me it had a round study on the ground floor, all windows, which she had converted into an atelier.

I was infected by her enthusiasm, watching her lose herself in her own excitement as the candle guttered in the breeze that came through the open window. "I think I do my best painting there," she said, "certainly my most exciting work. As a matter of fact, as soon as Felix is acquitted . . ."

I looked at her with mock astonishment, my eyes widened. She thrust out her jaw in response.

"Yes, Tommy, I meant that. As soon as Felix is acquitted—and he *will* be acquitted—I'm heading right back to Angers."

"What makes you so damn sure he'll be acquitted?" I asked.

She fielded the question smoothly. "For two *damn* good reasons. First of all, he didn't kill my sister. I know in my heart he didn't. He couldn't have. You know that and I know that."

I didn't feel like telling her that I didn't know that at all, so I didn't accept her invitation to agree.

"Second, and most of all, he has you on his side, Tom Tom." She used the name by which she had called me when she was so very young. My eyes got a little wet. She noticed it, and reached across the table and covered my hand with hers. A radiant smile beamed across the table and lifted up my heart. I hadn't felt so transported for years. I swear I began to hear angels sing.

Each of us drove off in our own car. I realized that I had not asked her a single thing about her private life. I guess I didn't really want to know.

29

I woke up to the scent of chicory-flavored coffee and perfume. Not a man to reject life's little offerings, I inhaled deeply. The scent was imbedded in the pillow beside mine, and the bearer of that frankincense was in the kitchen, proving she had further skills omitted from her résumé. I padded into that room and found Ida, wearing only high heels, standing over sizzling bacon, and frying eggs—sunny side up, like her. One leisurely hug was all each of us needed to rise to the occasion. Glancing at our ready breakfast, I whispered that in recognition of preempting exigencies we could start breakfast over later; but Ida, brought up to waste not and want not, opted to eat the bacon and eggs. Which we did.

After showering and dressing, I went into the living room. Using Ben's report on his interview at No Name Key, I wrote a series of notes, one item to the page, expecting the next witness to be Lester Melville. I wanted to be ready to cross-examine him, if his story hurt our case. Then Ida headed for the office and I for the courthouse. I wondered if she also wished we could play hooky.

Ben met me in the corridor outside the courtroom. "It's Lester Melville. He's around the corner in the charge of Susan . . . what's her name?"

"Harwick, bright eyes."

"Okay, Harwick. Are you ready for him?"

"I'm ready—barring surprises." I showed him my cross-examination notes and got back a look of grateful approval. I walked off by myself to study my notes, and was deep in concentration when the bailiff stuck his head out into the hall and bellowed for all parties and counsel to come into the courtroom.

Felix and Ben were at our table. Jeff Baker was at his. I

nodded at everyone and sat down. At precisely ten o'clock, the jurors were ushered in, and Judge Sperry took his seat on the dais. Susan Harwick brought in Lester Melville, who wore a crumpled linen suit and brown sandals. He carried an unlit pipe in his hands, apparently his security blanket. I noticed that his face brightened when he saw Reginald Archer among the jurors. He waggled a friendly wave. It had not occurred to me that they might know each other. No matter. The prof would play it by the rules. He looked through Melville as though he were plate glass and disregarded the salutation. Good for you, I said silently.

Ben had described Lester Melville to me when we went over the notes of their meeting. The old professor matched the physical part of the description all right, but in response to Jeff Baker's preliminary questions, a different person emerged. Ben had described his manner in two carefully chosen words. "Lazy diffidence," was the way he had put it. He had seen him as an affable, easygoing person with a tendency to ramble and repeat himself absentmindedly, possibly attributable to his having been hung over from the night before. Not so the man under oath. His posture was erect, and his voice was clear and penetrating, a lecturer's tone. He was not merely answering questions, he was instructing a class.

Taking the lead under the prosecutor's deft questioning, Melville told his story. I followed his testimony with Ben's notes in front of me. Mostly I simply watched him deliver his lesson.

The night before the tragedy, the Melvilles had thrown a clambake for a group of their friends. He discreetly avoided mentioning whether they had consumed more wine and beer than seafood. When the party broke up late in the evening, he said, and the guests had departed in their own boats, the Melvilles were too tired to clean up the mess. The next morning the professor, having awakened at his usual half past six, went outside to collect bottles and rake up clam shells and lobster claws.

Shortly after seven, he glanced out toward the sea, set shimmering by the rising sun. He thought he saw a figure on the spit of land called Round Key—actually nothing more than a sand bar running northeasterly from his No Name Key. Looking back minutes later, he noticed that the figure was waving something white. Since no one lived on Round Key, he figured the person might be in trouble, and after calling in to his wife, he took his boat over to the key.

A man stood waist deep in the Gulf as the launch pulled up in the shallow water.

"Hello, there! Are you all right? Saw you walking around and thought maybe you were in trouble." There was no response from the man. A look of confusion dominated his face.

"What do you say, young fellow, shall we call out the King's Guard or are you able to cope?" As he spoke, he dropped a light anchor off the windward side and climbed out of the boat toward the silent figure. As he approached, he noted that the man was naked but uninjured. By the time he reached him, the man had put on the white shorts he had been holding in one hand.

"What time is it, please?" Those were the first words the stranger said to him. As he did so, he clasped his hands together behind his neck. He can't be in big trouble, the professor thought to himself, or he wouldn't strike such a casual pose. Maybe he has a girl tucked away on the opposite side of the island among the mangroves.

"It's a little past seven. Are you sure you're all right?"

The stranger had shaken his head. "My boat is gone. I swam all night. It was horrible. I couldn't get any help. I swam and swam and then I reached shore—here. It was dark when I got here. There was a moon. The clouds had broken up. Yes, a full moon. I remember wondering why the moon was going down. It seemed just to have risen." As he stood in the water, his fingers thrashed at the surface convulsively and his voice became shrill.

"You'd better come back to the cottage with me. Come on, climb into the boat and we'll get you something to eat and drink and a chance to rest a while. Then you can tell us what happened to you." As he spoke he led the young man to his boat, and after considerable difficulty they managed to get into the bobbing craft. Reaching into the storage space in the prow, he hauled out a wrinkled but clean blanket which he draped over his companion's shoulders.

Neither of them exchanged any words on the short trip back. His passenger sat glassy eyed, mumbling to himself and shaking his head in apparent disbelief over something. When they reached the cottage, Mrs. Melville, who had been watching events through a pair of binoculars, met the two of them at the edge of the dock. She deftly looped stern and aft mooring lines over iron cleats, and with her husband helped the boat's other occupant ashore.

"What happened, Lester?" she asked.

"I don't know yet, my dear. Let's go inside and give him something to refresh himself with. As best I've been able to learn, he's been on Round Key all night. Boat's gone somewhere, and he had to swim for it."

By that time, they had reached the steps leading to the cottage. Halfway up, their charge stopped in his tracks and looked around blankly.

"Where's Lorna?"

"Who is Lorna?" asked Professor Melville.

"Where's Lorna, where's my wife?"

Mrs. Melville clutched her throat and whispered, "Oh my God!"

"Where did you leave her?" the teacher asked. "On Round Key?"

The man stood as though in a trance. Professor Melville took him by the shoulders and gently shook him. "Where did you leave your wife? On the island? In the boat? Where is the boat?"

The questions seemed to pull away his underpinnings, and letting all his weight fall on the professor, he began to whimper like an injured animal. Suddenly he tore himself loose and began teetering down the steps. "I've got to find her. She's out there in the water, swimming. She's been swimming since yesterday afternoon."

As he collapsed at the bottom of the steps the professor caught hold of him. It took both the Melvilles finally to get him into the cottage. Mrs. Melville immediately went into the kitchen to get some coffee reheated. The man stretched out on the couch and closed his eyes. Professor Melville thought it best not to disturb him. He thought about calling the authorities, but decided to wait until he had a better grasp of the facts. The young man gave all the indications of exhaustion. Yet when Mrs. Melville returned with a steaming cup, he sat up quickly to take it from her. My, that was a fast recovery, Melville thought, a most remarkable recovery. He stored the fact in the back of his mind.

Jeff Baker reinforced the last point for the jury.

"You said he sat up quickly, sir? What did you mean by that?"

"I mean that when I—we—had helped him into our cottage, he appeared to be close to total collapse, and when he stretched out on the couch, he appeared to fall asleep immediately. Three minutes later, he bolted upright at the scent of fresh coffee. That's all I meant."

"What happened then?"

"Well, Mrs. Melville asked him whether he'd like the coffee, that it would perk him up. He said yes he would, but that he took it with cream and sugar."

"With what?" asked Jeff Baker. I stirred uncomfortably, aware that Baker was simply forcing the point to be made again so as to bring home to the jury Felix's real state of mind.

"He said he'd like it *with cream and sugar*."

"What happened after that?"

"I asked him whether my wife could telephone someone for him. You understand, to let anybody know how things were. He gave me a Miami telephone number for her to dial, but there was no answer."

"Do you remember the number?"

"No. I think I jotted it down on the back of an envelope, probably threw it in the basket after I made the call. All I remember is that it was a series of descending numbers in the Miami area."

"Did he tell you whose number it was—his home, his family, his wife's, whose?"

"I don't recall that he did. It couldn't have been his home, because I distinctly recall asking whether I should notify someone there, and he said there was nobody there."

"Did you call the Coast Guard?"

"Yes, sir, I decided not to wait until I took him to the mainland." He paused and rolled the bowl of the pipe he was holding in the palm of his hand. "But I believe the Coast Guard had already been alerted. A cutter was cruising around here right before dark. I watched it for nearly an hour."

The witness looked a little uneasy. Maybe he had become

frightened that his den of iniquity was about to be busted, the old hypocrite. Ben had described the cottage as a filthy sink. Empty bottles all over the place. A real pillar of society, the professor.

"Did he ask you to do anything about his missing wife?"

"I told him about the Coast Guard's sweep the night before."

"What did he say?"

"That was the strange thing. He didn't say anything."

"Did he ask about the results of that sweep?"

Jeff Baker was making the most of a good thing. I stood up to shatter the jurors' concentration. Not too praiseworthy a ploy on my part, but worth the try. "Objection, irrelevant."

Judge Sperry waved me down with a flap of his hand. "Overruled," he said, brushing at his mustache as though he were wiping off egg.

Just to punish me for my bad manners, Jeff Baker got to repeat the question.

"Did Felix Evans ask you whether the search by the Coast Guard had produced any results?"

I cried a silent plea to the professor to answer yes, even though I knew the answer had to be no.

"That's another funny thing. He did not."

I stood up again, careful not to incur wrath. But this had to be stopped. "I object to the witness's constant gratuitous comments. Mr. Evans's behavior wasn't 'funny,' as he put it, or 'strange.' Traumas cause all kinds of temporary dislocations. Funny maybe to the witness, but not funny to my client, and certainly not strange."

"There you go again, counselor," said the judge quietly. "Just say 'I object.' I'll get the point and do the right thing. Save your arguments for summation at the end of the case."

But the old walrus knew I was on target. He turned to the jury. Kathryn Adelaide had her hands clasped under her chin, her eyes fixed on me. Reginald Archer was fussing with his damn stringy tie. Mollie Schneider was back at work on her fingernails. And Alex Raymond looked as though he was bored to death. The others seemed to be paying strict attention.

"You are to disregard the comments of the witness," the judge said. "Erase them from your mind. You must only address facts. Eventually it will be your task to interpret them as you deem proper. Got it?"

He certainly had a breezy way of speaking, but he made his point. I hoped the jurors "got it." As the judge nodded to Jeff Baker to continue, I asked Ben whether Melville had shown this kind of surprise, had told him that he found anything "funny" or "strange" during his interview. Ben gave me a vigorous negative shake of his head.

"All right, Professor Melville," Baker was asking in a conversational tone, as if talking to a neighbor across the garden fence. "Did you notice anything in particular about the physical appearance of Felix Evans?"

"Well, sir, he needed a shave, of course, and he was bleary eyed."

"Anything else?" I could tell that Baker was dying to lead him to something else but knew it would be improper.

When Melville still gave him a blank look, he tried a different tack. "Let me ask you this. Are you familiar with Round Key where you found Felix Evans?" It was clear that Baker was never going to dignify Felix with a Mister.

"Yes, sir, I am. Pat and I frequently crab hunt there. It's really not much more than an oversized sand bar with clusters of mangrove and some stunted pines."

"What about ground conditions?"

"Oh. I see what you mean. They're terrible, awful. Crabs all over the place. Some raccoons. And an infestation of sand fleas."

"Okay. Now let's get back to the morning you picked up Felix Evans. What was he wearing?"

"When I first saw him, nature's covering only. He had been waving his shorts to get my attention."

"Did he have any other clothing when he got into your boat?"

"No, sir, except for the blanket I threw around him."

"Shoes?"

"No, sir."

"Socks?"

"No, sir."

Jeff Baker faced the jury box and addressed the next question to them, although the foreordained answer had to come from Melville. "What, if anything, did you observe about his skin condition?"

"Oh, I understand now what you're getting at. . . ."

"Please!" I wanted him kept on a tight rein. He was doing damage enough without conducting an open seminar.

"Strike it. Answer the question, sir, just answer the question." The judge frowned, which happened to be the occasion for the sun to sneak mischievously behind a cloud, darkening the courtroom as if in direct response to Judge Sperry's beetling brows.

"What was the question?"

"Read it back." Judge Sperry to Donna Redmond. She flipped out a few folds of the continuous page nestled at the back of her stenotype machine and read their hieroglyphs with smug ease.

" 'What, if anything, did you observe about his skin condition?' "

The good old professor was playing it for all he could. Making everyone wait for his answer, he moved back in the witness chair. He wanted the jurors and all the others in the courtroom to lean into him, like students eager to suck up knowledge. And, damn it all, they did. The whole room seemed to tilt in his direction. A star is born, I said to myself.

"Well, sir, I noticed his feet as he climbed into the boat."

"What did you notice about his feet, Professor?"

"They were absolutely clean."

"What do you mean by clean?"

"They were completely free of bites, abrasions, cuts, and scratches. Not a single one that I could see. The reason I noticed all that . . ."

"No reasons, please. When you got to Round Key that morning, did you notice the ground conditions?"

Melville wagged his head vigorously. "Yes, I did."

"What did you notice?"

"Well, the first thing I saw was that my friends, *brachyura decapoda*—crabs, if you will—were racing all over the sands. Thousands of them. And to make matters worse, I could see clouds of mites—and fleas—as I scuffed along the shore. They are most active at dawn and sundown. Terrible beach pests. Also, there was much debris that had accumulated at the water line. Broken glass, cans, and the like. The key is something of an attraction to young people who use it for campfires, trysts— the usual purposes. When I go there to do my crabbing, I always wear shoes and slacks, and even then I get scrapes and flea bites that leave my skin itchy and blotchy for days."

"Did you notice anything about his skin—how did it look to you?"

"That was another funny—" As I started to jump up again, Melville stopped and drew himself up.

"Yes, sir, his skin. It was absolutely clean. No red spots, no bumps, no itch marks. Just clean epidermis. When we go there, we *always* wear slacks—"

Up I jumped. "ObjectSHUN!"

Jeff Baker voluntarily cleaned up the script. "Consent to strike the answer, beginning with words, 'When we go.' "

I sat down, trying to hide my dismay from the jurors, who were watching me. Juries disdain a sulky lawyer.

Jeffrey Baker took a minute to allow the significance of these observations to sink in. Ben had been alerted to this by Professor Melville when he interviewed him. We had questioned Felix. He told us that he had found a tarpaulin and had wrapped up in it during the night. When we asked him how he had crawled out of the water without getting into a scrap with the crabs, he told us he had no recollection of even reaching the key. So that was that. I had brushed aside the possibilities that flowed from those facts as incompatible with my rule for thinking positive. Call it wearing blinders if you like, but I had not been prepared for Melville's disclosure. It caught me off guard.

Jeff Baker then led the professor through the trip to shore. He and Pat Melville had brought Felix back to the mainland together. Pat Melville had some shopping to do. They owned a jeep, which they kept at the marina next to the Coast Guard station.

Felix, he said, had been quiet. Wrapped in his thoughts, he had sat huddled in the stern.

"Did he have anything to say at all?" Jeff Baker's voice gave away his excitement. I smelled a fuse burning. Even Ben leaned forward slightly. But Felix followed my instructions like a soldier. Relaxed, hands clasped, face immobile.

"As a matter of fact, he did." He paused. It was like a lost beat in a musical composition. Judge Sperry looked over at the witness.

"What did he say, Professor Melville?" The prosecutor repeated the question.

"Well as we were approaching the marina, he stirred and caught my eye."

"*What did he say?*"

"He said, 'I guess I killed her.' "

Jeff Baker turned and stared hard at Felix for ten long seconds, and then sat down. "You may cross-examine," he said curtly, glancing in my direction.

I stuck my fingers in my ears to see if they were bleeding from the explosion.

30

We asked for the luncheon recess and Judge Sperry granted our request. We had the right to demand copies of all statements Professor Melville had given before he came to court, and also the transcript of his testimony before the Grand Jury, if he had appeared before that body. He had. Jeff Baker handed me the transcript and a copy of the statement he had given to Deputy Sheriff Harry Carelton. This would allow us to see whether he had made any seriously inconsistent statements.

Ben and I hunched over the material as the jury filed out for lunch. Felix went down to the cafeteria to bring us sandwiches and coffee. Everything matched. Near the end of his Grand Jury appearance, I found the critical exchange.

Q. Did Evans talk to you in the boat on the way back?
A. Yes, sir, when we were approaching the marina.

Q. What did he say to you?
A. He said "I guess I killed her."

Q. What else did Evans say?
A. Nothing. I asked him what he meant by that but he simply stared at me.

Q. Are you sure he used those very words?
A. Well, sir, I believe I have it right. It did shock me, since I'd never heard anybody before then confess to a murder. But he confessed it all right in so many words.

In so many words. I would see about that. That's what you get, I said to myself, when you don't leave well enough alone, and ask that extra—unnecessary—question.

The statement to the deputy sheriff matched the Grand Jury testimony, and both corresponded to what he had just related to the jury. But none of the statements matched Ben Abbott's report. The so-called confession was conspicuously absent from his. My blood pressure began to build up like one of those old-fashioned pressure cookers. I was furious and they knew it. I teed off on Felix.

"Did you make that statement?"

"Never. Why would I have said a thing like that?" Felix dried his palms on a linen handkerchief. He looked as though he was about to give up his breakfast.

I turned to Ben. "So what's your story? Where does your case report on Melville deal with that choice morsel? You and your total recall." Ben blinked as hard as if I had thrown salt at his eyes. I had never spoken to him that harshly before.

"It doesn't, chief."

"Don't 'chief' me, Ben. Why the hell doesn't it? Did you think it was just an irrelevant detail, something unimportant?"

"Not at all, Tom," he said quietly. "I didn't write it down because Melville never said it to me. And there was no reason to suspect he was holding out on me."

As quickly as I had flared up, I quieted down. "Apologies, Benno," I said contritely. "I should have known better. I'm sorry I blew up." I really was. Ben simply shrugged. That made me feel even worse, but right now putting on a hair shirt would have been sheer self-indulgence. We decided to walk once around the block to compose ourselves. I walked by myself, planning Melville's cross-examination. As we reached the courtroom, the bailiff was bawling "Court in session." Walking inside, I wondered for perhaps the four hundredth time if there wasn't a less corrosive way to make a fortune and retire to Majorca.

Professor Lester Melville looked at me quietly, taking my measure. He placed his pipe on the table at the front of the witness box. He did not strike me as a witness I could safely badger or browbeat. He might bite me right back on my handsome nose. Well, we'd soon see. But for starters, gently, gently, I thought, mentally laying out my game plan.

"Professor Melville, how long have you walked the cloistered halls of academe?" That would show him how learned I was.

"Do you mean how long I have been teaching?"

"Yes, I do mean that."

"Over twenty-five years, sir, until I retired some years ago. To write," he added archly.

I didn't take the bait. I had no interest in his literary bent. "Good. Have you ever before been involved in a serious accident or a particularly stressful situation?"

Melville picked up his pipe and fingered it thoughtfully. "No, sir," he said finally. "I have been spared. Except, of course, with some of my students."

I had positioned myself at the end of the jury box again, and I noticed he was squinting at me, which inspired an idea. Asking the judge to excuse me for a moment, I walked over to Ben. On a piece of scratch paper I wrote, "Did he wear glasses?" Ben pondered, then picked up the pencil, and wrote a big YES.

I walked back on air to the corner of the jury box. Somebody in the courtroom dropped a metal object on the floor. Not one of the jurors looked around to see. They were totally absorbed in the matter before them. Even Mollie Schneider had let go of her pinky nail.

"Professor, do you recognize that your recollection and your perceptions of an event or incident can be affected by stress and excitement?"

"Yes, sir, that's sound. My students . . ."

"And you found the scene with Mr. Evans—the entire experience—an extraordinary occurrence, did you not?" I did not intend to let him wander even an inch from where I wanted him.

"It certainly was a departure from the normal routine of my life, yes. But all experience . . ."

"You found it stressful, even traumatic, didn't you?"

"Unusual, I would say."

Stop fencing with me, pedagogue. I'll have you pinned in short order. "I said you found it stressful, even traumatic." Then *con brio*: "Didn't you, sir." More a statement than a question. Again he fingered his pipe. He seemed to be genuinely considering my proposition.

Jeff Baker started to rise, probably to ask the judge to stop me from hectoring the witness or some such thing, but Judge Sperry pushed him back in his seat with a hand flourish.

"Yes, Mr. Attleboro, I did indeed find it stressful, somewhat traumatic. We were evidently caught up, Pat and I, in what threatened to be a great tragedy. Two young people . . ."

I held up my hand. "Please, Professor, no commentary. Now, then, bearing all that in mind, can you tell this jury with absolute, unshakable certainty as a matter of perfect recall that on your trip back to the mainland Mr. Evans spoke the exact words that you have attributed to him?"

He kept kneading his pipe in the palm of one hand, then straightened up and uncrossed his legs. "Yes, I think I can."

"Think you can. Only think you can. Is that it?" No answer was forthcoming.

"Mr. Evans had told you, had he not, that he had left his wife swimming—*swimming* since the previous afternoon. Don't I have that right?"

"Yes, sir."

"And that traumatized you in a way, didn't it?"

"Yes, it certainly did. In those shark-infested waters. I was terrified for the poor woman."

"He said he left her swimming, not that he killed her. *Right*?" I exploded the word and watched him jump. His pipe dropped on the floor with a clatter. Leaning over to retrieve it, he kept his eyes fastened on me.

"Yes, sir, right you are."

Where in hell did he get off speaking jauntily, I asked myself; and then stuffed my anger back into its place. "I put it to you that on the ride back to the mainland later on—you, your wife and Mr. Evans, all suffering from varying degrees of shock—what you heard Mr. Evans say were nothing more than words expressing his remorse at having left her swimming in the water instead of staying with her. Isn't that the fact?"

"I heard him say 'I guess I killed her.' "

I walked up to within spitting distance of him, and saw his hands trembling. "You heard him say that *in so many words*. Isn't that what you told the Grand Jury?" I shook the transcript in front of him.

"I may have said that, but really. . ."

"And you cannot deny under oath before Almighty God in this court of law that what Mr. Evans actually said—*in so many words*—was 'I *suppose* I killed her,' meaning he accepted a moral responsibility for her death in having swum off. You cannot deny that, can you?"

"It very well could be he said that, or at least meant that in so many words. The shock of it all—"

"*In so many words!*"

Jeff Baker jumped up, forestalling a further answer with his objection. But the question had been put, the answer had been given. Professor Lester Melville was pinned like a butterfly.

I had one more job to do before sending him back to No Name Key. I stood in front of him and asked him to describe my tie to the jury. Before answering it, he fished a pair of horn-rimmed glasses from his jacket.

"Can't you see my tie without glasses?"

"No, sir, not really. I should always wear them, I suppose." He made an unbecoming pout. The vain old cock, I thought.

"Did you wear glasses when you dashed over to Round Key?"

"I don't think so. No, I didn't. I didn't want to take the time to go inside for them."

"Did you put them on when you got back to your cottage?"

"Residence, if you please," he said primly, to the visible distaste of Molly Schneider, who looked away crossly. "No, I doubt it. I was too concerned. Besides, I'm always misplacing them." He got coy again, immersing himself in the role of absentminded professor.

"And yet you swore here today that you saw no scratches or other marks on Mr. Evans's skin, didn't you?" Not waiting for an answer, I added, "Without your glasses you couldn't possibly have seen any, could you?"

"Large ones, perhaps."

He left the stand like a chastened student. As he passed the jury box, he nodded shakily at Reggie Archer, his friend, who looked up at the ceiling. Kathryn Adelaide looked as though she was inclined to take his library card away. Mollie Schneider sucked the tip of her pinky thoughtfully.

And so ended that session. I walked out congratulating myself on a job well done, when my little friend with the big, shiny, bald head appeared back on my shoulder, and whispered that my triumph would probably be short-lived. He's such a killjoy.

31

Sandy Turner was a legend in her own time. In her own town, at least. She ran a boat charter for fishing freaks. Married four times, childless, and never divorced, she was a human man trap. Her first three husbands died of natural causes, meaning only that they were not the victims of premeditated murder. Persistent rumor had it that if she failed to wear them to death between the sheets, she frightened them to death. One of her peers explained her fishing prowess in the same terms, insisting he had witnessed with his own eyes that, after an hour's continuous stream of invectives and obscenities screamed at high pitch, whole schools of fish had been observed floating belly up in the nets around her fishing trawler.

Only the intercession of the Everglades City police force *en masse*, all three of them including the chief, had saved her current husband from an untimely demise, when, the month after they were married, they pulled her off his 200-pound frame before she beat his brains out with a marlinespike. No charges were preferred against her, however, it being the unanimous sense of the officers that she had clearly been provoked. So they wrote it up as a marital spat, and let it go at that.

Anyone who met Sandy was immediately taken by her personal appearance. She was invariably dressed in dungarees and a checked shirt. Her hair had, during the passage of some fifty-five years—give or take ten—faded from black to gun-metal gray. She was a formless block, five feet by three feet by three feet, perfectly structured to be planted on rolling decks, unmovable in the heaviest of storms. But on land in locomotion she resembled a scuttling robot. Her voice sounded like a shovel digging in a sandpile; hence her nickname. Yet she had reeled in at least four men, which to the mystified community in which she lived and worked indicated certain hidden attractions.

Sandy possessed an ingredient necessary for the state's case. As she sat in the witness box, her head hunched into her neck folds, eyes like bone buttons and her mouth a downward curving colorless slash, she looked like a 100-year-old snapping turtle. In response to preliminary questioning by Baker, she described herself as a pilot and navigator of the coastal waters and the owner and captain of the fishing trawler called *Sandy II*. She brought a titter to the courtroom when she described the demise of *Sandy I*.

"It was smacked in the ass by a Chris Craft run by a couple of smart aleck rich kids."

The judge stepped in—reluctantly I suspected.

"Captain Turner, you must mind your manners here. Do you understand me? You are not to swear. . . ."

"Who's swearing?"

"Be quiet! You are not to curse, and you are not to speak unless spoken to. You got that clear? Don't answer me! When this state's attorney asks you a question and you have sumpin' to say, then say it. And if you don't follow this friendly advice of mine, you may have to stay with us in a back room for a few days. You get the drift of what I'm saying, *Madame*? Don't answer me!"

Sandy looked as though she were about to lunge at His Honor. The bailiff began to inch forward. But the judge won the glaring contest. She settled back in her chair. I watched her mouth the word "shit" but it never became airborne.

Returning her attention to Baker, she told how she had been running the coastal waters since her daddy had bought her a skiff when she was twelve. She knew every eddy and current and reef and wreck from Fort Myers to Key West. "And," she concluded with proud disdain, "I kin read the weather by smell and swell, hours—sometimes days—before yer weather wizards at the Coast Guard Station kin unnerstan' their dials an' needles and balloons."

"Are you familiar with the inland waterways around Everglades City and its environs?" asked Jeff Baker.

"Everglades City and its what?" The glare returned to her button eyes.

"Everglades City and the neighborhood around it."

"I told you I've lived around these waters my hull life."

"Okay. Now do you remember the second day of June of this year?"

"Yup."

"How come you kin remember that paticuler day?" Her pronunciation was evidently contagious. Or maybe even Baker had to have a moment's fun once in a while.

"It's my birthday, that's how. It only comes once a year, thank Gawd." She guffawed like a burlesque comedian.

"Okay. Tell us where you were that afternoon and what kind of weather prevailed in your area."

She looked at him with amazement. "Whatcha mean? What kind of weather what?"

I noted that Baker looked awfully contented and showed great patience.

"I mean, tell us where you were and what the weather was like."

"I wuz out in the Gulf with a eight charter—four couples, that is. They wanted to fish barracuda even though I told them they would be better off eating camel meat. But that's what they wanted, and I give what's asked for. So I had took 'em to Devil's Hole—that's a big hunk of rock that's got holes punched in it by nacher, and they's always small fish in them holes and barracudas swarmin' around the rocks and coral that goes 'round it. Boat cain't get too closen to it, of course, but you kin cast and troll around and you'll allers pop barracudas. They're hungary sons of bitches. Oops!" She covered her mouth and glanced nervously at Judge Sperry, who pretended to have missed the line.

"Anyway, we wuz heading back, it wuz four-thirty, mebbie a little later. The eight of 'em were trolling to pass the time and maybe get lucky with a bonnie—a bonita—or is it bonito?"

"Go ahead, please."

"Anyhow, we wuz heading toward the boat dock with a fair catch to beat a blow that wuz getting kinda mean and heavy, along with clouds that wuz showing trouble ahead. I had told 'em that the smell and swell wuz telling me a good size storm, maybe force two, would hit in the late afternoon. And for once the weather wizards at the station had it right. They begun radioing small craft warnings around seventeen hundred hours."

"Did you pass anywhere near the delta—the exit of the inland channel from the Seaboard Motel?"

"Yup." She looked around as though she wanted to find a spittoon. "We crossed it right about four-thirty, mebbie a little later."

"How do you remember passing the spot?" Baker's voice was developing that strained timbre that meant he was going to light another fuse.

" 'Cause I saw one of them Seaboard jitneys heading out west nor'west with a low gale force tickling its ass—I mean pushing it along."

"How far from it were you?"

"About two hundred fifty yards."

"How did you know it was a Seaboard Motel boat?"

Sandy looked at him with contempt for his evident stupidity. "Because it wuz a gray-planked outboard with a yeller stripe round the hull."

"Could you see anybody in it?"

"Yup. I seen one man. He was perched on the port gunnel next to the throttle of the outboard engine."

"Was the engine running?"

"I think so, but it weren't easy to tell whether it wuz wake or waves. They wuz too much Gulf white—whitecaps—and wind, and I had my own hands full, to be sure. I *think* the God da—I suppose the widget was runnin'. The boat wuz opposite my port side. That's left," she added smugly, evidently proud that she knew her left hand from her right.

"Are you sure you saw only one person?"

"Yup."

"Did you see anybody stretched on the deck?"

"No way. I'da seen her—or him. The boat's shallow. Besides, she'd have been soaked from the splash. Or him."

Nicely coached, I said to myself grimly. "Her" first.

Baker sauntered over to the table and picked up the Seaboard map of the inland channel. He shook it open and placed it on the witness table in front of Captain Turner. She hunched over it with a blank look on her face. The jurors nearest her tried to get a peek.

"You told us you are familiar with the waters around the delta—the exit of the Seaboard channel?"

"Yup."

"Is there anything unusual about it?"

"You're damn right they is. They's a sandbar that stretches from north to south across the edge." She pointed to a pair of small islets on the north side of the mouth of the waterway, and an alligator-shaped formation on the south side. "From this'n on the north side to this'n on the south side they is a sandbar that praciley closes the channel off. 'Cept if you steer real tight to the north side." Jeff described for the record what she had pointed out on the map, and then passed it around for the jurors to see.

"What's the effect of the sandbar, Captain Turner?" The sudden deference was another one of Baker's signals.

"Well, on a good day, if you float slow and easy, you can skitch over it into the Gulf. But when you have an easterner of middle gale force, it empties the basin, and you kin see the bar laying naked like a big belly. And then the only way out to the Gulf, if you're damn fool enough to want to go out into that mean ol' lady in such weather, is to drag your outboard out over it ass—tail first with your mooring rope."

"No other way?"

"Nope. No other way."

"What way does the current run in that area of the Gulf?"

"So'west as a general rule. That's the natural drift."

"Can a boat drift northwest in a gale, like the one that was developing during the afternoon of June second?"

"Drift? No way. Impossible. Not natch'l."

The questions puzzled me, but my respect for Baker had grown to the point where I hesitated to disregard any of his inquiries.

Jeff Baker looked up sharply, as though he had just had an unexpected thought. It was pure camp, but admirably executed.

"Oh, by the way, is the man you saw in this courtroom?"

"Yup."

"Can you point him out?"

"Yup."

"Please do so, Captain."

She picked out Felix without a second's hesitation. Too damn fast, I thought to myself. I shook my head in a ploy of disgusted disbelief.

Baker gave me his sweet smile and a wink and sat down. "Your witness, counselor." He made it sound as though he were giving me the honors on the next tee, a murder trial transfigured into a Sunday afternoon sporting event. I was not amused.

I approached the matter of the identification of Felix by the sea witch.

"Do you see Felix Evans seated over there at my table?" I nodded my head in his direction.

"Yup."

"You said that it was that man whom you saw in the boat?"

"Yup, it wuz him all right."

"You're sure?"

"Yup."

"What was he wearing?"

She squirmed and squinted at me. "I cain't say that."

"Did he have a head dress?"

"A what?"

"A hat, a cap, something covering his head."

"I cain't say that."

"Could you see his eyes?"

"They wuz in his head."

"Did he have a beard at that time?"

Her eyes flitted over to Felix. He had his fingers laced over the lower part of his face. "I cain't say that."

"Did he have gloves on?"

No answer. Just lips compressed in a stubborn silence.

"Well, what was there about the man you *say* you saw"— I leaned on the word to show it was only her version of a fact, not conceded by me—"that led you to point him out in the courtroom today so dead bang fast?"

"Well, the law man, he called me in after I called and told him what I'd seen after hearing the story on TV news, and he fetched up a picture of this here man and here he is again."

"Did you see that picture again?"

Susan Harwick suddenly discovered a need to search for something under the table, and I knew I had the answer. The feisty captain looked over at the prosecutor's table to no avail.

"Well, did you see that picture again?"

"Yup."

"When and where?"

"Sue Harwick over there, she shown it to me this mornin' as we wuz waitin' t' come in. She fetched it out and told me

I should see if I could find him in the courtroom when I went in. She had it in her wallet, like it was a kind of permanent momentum."

Somebody giggled. I gazed back at the spectators banefully.

"You mean like a keepsake?"

"Yup."

"And that's how you were able to point out Felix Evans and say 'Yup, that there's the man I seen in the boat,' right?"

Again no answer. But none was needed. Her silence was my best reward.

I turned to the sandbar. "How long would you say it takes for the sandbar to show above the water after a storm hits?"

She looked up at the ceiling and pursed her lips. "Depends on the storm force. On that day I'd say it'd take about forty, mebbie fifty minutes."

"From when?"

"From when the storm broke."

"Didn't you tell this jury that when you first saw the boat, the wind was only at a low gale force?"

"Yup, but it wuz building up fast."

"You didn't get close enough to see whether the bar was exposed when you went by, did you?"

"Not exactly. But it had to be damn near exposed. No more'n ankle deep then."

"*Unless the boat drifted out earlier.*" I made the question a statement.

Sandy gave me a wide-eyed look as though I had just discovered an eternal truth that had never occurred to her before.

"I reckon so." The answer came out muffled from deep in her reluctant throat.

"You don't know how long the boat was outside the bar, do you?"

"It wuz just headin' out past me." She was tumbling her hands around as if drying them before an air blower.

"Did you ever see that boat again?"

"Yup. The sheriff showed it to me, when it was stored in the yard."

"When?"

"About a week ago."

"Did you recognize it as the very same boat you say you saw?" Silence.

"Well?"

Sandy Turner licked her lips and pleaded with her eyes for help from Jeff Baker. He had none to give her.

"Well, was it the very same boat or not?"

"It wuz the same kind of boat."

"But you cannot swear it was the boat *you* say you saw, the very same boat. You can't swear to that, can you?"

The captain squirmed uncomfortably. "You're asking me the same as *they* did," she said, pointing to the prosecutor's table. "An' I told 'em exactly what I'm tellin' you. I cain't say it wuz the same boat. And I cain't swear it wuzzn't. How could I?"

"And neither can you swear that the boat you say you saw had its motor running. Can you?"

"It looked like it wuz. . . . Okay, okay! No, I cain't say for sure." A few wrathful steps toward the witness box and an appearance of anger on my part had turned the trick.

So much for the mystique that surrounds eyewitnesses. I hoped the jury learned the lesson.

When I sat down, Judge Sperry looked at Baker. The prosecutor shook off the signal for redirect examination, whereupon the judge closed up shop for the day.

I was pleased with myself. But I knew that the indictment had to rest on a sturdier foundation. And despite my cleverness, I suspected that the jurors might have been satisfied that the wily old captain had indeed seen Felix in the boat that afternoon. Alone. And if they were, that would be bad news for the home team.

32

A trial has the same kind of tempo changes as a well-orchestrated symphony. So far, the case against Felix had proceeded from an opening *andante* to an *allegro* with Feeley and the professor, and then a lively *scherzo* movement provided by Sandy Turner. But I knew that we were verging on the part of the case for which all before had been only a foundation. It had been necessary testimony, but the jurors could from time to time allow their concentration to stray without inordinate risk. However, this was the trial of a man indicted for high crime, and it was time now for the State to present its evidence on the central issue: murder.

Ben Abbott made several attempts to see the boat that the newspapers had chosen to call the murder boat, but he had run into a stone wall. He had taken Harry Carelton out to dinner. The two of them stayed at the restaurant until closing time exchanging stories of investigations, serious and humorous. But every time Ben approached the subject of the boat the Coast Guard had found, the deputy moved off on a tangent. He was clearly under instructions, and no amount of conviviality was going to persuade him to allow us to inspect that critical piece of evidence. Ben was not even able to learn where it was stored so he could try by his own devices to see it.

When Ben delicately reminded him how the deputy had left the transcript of Felix's statement on his desk and gone out for a cup of coffee, Harry Carelton came right out and said that at that point there had been no charges against Felix. There had been only a missing person file.

Now matters were different.

During the luncheon recess, I had dashed over to my temporary office to deal with some matters that Amos had sent to me Federal Express. Just as I reached the courthouse on the way back, a squall struck, carried in the angry clouds that so often came scudding across the peninsula from the Atlantic. I parked directly across the street from the front entrance, but I had no umbrella. By the time I had raced up the steps and into the revolving door, I was rain spattered.

Felix and Ben were standing next to the window at the end of the corridor. They were dry, evidently having beaten the storm back to the building. When Felix caught sight of me, he dropped his cigarette and beckoned me over. I walked toward him, reflexively stooping to retrieve the flattened cigarette butt from the marble floor. There was a receptacle attached to the wall three paces from where the two of them had been standing. I tossed the butt in it with a show of irritation. Felix missed the lesson. He was nervously adjusting his frameless glasses on the bridge of his nose, his eyes seeking my attention. He evidently had something on his mind. Ben stood quietly, grooming his felt snap-brim hat on the sleeve of his suit jacket.

"We took a walk around the block after lunch, Tom." Felix's voice was edged with anxiety.

"What did you have for lunch?" The question was aimed solely at easing his tension. He paid no attention. He stood rocking slightly from side to side, his left hand balled up in the palm of his other hand, his glasses reflecting the ceiling lights. I moved slightly to the side.

Felix continued: "When we got around to the back of the court building, we found a paved courtyard inside a high wall. The gate door is guarded by a deputy sheriff. We figured it was used as a V.I.P. parking area, might also be the way they brought prisoners from the jail to the courtrooms. Anyway, as we walked by, the gate was opened to let a car in. And Ben and I saw the boat."

"You saw what?"

Ben took the baton from Felix. "Tom, they have the missing boat on a kind of old gun carriage in the back there. I guess they plan to bring it into the courtroom."

"Don't be silly, Ben," I said. "They would need a derrick. Besides, they couldn't get it through the door."

"Well, they're going to use it somehow." Ben was persistent when he was sure he was right. Felix was showing all the signs of a panic attack. His eyes were rolling, he was chewing on his lower lip, and he was perspiring profusely even though the corridors were still cool.

It was time for me to take charge. I dispatched Felix to the men's room to tidy up. When he returned, I cautioned him to remember my instructions on self-discipline. I had explained to him before the trial that jurors, being human beings with normal reflexes, would look at him every time either side scored a point. I reminded him how television cameras always focused on coaches and managers at sporting events when a big play occurred. Viewers often got more than the cameramen bargained for by way of lip printed obscenities, spit streams and the like. I wanted no reactions from him that might titillate the jury. Hands folded, head held high, expression bland. Over good news or bad.

And then Brian Sperry entered, sniffed with wrinkled nose the smell of wet clothes in the courtroom, twitched his mustaches, and gathering his robes around him, positioned himself on his high-back chair and signaled to counsel to fire when ready.

33

Peggoty Shea looked exactly as Ben Abbott had described her, except her pigtails were gone. She sat straight in the witness chair wearing a crisp summer dress uniform and hat. Reginald Archer subconsciously raked his hair with his fingers and adjusted the knot in his tie. Mollie Schneider gave her the kind of slightly disdainful look of appraisal that only fading beauty can muster.

Ensign Shea said she had begun her tour of duty on June twelfth at 0700 hours. She had received her orders of the day, which had not been remarkable. Her cutter was to make bihourly passes in an arc from Longitude 82 degrees West at Fort Myers and Captiva Island south to Longitude 81 degrees West in the vicinity of Florida Bay, and then reverse the course. Her primary targets were pleasure craft showing low waterlines, signifying heavy, unidentified loads that might be weapons, controlled substances or other contraband. She was instructed to make radio contact and inquiry only, and to report unsatisfactory responses to her home station, with vessel description and course. Her secondary mission was to respond to distress signals and keep an eye on outlying keys for suspicious objects or activities.

She testified that at 1300 hours while cruising off Cape Romano, just below the twenty-sixth Latitude North, her spotter noticed what appeared to be a brush fire on an unoccupied key in the Ten Thousand Islands area about one nautical mile northeast of the outlet of the Everglades inland waterway.

"What did you do, Ensign?" The questioning was lady to officer. Jeff Baker had turned the witness over to Susan Harwick, who carefully fingered the knife-sharp part in her hair as she began.

"Two middies and I took the powered dory ashore with fire extinguishers."

"What did you find?"

"A couple of kids playing with three buckets of tar they had lit up for fun and games," the ensign said ruefully.

"What did you do next, ma'am?"

"We sanded down the buckets, chased the kids off the isle, and then 'did' the key—that is, we conducted a routine sweep of the key per our S.O.P."

"Meaning?"

"Meaning that our standing operating procedure was to check out any area we touched for evidence of drugs, either caches or storage bins. Drugs and drug trafficking have become a dominant objective of our coastal survey operations."

"And what, if anything, did you find, Ensign?"

"It's about time," I whispered to Ben, just loud enough to reach the front row of jurors. The trouble was that my comment also caught the attention of Judge Sperry. He might have a bushy white mustache and white hair, but he had the ears of a young bunny rabbit.

"Something troubling you, counselor?"

"No, Your Honor, it's just the sun's timing. It just came out, and I was remarking to my colleague that it might have obliged us an hour ago." I looked piteously at my rumpled suit. Some smiles from Alex Raymond in the corner of the jury box and a couple of others in the back row comforted me.

"Go ahead, Ms. Hardwick . . ."

"Harwick, please, Your Honor," she corrected quietly.

"Ms. Harwick. Yes, of course. And you, sir, observe these trial proceedings, and allow the sun to pick and choose its own time to shine without further commentary."

I nodded humbly and shivered a little to emphasize my physical discomfort.

"Now, then, you started to tell us what you found, Ensign Shea," said Susan Harwick with an encouraging smile.

"Objection! Not her testimony. She was simply asked *if* she found anything." I was on sound ground, but it only delayed the inevitable.

"Sustained." Turning to the witness, the judge asked the proper question. "What, if anything, did you find?"

"I found a boat."

"Where?" asked the prosecutor.

"It was half buried in mud and sand about ten yards above the water line on the south side of the land mass. It was lying on its starboard side, the interior of the shell facing the water. South, that is."

"Can you describe its general condition?"

"Well, it was covered with a coat of dirt, as though someone had poured buckets of mud on it which had dried and caked."

I leaped up. "Move to strike the answer after the words 'coat of dirt.' They're hypothetical and opinionative. This witness is not an expert in geophysics. She's a sailor."

"She's an officer in the Coast Guard, Mr. Attleboro," said Judge Sperry, stepping on my tail feathers again. "But your objection is still well taken. Strike out the opinion. It is hypothetical. Just give us your observations, Ensign, what you saw or touched or smelled."

"Well, sir, as I started to say, the boat was caked with mud, just absolutely—well, from stem to stern, outside and inside, and half-buried."

"Was the ground around soft or marshy?"

"Well, you see that's the point."

I started to rise again. Peggoty Shea caught my movement and shifted her position, recognizing that she was going off course again. As she smoothed her skirt I noticed the Coast Guard Academy signet ring that weighted down the pinky of her right hand.

"The answer is that the ground around the boat was dry and firm, unlike the marsh in the inland bayous. There was sand and coral and rock and roots. But no water or swamp."

"Can you on the basis of your experience account for the level at which you found the boat?"

"No I cannot, not in my experience, except—"

I was ready. "Please! No guesses, no opinions. We have her answer, Your Honor."

Judge Sperry agreed.

Susan Harwick moved ahead carefully and slowly. I had to admit that she had excellent stage presence, and kept her objectives clearly in mind. She was wearing a beige linen suit over a light cocoa blouse, and conducted her questioning standing quietly in front of the lectern provided for the use of counsel, which was placed near the end of the jury box.

"Was this the first time you ran across what seemed to be an abandoned boat?"

"Oh no. We find them quite often, but usually along the shore line. When we spot one of them, we radio the local Sheriff's office and they follow up. But we don't usually find a boat deserted about a mile out. One can't just walk back to shore."

Jeff Baker strolled over and handed Susan Harwick six large photographs. They appeared to be about 24 inches long by 18 inches wide. She leaned them, faces in, against the side of the lectern.

"What, if anything, did you find in or near that boat?"

The officer paused as though collecting her thoughts. "Well, in the first place, the hull—the bottom of the boat—was staved in. The hole was about a foot wide. We also found a small infantry spade about twenty yards away under an exposed mangrove root formation."

"What else?"

"Well, the boat was gray and it carried a yellow stripe around it. It had the number eighteen painted on the prow." She stopped and looked at the state's attorney, waiting to be cued, I guessed.

"Did you notice anything else?"

"One more thing."

"And what was that?"

"There were no cushions in the boat, just wooden planked seats. Aft, however, near the stern, a plastic swivel chair was fastened to the hull."

"And?"

"The seat of the chair had dark stains on it. There were also some stains—dark splotches—on the starboard bench near the stern."

Somebody just behind me let out a breath between closed lips, making a penetrating hissing sound. I glanced over my shoulder. It had been Sophia Ward. Her spare frame was bent forward from the waist. Mervyn Ward held a restraining hand on her arm.

"Did you find an ax, a hatchet?"

"No, I didn't."

"Did you find anything else?"

"Well, no. But I didn't find what I should have found."

"And what was that?"

"Well," said the ensign, "I didn't find an emergency oar, which is required equipment on rented outboards. And the outboard motor was missing."

Ensign Shea's eyes widened suddenly. "I forgot something," she said apologetically. "We also found a Seaboard Motel courtesy map of the Everglades."

"Did you take any pictures of the boat?"

"Yes, we did."

Susan Harwick leaned over and picked up the six photographs and handed them to Donna Redmond, who duly stamped them as State's Exhibits. Then she placed them on the table in front of the witness. Peggoty Shea flipped them over one at a time and then testified that they were enlargements of the photographs she had taken, and that they fairly and accurately depicted the boat in the condition she had found it.

"Did you report the boat to your station?"

"Yes, I did. We had an open-end report on a missing person and missing boat from the Sheriff's office, and I thought . . ."

"That's enough," I interjected. "Your Honor, I'd like to have the witness's thoughts but they aren't proper evidence."

Susan Harwick did not wait for the court's ruling. She tossed the ball to me.

"Your witness," she said, and took the photographs back to her table and placed them face down on its surface.

She caught me by surprise, all right. I was all set to object to the photographs being received in evidence and shown to the jury, since it had not yet been established that the boat was the one that had been rented by Felix and Linda. But Susan had a firm grasp on the rules of evidence, and did not make that mistake.

What to do with the ensign was my problem. I had detected no cracks in her testimony. I stood behind my table with my arms crossed.

"Do you know how long those kids had been playing on the island?"

She was caught off guard by the question. Evidently she had been coached how to deflect a more direct cross-examination, but not this kind of question.

"No, sir, I didn't ask them."

"But of course you secured their names and addresses, didn't you?"

A very noticeable pause, and a little twitch of her manicured fingers. In two quick moves, I had placed her on the defensive. Among other games that came to mind, I decided I would like to play chess with Ensign Shea. She was probably a sucker for an enfilade bishop attack.

"No, sir, I didn't. It didn't seem . . ."

"Please, ma'am! We didn't ask you to explain your answer or give your reasons." Said with a friendly smile. "All we're searching for are facts, simple facts. All right?"

Her answer was a quick nod. Ben was right. Her blue eyes were captivating.

"Did you at least ask them where they had come from?"

"No, I didn't."

"Or whether they had been there before?"

"No, sir."

"Or whether they had played in the boat and tossed sand and dirt at it?"

Her face lightened, she had her bearings again. She thought.

"I hadn't seen the boat yet, sir."

"So you can't tell us whether or not those kids ever played with the shovel and boat or tugged it in from the water's edge, can you?"

"Of course not, sir."

Of course not, I repeated to myself. But the hypothesis had been neatly placed before the jury as though it had come from the witness.

"And since you never bothered to take down their names and addresses, we can't ever find that out. Can we?"

"Objection. Argumentative," snapped Jeff Baker.

"Withdrawn." The point having been made.

One more question to complete the counter-image I was building. "How old were the kids would you say?"

"Well, they were all boys. I'd say they were between thirteen and fifteen."

"Skinny, or well-built for their age?"

"Pretty big, I'd say. Taller than I, at least." Again that nice smile.

"Did you retrieve the shovel?"

The smile disappeared.

"No, sir."

I let a pause punctuate the last answer, and left to the jurors the answer to the unasked question, why not?

"Yet you reported the incident because you were aware that my client's wife had been reported missing in that type of boat. Have I got that right?"

"Then it was just a missing-person report, sir." It was not a proper answer but I let it stand.

"One more thing, please. About those dark stains you described—dark splotches, you called them, didn't you?"

"That's right, sir."

I was beginning to feel like a lieutenant commander from all the respectful "sirs" I was getting, but I didn't allow my head to swell unduly. "Did you determine what they were?"

"Did I, sir? No, sir, I didn't." With emphasis on the last pronoun.

"You didn't identify them as cranberry juice?"

"No, sir."

"Or beet juice?"

"No, sir."

"Or fish blood?"

"No, sir."

"Or menstrual flow?"

Jeff Baker rose before the answer. Judge Sperry anticipated him neatly.

"Mr. Attleboro, you're going a leetle too far, don't you think. You've made your point, agreed?"

"Oh, yes, Your Honor. Yes, indeed. But I wanted the jury to understand that all we have so far is a boat. Just a boat. Anyhow, I have no more questions." And beaming at the ensign to show how much I appreciated all she was doing to keep our coastal waters secure, I helped her down from the witness box like a gallant yeoman.

As she marched out of the courtroom I confirmed Ben's impertinent observation about her pert walk, and waited for the salvo that was sure to come after that little curtain raiser. The jury wanted to know more about the boat. Jeff Baker was in no hurry to appease their appetite. One little piece at a time. Just enough for them to chew on.

And leave them hungry for more.

34

The State summoned a deputy sheriff to the stand, who testified briefly how he had participated in the retrieval of the boat and its eventual storage at County Headquarters, thereby establishing an unbroken chain of custody and control to negate any suggestion of third-party tampering.

I waived cross-examination. I didn't even ask him why at age 56 he was still a plain ol' deputy sheriff and not a Congressman or at least a state senator. I make it a rule not to cross-examine every witness. Jurors had to recognize that that mighty weapon for the uncovering of falsehoods in the unending search for relative truth was to be used sparingly. They had to be made to understand that when I rose to cross-examine, something significant was going to be developed.

And then George Feeley came back to the stand with a vapid grin on his pasty face. I had not objected to the recall. It would have been a waste of my time to do so. He quickly identified the boat in the photographs as the one missing from the Seaboard Motel. The color, the faded yellow stripe, and the number all matched. It was the boat that had been rented to the Evans couple on June second last. Jeff Baker asked him a few more questions.

"Were there any stains—stains such as those you see in these pictures—in the boat when you let it out for hire to Evans—Felix Evans, that is—on June second?"

"No, it were a perfectly clean boat. And there weren't nothing wrong with the hull neither."

"Have you inspected the boat itself since it was found?"

"You mean when you asked me to go over to the Sheriff's Office an' look at it? I saw it there about three weeks ago."

"Did you look at the area where the outboard engine had been seated?"

"Yes."

"Did you see any fracture or splintering of the stern?"

"No, there weren't any."

Jeff had no more questions. He did, however, ask that, now that the boat had been identified as the motel's missing vessel, the six photographs be received in evidence. Before they were passed to the jury, we had a chance to see them. The first two were taken from a distance, showing the boat's half-buried position. The four others focused on the stains, two showed the seat and two showed the starboard bench near the stern. Each pair consisted of a shot taken at a distance of about six feet, and another shot close up. All the photographs were in color, of course. And while it was impossible to tell whether the stains were blood, it was nearly impossible not to imagine a scene involving something more chilling than a broken jar of cranberry juice. Even I, king of the positive thinkers, was much troubled by what I saw.

Still, I definitely had a couple of questions for George Feeley.

"Did you ask anybody at the Sheriff's Office about the missing spade and missing ax?"

"Yes, I did, but . . ."

"Did they show them to you?"

"They said . . ."

"Did-they-show-them-to-you?" Spaced out evenly like the boards of a picket fence.

"No, they didn't."

Another courtroom rule of mine is never to ask a question during cross-examination unless I know I can field the response. The trick, of course, is to know the rule exists as a caveat, not as an absolute bar. Occasionally, you have to take a calculated risk. I thought Feeley, a dullard after all, could be trapped. I rolled the dice.

"How often do you overhaul the outboard engines in the boats?" I asked innocuously.

"You mean all twelve of them?"

"I mean all twelve."

He stirred restlessly.

"Whenever a customer complains, I look the motor over. If I can't fix it, I call the service garage in town. They's a mechanic who comes over."

I stared at him, shaking my head in exaggerated disbelief. "Do you remember my last question? What did I ask you?"

Feeley gave me a blank look and stroked his thighs with his hands. "I dunno, what did you ask me?"

"Then listen, please, and answer my question. I asked you, how often do you overhaul the engines in all the boats?"

"No set time. Just when a customer complains or when one don't start up."

"I take it you're too busy with keeping the records straight and renting and receiving boats back to do much else," I said. "Isn't that about it?"

The question had to appeal to him. Few witnesses have any idea how understanding hostile counsel can be on occasions. Or pretend to be.

"You're so right! They think it's an easy job in the office. That ain't the case at all. I don't hardly ever get a chance to sit down and relax. It's always one thing or another."

"So I'm correct, am I not, Mr. Feeley, that you are busy from the time you start until the end of your long day with signing people in, getting them into their boats, showing them how to operate them, telling them about the water courses, taking the boats back, making sure they aren't banged up, taking cash or filling out credit slips, and so on. Isn't that accurate?"

"You said it, mister. That's exactly it."

He glowed with pleasure at my sympathetic appreciation of the awful burdens of his thankless, underpaid job. I could picture him running back to the manager of the motel and asking for a raise. He never once noticed he was walking backwards toward my lobster pot.

"One thing, though," he added as an afterthought, "I always made sure they was gas. I always give out a five-gallon emergency container, and I always take it back and check it when they come home. It ain't safe to leave it in the boat," he said with a flourish to emphasize the importance he attached to his procedure. And then to be sure that the jury recognized the full dimensions of his job, he said, "The management didn't tell me to do this. It was all my idea."

He was backing right up to my lobster pot. Now to get him inside.

"And so I take it, Mr. Feeley, that you see no need to check the contents of each boat each time it's signed out and each time it's signed back. Isn't that correct?" I put it to him blandly, as though it was obvious that such a procedure would be a waste of his valuable time.

"No need to do that. Whose gonna steal from the boat, right in front of me? An oar? A shovel?" He made the proposition sound ridiculous. "No, I don't have to do that, except maybe once or twice a season to be sure they wasn't getting rusty or too dirty." Into the lobster pot.

"Then Mr. Feeley, you can't tell this group of jurors, can you, that the boat you rented to Mr. and Mrs. Evans absolutely, positively, had a shovel in it, can you?"

"I don't see why not. They all had a shovel. And a ax. And a oar. They was standard equipment."

"Listen carefully, Mr. Feeley, to my question." I walked back to the swinging gate, stood there, and fairly shouted my question at him.

"On the afternoon when Mr. and Mrs. Evans rented one of your boats, did you—YOU—actually inspect that particular boat at that particular time to see whether it had an ax?"

"If you put it that way," came his reluctant reply, "I guess the answer is no, I didn't specially check for it."

"Did you inspect that boat at that time to learn whether it had a shovel?"

"No, I guess not. But as I said—"

"No buts, no ifs, please. And you have already told the jury that nobody showed you a shovel or an ax at the Sheriff's Office. Do I have that right?"

"I said that. But—"

"Thank you, Mr. Feeley. That'll do just fine." I sat down.

Jeff Baker stood up and walked over toward George Feeley. He had a big problem. No ax with which to kill. No shovel with which to dig. No *body*. He had a very big problem; and as he stood in front of the lobster cage, his face showed he knew it. He realized that there was no quick way to get George Feeley out.

"No redirect," he said abruptly, and returned to his seat, looking away from the jury.

It had been a tactical error for Jeff Baker to walk over, hesitate, and return to his seat. The jurors had to have caught his sense of helplessness.

It's a leetle early for you to be feeling smug, said the little bald-headed man on my shoulder.

35

Ben Abbott was right, as usual. On Thursday morning Jeffrey Baker told Judge Sperry's secretary that he would like to make an application before the jury came into the courtroom. The judge called down to Peter Hobson, the court clerk, telling him not to bring in the jurors, and a few minutes later he made his appearance. There was an unusual hush in the room. The spectators sensed that something unusual was about to take place.

"Your Honor," Jeff Baker began, his hands clasped together in front of his chest like a preacher, "I've had the boat brought over from the Sheriff's storage building. It seems to me that while the pictures we placed in evidence do highlight the main features of the boat and its condition, the best way for the jurors to gain full comprehension of the physical condition of this vital piece of state's evidence is to inspect the boat itself. It's outside in the rear courtyard of this building. I ask Your Honor to allow the jurors to examine the boat."

I was fuming, and I didn't care if Brian Sperry knew it.

"The state's attorney says that the photographs he put into evidence didn't give the jury full comprehension of the boat's condition. Then why, sir, if I may ask, did he place them before the jury, when all the time the boat was sitting outside this courtroom? Talking about comprehension, what did he think the jury was going to 'comprehend' from the close-up photographs of unidentified stains, except fear and horror that they might be bloodstains? Isolated, I suggest, to precondition the jurors and to create an atmosphere of prejudice. Just the kind of prejudice that usually keeps postmortem photographs of victims out of murder trials."

Judge Sperry held up his hand like Joshua bidding the sun to stand still, but I wasn't finished and my face told him so.

"Now, Mr. Attleboro," the judge said in a soft voice, "I didn't hear a peep out of you when the pictures got offered. Nary one leetle word of objection."

He was right, of course. I couldn't very well say that I had withheld any objection because it would have been overruled, and that I didn't want the jury to get the impression that I was trying to keep evidence from them.

"That's not the point, Your Honor."

"You just made it your point, though."

"The point I want to make is, having placed those pictures under the noses of the jury, the prosecutor doesn't need the boat inspection. If the pictures were no good, they shouldn't have been used. At least until he had first tried for this inspection."

Arms folded on the desk before him, the judge said, "Counselor, I'm gonna let the jurors inspect the boat. It clearly is the best evidence. Had you objected to those pictures, maybe—just maybe—I'd have reversed my ruling now, and since they are going to see the boat, excluded them from the record. Of course, the damage has been done in part. They have seen them. But I might have kept them out of the jury room."

He leaned back in his big chair. "Your application is granted, Mr. Baker." Turning to Peter Hobson, he said, "Bring in the jury."

In they filed. As they did, I saw the Wards get up and leave along with Christine. Sophie Ward looked as though she were about to faint. Mervyn Ward didn't look too hearty himself. I looked away before Chris could catch my eye.

Before the jurors were sent out to the courtyard, Judge Sperry told them they were "to look, smell, taste" but not touch. And not to talk about their observations either among themselves or to others present, then or later, until the case was closed and they had begun their deliberations.

The power of suggestion is a mighty force. But it pales like a candle to the sun when compared to the power of human imagination in the presence of what we lawyers call real evidence, which is to say corporeal objects such as guns and knives, dope, bloodstained garments, and the like. The human mind, following the law of physics, abhors a vacuum. It will take a gun or knife and place it in the hand of the defendant charged with its use. At least momentarily. The imagination will place the bloodstained garment on the victim and picture the accused person in the act of causing the blood to spout. At least momentarily. And it will connect up dope handed over in a plastic bag, bearing impressive labels and tags to identify it and trace its police custody, by placing the bag in somebody's pocket or closet, usually the accused person's. At least for a lingering moment.

But a moment is long enough to imprint an image on the brain, as a minisecond's light leaves its mark on sensitized film. And that is precisely the way prejudice is born; and that is when the presumption of innocence, always evanescent, disappears from sight.

The defense and the prosecution—all of us—watched together as the jurors circled around the boat in the courtyard. Judge Sperry was watching them, too. Their faces grew drawn and whitened when they saw the stains. I glanced at the judge, wondering if that look on their faces said to him what it did to me. Plainly, they saw little else. Turning to Felix, I saw a man about to collapse. I took his arm to steady him. None of the jurors noticed.

Alex Raymond, the black drugstore clerk, was the only juror who spent any time examining the stern, where the outboard engine had been bolted. He was just about to touch the area when a uniformed deputy stopped him. Just like the Metropolitan Museum of Art, I thought. I wondered what Raymond's experience was with small craft. Too late now to find out.

When everyone reassembled in the courtroom, there was an air of expectancy. But the jurors took their places with uniformly stolid expressions. Felix and I sauntered in, achieving an air of cavalier unconcern, a considerable feat under the circumstances. In fact, I used our physical proximity to tell Felix that now more than ever he had to keep in mind my rules for courtroom behavior. Upright carriage, even when seated, hands clasped or at quiet rest, and a serene, even blank expression, denoting patient waiting. And no matter what happened, not to show any sign of tension.

Jeff Baker announced the name of his next witness: Dr. Stephen Dennison Scott. The doctor stalked down the aisle, a tall, spare figure whose dark clothes hung in loose folds on his angular frame. He looked as though he had recently died, so pale was his skin. As he passed our table he exuded a whiff of formaldehyde, reinforcing that image. Here was the medical examiner of Lee County, whose curriculum vitae was fatter than he.

"Do you have a specialty?" asked the prosecutor.

"I specialize in hematology, which is the study of blood, blood characteristics and blood diseases."

His voice sounded as though it were issuing from the bottom of a well. It was a hollow, doleful sound, uttered with little visible movement of the lips. Each time he pronounced the word blood, he stretched the vowels into a low moan. Holding his hands in front of him, fingers slightly curved, he was a daunting figure, a sort of human lizard. But he was smart and knowledgeable, and his name and face were frequently in the papers in connection with his main job as a medical examiner.

He continued his answer unaided. "My work takes me into serology, which is the study of serums or body fluids, principally blood and related biologic stains."

Once again he stretched out "blood" into a brooding, sinister sound. I was paying close attention to him, aware of what he was going to testify to, and aware that my cross-examination of this expert would probably test my skills to the utmost.

The evening before, having been alerted to the fact that blood and bloodstains were coming into the case with a vengeance, I decided it was time to go back to school. I had sent Ida home from the office after a short mail session. Ben and I went to dinner, and then to the office of a leading physician in Fort Myers who had an extensive library on forensic medicine. He gave us a one-hour cram course on the identification, location, size, shape, and pattern, as well as individual characteristics, of blood and other stains of biologic origin. Then he piled some books and a medical dictionary on the table, and showed Ben how to use the small copying machine in the corner of his office.

I did some fancy speed-reading, handing pages to Ben from time to time, which he copied for me on the machine. We finished the first part of the cram course by midnight. We turned off all the lights, and locked the door behind us as we left. My work, however, had really just begun. It was three in the morning by the time I had mastered the selected material sufficiently to feel comfortable.

"Doctor," Jeff Baker was asking, "did you at my request examine particular stains in a certain boat?"

"Yes, sir, I did."

"When and where did you do that?"

"Two weeks ago today, in the closed shed maintained at the county offices of the Sheriff."

Showing the two close-up photographs to the expert, Jeff Baker had him identify the stains on the seat and bench as the ones that he had examined. He then gave the doctor his head, and off he went.

"I was asked to examine the stains. My first observation was that there had been a considerable efflux of a fluid on the bench, less on the seat of the anchored chair. The wood showed clear signs of absorption. I then made a careful inspection of the areas adjacent to the stain, using a high-power hand lens and strobe lighting." He paused, and then added apologetically, "I would have preferred to use a stereomicroscope but that wasn't possible in the circumstances."

"Did you find anything?"

"Yes, I did. On the floor beneath the bench I found two hairs embedded in a stain spot, and what appeared to be a bone spicule—that's something like a splinter—three centimeters long—about one and a half inches. And I found what was nearly a whole fingernail with bright red nail polish."

A gasp erupted in the courtroom from an olive-skinned woman in the middle of the spectator section. She hurried up the aisle, a handkerchief crushed to her face. It occurred to me that she and the man next to her had been in attendance since the start of the trial. Once during a recess I had seen them approach Felix as though they knew him and wanted to speak to him, but when they saw me too, they wheeled off in the opposite direction. I threw Felix an inquiring look but he had ducked my unspoken question.

As the flutter amidst the spectators subsided, I pressed a hand on Felix's thigh, a warning to stay disciplined. It was a very bad moment; and even though I was confident I could handle all this later on during cross-examination, there was no escaping the fact that the jurors were getting a word picture and forming a conclusion that would be difficult to eradicate even with an eraser dipped in the logic I would offer them.

Jeff Baker handed the doctor a small glassine envelope.

"Can you identify the contents of this envelope?"

"Yes. It has in it the nail I found—the fingernail, that is. I placed it in this envelope and sealed it and put my signature across the seal, which is intact."

"I ask that it be received in evidence," said Jeff Baker.

Over my dead body, I thought, as I stood up.

"Objection, Your Honor. The state has not yet connected that nail to anything or anybody, much less to the missing woman. And I am waiting patiently, along with the jurors, I suspect, for him to do so. But until he does, I submit it is not competent evidence." I sat down, confident of the ruling.

"Quite so, Mr. Attleboro," came the response from on high. "Your objection is sustained at this point."

Turning to the jurors: "It's just a fingernail, as yet, could be anybody's. Even the missing girl's. But then mebbie not. Proceed, Mr. Baker."

Jeff was shaken. "May I approach the bench and explain my position, Judge?"

"Nope. Not now. Jest ask your next question."

The judge's comments could not, of course, stop the jurors from making connections or hypothesizing. Mollie Schneider's lips were drawn tightly, a dyspeptic look on her face; and Reginald Archer was not looking too happy either.

Jeff Baker fetched another small glassine envelope from his table and handed it to Dr. Scott. He held it in the palm of his hand a moment and then placed it on the table in front of him.

"Can you identify the contents of this envelope?" Jeff Baker asked the question with visible resignation. He faced the same evidentiary bar, and he knew it.

"Yes, sir, it contains two strands of human hair."

I could have objected and made him go through the process by which he arrived at that opinion, but I elected to forgo that exercise, since I doubted he had any matching hairs. I had anticipated this, and checked with Felix: nobody had searched their home.

Jeffrey dropped the topic. He had no choice. Probably he thought he had more fertile lands to till.

"All right, Dr. Scott. Now, turning to the bloodstains—I mean stains—"

It was no mistake, and Judge Sperry knew it. Jeff earned a grimace, first class, from him.

"Please tell the jury, what procedures you followed with respect to the stain," he said in a chastened tone.

"Well, sir, tests to detect blood or to distinguish it from other reddish-brown stains usually require a demonstration of peroxidase with hemoglobin acting as a catalyst, an oxidizing reagent, to produce a characteristic color."

Jeff Baker got a glassy look in his eyes. He had bitten off more than he could chew. I smiled inwardly because the jury was looking glassy-eyed, too.

"Can you simplify your explanation for us, Doctor?"

"I think so. Let me put it this way. Organic stains are relatively perishable, depending upon environmental conditions. These factors complicated the job here. However, the stains in question retained sufficient specificity and integrity so that my visual inspection of them, based upon my experience, allowed me to reach the tentative conclusion that they were bloodstains. I then proceeded to darken the shed by covering up all the windows. I sprayed the stains with a Luminol reagent—which is simply a substance that reacts with another substance. When this reagent combines with blood, as distinguished from other nonorganic substances, the peroxidase activity results in the production of luminescence. In other words, if the stain which is sprayed glows in the dark, it is blood."

Dr. Scott looked at Jeff Baker with a dour expression, inviting another question. He got it.

"What were your observations?"

"The two stained areas glowed faintly in total darkness."

"Did you reach an opinion?"

"I did. It is my opinion that the stains were blood."

Again the doctor gave the word an attenuated, brooding sound. And once more a murmur sifted through the courtroom. At the rap of Judge Sperry's gavel, it ceased instantly.

"Did you conduct any further tests?"

"Yes, I did," came the response from the man with the sorrowful countenance. "I then proceeded to determine the species origin."

"Meaning?"

"Meaning that I then had to determine whether the bloodstains were of human origin. Basically, all such tests require the use of antiserums. The test procedure is quite simple. My testings allowed me to reach a definite conclusion."

"And what was that conclusion, Doctor?"

"It was and is my opinion that the blood was of human origin."

Jeff Baker stared at the witness; then he stared at the jury and nodded his head knowingly; then he stared at me. I stared back and, mimicking him, nodded my head toward him solemnly.

The judge ended charades. "Are you turning over the witness, Mr. Baker?" He sounded as though he might be talking about a portion of fried eggs.

"Your witness," said Jeff, and sat down.

I strolled over to my favorite spot at the furthest end of the jury rail, and leaned against it, my arms folded.

"Didn't you stop short in your testing procedures, Dr. Shott?"

I loved to mess up the names of adverse witnesses. It was a rare witness whose self-confidence wasn't at least slightly eroded by my having forgotten his name.

"Scott. My name is Scott. Stephen Dennison Scott."

"Dr. Scott. Anyhow, didn't you forget to finish your testing procedures?"

"I don't understand."

"I think you do. You told the jury how you determined it was blood . . ." and not delicious cranberries or flavorful beets, I said to myself ruefully. "Didn't you?"

"Yes, I did."

"And then you told the jury how you concluded that it was human blood and not fish, fowl, or animal blood, right?"

"Yes, I did."

"But you didn't tell us whether or not you determined that the human bloodstains derived from the body of a particular individual. *Did you determine that?*"

"No, I didn't, because I couldn't."

A mournful sigh accompanied the admission. Plainly, the doctor took the limitations of his profession personally.

"And you couldn't, Doctor, because biologic stains—bloodstains—are relatively perishable, aren't they?"

"Not entirely, but yes, to some extent."

"And the 'integrity' of the bloodstain—which is the way you put it, I believe—is affected by environmental factors such as the type and condition of the surface on which a stain is found, and the temperature and humidity. Isn't that so?"

"To some degree, yes."

"To a marked degree. Right?"

"Yes." Grudgingly.

"And you will agree, won't you, that environmental and surface conditions markedly influence attempts to identify agglutinins and agglutinogens?"

"Yes, they do."

"And in this case, and in this boat, with its dirt and sand and its debris, there was no possible way you could make a positive correlation between the blood found and the blood type of Lorna Ward Evans. *Isn't that a fact?*"

"Yes, it is."

"And that's partly because the warm, moist situation presented on the key where the boat was found promotes the growth of bacteria. And they in turn destroy erythrocytes—red blood cells. Am I correct?"

I was showing off. But I had spent a night cramming, I had forsaken Ida, and I had sacrificed my friend Jack Daniel to my professional responsibilities.

"Am I correct, Doctor?" I asked again, with a softness only self-assurance can afford.

"That is correct, sir." His forehead was beaded with perspiration. "But from all the connected facts and circumstances, the conclusion is really inescapable that . . ."

"But me no buts, Doctor. We have your facts, and we have your opinions as a forensic scientist of considerable renown. We need nothing more. Thank you. You have been a great help to us."

I sat down and then immediately popped up again—by design.

"One other thing. You didn't tell us about the bone fragment you found with your high-powered hand lens. By the way, that's nothing more than a magnifying glass, isn't it?"

"Yes, it's a magnifying glass, of a kind," he said. I detected a growing desire on the doctor's part to embalm me.

"What did you find out about the bone?"

"It was a human spicule, all right, from the wrist complex."

"Perhaps so, but whose? That's the key question, isn't it? Whose bone was it? Or is it?"

A silent stare was the doctor's only response until Judge Sperry broke the gridlock. "Doctor, you're a professional. You've been here before. Give 'em answers, not looks. C'mon now!"

I took the cue from the judge and repeated the question. "Whose bone was it? Tell us, Doctor."

The answer came forth from sullen, stiff lips. "Without the body, it was not possible to tell."

"What body? Did somebody tell you there *was* a body?" And then, before he could answer, "Are we to be left similarly in the dark about the hair, sir?"

"I'm afraid so."

"Don't be afraid of the truth, Doctor." I sat down.

36

Felix and Ben and I were at a bar and grill around the corner from the courthouse. It was one-thirty, and Judge Sperry had given us an afternoon off so that he could catch up on some other judicial work. The place was small and sedate, bearing the well-mannered name, Court Repose. Its patrons were mostly lawyers and court personnel and, infrequently, judges, who would sit off by themselves in a corner. There was no music, and rarely was a boisterous voice heard.

We took a table near the window and ordered drinks and food. We were all apprehensive, knowing what Jeff Baker's next scene would be. I decided to voice it.

"I guess all that's really left in the State's case, barring a surprise witness, is playing the tape of your statement." Looking at Felix, I added soberly: "I wish to hell you hadn't given it. At least until you spoke to me."

"You weren't my lawyer yet, Tommy."

"I know that, but you called for me before you gave the statement, didn't you?"

"Yes, but—"

"So you had some misgivings. Enough to want to speak to me or some other lawyer before you told your life's story." I could not keep an accusatory note out of my voice.

"By the way, who was it you tried to reach on the telephone from Lester Melville's place?"

No answer was forthcoming.

"Did you hear me, Felix? Who did you try to call?"

He looked at me with a blank expression that could have been honest or could have been dissimulating. I had my choice. "I'm thinking. I really am," he said. "I just can't remember. It could have been my office in Miami. It probably was. I was so beat I can't remember what I did. And I was in shock."

"Sez who?"

"Sez me."

"What's your office number?"

"483-7000."

"Melville said you dialed a descending number."

Ben cleared his throat. "What's the point of arguing? The call didn't go through."

"I just wanted to know if I was second fiddle," I acknowledged gloomily.

I didn't relish hearing Felix's narrative in the morning, but there was nothing I could do to prevent it. It could not be suppressed. It had been given voluntarily at the time when he was not in custody and he was not then the target of a criminal investigation. He would sink or swim, I thought, on the jury's reaction to his statement. Then I shuddered as I realized how unfelicitous were the words with which I had clothed that thought.

We sat there glumly, sipping our drinks. It was one of those moments in a trial when its pressures produce a feeling very like genuine depression. The main symptom is a kind of psychologic paralysis. One simply can't *think*. But Jack Daniel soothed me, I was able to feel *something*. Call it resignation. After all, there was no point trying to fight the inevitable. At my prompting, we spent some time discussing our options when the State rested its case. That was likely to be very soon, most likely tomorrow.

While I hadn't told Felix yet, I had tentatively decided not to put him on the stand. My strategy would be to rely primarily on what I regarded as a reasonable doubt whether there had been a death, and, if a death, whether there had been an act of murder. The State had to prove that to a moral certainty.

Since tomorrow was Friday, we finally agreed to ask the judge to give us the weekend to ponder over our options.

When we finished our drinks, Felix picked up the check. Maybe he was trying to make up for having given the statement to the deputy sheriff, and heartburn to us. Heartburn goes away, I thought. Statements don't.

37

A fight erupted in the courtroom the next morning. A feature story in the newspaper was responsible. Barbara Murray, who had been doing a story a day on the trial in the local paper, must have met with Jeff Baker the night before over drinks or better, and together with him had created her masterpiece, which filled the courthouse.

EVANS ACCOUNT OF WIFE'S DEATH
LOST OR KILLED AT SEA?
By Barbara Murray

The trial of investment banker Felix Evans for the murder of his wife Lorna will reach a climax today when the state's attorney Jeffrey Baker plays the recorded statement of the defendant, given the morning after her unaccounted for disappearance last June 2nd. Yesterday's testimony by Dr. Stephen D. Scott, Miami's renowned medical examiner, rocked the courtroom when he identified the stains in the recovered motor boat as human blood. He also identified a bone fragment found on the floor of the boat as having come from a wrist, and a torn fingernail with vestiges of red polish still visible.

Earlier in the day, Judge Brian Sperry, over bitter objections from New York attorney Tom Attleboro, allowed the jury to inspect the bloodstained boat, which had been hauled to the back of the courthouse building in a covered van.

It was a sobering scene as the jurors, forbidden by Judge Sperry to converse with each other, circled around the vessel and peered at the bloodstains. One of them was observed to be suffering from an attack of nausea as she pressed a tissue to her mouth. Prosecutor and defense counsel, together with Judge Sperry, stood some distance from the jury. When the jury returned to the courthouse, Attleboro and his New York investigator Ben Abbott closely inspected the bloodstains. Attleboro and state's attorney Jeffrey Baker both declined to comment.

Evans's wife is said to have disappeared in the Gulf of Mexico after the couple's boat "broke down and drifted into the Gulf" from the inland waterways in a sudden squall, as Attleboro put it in his opening statement. However, it is the prosecutor's contention, as disclosed to this reporter in an exclusive interview last evening, that Evans took the boat into the Gulf deliberately, and axed Lorna Evans to death.

Et cetera, et cetera. To make matters worse, the front page carried a picture of the boat with Jeff Baker and his teammate, Susan Harwick, sitting on the gunwale, pointing to the bloodstains with a look of distaste that was pure Drama-101.

I wondered how our jurors would react to the news item, had they read it. Of course, they were not *supposed* to read or listen to any accounts of the trial, but morning papers to sitting jurors are like open cookie jars to children. All I could do was to gulp down the indigestible story and hope against hopelessness that it would not be as damaging as I knew it had to be.

Disorder reigned in the courthouse. The crowd seeking to gain entrance to the morning's proceedings acted as though there were going to be a rock concert inside. Only one hundred ninety persons could be accommodated, and that included seats reserved in the front rows for newspaper reporters and visiting V.I.Ps. For the case had not only drawn local courtroom buffs, it had also attracted reporters and lawmen from other regions. No doubt about it, our little MP case had become national news.

The bickering and shoving in the hall swept into the courtroom and, finally, erupted in the last row when two well-dressed women both struggled for the last remaining seat, using swinging pocketbooks as persuaders. The bailiff quickly moved in and escorted both women out.

I scanned the spectators as we waited for the jury. Apparently one juror was late, probably so engrossed in the newspaper story, that he—or she—had had to reheat the coffee. The Wards were in their appointed places, looking much like waxen figures at Madame Tussaud's.

The jury finally arrived, and so did Judge Sperry. Silence dropped like a velvet mantle over the spectators. Speakers had been placed at each end of the jury box. It looked as if we were in for a stereophonic performance. The microcassette was set up on a small table next to Donna Redmond.

Deputy Sheriff Harry Carelton walked up to the witness stand, clutching a small box. He began his testimony by describing the condition of Felix the day he was brought in by Lester and Pat Melville.

"He seemed to be dehydrated, so I gave him a lot of water. He was wearing slippers, slacks and a cotton shirt. Professor Melville's. I had called you, Mr. Baker, but you hadn't gotten there yet when the three of them arrived. That is, the Melvilles and Felix Evans."

"Where did you go?"

"Mrs. Melville waited outside; probably went to her car. Her husband, Mr. Evans and I went into the conference room on the main floor of the building. It has a permanently installed recording unit, a table, chairs, and a built-in screen for viewing slides and films. No telephones, no windows. It's secure."

"Secure in what way?"

"It's escape-proof."

I smiled to myself at the delusion of the Sheriff's office. No room, no prison is escape-proof. At best it is escape-*resistant*.

The deputy then described how he took notes on Lester Melville's story. Using the notes to refresh his recollection, he retold the Melville story. It was a clever strategy by Jeff Baker. Since Melville had been speaking to Harry Carelton in the presence of Felix, what the deputy sheriff had heard was admissible evidence. In its retelling, the story became fresh in the jury's mind and, following yesterday's disclosures, had new and possibly greater significance. So off went Harry around the Melville track a second time.

He didn't miss much. He told how the professor had caught sight of Felix waving his white shorts. How he had taken his boat over and picked up Felix, noting that he had no scratches and bruises and that his legs and feet were not cut. Jeff Baker interrupted him.

"Where was Evans—Mr. Evans—sitting in relation to Professor Melville and you, while you were at the Sheriff's office?"

"We—Professor Melville and I, that is—were facing each other across the table. Mr. Evans sat at the head of the table between us."

"Was he listening?"

"Of course."

"What did he say, if anything, when Professor Melville made those observations about his physical condition?"

"Not a word."

"Please continue."

He did, recounting for the jury how Melville told him that Felix had asked what time it was. A little past seven. How Felix had followed Melville into the cottage, where for the first time he had asked, "Where's Lorna?" He told the jury how Felix had asked for cream and sugar for his coffee. How the only telephone call Felix wanted to make was to some number in Miami. No call to his wife's family. Finally, he told the jury how Melville had told him that on the way back to the mainland Felix had said to him, "I guess I killed her." It was a deadly performance, regularly punctuated by the same question from wily Jeff Baker: "What, if anything, did Mr. Evans say to that statement by Professor Melville?"

And the answer: "Not a word." The inference was that Felix had agreed to the truth and accuracy of Melville's account.

By the time Harry Carelton finished his recital, I felt as though I were wearing a hair shirt. I itched all over my chest and back. But Felix sat next to me impassively. He either had nerves of steel or supreme confidence in his attorney.

"Did Mr. Evans make a statement?"

At last. Every juror inched to the edge of the seat. A reporter dropped a pencil. It sounded like a gunshot in the fragile silence of the room.

"Yes, sir, he did." Harry Carelton handed a cassette to the prosecutor.

"Did you record it?"

"Yes, sir."

"Did you tell Mr. Evans you were going to do that?"

"Yes, sir. That's S.O.P. Although," he added, "our instructions are that we don't have to inform a party who is only involved in a boating accident or an MP—missing person—case. We can tape a face-to-face on our own."

"What did Mr. Evans say when you told him?"

"He said it was O.K. with him, or words to that effect. It's on the tape at the opening."

"Is this the tape?" Showing the cassette to the witness.

"Yes."

"Where have you kept it since making the recording?"

"It was inventoried in on the property clerk's log, and wasn't signed out until I picked it up yesterday. Oh, yes. It *was* out once to have a duplicate tape run off. But I stayed and watched, and then I gave it back to the property clerk."

"Did you alter the tape in any way?"

"No, sir, of course not. It's absolutely intact."

Jeff Baker offered it in evidence. I was helpless to object. He also produced a set of typewritten sheets which the deputy sheriff swore was an accurate transcript of the tape recording. It was duly marked in evidence as I sat on my hands, unable to find any basis for objecting. The electronics man who had hooked up the speakers and the microcassette inserted the tape into the machine. A copy of the transcript was distributed to each juror and counsel. The original was handed up to the judge. The electronics man turned the unit on.

38

A voice boomed through the room like a wave breaking on a rocky shore. The electronics man quickly leaned forward and reduced the volume.

"My name is Harry Carelton. I'm a deputy sheriff of Lee County. Do you mind if we make a tape recording of our conversation? It's easier than taking notes, and it's quicker."

"Should I mind? Does this mean that I'm in trouble because my wife is lost?"

"Not at all, sir. It's just a matter of convenience."

The jurors were following the exchange on their copies of the transcript, as was Susan Harwick. She was using a pencil to mark certain places. Ben Abbott did the same. Judge Sperry simply listened to the voices, brushing up the corners of his mustache, his eyes focusing on his favorite ceiling square. I sat with my hands clasped, chasing my thumbs. To my left, Felix was immobile.

"Okay. Go ahead, if you want to."

"First of all, tell us who you are."

There was a pause. Felix was evidently nonplussed by the fact that his words were being taped.

"Do I need a lawyer?"

"Well, do you?"

"I'd like to call one."

Jeff Baker gave the signal to the electronics man, and the machine was switched off. He turned to Harry Carelton, who had been sitting quietly in his chair, glancing occasionally at the jury, and sometimes doing a sweep of the spectators packed in the seats in front of him.

"What happened at this point?"

"Well, I took him—" indicating Felix—"to my office and let him use the telephone. He was only in there a minute. When he came out, he said that he hadn't been able to reach his lawyer. I covered it in my questioning."

"How did he look?"

"Calm, collected. He was sweating, but so was I. It was very warm, and our air conditioners were not too effective."

Jeff Baker nodded to the electronics man. He flicked the switch. The tape began again.

"Okay? Did you speak to your attorney?"

"I didn't reach him. His name's Tommy Attleboro and he's in New York. I left a message with my sister-in-law to get hold of him. But I see no reason for me not to speak to you. For God's sake, all I want to do is find my wife."

"Well, you're the one who wanted to call your lawyer. So go ahead now."

"My name is Felix Evans. I'm thirty-seven. I live in Palm Beach and Miami. I work for my wife's father, Mervyn Ward. He's an investment banker in New York. I run the Miami branch office. My wife's name is Lorna."

Felix's voice emerged from the speakers high and reedy. I noticed some of the jurors, particularly Kathryn Adelaide, looking quizzically at Felix as though trying to match the voice with the man. He sat quietly at my side, back pressed against the chair, white knuckles beginning to stand out on his clasped hands. His eyes seemed fixed on the gold-lettered legend on the wall over the judge's head. I wondered on which word, "God" or "Trust."

Ten seconds of complete silence followed his last remarks. And then Felix began to speak again. It seemed to me that he was in shock, or giving a winning performance of it. His voice was strangely incompatible with the features and person of the man sitting to my left at the end of the table. He began, not surprisingly, with an explanation of the purpose of his trip along the west coast of Florida. Then, unexpectedly, as I knew from Ben, he meandered into lanes and byways that had nothing to do with the circumstances that had brought him to a small room in the office of the Sheriff that early morning. It was eerie. As Felix spoke, it was as though he were peeling away layer after layer of the tissue of his being. There was a hypnotic quality to his voice, which grew even more distant, attenuated, as it drifted backward. . . .

I was looking to open a branch office on the west coast of Florida. Ward and Stenrod is an old-line company in New York City. My father-in-law and his partner have always resisted change. He's a bedrock organization man. By the numbers. You know the type. Getting him to let me open a branch in Florida took me a year. I suppose it would never have happened if Lorna hadn't told him I intended to walk out of the business unless we opened a Florida office. So when I told him a couple of months ago that I thought the branch should be moved from Miami to St. Petersburg or Fort Myers so as to follow the migration of venture capital over there, I wasn't the slightest bit surprised that he called my idea harebrained.

I decided to look for myself, maybe leave the damned business and get into something else. All right, all right so it seems silly to you. I can read that look. You think that because I was— am—married, have a secure position in the family business, mucho dinero, that with all that I should be satisfied, happy, count my blessings. Well, you're wrong. It's not all that great. If you must know it's boring. Bor-ing! Figures and printouts and statistics all day long, choking to death on the wealth of others who were looking for ways to invest and spend and lose money that was choking them to death too.

I had to join the family business. It was expected of me, the only son, as it were. I was to take the torch from my father-in-law some day, as if the whole thing was a kind of relay race from one generation to the next. Well it's not that simple. I have a right to make my own decisions once in a while. I mean after all what I want counts, too. My own decisions! That's not so farfetched, is it? My whole life others have pushed decisions at me. When I was a kid, my mother used to tell me what clothes I liked. Tell me, not ask me. It was never my choice. What I liked just didn't count. I can still hear her coaxing and wheedling "Felix, you really like that suit, don't you?" "Yes, mother." "And that shirt is exactly your taste, isn't it, Felix?" "Yes, mother." On and on and on, year after year.

I thought I would never escape from it. It was like being in bondage. School and home. Home and school. Stuck like a fly on flypaper. And then escape seemed possible. Marriage and new horizons. God's in his heaven, all's right with the world! Bullshit, pure bullshit. I ran away from bondage and ended up in a tiresome world of audits and balance sheets and assets and liabilities. [Pause.] Well, not quite. I developed other interests. But that's another matter. The thing is that my life mostly seemed to be turning back on itself. The years ticked away, but I kept growing smaller and smaller. And I got scared. For the first time in my life, I was really and truly scared that I would never ever be free.

Felix had then asked Harry Carelton for another glass of water, and just then Jeff Baker walked in and introduced himself. When they all settled down again, Felix resumed his narration. But instead of returning to the incident at hand, he rambled on for ten or fifteen minutes, dredging up things from his past. He spoke about his school days; about how his classmates constantly picked on him for no reason at all. He mentioned how, as a kid, his best friend, Tommy—Tommy Attleboro, had always protected him. He complained about his home life as a child; he railed at his poverty-stricken years: at his distant and severe mother.

Then he picked up the thread as suddenly as he had dropped it earlier.

I suppose it really started when we about reached the Tamiami Trail. To beat the heat, we had started driving very early that morning. I had a couple of people I wanted to see along the way south, so we knew it was going to be a long day, and it was. By five we were pretty tired, but I wanted to cross over and get home to West Palm. Lorna was getting irritable. . . .

The road stretched out ahead, a glaring track of reflected sunlight shimmering up from the pavement in waves containing mirages. In the front seat next to Felix, Lorna stirred fitfully. A white sign along the road rushed into view and snapped past them as though drawn by a giant rubber band, but not so fast that she did not catch a glimpse of its message that a rest area lay ahead. She spoke above the wail of a forlorn country singer on the radio.

"Felix dear, let's stop off for a little while. We've been on the road since eight. We could both use a break. Maybe coffee and Danish. Okay?"

He paid no attention. He thought to himself how she had been complaining all day. First it was over the breakfast in Sarasota. The eggs were overdone, she said, the coffee too weak. The car too hot, then too cold. Then she had wanted to accompany him on his stops. She didn't accept his word that it was best for him to handle them alone.

He sped past the rest area.

And then, as though released from a string, the blazing sun dropped into the waters of the Gulf of Mexico to the west, leaving a salmon-colored curtain in the sky. As darkness quickly followed, Felix reluctantly agreed not to drive across the Trail to West Palm Beach that evening, but to bed down on the west side of the peninsula and return home the next day.

They ended up at the Seaboard Motel in Everglades City.

Lorna and I tucked in early, after a pretty decent shore dinner. We split a bottle of wine and got a little heady. I guess the driving and the heat had their effect. I asked my wife if she'd like to call her parents at West Palm to tell them we were staying over a day, or at least let our housekeeper know. She said no, her parents wouldn't worry, and the housekeeper was better off not knowing. She always had the idea that the housekeeper was sneaking some man in the house whenever we turned our backs. She said if she expected us home, she'd be careful. I didn't tell her how foolish her reasoning was. The house was not my concern.

Anyhow, we slept late, until about eleven. We had a crummy brunch in the restaurant, and then I told Lorna I'd like to take a boat out into the Gulf before we headed east. She thought it might be fun. So we went down to the dock later and rented an outboard. The weather wasn't so great, but it didn't look like it would build up into anything heavy. And, anyhow, I figured the Gulf was not like the ocean. So we took off in the boat. I got a sort of road map at the office. It was a layout of the channels showing the markers in red and black. I stuck it in my pocket.

I knew the water marking system. You know, red-right-return, and all that stuff. We headed due west. The first marker we saw was 26. The boat was running fine. It had about a nine-horsepower outboard on it. The fellow at the Seaboard Marina had told us to stay inside the Gulf, in the channel, and of course I took his advice. We had gotten to a kind of lagoon, very wide, about halfway to the mouth of the channel. The water was beginning to ripple up a little. Lorna said to me, "Let's go back, we've been out long enough." I looked at my watch. It was a little before four o'clock. I told Lorna that it was great, relaxing out there in the channel. There were hundreds of small islands covered with mangroves and scrub pine, and channel markers showing the paths through them. I told her I would like to stay out longer, but she kept grumbling that it was getting very cloudy and that the wind was getting stronger and she wanted to go back. So I decided it wasn't worth arguing about, and I began to make a big circle, an arc, to turn around and head back to the marina.

All of a sudden the handle, the throttle whipped out of my hand. I was surprised because I didn't think I had hit anything. There I was just making a wide turn and the handle leaped out of my hand.

I looked back at the motor. I was seated on the rear board. Lorna started climbing back toward me. I told her to sit down, she was rocking the boat. I saw that the two clamps that held the motor plate to the rear end of the boat had come loose. The motor had stopped and the propeller was dragging. I couldn't even reach it.

She started crawling over toward me again. I told her to stay in her seat, and I reached down and took an oar from the bottom of the boat. I tried to paddle the boat but I couldn't steer it toward land because the damn motor was dragging. It seemed almost ridiculous. I was so close to one of the markers in the lagoon, number 13, that I could have reached out and grabbed it. But I didn't because I was sure that I could paddle over to a shore about twenty-five yards behind it to the east, back towards the Seaboard Motel. I guess I underestimated the wind. We kept drifting down the channel.

And then the wind suddenly got much stronger. It was like it came at us in gusts from every direction. The water began to develop crazy currents. Once the boat spun completely around. I tried to touch the bottom with the oar. I couldn't. In less than thirty minutes we were out in the Gulf. I tried to pull the motor back against the boat, using the anchor line as a pulley, but I couldn't do it. When I looked up, we were so far out that I could hardly see the channel we had left. The waves really began to rock the boat. Lorna began to cry. I didn't feel too happy either, to tell you the truth. I told her to lie down on the bottom of the boat—that since we hadn't gotten back in an hour, the boat man would send out a search party. I got down on the bottom with her. It began to rain. Hard.

It must have been close to seven o'clock and still no help came. The water had gotten very rough and was beginning to splash into the boat. I took the spare container of fuel and emptied it in the Gulf so I could use it to bail out water. When I wasn't bailing, I huddled with Lorna, trying to keep her calm. We decided to wait a little longer before doing—what? We really didn't know what to do.

We couldn't understand it. The rain had stopped, but there were heavy clouds all around us. No help came. Nobody at all. Not one soul in the universe seemed to know we were in trouble, that we were missing. It was getting dark when Lorna and I decided we'd have to swim for it. Actually, it was her idea. When we faced a real crunch, she always had more courage than I. She got to her knees, looked all around the circle of the horizon. I thought I saw a couple keys, off to the north, I think. I'm not too good on direction. It seemed we were also drifting further into the Gulf. I told Lorna she could slip her arms through the straps of a cushion in the boat and use it as a life preserver. We'd swim toward the keys before we were too far beyond them.

We took off most of our clothes. I wasn't so happy to go into the water, but Lorna jumped. When I saw the boat drifting away from her, I jumped over the side. We swam and swam and swam. After a while, I could tell that she was tiring. It was getting very cold. Her face was very white and she was clamping her teeth as she half floated, half swam. We could hardly see each other because the waves were getting too high. And then all of a sudden I saw her head go below the water. That's when I decided to give her my cushion, to help her float more easily. I made my way over to her, and helped her slip the extra cushion on and up to her waist. The roar of the water and wind were so damn loud. Right beside her, I still had to shout to her that I was going to swim to the nearest key. I even thought I might get there faster without being wrapped in the cushion. I told her to take it easy, not to swim and exhaust herself, and that I'd get help.

The last thing I saw were her eyes. She kept looking at me. And then I had to start swimming. There was just no other way to get help.

I don't remember reaching the key. I don't remember anything until I woke up early this morning. I had no idea where I was. But I thought I saw somebody walking around on a key not too far off. So I took off my shorts and started to wave them. Then I saw somebody get into an outboard and head over to me. It was Professor Melville. I think I began to cry. I was out of my head. After that everything is hazy. I don't even remember who brought me over here. I think it was Professor Melville, maybe his wife. But I'm not sure. I'm very tired. I want my wife. Where's Lorna? Where is she? Where is she?

The electronics man turned off the machine.

39

The murmuring in the courtroom sounded like zephyrs passing through willows. Judge Sperry gently tapped a pencil on the scarred edge of his desk.

"Deputy Carelton, have you to this day ever located the ax that was in the boat?" Jeff Baker asked his question quietly, making several jurors lean forward to hear his words.

"Objection! Who testified that there was an ax in the boat? Or a shovel? The question assumes a state of facts not in the record, Your Honor."

"Sustained. Rephrase, Mr. Baker."

He didn't because he couldn't.

"Have you, to this day, ever located the oar?"

"No, sir."

"Have you to this day found the body of Lorna Ward Evans?"

"Objection!" I was on my feet, hand held out to stop the witness from answering. "Again, the question assumes a state of facts not in the record. The question as to a *corpus delicti* is a critical issue to be submitted to the jury. I submit that the jury should be so instructed, and also reminded that questions that include facts do not become facts unless a witness adopts them."

The jurors looked a little mystified, but I was not taking chances.

"Quite so, Mr. Attleboro, you are quite right." His Honor dealt a grave glance at the prosecutor. "The record, ladies and gentlemen, reflects evidence of the disappearance of Mrs. Evans, and nothing more than that. Yet. It also contains some evidence bearing upon the circumstances under which Mrs. Evans disappeared. It will be your task to weigh that evidence later, when I give you the case and do some teachin' to you on the law you must apply." Turning to Jeff Baker: "Your question was improper, you stated something that is not a fact. Juries make facts by their verdicts. Not you, sir." As he worked himself into a judicial pique, Judge Sperry's comments increased in volume. "Rephrase your question."

Baker nodded respectfully. "Let me rephrase the question, Deputy Carelton."

"Thank you!" I interposed ironically.

"To this very day, has your office located Mrs. Evans?"

"No sir."

"Any signs of her?"

"None at all."

"Thank you."

I meditated a moment, deciding whether to leave matters as they were or try to plant a few seeds of my own.

I stood. "Deputy Carelton, have you and your brother officers closed the book on the case?"

He hesitated, as though puzzled by the question. "I'm not sure I understand what you mean."

"Sure you do, Deputy, you know exactly what I mean. When you took jurisdiction over this matter, you opened a file, didn't you?"

"Yes we did, sir."

"Do you have your file in court?"

Harry Carelton looked at the prosecution table and nodded his head in that direction. "They have it."

I walked over and stood next to Susan Harwick, who ducked down in her customary fashion, and, after riffling through packets of papers under the table, came up with a white manila folder. I noticed that the knifelike part in her hair remained undisturbed. I squinted to see if she kept the seam in place with scotch tape. She looked questioningly at Jeff Baker. He whispered something, and she handed the folder to me.

I quickly found what I wanted, so I walked over and had the envelope and an enclosed Incident Sheet marked as defense exhibits. Jeff made no objection. Donna applied her stamp to the ink pad, whacked it on the envelope and sheet, numbered and initialed them, and handed them back to me with a radiant smile.

"Deputy Carelton, did you open this file on June second of this year?"

"Yes, sir, I did. Actually, it was opened by another deputy who was on duty that night. I came on at seven A.M. on three June."

"Do I properly assume that the other deputy filled in the opening entry on the 'Incident Sheet'?"

"Yes, sir."

Pointing to the letters in the upper right-hand corner of the folder, next to the word "Matter," I asked him:

"What do the letters MPR stand for?"

"Missing Person Report."

"Is the record kept in the regular course of your duties?"

"Yes, sir."

"Are the entries made contemporaneously with the occurrences recorded?"

"Yes, sir."

"Thank you." The report was received in evidence as a defense exhibit. It was a printed in columnar style. The headings and first entries read:

DATE	HR.	INQ/~~COMPL~~	NATURE	ACTION	ENTRANT
6-2	1815	RANSOM, LEO (SEABOARD MOTEL)	BOAT MISSING W/EVANS (2)	INFORMED C.G. @ 1820	T.W.

With the permission of Judge Sperry I loaned the sheet to the jurors. Each group clustered over the exhibit, and then passed it along. When I got it back from the bailiff, I walked to my perch at the furthest corner of the jury box, where I stood next to Number 6, a portly sixty-year-old retired realtor appropriately named House, who fancied florid ties. I had selected him for no better or worse reason than that his first name was Thomas. I picked horses in the same analytical fashion.

"Will you interpret the first entry, please."

"It means that on June two at six-fifteen P.M., Leo Ransom from Seaboard Motel reported a missing boat of theirs with a party of two named Evans. Ted Wilson, the deputy on duty, notified the Coast Guard at six-twenty P.M."

"What does INQ slash COMPL signify?" I knew, and I supposed anyone could guess correctly, but there was a method to my meticulousness.

"It identifies whether the matter originated as an inquiry or a complaint."

"And this one?"

"As an inquiry. That's why there's a line through the word 'Complaint.' "

"Ah so!" I said, with feeling.

"And 'Entrant.' What does that mean?"

"It identifies the deputy who logged in the item. In that case, Ted Wilson."

A series of entries followed below, which traced the action at periodic intervals during the evening, showing "N.D."—no developments—until the next morning. Then it showed the arrivals first of the Melvilles and Felix, and later of Jeff Baker. Then it had an entry on June 12, when Ensign Peggoty Shea found the boat, indicating its location at an unnamed island one mile northwest of the channel exit, and it noted the tentative "ID" of bloodstains. The last entry was made on June 13th. It simply read: "Ref to State's Attorney."

"Am I correct," I asked, "that so far as your office is concerned, this matter is still treated as an open missing person report?"

"It's a prosecution, sir."

"I'm not talking about the state's attorney. I'm referring to *your* file. It isn't closed, is it?"

"No, sir, it isn't."

"Why not?"

"Well, because . . . I guess it's . . ." He stumbled to a halt.

"The reason the file's open is because you still have a missing person. Isn't that right?"

"We have blood, a wrist bone, a fingernail, and so forth."

"Whose, Deputy? Whose blood, whose wrist bone, whose fingernail? Yours, sir?"

"Now, now, counselor. Objection sustained. Why dont'cha try that question in proper form?" There had been no objection, but there would have been one if the judge hadn't beaten Baker to it.

"Whose blood, whose wrist bone, whose fingernail?"

The deputy sheriff had no choice but to answer the question. "That's for the jury, I guess."

"You guess right. And what else did you have in mind when you said 'and so forth'? There aren't any 'and so forths,' are there?"

"That's a sort of figure of speech," he offered meekly. He tried on a smile but it didn't fit. The way he was shuffling his feet, his size eleven shoes, triple E width, must have begun to hurt.

"Am I correct, sir, that your file is not closed *because you still have a missing person?* That's a fact, isn't it?"

"Yes, that's so, Mr. Attleboro."

"And a missing person doesn't have to be a dead person or a murdered person, does it?"

"Objected to, Your Honor," came Jeff's response.

"Sustained," came the judge's predictable ruling, too late.

The seeds were sown. Plenty of time left for germination.

40

That, I supposed, was the State's case. Not too bad a case, all things considered. It had emotional appeal, and juries can easily be swayed by factors that are not strictly factual. My supposition, however, was wrong. Jeff Baker was not yet ready to rest. He had another witness.

He called for Sophia Ward to take the stand.

Damn, damn, damn, I said to myself. Had I known that she was to be a witness, I could have had her excluded from the courtroom until she testified. I remembered too late I had simply forgotten to ask for the exclusion of *all* witnesses. Not that it made too much difference in this case, I thought, since Mrs. Ward would never tailor her testimony—whatever it turned out to be—to fit that of earlier witnesses.

She was dressed severely in an expensive black dress. She wore no jewelry, nothing to relieve her starkly tragic appearance, except an oval pendant with an ebony-latched cover. I suspected it contained a picture. She approached the witness chair with her head held high, walking stiffly to maintain tight control of herself.

The oath was administered. She nodded her acceptance. When Judge Sperry told her she had to articulate her acceptance of the oath, her voice came out as thin and tremulous as tissue paper. Her examination was conducted by Susan Harwick, who stood directly in front of her and spoke in subdued tones as though extending condolences at a funeral chapel.

"Mrs. Ward, are you Lorna Ward Evans's mother?"

At the name Evans, Mrs. Ward flinched. "I am," she said in a tightly reined voice.

"Do you recall an episode at Jones Beach when your daughter was eight years old?"

"I do."

"Would you relate it, please, to the jury." Susan Harwick faded back to her table, giving Sophia Ward stage front.

"Well, little Lorna had a friend named Geri Miller. They were best friends, you know. It was Geri's birthday—August tenth—and it happened to fall on a Sunday that year. The girls asked us, Geri's mother and I, whether we wouldn't take them to Jones Beach out on Long Island. It wasn't our sort of place, really, but Geri was crazy about swimming, and while Lorna had not learned to swim yet, she liked to splash along the edge. And, after all, it *was* Geri's birthday. I agreed to take the girls while Geri's mother prepared for the party that afternoon.

"They had a summer home on the Island about half an hour from the beach. So I drove out early with Lorna, picked up Geri, and we went over to Jones Beach. It was a glorious summer day, but the beach wasn't crowded yet."

Sophie Ward paused. She took a small pill from a vial in her purse, swallowing it with a sip of water. Judge Sperry asked her if she was all right. She nodded, brushed back her hair with a sweep of her hand, and resumed speaking in that tissue paper voice which had the jurors all leaning forward to catch her words. It occurred to me that whatever the end of the story was, Lorna had never told it to me. I was as much in the dark as everyone else, except perhaps Felix.

"We settled down on a couple of beach towels near the edge of the water. The tide was going out so we didn't have to worry about moving back. I gave the kids the usual warnings and off they went. I took out some needlepoint." Sophie Ward's hands were making a ball out of her handkerchief.

"All of a sudden a wave developed some distance out. I noticed it building up as it moved in toward the beach. Lorna was waist high in the water, Geri beyond her, splashing and swimming on her back. I didn't like the sight of that wave but it all happened too fast for me to do anything but watch." Her voice had developed a tremor. "As it reached the shore, it broke with a fearful roar. I saw it pour over Lorna and suck her out. It seemed to be alive, like a giant white monster. I couldn't see either of the little girls. I rushed to the edge of the water and saw Lorna surface about ten yards out, way over her head. She was thrashing and choking. She couldn't swim. My little girl couldn't swim! I was panic-stricken. And I couldn't find Geri at all."

Tears were coursing down her cheeks. I noticed that her pocketbook had fallen to the floor, but she made no attempt to retrieve it. She didn't need a pocketbook. She was on Jones Beach.

Gently, Susan Harwick prodded her. "And then, Mrs. Ward?"

"I became hysterical, I'm afraid. There were no other swimmers near them. Then I heard whistles and voices, and suddenly a bunch of lifeguards raced into the water with lines tied around their waists. I guess there were life preservers or something tied to the other ends. I was beside myself. Two of the boys got to Lorna, but I could tell the others were looking for Geri. They finally found her, way, way out, and brought her in. Lorna was all right. She had swallowed a lot of water and was frightened out of her wits, but she was all right." Her voice was a quivering whisper. "Geri was unconscious. She must have hit her head on a stone as she was tumbled over and under. It had been the undercurrent, the lifeguards said, that had done the damage. They worked on Geri right at the edge of the water for fifteen minutes. Then the fire department got there with a respirator. But nothing worked. She was gone. She was dead."

"Just one more question, Mrs. Ward, and I'll be done." She walked a few steps away and stood quietly, fingering a pencil.

Then: "Mrs. Ward, did your daughter *ever* learn to swim?"

There was a long, dense pause.

Finally, with infinite sadness, she said, "No, she didn't. In fact she never, ever went near the ocean after that day. Never. She never *dared* to jump in it."

Susan Harwick sat down. Judge Sperry looked over at me. I gave him a barely perceptible headshake to indicate there would be no cross-examination. The bailiff assisted Sophie Ward from the room. Mervyn Ward trailed after her.

Jeff Baker stood up, said, "That's the State's case, Your Honor," and sat down.

I was in no shape at that moment to pick up the pieces. The jury was given a recess to allow me to talk to Judge Sperry out of their hearing. I told him that I needed some time to decide whether to put Felix on the stand or to rest entirely on the State's inadequate case, dramatics to the side. My unexpressed guess was that, since it was Friday, His Honor could find better occupation for the afternoon than presiding in the courtroom. I guessed right. Proceedings were put over to Monday morning.

It was destined to be anything but a pleasant weekend. Not for Felix. Not for me. As we left the building, the usual covey of television people gathered about, pressing us for comments. I had mislaid my sense of humor. There was nothing I cared to say. I walked through the group silently and into my waiting car. Ben got in next to me. Felix got in next to the driver. I had a very bad taste in my mouth that would take more than one or two Jack Daniel's to wash away.

41

"Putting you on the witness stand is easy. It's getting you off that may be the problem."

I had gotten to my temporary office at eight o'clock on Saturday morning to turn on the air conditioning before the thermometer began to climb, and to set out a modest breakfast before Felix and Ben made their appearance at nine. I also wanted to reread the transcription of the statement Felix had given at the Sheriff's office.

Just as I finished, Ben's rapping rattled the door. He walked in, hat in hand, dressed in a gray business suit, a white shirt, a dark tie, and black shoes. He was a credit to his parents. A surge of affection for him swept over me as he followed me gravely and deferentially.

Felix had arrived minutes later, wearing cotton slacks and a yellow terry cloth shirt. He looked like a beach bum rather than an investment banker on trial for his life. The three of us beleaguered the coffee table with its onion rolls, sweet rolls, bagels, and cream cheese and jams, and two large thermos bottles, one filled with Colombian coffee, the other with a decaffeinated brand.

Felix finished first, and began to saunter around the office as though he hadn't a care in the world. There was a world globe mounted on a stand in one corner of the room. He walked over to it and started spinning it around, all the time humming softly to himself.

How little I really knew about him, I thought. Part of me wanted to believe that he was still the same boy whose dependence upon me during our school years had given me such pride and pleasure. He looked the same. Narrow shoulders, a slight hunching of his back as he moved, soft liquid eyes, his head balanced as though it might fall off if he was not careful.

Yet I realized he might have become a completely different person. A stranger to me. I pushed the troublesome thought aside, but leftover uncertainty over its possibility made me lash out at him.

"For God's sake, come over here and sit down! We're here to work, not play geography games."

Ben stopped munching his cheese Danish and looked at me curiously. Annoyed with myself, I sat down at the desk in front of the window and pulled over a yellow pad. I motioned Felix to a ladderback chair in front of me. Ben took a chair to the side, whose soft leather burbled as it resigned itself to the intrusion.

Felix broke the silence. "Don't worry about me on the witness stand, Tommy. I can handle myself." The slight laugh that accompanied the statement conveyed quite the opposite to me.

"Putting you on the witness stand is easy. It's getting you off that may be the problem. One of the reasons we're here is for me to reach a decision, which I won't make until we review the State's case and see what, if anything, can be gained by exposing you."

"Until *you* decide? What do you mean, until *you* decide? What do you mean decide? It's my life that's at stake, isn't it? I have to make decisions, old boy, not you. Anyhow," he added in more modulated tones accompanied by a wry smile that reminded me of the Felix I had known, "when do you tell me what I need to know so I can make this big decision?"

I refrained from telling him that trial strategy was an attorney's call, although he had every right to be consulted. Indeed, I had never refused to let a client testify in his own defense, if he insisted, even when I thought it was a mistake. But that rarely happened. Most clients listened.

"It's not so simple, Felix. We've got a number of pros and cons to weigh. We can put you on and fight back by letting them see the real Felix Evans, shy, even-tempered, not likely to hurt a fly." My mind's eye suddenly conjured up the picture of a boy with black ink dripping from his face and clothes. "We can have you trace your life to the jury so you become a three-dimensional being they can see and understand. Or we can keep you off the stand and rest on the State's case, arguing that it's so damn weak we see no need to respond to it." I paused to make him look at me. But then my own eyes shifted as I added, "Even if we don't believe that completely."

Because I was unsure myself whether it was a confession, a warning or a plea, I raced on. "In other words, we can rest on the presumption of your innocence and argue that the State has not destroyed that presumption by proving your guilt beyond a reasonable doubt. But if we don't put you on the stand, there's always the chance that one of the jurors will push aside your presumption of innocence—which is wrong but human—and wonder what you're afraid of." I took a sip of coffee.

"So where do we begin?" Felix asked quietly.

"At the beginning," I said in my most authoritative tone. "Let's start off by acknowledging that the State's case is a good one. Not great," I quickly added, when Felix leaned forward as though to take issue. "Not great, Felix, but certainly there's enough to give the jury something to chew on. Lots of unanswered questions, blanks they can fill in that hurt you."

"What do you mean, blanks? There are none I can't answer. You think I can't handle myself?"

Ben cleared his throat. I'd nearly forgotten he was there. Felix still had that effect on me.

"Tom," he said, "is trying to tell you that both of us have a feeling that we don't have the full story, that you're holding back something. We may be wrong, but that's our feeling. Maybe you think something is not important, but that's for Tom to decide. And if it comes out for the first time during your cross-examination, it may hurt you badly."

Felix gave a snort of derision and waved a hand at Ben. "Do you mean to tell me—"

"Meaning, Felix," I interjected, "that Ben's got it exactly right. I'm not convinced—which means the jury's not convinced—that you simply acted like a damn fool that afternoon, joyriding in a motor boat with an unwilling wife because *you* wanted to go, and the hell with the way Lorna felt. So like you to have things your way. Still, there are too many missing pieces, too much left unexplained, and I don't know whether you can give answers the jury will buy."

"Such as?" It was half-question, half-challenge.

"In the first place, why *did* you insist on taking Lorna out in the boat? Why did you go when you were told the weather was going from bad to worse? Did you really just drift the way you said into the Gulf?"

Felix stood, walked over to a pitcher of orange juice on the coffee table, filled a glass and walked back to his chair. He sat there, looking steadily at me but saying nothing.

"Why didn't you take your emergency oar and row to a bank? Why did you let Lorna get out of the boat? And why did you leave her? And, most of all, where in goddamn hell did those bloodstains come from?"

I might as well have been talking to myself. Felix sat, legs crossed, fussing at a speck on his white ostrich leather moccasins. Nothing I was saying seemed to faze him. I couldn't help thinking of our school days. "You're my guardian angel," he used to say. "When I'm with you, nothing can happen to me." And strangely enough, nothing had happened to him that I had not been able to handle. At first when he started saying that, I would laugh; but after a while I began to think he really believed it. Maybe a piece of that boy still remained in the man and was doing tricks with his grip on reality.

Felix kept looking into my eyes, apparently at peace with the world. Ben pretended to be looking for something in his notes, and then stood up. He often walked his ideas to the surface. I watched him curiously, waiting for the progeny to issue forth. He went back to his leather chair and, leaning forward over the back of it, said, "How about the three of us taking the morning off?"

I waited. Sometimes Ben liked to toy with his thoughts, push them around like a cat with a ball of yarn. He would stop playing when he was ready. It took less than a minute.

"Why don't we take out a boat and run the course that Felix took, actually cover the scene of the . . . I mean, let's go out with a camera and put some flesh on Felix's story. Right now, all the jurors have is a boat. Let's put it in the water and show them how it all happened. And where. Take pictures of the channel, the marker, the lagoon where the boat broke down. Give them a sense of the actual surroundings, make it all real for them. Sort of a reconstruction."

I endorsed the idea at once, but Felix refused. He said he would not go back there—could not. He told us that we had his statement and didn't need him as a tour guide.

I hesitated. That meant we wouldn't have Felix's reactions to what we encountered. Well, I wasn't sure how genuine Felix's reactions to anything were anyhow. And we would have our own responses, which we could share more openly if Felix wasn't with us. His refusal to come along annoyed me, the way everything he did or didn't do seemed to be troubling me these days. But I could see the benefits to his not being along. So the upshot was I told him he had a free day, and that we'd meet him here tomorrow morning, when we'd make decisions.

When we left the building, Ben and I separated. I went ahead to the Seaboard Motel to reserve an outboard, and Ben headed for his room to drop off his briefcase and pick up his camera and some film. At the thought of a day of relaxation, my spirits started to lift. I even considered asking Ida if she'd like to come along for the ride, but decided that Ben might misunderstand. Or worse, understand.

As I set off for the motel boat dock, I privately thanked Ben for his suggestion. I was convinced that it was the right thing to do. It would give us a clearer picture of the accident Felix had described, and where it had occurred. I looked up at that inverted bowl we call the sky and began to whistle happily as I saw only blue.

I forgot that I was color blind.

42

Ben arrived at the Seaboard Motel in about half an hour. Wonder of wonders, he had shed his hat and jacket, but he still was wearing his tie up against his collar. A Nikon camera was slung over one shoulder and binoculars over the other. We must have looked like a pair of amateur bird-watchers out doing a head count on gulls. George Feeley was not at the boat dock, which was just as well. It eliminated the need for explanations and a possible leak back to the office of the Sheriff or to Jeffrey Baker's bunch.

The boats all looked the same except for their numbers. We picked out one, noting it had all the equipment Feeley had described. An emergency oar, an olive-drab metal container of gasoline, an infantry spade. And a wicked looking short ax with a grainy wooden haft. The spade and ax were mounted on clips in the storage area inside the shell at the front of the boat. The young girl in charge had bright yellow hair, the result, I guessed, of do-it-yourself bleaching. She was dressed in a very-mini-skirt and a wide open blouse. I wondered if Ben was wondering what she wore on her time off. Since we weren't guests, we left a deposit and a driver's license as a form of "identification" as she called it. She gave us another accordion map marked "With the Compliments of The Seaboard Motel." It was the same vintage as the one introduced in evidence. Ben settled down next to the throttle, electing himself captain, and then surprised me by opening his attaché case and pulling out a pair of sunglasses and a baseball cap. He smiled almost slyly when he saw me gaping at him.

He immediately established himself as an experienced mariner. He flicked on the switch, primed the engine, raced it for a minute to develop an even throttle and, signaling to Miss Miniskirt to cast off, spun the boat around as though he had been trained at the Merchant Marine Academy. I took the transcript of Felix's statement out of Ben's case, and left the map open on the planked bench near the prow where I was sitting. Ben had the binoculars slung around his neck and the camera wedged in his crotch.

The sun on the eastern horizon behind us was filtering through the mangroves and dwarf pines that dressed the broken-up land masses to either side of us, creating a kaleidoscopic effect of constantly changing patterns of light and dark on the quiet water lanes. The air was filled with shrieks and whistles from unseen birds and water fowl. Every so often something scuttled off in the brush. Huckleberry Finn would have given a tobacco-stained eyetooth to raft in those waters.

And then we saw the first marker.

It was a red metal triangular pennant about eight inches across at its base and a foot long. It was mounted on a black staff which in turn was fastened to a thick wooden post. The number was stenciled on a red background: 30. I called to Ben to throw the engine into neutral as I pored over the map, searching for the number. It wasn't there. A light flashed in my head like a digital print-out on the dashboard of a car warning of a malfunction. I ran through the transcript and found what I was looking for on page 41:

> I knew the water marking system. You know, red-right-return, and all that stuff. We headed due west. *The first marker we saw was 26.*

And there it was also, on the Seaboard Motel map, the first marker, just a short distance west of the boat dock.

But clearly not so in the water lane we were traversing. The first marker we caught sight of was red 30.

I motioned to Ben to take a picture as I sat silently in the slightly rocking boat listening to the derisive cackle of an unknown waterfowl as it mocked my confusion. The thought crossed my mind that we should turn back, go home and enjoy the rest of the day at the hotel instead of looking for more trouble, maybe finding it. I pushed the thought aside. I had to know; I had to see this through to the end.

Ben started the engine up again, and in a moment we sighted the first black pennant: 29. Markers followed in descending order, each one, however, four digits higher than the ones shown on the map. Marker 26 was a good 500 yards below its original location. As we progressed, I corrected my map to show actual numbers and locations.

We passed through a narrow neck staked with Markers 22 and 21. We identified the spot on the map. The markers shown on it were numbered 18 on the left and 17 on the right. Just beyond the neck in the channel, we entered the lagoon that Felix had described, where his outboard had broken loose. He said. Once again, I told Ben to throw the engine into neutral so that we could drift into it slowly.

"Should we track the way Felix said he went in here?" Ben's voice caused a rustling in the isle to our right, and a large white crane lifted up and flapped off, startled by our intrusion. He started the motor again without waiting for my answer. I was thinking ahead to Monday morning. As Ben began to nudge the boat into a broad circle, counterclockwise, passing a Marker 19, I found my place in the transcript.

The motor had stopped and the propeller was dragging. I couldn't even reach it . . . I tried to paddle the boat but I couldn't steer it to land. It seemed almost ridiculous. I was so close to one of the markers in the lagoon, *number 13*, that I could have reached out and touched it.

The marker lay dead ahead to the right. But it was not lucky 13. It was unlucky 17. I told Ben to cut off the motor. I pulled out the oar and poled the boat that Felix said he couldn't paddle or steer. Within a minute I reached the marker and touched it, like a kid playing tag who got home free. But I was no kid and the game was turning into a deadly exercise. I slammed the oar with fury into the water, splattering Ben's clothing and sending a family of crabs on the nearby crust of land scuttling off in a mindless search for safety. The oar bobbed off toward the center of the lagoon.

My head began to buzz as a migraine seized my temples in a fiery grip. I sat down quickly and grabbed my head in my hands. Ben came forward to see what was wrong with me. The boat edged into a land spit on the starboard side.

"What's the matter, Tommy? Are you all right?" Spoken gently.

"I'm not all right, I'm terrible." The migraine continued to bore into my brain like a blue flame from an acetylene torch.

Ben went back to his seat and took a picture of Marker 17. I updated my copy of the motel map. Ben also photographed the lagoon. Then he did a strange thing. He sat down, took off his shoes and socks, slipped out of his trousers, and hitched up his shirt. I was flabbergasted. He sat on the gunwale, swung his legs over, and gingerly lowered himself into the water. It reached his waist. He began to move out into the lagoon. After some ten or twelve steps, he stopped. The water had reached his chest. It looked as though he could have walked across the whole damn area without getting his chin wet. He returned to the boat.

Without uttering a word, he had made a vital point—for the prosecution. But had they learned how shallow the water was at that spot? I wondered if Felix had tested the depth. And if he had, why hadn't Lorna and he walked to dry land and just waited for the help that was sure to come sooner or later?

We sat in the boat for a long while, waiting for Ben to dry. I was in a murderous state of mind, sensing another betrayal by Felix, but at the same time glad he was not there. After Ben had dressed, and remade his tie, of course, he looked at me inquiringly.

"Now what?"

"Let's start circling again. When we get halfway round, cut off the motor and let's see what the hell happens."

When he turned off the engine, we sat and waited to see how quickly we would drift into the Gulf of Mexico a thousand yards away. We drifted two hundred feet into muck on the south side of the neck at the foot of the lagoon next to Marker 16. We repeated the procedure, circling clockwise and again we drifted toward Marker 16. The map, however, identified it as Marker 12. The boat scraped to an abrasive stop on the south side of the lagoon between Markers 16 and 18—old 12 and 14.

We spent over an hour testing the drift of the boat from various positions in the lagoon. And while on a few occasions the boat did drift through the neck, and swiftly at that, it never got past the sandbar just inside the Gulf. Eventually we reached the Gulf, but we did so under power, not by drifting, and by carefully skirting the sandbar, on its north side, visible approximately four feet below the surface.

When we satisfied ourselves that there was nothing more to be gained by further test runs, we motored out to No Name, the key the Melvilles called their home away from home.

Professor Melville came out when he heard the engine. He was carrying a glass in one hand, and a beer bottle in the other. He was back in his dirty bathrobe and yellow slippers. A true patrician. We turned away before he could recognize us.

Finally we went over to Round Key where Felix was found. He had told us that he had slept under a large tarpaulin that fateful night, and I wanted to check it out. Finding the leathery cover just about where he had said it was, I started walking quickly back toward our boat. I had gotten about half the distance when I heard Ben call to me to come back.

He was standing next to the tarpaulin. He had flipped a large corner of it over. Ben did like to turn over every stone. I walked up and followed the line of his eyes to the ground. A shoelace lay on top of the flattened sand. I tugged on it. It broke. I took a stick and dug down about six inches and uncovered a sneaker. Its mate was buried next to it, a sort of double interment. Together, then, we dug up the rest of the compressed area and found a cotton shirt and a pair of linen slacks. They were both covered with dark brown stains. Ben walked back to the boat and, returning with his emptied attaché case, stuffed the clothing and shoes and shoelace inside. We walked in silence to our boat, got in, and pushed off the key.

It took us well over an hour to return to Seaboard Motel, where we signed out. In all that time neither of us had said a word. Driving back, I finally broke the protective shell of silence. Even then, our conversation was restricted by unspoken agreement to what absolutely had to be said.

Ben dropped me off at the office, where I wanted to reconstruct the jigsaw puzzle, using the new pieces. On my instructions, Ben made a beeline across Alligator Alley to the Coast Guard's offices in Miami to determine when the markers had been moved around in the inland waterway. He also wanted to find out whether, and if so when, new maps were going to be issued. I commissioned him to get the answers. Saturday notwithstanding. Regardless of cost.

43

It was six o'clock before Ben got back to the office. Ben noticed the sand and shell fragments that had scattered on the carpet when I had taken the clothes out of his case. They had offered me nothing helpful, at least nothing that said they could not be Felix's garments. He walked carefully around the debris and briefly fingered the clothes, sniffing at the brown stains like a bloodhound. I had done the same thing, but all I'd been able to detect was the musty odor of sand and seawater.

He sat down heavily on the couch. He looked tired, but he would never admit it, I knew. Not my Benno. I called our little meeting to order by slapping the palms of my hands lightly on the table in front of me. "Well, what did you find out?"

He paused before he answered, looking at me anxiously. "How do you feel?"

"Fine. Why do you ask?"

"You look—well, you know, a little out of it."

I thought I had a good hold on myself, but I ducked answering him.

"We were in luck, Tom. Most of the bureaus closed at noon. But the geodetic-survey people were at work to meet a deadline. All very interesting. They work from aerial photos, underwater photos, sonic readings, and some other data bases that were beyond my comprehension. Heavy algebraic stuff and computer printouts. Some of the map product is so complex that it can only be read by trained geographers. Reading tea leaves has to be a breeze by comparison. Anyway, I got the answers you want."

"I don't know what answers I'm looking for any more," I said, searching in the bottom desk drawer for a fresh bottle of Mr. D. Unsuccessfully.

"There are a whole bunch of waterways like the one at Seaboard Motel. Maybe as many as twenty between Fort Myers and the tip of the peninsula. None of them is within the jurisdictional waters of the Coast Guard. They're Florida property, private or state. But because the Coast Guard has trained personnel, and because they have to get into those waters for map making and map corrections, they help position safe-water markers." Ben pulled out a large geodetic-survey map that had depth soundings shown by shadings and numbers signifying feet. It included Everglades City and its watery environs.

"This map," Ben continued, "is fresh out of the oven. It won't be released until certain soundings are rechecked." He pointed to the lower left hand corner. "No certification signature yet. But the thing of it is that the surveys for this sector were completed last spring. And here's the most interesting part—what you wanted to find out." He put the map down and perched on the edge of the desk. I was wedged in the chair behind it, a little fuzzy, but not missing a syllable. I had poured myself a cup of black coffee from the small coffee machine I kept on the table next to the wall.

"When the survey team gets to an inland channel such as Seaboard's, they team up with reps from the State Conservation Department and check the channel markers to see whether surface or subsurface changes in the terrain call for moving any channel markers or adding any. It's all done so as to avoid disrupting nesting areas. The last check-up was back in 1983. That's a long time where the waters are tidal and the bottom is sand and silt."

I was growing impatient and my head was beginning to throb again. "Bottom line, Ben. Please. When did the Seaboard channel get a face lift?"

"Around March of this year." Somewhere in the distance an aircraft broke the sound barrier, producing a sonic boom that played havoc with the windows and my head.

"That means," I said stonily, "that the Seaboard Motel Map was outdated last March."

"At the latest."

"And a new schematic map—"

"Hasn't been made, can't be, until this one is certified and released. You see it locates new low-numbered markers in the Gulf waters. Those are what threw the old inland markers out of kilt. The rest of the job is up to the motel people who make their own inland map." Ben scratched his head. "But I don't see how Felix could have missed the new number of the first marker he saw as he started out—number 30. Or the one he said he could have grabbed—" He stopped and found the new number of the marker in the lagoon. " . . . number 17. Here it is," he said, showing it to me. "In the lagoon. Old 13. How could he have messed up the numbers? I can't understand that."

I glared at him. "Of course you can," I said. "It's as simple as can be. He didn't see *any* numbers in the lagoon on his way out. He just saw red and black markers. He wasn't *looking* for numbers. He had other things on his mind, other priorities. The fact that later on he said he has passed close enough to touch number 13 *proves* he hadn't stopped there. If he had, he damn well would have noticed that the number was 17." I stopped to draw a deep breath, and Ben took the opportunity to speak.

"That means he could only have gotten the wrong number later on, from the old map. The one he got from Feeley when he rented the boat. He must have studied the map and the markers after—"

"Ben, do me a favor." I had to interrupt him. I couldn't handle his giving voice to my own thoughts. Damn it, I was Felix's lawyer. I had to deal with this mess myself. With Felix. "Leave a message for Felix to be here tomorrow at nine. No breakfast, no snacks. He'll probably ask how we made out. If he does, tell him that we'll see him in the morning. Nothing more." I gave Ben a mirthless smile and turned off the lights. Neither of us so much as mentioned the stained clothing.

"Have a nice evening," I said, "I'll see you in the morning."

"What about you? You look like you could use some food to absorb the liquor." Gently put, but there was a reproof tucked in there somewhere.

I frowned.

"Don't you want some company?" Ben asked. His face colored. "I meant me, of course."

"Company isn't among my desires," I said grimly, "not tonight. But thanks."

Ida had soft music sifting through the air-conditioned suite, and a bucket of ice and glasses on a tray. And Mr. Daniel, of

course, in his place of honor on the sideboard, kissing a bottle
of 100-proof Stolichnaya, Ida's pride and joy—after me. There
was no way for her to have known that I had reserved the
evening for myself, away even from her sweet ministrations.
She stood there quietly, wearing a canary blouse and shorts and
a look of sympathetic concern. It was never clear to me why
some perceptive male had not snatched her from circulation.
Whenever I ventured to say as much, however, her pretty face
closed down. I didn't want any part of her closed to me like
that, so I always dropped the subject. And then, always, she
would smile again. It was like the sun coming out.

Tonight, though, I looked at her with unseeing eyes. They
were too busy looking inward as I slipped deeper and deeper
into a black mood. I pinched her absentmindedly on a tempting
buttock. I told her that the game had been called because of
darkness, and sank gloomily into the club chair next to Mr.
Daniel's place of repose. She stalked off to the bedroom with
a hauteur that boded ill for my nights ahead. Had she been a
Siamese cat, she would have flicked her tail and spit at me.
She closed the door hard enough to convey her displeasure. I
knew she would be asleep by the time I got to bed, at least
pretending to be. And I had no intention of calling her bluff
that night. No, not that night.

When she had gone inside, I called Amos. We spoke for
over an hour. He warned me again of the ethical morass I was
wading into. This time I had to agree with him, but I told him
it was too late for me to change my course. He pleaded with
me to have it out with Felix in the morning, and to disengage
from the disastrous course upon which I was set. I thanked
him for his advice. I knew I left him unsatisfied. He left me
unmoved.

As I crawled into my twin bed alone, I murmured *caveat
emptor*. I fell asleep before I had figured out whether I was
speaking to Felix or to myself.

44

When I got to the office on Sunday morning, Ben and Felix were waiting for me in the building lobby. I nodded at them, but remained silent as the elevator carried us up to the third floor. No doubt the expression on my face conveyed the message that not following my lead would be risky. For neither man said so much as good morning.

Before leaving on Saturday, I had changed the position of the ladderback chair so that it half faced the couch. It also directly caught the waves of sunlight splashing through the windows behind my desk. I expected the two of them automatically to take the same chairs they had previously occupied. People nearly always did that. Immediately, and perversely, Ben upset everything by walking over to the couch and straddling the arm nearest me, throwing into shadow the slacks, shirt and shoes I had placed there, covered for the time being by some scattered files. Still, I could not blame him for wanting a head-on view of Felix's face during the denouement.

Felix sat down apprehensively. He could hardly fail to note that something was in the air. He looked into my face, squinting slightly because of the sun.

"We made the run, Felix, from the Seaboard Motel dock out to the key you were found on and back. And we had some luck. Only thing is, it wasn't good luck."

His face stiffened. As I looked at his fixed expression, the part of me that didn't want to choke him wanted to find some way to get past his guard. I had a momentary wish that I could spirit us both out of this room filled with distrust, and terrible road markers to disaster, and ask Felix once again to walk down Broadway with me to the public library branch on 100th Street. I wanted to put off to some indeterminate future day this one of confrontation. Back to the library, breathing its musty scent of old books, browsing through the aisles where I had first met Lorna. Felix's wife. I jerked myself out of my fantasy, thinking Lorna is probably—more than probably—dead. And my friend, my oldest friend probably—more than probably—had killed her.

Felix had not glanced over at Ben yet, hadn't noticed the pile on the couch. "C'mon, Tom, stop setting me up. Get to the point." Spoken calmly. He reached into a pocket for a slice of gum, which he folded neatly into his mouth, playing cool mouse to my cat. I said silently, *Did you kill Lorna, Felix?*

Then out loud: "When you left the dock, Felix, where were you sitting?"

"Back on the seat, next to the throttle on the outboard. Lorna was right next to me. Why?"

"Did you have your glasses on?"

"Of course. You know I can't see worth a damn without them. Why?"

Again, I ignored his question. "You told us, and you told the sheriff, that the first marker you saw was 30, didn't you?" My mistake was deliberate.

"No, I said that I saw Marker 26 first. Red. On the left as I cruised out."

I opened the motel map on the desk in front of him. He leaned over, scanned it for a moment, and then pointed to the number. I kept my eyes on his face.

"The first marker is 30," I said.

"It is like hell."

"*Felix.* We saw it with our eyes, Ben and I, when we left the dock."

He bit down hard on the gum. "I must have missed it then. Some of them are hard to find. Anyway," he added easily, "I wasn't paying too much attention yet. We were just starting out."

"You paid enough attention to mention the number specifically at the Sheriff's Office, didn't you?"

From Felix, only silence.

"Well, didn't you, Felix?"

Still, deadly silence. His eyes were focused on some distant object.

Ben cleared his throat. "Did you also miss 29? How about 28, and 27?"

"I guess I did, Ben," said Felix, still smoothly. "But I did catch 26. It was red, left going out." He said it as though his description validated his answer.

Ben nodded slowly. He opened his mouth, then closed it, evidently deciding that it would be best to leave the rest to me. When he looked over from Felix, I continued.

"Okay. Maybe so, Felix. Maybe so. Anyhow, we continued down the channel and finally reached the lagoon, where you said all the trouble started. See it on the map?"

Felix found the spot. "Yes, there it is. That's where the damn engine stopped as the throttle kicked up in the air. And there's black 13. . . ." His voice went up, as though he were asking me.

"The one you got so close to that you could have reached out and grabbed it," I said coldly. "Right?"

"I could have. Yes, that's what I said."

"Black 13?"

"Whatever the hell the number was. I wasn't in a frame of mind to memorize numbers." Finally, Felix was becoming wary.

"But you made it clear and specific to the Sheriff, didn't you? That's precisely what you said. 'I was so close to one of the markers, *number 13*, that I could have reached out and touched it.' Well, did you or didn't you see 13?" I was having trouble controlling my voice. My anger was bubbling just below the surface.

"Look here, Tom, the numbers don't mean a thing. What's important is that the engine snapped, I hit a panic button, we drifted over to a marker—whatever in hell the number of it was, and then we drifted—"

"*No.*"

He stared at me.

"You drifted *nowhere*, Felix. We went through the drifting routine, and grounded our boat every time we tried it. You didn't drift into the Gulf of Mexico, you steered a course into it. You've got the markers wrong because you weren't paying a damn bit of attention to them when you took Lorna out in the boat. You just kept your eyes peeled for a place to do what you planned to do on that trip. And I'll tell you something else. You could have walked to land, that's how shallow the lagoon is. I don't believe you ever tried to paddle anywhere. *No way.* And another thing. Your boat didn't drift to the key it was found on, either. The current was against it, and the wind against it. I still don't know what happened to Lorna, and I'm not sure I want to know. But this much seems clear to me, and I suspect to Ben, too, although neither of us has said it out loud yet."

I had walked over to Felix, and now I stood over him. I noticed that Ben had slipped off the couch arm, and was standing in a posture of readiness. Through the turbulence of my senses I said, "I'll tell you what I think happened. At some point, before you motored that boat to where it was found and swam to the key where Melville picked you up in the morning, you studied the map and you memorized those two markers so you could refer to them by number later on, to give credibility to your story. At least you thought they'd do that. But, you stupid bastard, you never noticed that the numbers had been moved around since the map was made. So you referred to the old markers on the map."

I began to shake with rage. Ben walked over and placed a restraining arm on my shoulder. I shrugged it off. Felix looked up at me, his liquid eyes shining directly into mine. And once again for a split second the years slipped away from me and I had to wrench my eyes from the faintly supercilious look he so often affected when he felt insecure.

"He *could* have seen the numbers, Tom, and mixed them up when he got to the Sheriff's Office." As he spoke, Ben kept his eyes on Felix. "Shouldn't we try to find out a little more before we jump—you know, get to a conclusion?"

I recognized the sense in what Ben was saying but I was in no mood to acknowledge it.

Looking at him I said, "Do you know what Baker can do to him with this kind of information—not to mention the other stuff?" I looked at the couch. Subtlety was my middle name.

"What other stuff?" Felix asked right on cue.

Ben kept at me, ignoring Felix. "Okay. I know that you have to assume that Jeff Baker has the same information we have, and also reconstructed the boat trip. I agree you have to be ready. But I don't think they did the run, I really don't. Because if they had, they would have had Carelton or somebody else from his office on the witness stand tracking the route and showing what we discovered about the markers, drift, current, and the rest of it. They wouldn't have risked losing that opportunity to bolster up their case by saving it for rebuttal. Because if Felix doesn't testify, if he doesn't run through the story, the State can't come back to it in rebuttal. Can they?" Ben knew they couldn't, but he was trying to be deferential.

"You have a point, Benno," I muttered with less than good grace. "But *we* know these facts. And that puts me in one helluva spot as a lawyer with a license. Must I report our observations to Baker? Don't answer that."

I was treading water, so Ben decided to seize the moment. He took a wild shot. "When you got to the Sheriff's Office, did you have the motel map with you?"

"I told you before, I left everything in the boat."

"Everything? Clothing and all?"

"I said everything. Except, of course, our underwear, which we left on when we abandoned the boat and decided to swim for it." Ben didn't glance at me. I could see the effort it took. About the same effort I was expending on not sneaking another look at the lumpy files on the couch.

"Didn't you have a talk with Carelton when the Melvilles dropped you off, before they took your statement?" Ben asked.

"I was taken to Carelton's office straight off. He was waiting for me. Melville had called in from his place before we came over on his boat. When I got to Carelton's office, he and two other deputies were standing around his desk. . . ."

He pulled up sharply, as though someone had jerked on invisible reins, and his jaw dropped. We waited. My heart was beating as loud as a dime-store clock.

"Now I remember. Funny how your mind opens and closes when you try to remember things." He slapped his knee. "They were standing around Carelton's desk looking at a large map of the area. I walked over after they introduced themselves— I only remember Carelton's name. One of the other two was a little guy with red hair. I remember wondering how such a gnome had made it into the Sheriff's Office. The second man looked like a clerk. He had standard sheriff's slacks on but was wearing a striped shirt and didn't have a gun belt on like the others."

"So?" My voice sounded ridiculously normal.

"So Carelton asked me to look at the map and show him about where Lorna and I had left the boat. I told him I couldn't do it, I had no idea where the spot was. Then he pulled out one of the Seaboard maps and asked me to point out where the boat broke down. So I traced our trip on that map through the inland waterways and out into the Gulf. I showed him red 26 and said that was where we started. Then I pointed out black 13, where the engine broke loose."

He looked up; his eyes latched onto mine. "Is that helpful?"

Ben stepped in again before I could think of something sufficiently devastating to say.

"Tom, don't you see what may have happened? Felix *blacked out* on the actual numbers he saw or just forgot them. When he looked at the map, he just assumed they were the right numbers and referred to them when he gave his statement. See what I mean?"

I glowered at Ben. If he had tried as many cases as I had, he would have realized how fecund is the imagination of a trapped witness, how quickly he can construct a response. We call it recent fabrication. Sometimes it works.

"Well, well, Benno," I said. "You certainly have come around. When you first reported to me after your Florida investigation, you were ready to nail Felix to the wall by his thumbs. Now you're championing his cause like a bloody lobbyist. How come?"

Even Ben's face was silent. Felix sat there like a disinterested party, placidly chewing his gum. What he had just told us had a certain ring of truth to it, but there was no way for me to know whether the bell was cracked. Of course I could call up Carelton and, if he was on duty, ask him about the map. But what if he were to contradict Felix, to say that he never showed him a map? The whole thing was too risky.

Besides, we weren't finished here yet. There was a much more serious matter at hand. I gave Ben a sign, and he went over and gathered the files off the clothing. Both of us watched Felix's face as the stained shirt, the trousers and the shoes were uncovered. I focused on his Adam's apple. Experience had taught me that a witness about to lie does a lot of imperceptible swallowing with his lips closed. Only his Adam's apple can give him away. Felix's Adam's apple was bobbing up and down like a yo-yo.

Without a word he got up, walked over to the couch and picked up a sneaker. He loosened the laces and folded back the tongue, peering closely at something or other. I watched his Adam's apple, still bobbing up and down. He put down the sneaker. He was standing right over the clothes but he didn't touch them.

Neither Ben nor I moved; watching Felix was, for the moment, an all-consuming activity. A siren some distance off wailed its way through a street.

"What's all this?" Felix asked.

If I'd been in a different frame of mind, I might have congratulated him on his sangfroid. As it was, it was all I could do to keep my turbulence under control and speak to him quietly. "Just some clothing we found yesterday," I said. "Want to know where?"

Felix finessed. "Whose clothing?"

"That's what we want you to tell us. Is it yours? Go ahead. Pick it up, look at it. *It's yours, isn't it?*"

Felix stood there staring down at the clothing, but he didn't pick any of it up, or bend to get a closer look. I walked over and picked up the sneaker that Felix had dropped back on the couch. Rolling back the tongue, I noticed a black smudge. On closer inspection I was able to make out that it was some kind of monogram.

I looked inside the other shoe, and there it was again. Legible, yet incomprehensible. Initials are not usually expressed in terms of an algebraic fraction. I showed it to Felix.

"Was this what you were looking for in the sneaker before?" I asked.

$$\frac{\beta}{\pi}$$

"I was looking for my initials. Plainly, those aren't."

"So you say they're not your shoes?"

"They all look about the same, Tom. No, the initials aren't my initials. And the clothes aren't mine, either."

"How do you know? You haven't even picked them up. The shirt is white, the pants are white—George Feeley swore you were wearing white slacks and a white shirt. Want to try them on for size?"

He walked away, going over to the table by the wall, where

he picked up a paper napkin and spit his gum into it. His hands were trembling. I had the feeling, clear and strong, that the clothes were his. There was no way I could prove it or really wanted to; but as a coincidence it flew into the face of reason, and the place we found them made the inference that they were his close to a certainty.

Felix walked back to the couch. After another moment, he picked up the shirt and stared at the brown stains spattered over the front. "Even if they were mine—which they aren't—but even if they were mine, how could anyone show that I hid them or that the bloodstains were mine? Or Lorna's?"

A crack shattered the stillness that followed his question. Ben looked up sheepishly, holding the two pieces of a broken pencil.

"Who said they were hidden? And who said those are bloodstains, Felix?" I asked in a voice as smooth as cream.

"You did."

"I did not. I only said we found the clothes. I didn't say where, and I didn't say they were bloodstained. Are they, Felix?"

Felix poured himself a glass of ice water from an insulated carafe on the side table. His hands did not appear to be shaking any more. Then he sat down again in his chair. Clearly, he had regained his composure. His hands wrapped around the cool glass, he said, "Look, Tom, you're my lawyer, not the state's attorney. So why not stop treating me like the enemy and remember you're here to defend me?"

I reached him in three strides, grabbed his sport shirt at the throat, and hauled him to his feet. Ben rushed over but I pushed him away. I held Felix close enough to smell the sourness of his body.

"You *are* the enemy," I spat at him. "The clients are always the enemy. They hide, they lie, they cheat, and if they can avoid paying, they do that, too. I can figure out my courtroom adversary, but I can never trust my client. I want the story, Felix. Now. I'm stuck in your case up to my neck, thanks to Chris. You know damn well that I didn't take you on for your sake alone."

I was entitled to a lie of my own now and again.

Felix wrested himself free. "Don't pull that 'I did it for Chris' crap on me. The big bucks hooked you, not Chris. You took me on for the money. You'd probably take on any case, if there's enough money in it."

I pushed Felix against the wall. Hard. The water glass fell to the floor, staining the carpet at his feet.

"There was no accident, there never was an accident, was there? You knew exactly what you were doing when you rented the boat. You didn't break the motor and drift into the Gulf, you *steered* into the Gulf. And then you killed her, didn't you? What did you do, brain her with an oar? Did you hit her over the head and splatter her brains over the boat? Why? For God's sake, *why*? What did you do it for? Tell me dammit!"

I slapped him across the face so hard that he reeled. Mucus appeared at the openings of his nostrils. He began to shake uncontrollably.

And then he told me how much I meant to him.

"All right, you self-righteous bastard. Mr. Perfect. Let me tell you something. I'm as sick of you as you are of me. When I look at you I want to vomit. It's always been Tommy this, Tommy that. '*Tommy* wouldn't do that.' '*Tommy* used to say.' Tommy, Tommy, Tommy. From my mother, from Lorna, from my sonofabitch in-laws, and now this, you trying to run my life. You think you know what's going on? Nobody knows except me. I'm not the fool you take me for. Our Boy Scout days are long over, Tommy boy. Let me tell you, I'm tempted to let you have the full story, for all the good it can do you. It sure can't hurt me to talk. Remember, I'm your client. Your lips are sealed. This is a priv-i-leged comm-un-ication." He dragged out the last words with mock gravity. He was wrong, but it didn't matter. I stood off, my eyes riveted on him, watching his fist clench and release spasmodically.

Suddenly he dropped back into his chair, his legs outstretched, his arms dangling at his sides. His eyes became glassy and he started swearing, a long, endless stream of curses that even singed my fireproof ears.

Quietly, I walked to the door and left. Left them. Left *him*. Left Felix's stories and his lies and the lethal truths that were beginning to bubble from his lips. Left him with his nightmares and his dreams. Left the whole rotten, sordid mess behind.

Knowing full well that in the morning, with the inevitability of morning itself, I would have to face the jury and present Felix's case, or find a viable alternative.

I did not need my little friend with the big, shiny, bald head to tell me that I did not want the truth. Not yet, anyway.

And I did not need his accusatory finger stuck in my eye to tell me why.

45

I woke up on Monday morning with another monumental head-ache. It would be the last day of the trial. Baldly put, I had to finish the case before I became fatally tainted with the truth. Felix could not be permitted to testify on his own behalf. It didn't bother me that if he took the stand he might be forced during a deft cross-examination by Jeff Baker to convict him-self. That he deserved that was becoming clearer and clearer. But I did care that I might lose the case. I had lost Lorna over him, but that was done and gone and, as Ben had told me and Chris had also said, I had come to accept it as a defeat I had subconsciously invited. So it really wasn't a defeat. But I was not going to let him bring me to the first loss of a murder case in my career. Felix the Spoiler wasn't going to spoil my perfect record. Not Felix, my enemy. Not Felix, my friend.

Ben had awakened me at seven o'clock to find out what the morning line was going to be. I did not ask him what had happened after I pulled the door closed the evening before. That was precisely what I did *not* want to know; that was the real reason I had left when I did. I did not have to tell him that I had decided not to call Felix to the stand. He guessed as much when I slammed the door behind me the night before. I told Ben to have Felix at the courthouse an hour before the trial was scheduled to resume so that I could tell *him* my decision. Which was firm, and would not be reviewable by him, unless the private hell he must have visited during the night had given him the incentive he needed to insist upon taking the witness stand for the sole purpose of confessing. That is, if indeed he had anything to confess.

I hated not knowing almost as much as I would hate having to know.

We had our meeting, Felix and I, in the cafeteria in the basement of the courthouse. He accepted my decision calmly, almost meekly. For my part, I refused to recognize the plea his eyes made that I forgive yesterday's behavior and that I remain his champion. Nor did I disclose what I planned to do in court that day, what I had so carefully rehearsed during the predawn hours that morning. Like an innocent man—or a condemned one—Felix enjoyed a full breakfast: fried eggs, bacon, toast. And coffee—with sugar and cream of course. All I took was black coffee.

We walked into the courtroom together, Felix and I. He headed toward his seat at the counsel table as I paused to perform my ritual bow before Mr. and Mrs. Ward, who were in their usual seats. They ignored me totally. Christine was not there. How strange, I thought.

Seated directly behind them was the couple who also had not missed a court session. The lady gave me a friendly glance and a slight nod. I could not help noticing her sensuality. Her face was beautiful despite a darkness under her eyes and vertical lines forming near her mouth. She was dressed severely, her black hair pulled tightly across her temples. She wore an interesting gold figure hanging from a thin chain, which nestled in the small of her throat. I could not make it out, but it looked like some kind of horse or dragon. Probably an Aztec or Mayan god. The man gave me a look only a certain kind of husband would give when someone paused to admire his selection. She must have given him plenty of opportunities, I thought, to practice that look. Not likely a one-man woman.

At precisely ten o'clock, Judge Sperry made his appearance, and rapped for order. The spectators settled down. How hungrily they looked at me, expecting me to feed them Felix as a witness.

I took the glance of inquiry from the court and responded by standing up behind the counsel table, arms akimbo. "We don't see the need to call any witnesses for the defense, Your Honor. We are satisfied to rest lightly on the State's very thin case."

"Now, now, counselor. No summations yet. Just tell me the defense rests."

"The defendant rests, Your Honor."

As I stood at parade ease, Judge Sperry tugged at the ends of his mustache.

"All right," he said finally. "Then the defendant will not be taking the stand on his own behalf?"

His face turned beet red as he realized the gigantic gaffe he had made. Before I could take him to task, he raised a hand. "My comment was entirely improper. I don't mean to suggest in any way that the defendant needs to testify, or should testify." He turned to the jury, clearly embarrassed over his slip of the tongue. "Don't any of you dare ask yourselves that question."

Of course not, I said to myself with disgust.

"You must clearly understand that the defendant has the absolute right to refrain from testifying. Only the State is required to make a case and, if it can, establish guilt beyond a reasonable doubt. The defendant need not respond to it, if he chooses not to do so. If he exercises his absolute right to remain silent, you may draw no inference of any kind from that decision. None whatsoever. I'll cover this point more completely right before you start your deliberations, when I teach you a few rules of law you must follow. Is that understood?"

A chorus of silent nods stirred the air.

Damn it, I thought, that's the Fifth Amendment for you. Everyone always has something to say or to think about when a defendant stands mute. Even judges, who should know better. Ben was looking at me. I guess he knew I was still angry.

But he had no idea how angry I *was*.

Jeff Baker was sitting in his seat with his mouth ajar. His beautiful blond assistant looked as though she had just found half a worm in an apple. Each of them had a pile of notes in anticipation of an earth-shattering cross-examination. Instead, summations stared them in the face, and they were not ready.

Judge Sperry beckoned the state's attorney and me to the side bar away from the jury box. He cupped his mouth with a hand to prevent lip reading by the jurors, although how anyone could detect lip movements beneath the scrub of wiry, white bristles on his upper lip was a mystery to me. Baker stood next to me, half facing the jury, allowing a silly smile to play across his face in plain view of the jurors, as if he found it highly amusing that Felix was hiding behind his constitutional rights. He erased the

smile quickly with his cuff, however, when Judge Sperry threw
him a lethal glance for his transparent ploy.

"Tom, you remember, don't you, telling the jurors in your
opening address that you were going to put the defendant on
the stand? Now that doesn't mean you're bound to do so. But
there's going to be questions in some minds. Does Mr. Evans
agree with your tactics? I won't permit you to gag him over
his objection."

I flushed as I recalled yesterday's confrontation. If he only
knew, I thought. What would he tell me to do? What the hell
would he do in my place?

"We talked it out yesterday, Judge, and he knows exactly
why I'm doing this. Why I have to do this," I added after a
moment's pause.

Jeff Baker began to smile again.

"Watch yourself, Mr. Baker," snapped the judge. "Don't
force me to smack you. This is a courtroom, not amateur night
at a country the-ater." Judge Sperry was testy this morning.

Once again Baker washed his face clean. The judge sent both
of us back to our seats and tapped with his pencil on the front
edge of his table to halt the buzz that had welled up during
the side bar conference.

"Remember what I told you, ladies and gentlemen. The
defendant is exercising the fundamental right guaranteed by
the federal Constitution—and by the constitution of this State
as well—to all citizens: to stand silent. His decision carries no
implications at all. Don't you ferget that."

He pivoted back to me. "Mr. Attleboro, are you ready to
sum up, or do you need time?"

Yes, I thought, I'm ready. I'm ready all right. Ready to be
done with Felix, the user. Ready to be done with the whole
goddamn case.

"Ready, Your Honor."

I stalked over to the jury box, running my fingers through my
hair as I collected my thoughts. I stood with my arms spread,
my hands grasping the front wall of the jury box. Slowly I
combed the jurors with my eyes.

"Ladies and gentlemen, it is my job now to review with you
the facts which have been presented to you and the exhibits
which have been placed before you. To show you which of
them are important and to analyze those with a meaning that

may not be clear. And it's my job to argue how these facts and documents establish my client's innocence, or at the very least show you why there is a reasonable doubt that he is guilty of the crime charged. That's my job, I say. But I can't follow that procedure in this case. And I won't. There's more to this case than that. This morning my job is not that simple."

I paused and waited for the reaction. Predictably, it came. Judge Sperry, who had been leaning back in his chair listening quietly, his glance fastened on his pet spot on the ceiling, turned his eyes to me. Felix placed his hands along the sides of his face, using his fingers to shield his eyes like blinders on a horse. The brows of some of the jurors puckered as though they had not quite caught what I said. I didn't look at Ben's reaction.

I drifted backwards toward the chair occupied by the defendant, keeping my eyes riveted on the jurors. Stepping behind the chair, I grasped Felix's shoulders with my fingers, pinning him down. Then I swiveled his chair so that the jurors could look directly into his face.

"Ladies and gentlemen, there are two kinds of innocence. And I will show you why you cannot convict my client. Why in fact you must find him innocent. That's the easy part. But before I address that issue, I am going to talk to you about a different kind of innocence. I am referring to moral innocence, a pureness of heart. And in that respect I am not going to summarize the evidence and argue how it establishes my client's moral innocence. And the reason I won't is that I can't. Because to do so would go against the clear weight of the evidence."

Quietly Judge Sperry rose from his chair and stood behind it, his hands grabbing the soft, rolled top.

I continued implacably. "Even a villain is entitled to be represented by counsel of his choice. The Constitution says that. The Sixth Amendment. The Bill of Rights. And Felix Evans chose me. But remember, too, that I carry a brief for his defense, not for him as a person. I'm not paid to serve as his character witness."

I looked down at Felix, boring a hole in the top of his skull. "Look at this man, look into him—and see him for what he is. Egocentric. Vainglorious. Ruthless. A born user. A man who doesn't give a tinker's dam about a solitary human being but himself. Not his friends, not his family, and as surely as God made little green apples, not his wife."

The courtroom exploded.

Felix strove unsuccessfully to pull away from my grasp. He twisted his neck around. His eyes were bulging. A feathery pulse fluttered in his temples.

"Approach the bench please, Mr. Attleboro," said Judge Sperry, at the same time pounding the gavel to regain order, while the bailiff shouted, "Quiet! Quiet!"

Baker and I walked to the far side bar. Judge Sperry's mustache was quivering. He was stewing like a fricassee. "What in hell are you up to, Mr. Attleboro? Have you lost your senses? Or are you trying to force a mistrial? Because if you do I'll have your bleeding head on a plate before the Grievance Committee, and see to it that you don't ever again walk into a courtroom in this State."

I looked impassively at him. "I've never been called to the bench during a summation," I said coldly.

"You have now!" he snapped back.

"I can assure you, Your Honor, I am sane and well. And I know exactly what I'm doing. I'm not going to throw my client to the wolves, although I admit I'm sorely tempted to do so. I'm going to see him acquitted, if I can, as I have been paid to do." I could feel distaste involuntarily contort my features. "Please believe me, I don't want a mistrial, I won't cause one. And," I added sardonically, "I want my license to stay shiny bright."

"All right. But remember, you're on thin ice. One more thing." He fastened his look on Jeff Baker. "You're on thin ice too, sonny. One more grin out of you at your table and you'll be in private practice. I remind you for the last time that it's improper to send those messages to the jury."

"Judge, I couldn't help it. I had gas pains."

"Then fart. But fart with a straight face. Do you hear me? Okay, both of you, watch your steps."

We walked away from the bench. Jeff Baker sat down, self-consciously aware that Judge Sperry would be watching his every expression. I positioned myself at an angle which allowed me to see both the jurors and Baker.

As I resumed my summation, I could hear the harshness of reviving anger in my voice. "Now, then, as I was saying a moment ago, it is not possible for you to reach a reasoned conclusion other than that this man sitting in judgment before you took Lorna Ward Evans, his wife, out in a motor boat in the teeth of a storm and proceeded deliberately to steer it into the Gulf of Mexico as part of a premeditated plan and design—for reasons not clear. He probably *intended* to kill her—"

Over the sound of Judge Sperry's gavel, I raced ahead.

"But, and despite all I have said about this bad man, you simply cannot, on the flimsy record which the state's attorney has made before you, reach the conclusion that he did so. You cannot find him guilty of murder. There is a question here that cannot be answered. And without an answer you cannot judge him guilty of murder. For no matter how miserable a specimen of humanity sits here before you, he is surely entitled to a fair trial. If Satan himself were on trial in this court, he could not be prejudged. Under our system of justice, every defendant is presumed innocent until *proven* otherwise. Hear me and remember this. Our system of law and justice has no more vital a concept. It's the only way the system can work safely. The learned justice who is presiding here has seen to that, thus far, and he will continue to see to it during the rest of the trial. The point I make is that guilt cannot be determined on the basis of character defects, or for that matter evil intentions. Let's face it, folks. Few of us are perfect. All of us have harbored evil thoughts and have fantasized irresponsible acts at one time or another. None of us is above reproach. 'He who is without sin among you, let him cast the first stone' is no idle teaching."

Waiting a moment for my Bible lesson to sink in, I noticed that Felix had visibly relaxed.

"So it is that the law of our land deals with facts, not mere thoughts and intentions. With proof, not mere supposition. It does not permit you to reach a verdict of guilty unless that proof, those facts, lead you to a judgment beyond a reasonable doubt. That is to say, to a moral certainty. This, I submit, cannot be the case here. You simply cannot reach such a judgment on the basis of a snippet of fact here and a dash of fact there. A fingernail—whose? A bloodstain—whose? A tiny bone fragment—*whose*? You have no answers, and you may not speculate in that area. You are not watching a sporting event. You are judging a human life. At the very least, a human being's freedom."

A shadow passed over the faces of several of the jurors, obviously coming to grips for the first time with their awesome power. And responsibility. Few people *really* want to play God.

Judge Sperry stood leaning back against the red velvet drape behind his high-back chair, twisting his gavel so that its head spun like a top. Kathryn Adelaide had a white handkerchief pressed to her mouth. Reginald Archer was wearing the fixed frown of a wooden Indian. A forefinger was pressed against the center of Mollie Schneider's carefully painted lips. No one sat back with his arms crossed.

I started pacing slowly back and forth along the jury rail.

"In this case there is not one issue, there are two. Not only are you called upon to decide whether Felix Evans had the premeditated design and intent to destroy his wife—to kill her. You must also decide, before you can find him guilty as charged, an overriding second issue. You know, of course, what that issue is."

Of course the jury didn't, with one exception. Professor Archer, whose attention never flagged, gave two sharp nods despite his grim expression. I knew intuitively that he had raced to the next station ahead of me.

"In a word, you are also called upon to decide, on the *evidence* before you—notice I emphasize the word evidence, for guessing and conjecturing won't do—whether the State has proved to the exclusion of a reasonable doubt that Felix Evans did in fact *kill* Lorna Evans. And there, I say to you insistently out of respect for the system of justice that prevails in our land, there the case of the State of Florida against Felix Evans founders." A pause. "And sinks. Sinks no matter how you feel about Felix Evans, the man." Judge Sperry sat down and resumed his study of the ceiling through half-closed lids. I had no time to stop and interpret the resumption of the customary posture of most judges during summations. I had more to accomplish here.

"The usual way a state proves that a homicide has taken place is to offer evidence through the medical examiner that the victim is dead and to show that the cause of death was a bullet wound, a stabbing, a poison, or such other medium as the accused party is alleged to have used. *And that the accused party used it.* Remember that. Such evidence, of course, comes from an examination of the body, properly identified as that of the victim."

Kathryn shuddered. A little leavening was needed, not too much, but a touch.

"The expression *corpus delicti* doesn't mean what you think. It's just a fancy way of referring to the subject of the criminal act, which is to say, proof that a crime was committed.

"And so we reach the deadfall in the State's case, the trap into which you may not be allowed to fall. Ladies and gentlemen, where is the body of Lorna Evans?"

I stood with my arms stretched out in feigned perplexity, looking into each individual face of the jurors in front of me as though I might find the answer in one of them.

"A still better question is, is Lorna Evans really dead? She could not swim, said her mother, but she had two flotation cushions, so she could have floated easily enough. The question remains, did she? I have my private views but I cannot share them with you. You have yours. Can you say that yours are right to a moral certainty? Where is she? What happened— *actually* happened out in the Gulf? Only echo answers us. To these questions the State has not provided you with a single, hard fact. Only suppositions and conjectures. Worse than that. With hypotheses. And what's a hypothesis? An *assumed* fact. A house of cards. Nothing more."

I walked over to the counsel table to give the jury a moment's breather; then back to them. I wanted us all close together as I carefully inched my summation to the apex I'd rehearsed in my mind for hour after hour early that morning.

"You may ask yourselves, Well, where *is* Mrs. Evans, if she is indeed alive? And there are answers, of course, which may occur to you. But they, too, are speculative and hypothetical.

"A more telling issue to consider is this. Even if you were to conclude that she is not alive, what hard, reliable evidence is there that she died at the hand of her husband? Again you are left leaning on weak reeds: somebody's fingernail, somebody's wrist bone, somebody's blood. A missing ax. But no proof that the blood was Lorna's. No proof that the fingernail or bone was Lorna's—or for that matter were the consequence of any act by the defendant. There isn't even any proof that the boat *contained* an ax or a spade!

"And then, at last, you must face the ultimate question, to which no clue, much less any answer, is offered by the prosecutor. What motive did this defendant have? Not a word has been spoken of another woman or of hate or of jealousy or of greed or of financial gain. Ladies and gentlemen, there simply was no motive."

Motive was, in fact, what was driving me crazy. The absence of an answer to that big, never more important question: Why?

I turned and pointed an index finger at a haggard Felix. My oldest friend. Or had he always been my enemy? He sat erect in his seat, his secret a secret still.

"I said that even Satan is entitled to justice and a fair trial in this court. Even Felix Evans, ruthless and heartless though he may be, cannot be found guilty by you, absent an explanation of the disappearance of his wife and the cause of her death by proof that satisfies you beyond a reasonable doubt that her disappearance *and* her death were both brought about by this man. Proof beyond and to the exclusion of a reasonable doubt. Proof to a moral certainty."

I pulled out a handkerchief and dried my hands of the matter. I backed away from the jurors to allow the curtain to descend as I uttered the last words I would ever address to these twelve judges of the facts.

"Is there any alternative to these obvious conclusions? I think not. Simply put, you must set Felix Evans free. If our system is to work, your verdict must be not guilty."

46

When I returned to the counsel table, I motioned to Ben to change seats with Felix so that I did not have to sit next to him. Chances were, Felix didn't want to be sitting next to me, either. A buzzing of whispers came from the spectator section, but the courtroom quieted when Jeff Baker got up to exercise his right to equal time before the jury.

He spoke briefly. He should have been an accountant. Everything was add, subtract, carry over, balance. He presented a whole series of equations.

Fact: Lorna Evans resisted going out in the boat, was forced to do so against her will. *Fact:* George Feeley warned both of them against the trip, told them to stay in the inland waterways. *Fact:* Sandy Turner saw Felix Evans at the mouth of the Seaboard channel, in the Gulf; the engine of the boat was running. *Fact:* Felix Evans was alone. *Fact:* There was a storm coming out of the northeast; so was the current. Therefore the boat could not have *drifted* one mile northeast against that current to the place where it was found. It could not even have *drifted* across the sand bar into the Gulf. *Fact:* Felix Evans turned up without a mark, bite, scratch, or bruise. *Fact:* The key where Professor Melville found him was teeming with crabs and sand fleas; the shore was littered with broken glass and crushed sea shells. Hence, his story of having spent the night there naked, was a palpable lie. *Fact:* When Lester Melville rescued Felix Evans from the key on which he was found, apparently in shock, seemingly distraught over his experience and terrible loss, and presumably dehydrated from exposure to salt water and a night on the key, he requested cream and sugar with his coffee!

"Think of that, ladies and gentlemen," said Baker with a look of pretended astonishment. " 'Cream and sugar, please.'

Which would lead anyone with a grain of common sense to wonder whether he was suffering shock. Or faking it. Felix Evans himself unveiled the fact that he was faking it, that his entire story was contrived to hide the truth. For he *told* the truth. To Professor Lester Melville. On the way back to the mainland on June third. What did he say? 'I guess I killed her.'" And following a pregnant pause, he added darkly, "And that, ladies and gentlemen, is what I ask you to find to be unvarnished truth.

"*Fact:* The boat was found. On the floor was a broken fingernail and a wrist bone. And on the chair and bench, blood. Human blood. It overtaxes credulity to believe they came from anybody but one of the occupants of the boat. Felix or Lorna Evans. And Felix Evans didn't use nail polish, his wrists were intact, he had no cuts, certainly none that could have left the gouts of blood found on seat and bench of the boat. *Fact:* Lorna Ward Evans is gone.

"It all adds up," said the prosecutor, arms spread, palms to the jury. "You have all you need to see clearly, without room for doubt, the premeditated design of this man to murder his wife, which most assuredly he accomplished. And I am talking about a man whose own counsel just branded him a ruthless egomaniac." The state's attorney rolled his eyes in pretended incredulity that I had dared to describe my own client in those terms.

"And you have equally clear evidence of what ultimately happened to Lorna Evans. The disappearance of her body is no enigma wrapped in a mystery, as defense counsel suggests. You are not expected to leave your reason and common sense outside the jury room. And you are not called upon to play detective. You needn't search for her. She's not in hiding. She's dead. A chopped up human body thrown overboard together with a bloodstained ax. Her parts will never be found for the reasons you heard from Professor Melville and Captain Turner. I don't have to restate those grisly reasons." Jeff Baker let that one sink in as he gulped down a paper cup of water.

"And just because George Feeley had not checked the boat when it was rented by Felix Evans to see if the ax, the spade and the oar were in place, doesn't mean they were not there. It means nothing more than that Feeley didn't check to find out whether they *were* there. As a matter of fact, the oar had

to have been there. You heard about it from Felix Evans. He
tried to paddle with it. You may therefore conclude that the
spade was there, too. And the ax as well." Again he paused
to take another sip of water.

"Finally, we have the ultimate fact. Not a conjecture. Not a
hypothesis." He glanced over at me, carrying the jury's eyes
with him. "A hard fact. Lorna Evans couldn't swim. She hated
the water. She feared it. Do you really believe she jumped into
those waters? Voluntarily?"

For the first time during Jeff's summation, Felix drew attention to himself as he shook his head violently as though to
indicate that the prosecutor had it all wrong. And then, wonder
of wonders, tears came from the eyes of Felix. The jury saw it
happening. Right in front of their eyes, Felix was transformed
from a stone image into a breathing, sentient being with feelings and emotions. They saw suffering and they saw pain. And
they heard a whispered, anguished "Lorna" breathed from a
mouth drawn down at its corners as he controlled a sob.

Kathryn Adelaide's eyes filled up as she pressed a handkerchief to her mouth. The men were harder to read, except for
Alex Raymond, who was frowning, whether over the horror
envisaged by the prosecutor's remarks or the agony displayed
by Felix, I could not tell. But the one thing everybody knew,
could not mistake, was that Felix was not playacting. His
suffering was real, and it had a real effect. The whole scene
troubled me greatly; it shook my belief in the private hypothesis
I had built up. There was no way I could tell whether his pain
was really over his lost Lorna or was simply a sudden revulsion
over his own brutal acts.

Jeff Baker saw his lesson in simple mathematics sinking
under the human equation. He moved to his closing comments
quickly. "So go into that jury room," he said in a matter of
fact tone, "and add up the facts. You can't make a mistake.
And then do your sworn duty. Reach a verdict on the sum
total of those facts. Just the facts. Their sum total. Guilty as
charged."

In the noisy stirrings that followed Baker's return to his
seat, it occurred to me that he, too, had been unable to come
up with a motive for what appeared on its face to have been
a senseless killing—indeed led to the insistent doubt whether
there had been a killing at all. Had I stayed with Felix and

Ben the evening before, I might have been enlightened. But the one thing certain was that the jurors were left in the dark on a crucial factor in any homicide case. Absent an insane or random act, the Why is always the biggest question, and its answer the strongest circumstantial proof.

Jeff sat at his station and adjusted the knot in his tie, almost choking himself in the effort. He looked expectantly toward the dais as though waiting for the teacher to grade him, while Susan Harwick looked adoringly at him, her evaluation of his performance no secret. Several jurors stole a peek at the clock on the rear wall above the doors. Both Baker and I had been spoon feeding them all morning. It was no wonder they were ready for lunch.

So was Judge Sperry. Court recessed until two o'clock.

All that was left to do then was for the judge to teach the jury guiding legal principles in an hour, which had taken me two full semesters in law school to learn. Some of them I never understood.

The bailiff locked the doors. There would be no interruptions as Brian Sperry instructed the jurors on the legal rules they had to follow when they went about their deliberations. No more quips, mispronunciations, eye twinkling, mustache-twitching—all the little tricks he had employed to keep the steam pressure low in the cauldron called trial proceedings.

Giving no indication by word, gesture or intonation of his views on the merits of the case, Judge Sperry arrayed the conflicting contentions of Jeff Baker and me before the jurors as so many serried ranks of soldiers. He skillfully avoided such telltale phrases as "the State established" or "the defense showed," since they carried a judgmental implication. And then he addressed the matter of the missing body, the principle of *corpus delicti*.

It was really a simple proposition to grasp, he said. "The term *corpus delicti* means nothing more or less than evidence of the crime. It doesn't necessarily mean a body. The principle applies to all crimes. For example, a person cannot be convicted of arson unless there is shown to be a burned building. There can be no conviction for counterfeiting without proof of a counterfeit plate or a counterfeit bill. And, there can be no conviction of murder unless there is a body. Or," he continued after a weighty pause, "when the body of the supposed victim is not found, where the disappearance of that supposed victim is accounted for by evidence which not only explains the disappearance but also leads to the conclusion beyond and to the exclusion of a reasonable doubt that the supposed victim is indeed dead."

He paused to allow the legal rule to sink in. Yes, he pointed out, there was evidence before the jurors that Lorna Evans could not swim. On the other hand there was evidence that the boat had flotation cushions. Then too, said the judge, "there was some evidence of the presence of sharks in the waters of the Gulf."

"Do not cast aside that evidence," cautioned Judge Sperry, "if you find it believable, simply because it conjures up in your minds an image you would like to reject. But," he quickly added, "also weigh the testimony of Professor Melville that the presence of sharks in the waters off Everglades City had not been noted for several years and that not all species are carnivorous." The faces of the jurors reinforced his need to remind them that unpleasant possibilities could not be dismissed on those grounds alone.

He stood up and positioned himself in his favorite spot behind his chair, his arms resting on the leather roll top.

"Defense counsel emphasized the fact that the State had not shown you a motive for the killing, if indeed you find that Lorna Evans is dead, and if you find that she was killed." Judge Sperry looked at me impassively as he continued, drumming his fingers lightly along the top of the chair. "I charge you that motive is not an essential element of proof of premeditated murder. If, therefore, you find that Lorna Evans is dead by the hand of the defendant, you need not be concerned that his motive remains a mystery. In such case, a motive, while not known, is conclusively *presumed* from a finding of a deliberate and premeditated killing."

There was nothing I could do to counteract the force of that statement. So I settled for gritting my teeth and wishing on His Honor a case of the shingles and a dull razor blade.

"These, then, are the legal rules you must heed during your deliberations. And if, after weighing all the facts in the light of the legal principles I've explained to you, you conclude beyond and to the exclusion of a reasonable doubt that Lorna Ward

Evans is dead, and that her death was caused by the intentional, premeditated act of the accused, then you must return a verdict of guilty.

"However," continued the judge, shifting his weight to his other leg, "if you cannot conclude beyond a reasonable doubt that Lorna Ward Evans is dead, then whatever you may think, however you may feel about the accused or view his acts, you must put those subjective considerations to the side and, in accordance with your sworn oath to serve dispassionately and to give your judgment only on the basis of the evidence before you, you must return a verdict of not guilty."

Judge Sperry walked around the chair and stood over his table desk. He looked squarely at me. I got the distinct impression I was going to be boiled alive, and I winced in advance. His face was stern, and as he spoke he pounded his words in, his clenched fist making rhythmical thuds on the table.

"I must tell you that I disapprove, I strongly disapprove, of portions of the summation presented by Mr. Attleboro. While he is allowed great latitude in his closing argument, his comments should never appeal to the emotions or introduce matter alien to the issues before you."

If only he knew, if only I could tell him, I thought. What a farce the best-managed trial can become when rules of law and professional ethics meant to protect the innocent become shields for the guilty. I made myself listen to him.

" . . . his reputation at the Bar, with which this Court is familiar, his unblemished record for integrity and loyalty to the individuals he has defended, and the legal causes he has espoused, all these circumstances led me to refrain from chastising him before you. Nevertheless, ladies and gentlemen, you must give no weight at all to his improper observations concerning his client. You must stay with the evidence in the record before you."

I let out my breath. It could have been worse.

Judge Sperry sat down and rapped sharply with his gavel. "You may now retire and consider your verdict." He motioned to the bailiff, who led them out toward the jury room. He rose from the bench and stalked off the dais between the parted red velvet curtains, leaving justice to be done.

Justice to be done. Who was to say it would be, if the jury acquitted Felix? Or convicted him?

47

The agony of waiting began. I sat at my table, emotionally spent. I felt as though I had been buffeted by a fierce storm. Glancing idly at the wall over the dais, I read the inscription again. Sometimes, as now, it bothered me. What about the separation of church and state? Why bring God into the courtroom? Did we have to pray for justice too?

I told Ben and Felix they could go down to the cafeteria, if they wanted; that I'd call them if anything happened. Felix, to my surprise, went over to where the Wards were sitting, alone in their row. Most of the spectators were milling around in the hall; few had left the building. When Sophie Ward saw Felix, she turned her back to him. Mervyn kept his eyes out of focus. Felix gave a slight shrug and walked on, a frail-looking figure, his head precariously balanced on slightly hunched shoulders. The couple seated in the row behind the Wards slipped out of their pew and followed Felix through the swinging doors. And if my curiosity was stirred, I was in no mood to chase after anyone.

My head felt like a wrecking ball, so heavy that I had to rest it between my two palms, elbows planted on the table. A verdict of guilty, I said to myself, was a real possibility, and richly deserved by Felix. Once I achieved that detached frame of mind, I began to rationalize the situation in a different light. What if Lorna were not dead? What if she had been rescued and had grabbed the chance to run away from it all? She certainly would not have been the first person to start over with a new name. Even a new face. She had her own resources. All she was leaving behind, besides a sister of questionable loyalty, were her parents, whom she could arrange to inform and see occasionally in a discreet way. There were no children, no imperatives that rooted her to Florida or New York or any other place for that matter—except for a murderous-minded husband who deserved to be convicted on that score alone.

Realizing I was rambling in profitless fashion, I turned off the revolving motor inside the lead ball I was holding in my hands and lowered it to the table top. I was bone weary. There really was nothing to do but wait.

Even though the deck of the sloop was at least fifteen feet above the water line, I was able to stretch out my arm to Christine, who was floating on her back in the water, and touch her naked body. I tried to read the name on the boat, but it was painted in Greek letters. The name danced mischievously beyond the range of my vision. Christine kept telling me to jump in. It must have been the Mediterranean because she was speaking French, and so were the others on the boat. The funny thing about it was that, although I had never learned the language, I understood every word she uttered. I also grasped for the first time what a born linguist was.

The boat was anchored about a mile from shore; still, I could make out the features of a number of people lolling along the sand in striped beach chairs. The couple was there. The woman was wearing a bikini. Her skin glistened in the sunlight. Her husband stood in front of her, trying to hide her, but she kept shifting in her chair from one side of him to the other. I thought I caught a glimpse of the Wards but I was not sure because their chairs faced away from the water. I looked all over for Felix, I even called out his name, but could not pick him out. He had to be there, I was somehow sure of that.

As I looked down at Christine, I noticed someone swimming up to her behind her head, propelled through the water effortlessly by long, thin legs. Curiously, the figure never raised its head from the water, so I was not able to see a face. I was convinced that Christine was in great danger; there was something sinister and threatening about the form moving toward her. Suddenly I knew who it was. It was her sister. It was Lorna. And she had a long, curved knife clutched in her hand. I tried to warn Christine, but I still could not speak French. I started to scream, but she didn't hear me; she just lay floating on her back smiling, her breasts exposed above the water, the dark triangle of her pubic area highlighted just below the rippling surface, caught in the refracted rays of the sun. I tried to take off my clothes and jump in, but I couldn't move; someone was holding my shoulders down. The more I tried to free myself, the more the hand shook my shoulder. I managed to twist my head around, and I looked into the liquid eyes of Felix, but they weren't in *his* face. The mouth that was his was trying to say something to me. I raised my head, the better to hear him.

The bailiff woke me up, shaking my shoulder. Slowly I recovered focus. I glanced at the clock on the rear wall. It was a quarter to seven. The bailiff was trying to tell me something. In English. I finally grabbed hold of the words he was whispering. The jury was returning. They had reached a verdict.

Too quickly, I thought.

48

The crowd filed back into the courtroom like a theater audience that had finished its lemonade and smokes and was ready for the last act. Sophie and Mervyn Ward had moved up to the front row, positioning themselves directly behind our table outside the low wooden partition. I hurried into the corridor to find Felix and Ben. I saw Felix talking to the couple, and I told him to go on into the courtroom. He said that he had left Ben downstairs, so I went to the cafeteria, which had been kept open to take advantage of the surge in business. Ben was off in the corner reading a newspaper and sipping strong tea. He saw me hurrying over and, sensing something was up, gathered himself together quickly.

By the time we returned to the courtroom, the stage had been set and the curtain was slowly rising. Donna Redmond, our court reporter, was seated in front of the jury box, her plaid skirt hitched up to allow her to straddle the single chromium leg on her stenotype machine. Peter Hobson, the clerk of the court, stood in his corner. If he lifted one leg, he would look exactly like a great blue heron. His skinny neck stuck out of a vastly oversized collar with a grimy edge, and his nose was elongated by some trick of light and shadow. The bailiff stood at the bar rail, maintaining an absolute silence in the courtroom. The atmosphere was tense.

I walked over to Jeff and congratulated him on his fine job, and he reciprocated; done like a couple of tennis players at the end of a match, except this was no sporting event, and the match was not quite over. As I returned to my seat, the red velvet curtain parted and Brian Sperry entered. He motioned to the bailiff, whom I had gotten to know as Don, to bring in the jurors. While he was out fetching them, the judge addressed the assemblage. It had started to rain and drops hit the window panes like a muffled tattoo played on draped drums at a military funeral.

"Now remember," he said, "this is a court of law. You are to remain absolutely quiet as we take the verdict of the jury. Not a peep out of any of you." His eyes were not twinkling and his mustaches were not twitching. "And when the verdict is rendered, whatever the outcome is, you are to make no demonstration. Just sit quietly and observe, as is your right in this open court."

As the jury entered with their shepherd following closely behind, I tried to read them as I had done with only mixed success countless times before. As usual, Reginald Archer, my college professor, was fingering his skimpy tie. He was also sucking pensively on his lower lip. Kathryn Adelaide, my librarian, was red-eyed, a clear sign she had been weeping— but no indication of to what end. She clutched her ever-present book in prayerful fashion, hands clasped over it. Alex Raymond, the drugstore clerk, deliberately avoided eye contact with anyone. He walked to his seat, looking at it as though it required his undivided attention. Mollie Schneider waited until the five seats to her left in the front row were filled, and then slipped into her chair at the end in the Number One position. She tugged at a long strand of rather large cultured pearls. She gave me a shadow of a smile, and my heart quaked. She had a kind of sleek attractiveness. But fine feathers are not always the sign of fine birds, said I to me, and took my eyes off her.

All the others looked vacantly into space. They gave the impression that while a unanimous verdict had been reached, it was not one they were fully contented with. Missing was the sense of camaraderie that frequently develops among members of a group thrown into close contact for a length of time.

When all of them had settled down and the spectators had returned to silence after a seizure of murmurs which had broken out as the jurors entered the room, the judge nodded to Peter Hobson, who teetered over to the spot directly in front of the dais and addressed the jury.

He looked bored, as though he had seen the picture before. He had, of course. So had I. But to me the publishing of a jury's verdict is always high drama. It is the moment of truth to which the entire legal justice system points. Adversaries at the bar each offer fact versions. They do not count. Facts are made by the verdict of the jury, for better or worse, and for good.

"Ladies and gentlemen, have you reached a verdict?"

"We have," came the reply from Mollie Schneider, who was still fingering her pearls, but held the verdict sheet in her other hand.

Peter Hobson twisted his head around toward our table without otherwise moving his body. "Will the defendant please rise and face the jury."

Felix did as he was told, and as his counsel, I stood, too. I looked over at Jeff Baker. He was stretched out, legs extended, the base of his spine at the front edge of the chair. His elbows rested on the arms of the chair and his hands were clasped. His face was expressionless but I knew that his blood, pressured like mine, was churning through arteries and veins at a much stepped-up rate.

The court clerk had twisted his head back toward the jury box. "Will the forewoman please rise and face the defendant."

Mollie Schneider dropped her hands from her pearls and stood, her chin thrust out, her mouth grimly set, her red-tipped fingers wrapped over the edge of the jury box.

I suddenly realized that I was holding Felix's right wrist in my left hand, and was squeezing it tightly. Our bodies were close together; our heads nearly touching. There we were again, back in school, facing a group of jeering bullies. But he had nothing to fear. I could tumble the whole damn lot of them like a stack of dominoes, and I would if they took one more step toward us.

"Madam forewoman," Peter Hobson continued, "how find you the defendant, as charged in Indictment A-621, People of the State of Florida against Felix Evans, upon which he stands trial before you, his peers: Guilty or not guilty?"

Mollie Schneider stared directly into Felix's face with eyes so cold, so devoid of feeling that they might as well have been carved out of marble. She drew another piece of paper from her purse, which she proceeded slowly to unfold, and began to read from it in a loud, clear voice.

"We, the jurors, unanimously condemn the defendant, Felix Evans, for his heartless indifference to the life and safety of his wife, Lorna Ward Evans. . . ."

Judge Sperry rapped his gavel sharply. "The verdict of the jury, Ms. Schneider, must be either guilty or not guilty."

"We are unanimous in insisting, Your Honor, that the words I am reading be a part of the record of our verdict." And she proceeded imperturbably to finish reading from the sheet.

" . . . his heartless indifference to the life and safety of his wife, Lorna Ward Evans, which we find showed a criminal intention to cause her death." She put down the paper and, looking straight at the judge, finished her statement.

"We the jury, however, regrettably find the defendant not guilty."

There was a gasp directly behind me, all the more audible because of the otherwise total silence in the courtroom.

"Harken ye, members of the jury, to the verdict as published. You find the defendant not guilty. So say you all?" Eleven nods confirmed their unanimity.

Not one smiling face.

There was a scuffling behind us. I looked around, and saw Sophie Ward standing ten feet behind Felix and me, holding in her outstretched hand a small, short-barreled pistol, probably a derringer, pointing in our direction. Mervyn Ward was looking at her with his mouth agape, his face the color of chalk. A shot rang out. I felt a pain on the left side of my head as though someone had drawn a hot knife across my temple. I saw two guards racing down the aisle from their stations at the back of the room. I heard screams, and I heard the judge rapping, rapping, rapping for order. And then, as a haze settled over my eyes, I heard myself say, "Now why did you have to do that?" And amidst shouts and screams coming from somewhere far out in a distant galaxy, I lost consciousness.

Christine

49

Between the small, porcelain factory town of Gien and the ancient, fortress city of Angers, which for centuries was the traditional home of the Counts of Anjou, the Loire River flows through sunny slopes and the vineyards of central France. Just southeast of the River Main, which cuts Angers in two, runs a quiet street called Rue de Port, lined with flourishing plane trees.

Slightly set back on the street stands a brick house of great age. Its white walls had been freshly painted and black, hand-carved shutters provided the bold contrast of a typical Norman home.

Christine Ward owned it. It was more than a French home to her, it was the epicenter of her universe. She called it Sans Souci, meaning "without care." She stole the name from Frederick the Great, who so named his summer estate. She would tell any of her friends literate enough to call this to her attention that if the Emperor made an issue over it, she would change the name. Otherwise, it stayed Sans Souci.

I lay on a beach chair at the side of the pool which was located at the back of the house. The pool had been constructed so that one branch flowed under a partition into a glass-enclosed room that was part of the house. The interior had been designed like a rain forest. Exotic trees and shrubs were planted over boulders and rock gardens that bordered the pool's edge. I liked to swim in that enclosed area. No insects, no sunburns and, best of all, a well-stocked floating bar that was accessible from the pool. The whole layout spelled beaucoup de francs. Chris must be doing just fine as an artist, I thought.

I had arrived there a week before, which was three weeks after the trial had concluded, nearly ending my life in the process. Sophie Ward had been arrested even though I had refused to aid and abet the State in any way. Luckily, which was defined in terms of millimeters, I had only received a close haircut and had lost a little blood, not even injuries enough to earn a day's repose in the hospital. Sophie was released on her own recognizance while Jeff Baker and his boss decided whether to make a big case of it, or let her enter a psychiatric institution in Miami for a short stay. Meaning, time to allow her attorney, a prominent member of the bar and a former president of the Florida Bar Association, to argue that she had suffered a temporary mental imbalance caused by the trial and the loss of her daughter, and thereby to persuade the Grand Jury to decline to indict her. The State backed off. Sophie Ward voluntarily entered a private hospital for a short stay.

She had collapsed after she was tackled by the guards and made no statement. She never said whether she had aimed at me or Felix. Or for that matter, at anyone. Maybe she intended to shoot herself, and the damn thing went off before she could point it properly at herself.

I had thought those palm-size derringers had gone out of style at the time of the Civil War. They were notoriously inaccurate unless virtually pressed against the flesh. The old joke was that a man was never safer than when such a weapon was aimed at a spot between his eyes.

Mervyn Ward was dividing his time between his offices and his wife's temporary address. Felix had disappeared. When I had asked Ben Abbott what had happened to him, he told me that Felix had walked out of the courtroom after the shouting and tumult had died down. What hurt me more than I liked to admit was that after she learned I wasn't badly hurt, Christine hurried away too.

Amos Stern flew down two days later. He had to buy a first-class seat, unheard of for him. He must have thought I was dying because he arrived shortly after midnight with a wreath. He said that was all he could get at an all-night florist in the Fort Myers airport, but I had some trouble with that explanation.

He was slightly shocked when he met Ida, who had transformed herself into a practical nurse. She was wearing a white satin housecoat with a broad lavender sash and insisted upon tending to my needs as I lay stretched out on the sofa watching a late, late movie. My head ached too much for me to get to sleep. The only outward indication of my recent encounter with the angel of death was a two-inch strip of gauze taped to my temple. Ben was still there, and gave Amos a summary of the last day of the trial.

While the two of them were talking, and Ida, uncertain where to put it, walked around holding the wreath like a Wimbledon trophy, the telephone rang. Ida answered it, asked three times "Who?" and then said to me, venomously, "It's for you." She handed me the telephone, a cordless device, and I sat up to take the call. A trans-Atlantic operator announced in a delightfully accented voice that Mademoiselle Christine Ward was calling from Angers, France. I looked at my wristwatch. It showed close to one o'clock in the morning. That meant it was early Tuesday morning there. When I mentioned out loud who was at the other end of the cable, Ida flounced out of the room, but Amos sat by quietly. My heart jolted when I heard the sound of Chris's voice. The anger I had been nursing vanished.

"Tom, darling! How good to hear your voice! First of all I want you to know I waited and made sure you weren't badly hurt. Then I had to hurry off to take care of Daddy. You know, don't you, that Mother actually had to spend a night in jail. How cruel!"

"She would have spent a lot longer in jail if her aim had been better."

"Yes, yes, I know, darling. But thank God you weren't hurt seriously. And Daddy insisted that I get out of the way. So I flew back here yesterday. But I had to call you and say thanks. Thank you with all my heart, love, for what you did. That was another reason I had to get away from the courthouse. I couldn't bear to hurt Daddy more by letting him see me hovering over you or thanking you."

"Sure!" The explanation left me unsatisfied. She could have called me before she flew off into the blue yonder. Also, as I saw it, she should have insisted upon staying until matters were worked out over her mother.

"Anyhow, thanks once again, my darling. When are you going back north?"

"In a few days, I think."

"Okay. I'll call you again when things settle down here. My place is a mess. There seems to have been a break-in. My housekeeper was away. Not much taken, but a big mess.

I've got to go now. I'll call you in a couple of weeks in New York. Goodbye, love."

The crackling line told me the conversation was over. I felt dazed. My head began to hurt. So Amos and Ben left, and Ida came to my aid with a tenderness that did her credit. She aimed at making me forget Christine. She succeeded.

Ben and Amos returned to New York the next day. There was nothing to keep them in Florida, since my remains were ambulatory. I told them I would be up in a couple of days, when I had gotten my strength back under the restorative powers of Ida.

Besides, I owed her. It took me two days and nights to pay off my debt. By the second morning I had lost my headache. Our parting was very sweet sorrow.

Two weeks later Chris called me from Nice. Would I like to spend a week or so with her at her house?

Her invitation was the last thing I expected—next to an invitation from Felix to join him wherever he was celebrating his freedom from care. I declined, politely, but then jumped on a seesaw of indecision. It turned out to be a short ride. Within two minutes I was writing down directions on how to get from New York to Paris to Angers to Rue de Port. That night I dreamed about Venus rising from the sea, standing naked in an open shell lined with iridescent mother-of-pearl, and answering to the name of Christine.

The following Saturday, I left for France.

50

As I twirled the tall glass around in my hand, the ice cubes in the drink clinked cheerily, inviting another sip. Sitting poolside at Christine's house in Angers, I silently toasted bliss. Today, the Saturday following my arrival, I looked forward to the party Chris had arranged for tonight in my honor.

When I had first arrived at her house in Angers, I was met at the door by a wizened old woman with a toothless smile and leathery skin the color of river mud. Evidently she had been expecting me because she chattered away in French, which might just as well have been Chaldean for all the sense I could make of it.

A voice called a question from a distant room, to which the old woman called an answer that included words that sounded like my name. The questioning voice belonged to Chris, who came padding into the foyer barefooted, wearing a big grin and a paint-smeared khaki jumper. Her light hair bore traces of ocher, from which I guessed she might be working on a painting of one of the wheat fields I had passed on my way.

"Bienvenu, cheri! Welcome to Sans Souci." She accompanied the greeting with a big hug and kiss on my mouth, with the tip of her tongue still suffering from wanderlust. "How was the flight? And the ride down, did you get lost? You must be tired. I forgot to tell you about the fork at the bridge. I'll bet you ended up on the wrong side of the river!"

She suddenly realized that the little old woman was standing by waiting for instructions. "Darling, this is Mme. Claire. Marie-Louise will do. My housekeeper, hairdresser, cook, back washer, you name it. Without her, I'd need three other domestics. She also can prune rose bushes, do elementary electrical repairs, and she drives like a demon. She can't speak English but you'll be able to make yourself understood, I'm sure. She's indispensable to me."

Marie-Louise sensed the flattery and beamed. After a direction from Chris in rapid-fire French, she took my one large suitcase and disappeared up the hall staircase. I was going to follow, but Chris took my arm.

"What's your hurry? So long as you're not too tired, let me show you the house. We'll end up in your room."

I didn't remember telling her I was not tired, but I liked the way we were going to end up the tour. The fact was, my head hurt from a sleepless night on the plane to the uninterrupted accompaniment of a wailing infant directly behind my seat; and my eyes ached from the glare of the sun as I drove south. I had reached Paris at 10:30 A.M., had waited an unconscionable length of time for a rental car I had reserved in New York. I didn't reach Rue de Port until 5 P.M. local time. Chris had guessed right. I had gotten very lost.

Hers was a house of which Chris could justly be proud. Her own talent was well displayed. She pointed out painting after painting on the walls, signed in a flourishing hand with her first name only, always in red paint.

A large living room with a low, beamed ceiling was situated to the left of the foyer, separated from it by a paneled sliding door. The floor was made of highly polished, dark oak boards fastened down with pewter nails. Its only relief was an antique silk Persian story rug of considerable beauty. There was a large sofa, several interesting occasional tables, and carved wooden armchairs with multicolored tapestry seats. French doors in the wall to its right opened on a large garden brimming with rose bushes and flowers. On the wall opposite the entrance was a large fireplace framed in green Carrara marble. Over it hung a painting of Bacchanalian abandon, a canvas arrayed with intertwined human figures. It was vividly erotic, but neither coarse nor crude. The fact that Chris had painted it heightened its interest for me.

The dining room was across the hall to the right, brightened by a red Moroccan rug. A country French table and chairs gave the room a comfortable, informal feeling.

Upstairs were three guest rooms and Chris's master suite, which was done in pastels. In my room, Marie-Louise had already unpacked my bag and was putting away the contents. A large window overlooking the garden was open and the wooden shutters thrown back. Chris showed me a second guest room opposite mine. At the end of the hall furthest from the master suite was another room, presumably the third guest room. But Chris did not offer to open it.

The last room she took me to was back downstairs. It was behind the fireplace in the living room. The door to it blended in with the stained wall paneling, and I missed the small black knob, which at first looked like a knot in the wood itself. It must originally have been a kind of family room, perhaps a child's playroom. But Chris had converted it into her studio. Three of the walls were louvered glass with bamboo blinds that could throw a variety of lights and shades as the slats were adjusted. Its principal furniture consisted of a group of easels of different sizes, each holding a covered canvas. Paintings, some framed, others on stretch boards, were scattered around the room. There was a wooden bench, a couple of high stools, and a bewildering variety of paints and brushes in tubes, boxes and jars. It was more than a workshop, it was clearly the sanctum sanctorum, the altar room in which Chris performed her rites. Chris restrained me gently at the entrance, not actually allowing me to enter. I was a visitor with a limited visa. I wondered whether her bedroom was also off limits.

By the time I had cleaned up and changed clothes, it was close to six o'clock, and I met Chris in the garden, where Marie-Louise presented a tray with a bottle of Roederer Cristal in an ice bucket, chilled tulip-shaped glasses, and a platter with brightly colored square hors d'oeuvres. La vie en rose, indeed. Chris and I talked of many things: of her, mostly, her love of painting and the sense of freedom she enjoyed in Angers. How she loved to wander alone through its cobbled streets, stopping to talk to local artisans and tradespeople. How she often drove into the countryside, sometimes far to the south, where she would pass the time of day with farmers and housewives and children. All this, she said, gave her the sustenance and inspiration she needed to paint not only *in* France but to paint France itself. She was obviously enthralled by her environment.

But there was also a shaded side to her. She simply refused to talk about the trial. She veered off the subject of Felix, and said not a word about her parents. It was as though family, friends, associations, indeed the land itself that lay across the ocean, had sunk into the sea like Atlantis, and all that existed was her *presentness* now in France, in Angers, in the microcosm that was her house on Rue de Port. It was uncanny how complete the separation appeared to be.

The sun had disappeared below the horizon when Chris, glancing at her watch, jumped up. "My poor darling, you must be famished. Here I am chattering away and you haven't had a decent meal in God knows how long. I'll go inside and see what Marie-Louise has created for you. She's a miracle worker in her kitchen."

She leaned over my chair and brought her pouting mouth to within inches of mine. I seized the invitation with my lips, feeling a quickness in my groin with unmistakable objectives. The magic of the moment I had experienced on the deck of the white yacht, when I had first met Chris as a grown-up woman, swept over me again with the same intensity, and the wish came to me that here and now fantasies might be transformed into flesh and blood reality.

But my timing was off. Chris, it seemed, had other plans for that evening. Standing up, she planted a dainty, moist kiss on the end of my nose. I was still living in the most recent past, savoring the taste of her lips, when she gave me the order of the evening.

"Don't be annoyed with me, cheri, but I have to leave you alone now." She arched her shoulders and adjusted her blouse. "I have to be in Angers for a couple of hours. Even your wonderful visit could not give me an excuse to change my plans. So stay here, enjoy the house as if it were your own, and I'll look in on you when I get home."

To my chagrin, I stammered something about understanding, disclaiming any preemptive call on her time. Where had all my worldliness gone? I knew. It had gone into building high hopes out of her casual promise "to look in" on me later. Could I so quickly—so rashly—be a goner, trapped again in an emotional web? Not I. I was just caught up in the moment. It would pass. Like all such moments in my life, since Terry died.

As Chris tripped off toward the French doors to the living room, she called back to me gaily. "I've arranged a party in your honor next Saturday evening. Artists, businessmen, beautiful women, some *femmes soles.*"

"And none of them speaks English, I'll bet," I interjected,

to hide how little I cared what they spoke, these unknown women, as long as Chris spoke to me. Damn, I *was* a goner.

Still, my linguistic shortcoming did annoy me. It left me without my favorite weapon of attack, a sharp tongue with the precise timing of a military band. I liked to lead the verbal march.

"Wrong, my little darling," Chris was saying. "Some of the people are former Parisians, one couple is from Brussels. Their English is as good as yours. Most of the others can feel their way around in English—and in Italian and in Spanish and even minimally in German. So don't be so insular, mon petit couchon, and *faîtes attention*—watch yourself! Some of the women are very beautiful—former models—and you will see they are morally emancipated." She made a damn near irresistible pout and touched my lips with a slender forefinger. My whole body quivered, I hoped imperceptibly.

"Remember," she said. "You are my house guest, which makes you mine, mine, mine!" Her light laugh left me tingling. But I could not decide whether her tongue was in her cheek or reaching out to mine again. It was taking considerable effort on my part not to find out the answer immediately, one way or the other. But I knew I should wait, bide my time, and I managed to act as though I found that as easy as breathing. I threw every last bit of aplomb I had into a disciplined smile I hoped looked positively content.

Chris slipped through the French doors and gently pulled them closed. I sat alone in the darkening garden, wishing I still smoked, while mental images of Chris and me steamed the windows of my mind. But I could still see the dangers lurking outside those misted windows. I could see the risk of my playing the collared pet to her Blue Angel. I blew the windows clean.

Marie-Louise came out and motioned me into the house. I noted that her manner was deferential but not servile; I liked that. The dining room was candlelit. The table, a shimmering pool of highly polished satinwood, was set with dramatic burnt orange and blue plates and oversized European silver. A cut crystal decanter filled with a ruby-colored wine was placed to my right next to a bottle, empty except for cloudy dregs. I looked at the label. It was a Château Palmer 1959, one of the great Bordeaux Rouges. Great care and a great deal of money had gone into these details. A disquieting question flitted across my mind about the source of the kind of wealth that allowed a young artist to enjoy such opulence. And again I brushed it aside as tomorrow's question.

The meal was superb. I finished the wine. Heavy-headed, I climbed upstairs. I intended to read for a good hour. But before the French clock on the wall chimed the next quarter hour, I was fast asleep.

And dreaming to a slow tango.

51

The caress was as soft as a whisper as it brushed across my chest. I also felt the cool breeze which had whisked out the heat of the day and was making sails of the batiste curtains ballooning in and out the open windows. Happily, I sailed back into a light sleep.

Another caress, this time over the tightness of my abdomen, as weightless as those gossamer sails. Drawn by the refreshing caress of the sail wind, I rolled over slightly to my left, the side the wind was coming from so silently. Curiously, the breeze began to tickle my ear. I raised an arm to brush it away. I wasn't finished dreaming.

I touched a head. I knew, somehow, that this head was not conjured up by me. Not part of my dream. Slowly I opened my eyes. A figure was lying beside me, nearer the windows. A silhouette emerged. A tousled head, a rounded shoulder, a curve gently inclining inward to a swelling hip. I saw no further. I looked no further.

I touched Chris's soft hair and my seeing fingers moved down to her temple, cheekbone and lips, slowly, ever so slowly. As she moved her body closer to mine, it made a delicate rustling sound on the sheet. Like whispered praise.

Her left leg touched my calf and she rubbed it gently until the hair on it stood up. She passed her leg across mine and I felt the brush of her pubic area on my thigh as she slowly rubbed back and forth. I rolled over on my back again to allow my tumescent member its full freedom, and she put her hand around it, loosely at first, and then in a deliciously brazen grip. Our kisses became frenzied and our breathing, short, stolen gasps. She mounted me as I lay across the bed, my head partway over the edge. She guided me into her silken interior with deft fingers and, placing her hands on my chest, started rocking back and forth. I began to sweat as I felt myself hurtling toward a climax I could no more stave off than I could brush back the sea. I pulled my head up and cupping her breasts, licked the perspiration between them, tasting the salt that was sweet to me. Not a word had passed between us that could be classified as speech, but our understanding was perfect. Back and forth she rocked, with me locked inside her, faster and faster, her head thrown back, her eyes closed. Just as I reached a point beyond which I knew there was no stopping, and grabbed her by her hips to signal that I was losing control, she raked her nails across my chest and spasmed with a cry that was all elemental ecstasy and triumph. She collapsed forward on me, panting, wet, utterly drained.

For a while, our breathless breathing was the only way we communicated our contentment to each other. Then, for the first time, she spoke, her voice a husky whisper. "I wanted you this way the day I first saw you on the deck of the boat. Even before I knew who you were, I knew we had met before and that I loved you then." Her lips, now as cool as a sweet fruit-flavored sherbet, brushed across my cheek.

"Chris, you were a baby the first time we met. You loved milk and cookies and bubble gum, not old men."

"I was fourteen, Tommy, and I did love you," she replied firmly, rolling off me forcefully, nearly taking me with her. "I used to cry myself to sleep on the nights when Lorna and you went off together. You can't understand, but a young girl is far more mature, her sensibilities far more advanced than a boy even several years older. A boy begins to think of his penis, but a girl starts to think of her heart."

I brushed back her tumbling hair. I could not read her face because it was turned away from the moonlight streaming across the bed. I told her things that lovers fresh from passion say to each other. We exchanged praises and words of endearment, and we loved again and again during the star-spangled hours, while the moon glided to its morning rest. Eventually we fell into a deep sleep, Chris lying on her side in the lap I made with my legs drawn up, my arm resting lightly across her breasts.

When I woke up, she was gone.

After I had showered and dressed, I went downstairs, humming "The Serenade" from *Eine Kleine Nachtmusik*.

Marie-Louise made me understand by sign language involving my wristwatch that Chris had been in her studio since six. I headed for it, wrapped in my dark blue silk robe, but the little French majordomo brought me to a quick halt with a "S'il vous plait, monsieur," spoken like a true company commander. "Jamais sans sa permission!" Only the "jamais" was a familiar word: Never! I brightly deduced that the studio was impenetrable. So I changed my course and headed for the dining room and a solitary but sumptuous breakfast of fresh orange juice, perfectly fried eggs with high, deep orange-colored yolks, freshly baked croissants, thick bacon, country butter, café au lait, and finally, a thimbleful of Pernod.

I would not permit myself to think I was in love with Christine. That emotion was alien to my entrenched independence. Too many years had passed since my marriage, years during which I had told myself, and eventually came to believe, that I was not meant to be domesticated. Besides, there was so much of Lorna in Chris that it made me vaguely uncomfortable, as if I were cheating on my first love.

Nevertheless, like it or not, I felt my ship of state keeling dangerously in a submissive direction, disregarding the storm warnings that were being shouted excitedly in my ear by that little fellow with the big, shiny, bald head, who was hopping up and down on my shoulder. After all, I asked him, who's in charge of the ship, you or I? I pushed him off before he could answer.

The rest of the day passed pleasantly, as did the week. Occasionally, I walked through the streets of Angers, past balconies dripping with red geranium plants. I filled my lungs with the sweet incense of lingering mimosas; nodded at the tradespeople and greeted passersby. I managed, in brief, to spend those days doing nothing at all with great pleasure. And when the sun began westering over the tops of the trees, I headed back to Rue de Port like a homing pigeon.

On other days, I stayed around the pool, reading, swimming and hurrying along the cocktail hour, when Chris would emerge from her chrysalis, spattered with paint but wearing a beatific smile, teaching me there was more to life than the law. Each evening, she would meet me in the garden, where she taught me the refined pleasure of fine champagne, trying to wean me from what she called my ruffian friend, Jack

Daniel. Each night we slept in each other's arms after exhausting ourselves in the myriad pleasures we discovered as we tested the extent to which we could climb the silken ladder of ecstasy.

52

The party broke upon Christine's home like a cloudburst. In the last quiet moment before the guests arrived, I lounged in the garden, sipping an iced vermouth. My regular American friend didn't suit the image I planned to project. Chris told me the men would dress casually, meaning no ties, but the women would take the occasion to show off their newest finery. I had put on white slacks and a dark sports jacket over a silk shirt open at the neck. I wore sunglasses to give me a sort of French Colonial look, to play down my American heritage. As it turned out, it fooled nobody. One of the first persons to approach me later on took one quick look and said, "You must be the American friend Chris told me about yesterday!" But then I never claimed to be a master of disguise.

In any event, I sauntered around the back edge of the garden, thinking impatiently that it would be hours before Chris and I could be alone again. As distant church bells paid their last respects to the departing day, a cavalcade of cars drove up to the house and spilled out its boisterous contents. I peeked around the side of the house and watched ten to fifteen people, mixed and matched. Most of them trooped inside, but several couples strolled together around to the back of the house toward the swimming pool, around which Marie-Louise had hung candlelit Japanese lanterns. The pool itself was illuminated by underwater lights. I counted to ten about twenty times, and took the plunge, walking back into the living room through the French doors.

Almost immediately, the party had moved into high gear. Glasses were clinking inaugural toasts; people began filtering into the living room and past me into the garden beyond; the air was becoming a wreath of swirling blue smoke. The American campaign against smoking, I thought to myself, had not yet touched French shores. And then I revised my judgment as I recognized with a sinking feeling the unmistakable scent of burning corn silk, just as I had detected it on the boat the day I met Chris.

I spied her talking to a couple, and walked over to join her. She had on a pale pink gown and a choker of angel-skin coral beads. On her right hand she wore a large square-cut ruby ring. Her golden hair was combed straight down to her shoulders. The man and woman to whom she was talking were both tall and thin. If the monsieur had not been brushing his hand gently back and forth against the woman's buttocks, I would have thought them to be father and daughter. He wore his white hair combed back neatly, and had on white slacks and a fitted white silk shirt with broad red stripes. She wore a loose-fitting green flowered print and flat-heeled shoes to minimize her height. As I walked up, Chris caught sight of me and her face brightened. She gave me a smile that would have made the sun pink with envy. My heart, carefully trained to behave itself in the heat of court battles, tried to free itself from my chest like a bird wildly fluttering in a thicket.

"Darling, this is the Belgian couple I told you about, Claude and Colette Brandt. Claude was—still is—a very great architect. If you've been to Paris, you'll have seen much of his work there."

I shook hands. "The Arc de Triomphe, perhaps?" My smile died before his withering glance, and Chris called me a naughty boy. So I applied ingratiating words to the scratch, and quickly detached myself. Having decided then that I needed more than vermouth, I poured myself a generous dose of Jack Daniel's. As I drew myself up to my most formidable stance, a quiet voice spoke into my left ear.

"You must be the American friend Chris told me about yesterday." The words were uttered in English lightly salted with a delightful French accent. I turned around and looked into a boyish face framed in brown hair. Misty freckles hid beneath the skin around her cheeks and hazel eyes. She was wearing a tailored white linen dress pinched at the waist by a broad, black leather belt with metal studs.

"I'm Nanette Phillippe. Nan will do." She stuck out a hand. Her grasp was firm. There was none of that "I-hate-to-touch-skin" message.

"Yes, I'm Tom Attleboro. How did you know?"

"It was trés simple. You are the only stranger here. Non? Besides, no one in this group would have the—how you say— the fun?—to wear dark glasses at night." There was no malice in her voice, just friendly banter. I was about to riposte, but decided to make friends instead. I put the glasses in my pocket. She was drinking a Bellini. My eyes, drawn by a cabochon star sapphire on her right hand, noticed also that she wore natural polish on her nails. I saw a faint brown smudge between the pinkie and ring finger of her left hand.

"You are a left-handed painter," I said with the confidence more natural to me in the courtroom.

"You are—how you say—Maître Shylock Holmes, perhaps?"

I did not correct her. The misnomer may have been Gallic humor.

"It was elementary, my dear Watson. There is a brown smudge between the fingers of your left hand. Voilà!" Which just about exhausted my French vocabulary.

She looked down at her hand, said something in French that sounded like "mad," and then threw me a shining smile that showed the refreshing absence of personal vanity. "How careless of me. But—how you say?—you make a wrong. I have a gallery in Angers and I was touching up a frame just before I left. I am no painter, but oui, I am writing with my left hand."

We laughed together, and I accepted her invitation to tour the party and allow her to give me a thumbnail sketch of some of the guests. Chris, to my displeasure, evidently was too busy elsewhere. But Nanette was a delightful alternate.

She introduced me to Monsieur and Madame Roule, the proprietors of the largest department store in the city. Monsieur Roule's English was barely passable, but he gave me a gracious bow while Madame stifled either a yawn or a belch. I met a young painter who walked around by himself with a notebook, pencil, and a curved pinky nail, doing quick sketches of the rooms and guests and constantly looking furtively over his shoulder to make certain no one could see—and steal—his studies. She introduced me to a German couple who spoke no English but welcomed me in guttural French to the shores of La Belle France. Nan translated, and told me as they stood there smiling, possibly understanding more than they admitted to, that he was the managing director of a prestigious hotel near Chinon. She said they had an enormous château halfway between Angers and Ninon, where they threw lavish parties. Once they had engaged a full ballet troupe from Paris to provide one hour's entertainment for two hundred guests in a fully equipped theater on their estate. From his girth I suspected that a large part of his wealth was consumed at the table. I envied him his hedonistic unconcern.

Then there was one of the models Chris had mentioned who, seeing me already in tow, steered a course directly to our side and introduced herself, to Nan's visible annoyance, as Chris's best friend. She towered over me, a graceful figure sheathed in a dark blue gown with a V-neck that dared me to a game of peek-a-boo.

"Darling," she hissed to Nan, keeping her obviously store-bought green eyes fastened on my face, tilting back until her spine was curved like a bow. "How do you dare capture this lovely man to yourself? You must share him. I insist!" She offered me a limp hand with nails so long that it must have taken half a bottle of polish to give them one coat. Her other hand held a tall glass of some amber liquor and a thick joint. She offered it to Nan and me but we declined after glancing at each other. When the gushing ceased and introductions were completed, and a few desultory words were exchanged, Nan and I, on an eye signal from me, moved on.

"What's her story?" I asked as soon as we were a safe distance away.

"Pardon?" Apparently she was puzzled by the colloquialism.

"What does she do besides walk around like the leaning tower of Pisa? What does she have in common with Chris?"

Now Nan seemed uncomfortable. Suddenly, really quite uncomfortable. Repeatedly, she stroked the back of her shingled hair. "I suppose she is just a friend. One meets all types of persons when one moves about, painting. N'est-ce pas?"

"A model in Angers? She has Paris and London and Rome written all over her. What's the connection? And why is there so much pot being smoked here, anyway? Do you smoke it too?"

"Attendez, attendez, mon ami! Slowly, please. You put me in the witness box, no?" Plainly, Nan was vastly discomfited by my questions. We were momentarily distracted by a roll of thunder off in the distance, ominously deep. Nan shook her head and pointed in that direction. "It will not come this way. Not tonight at least. No, I do not smoke at all. Do you?"

Back to me. Clearly, she did not propose to respond to my main questions, and I realized I was being rude to press her. But there was something being hidden here, something out of balance in the equation. I got the same feeling I had on the boat. It was more than that. The whole milieu, like Mary's little lamb, seemed to follow Chris wherever she went. I was sure Nan knew more than she chose to disclose, but I asked her no more questions. Instead, I resolved to corner the slinky model—Mademoiselle Valentère was the name she had offered me—before the evening was over.

Nanette was corralled herself a short time later by a young man who kissed her on each cheek and pulled her away without bothering to introduce himself to me. Nan looked back at me and rolled her eyes in despair before she disappeared in the haze. Her departure gave me a chance to do a little private investigating on my own. I refilled my glass to maintain the image of a casual guest, and headed upstairs. There was a large guest bathroom on the main floor behind the staircase. Yet I had noticed a steady stream of guests going up and down the stairs, and I was curious to find out why.

First I sauntered into my room, where I fussed for a few minutes behind the closed door. When I came out, the hall was empty. I rapped on the door to Chris's bedroom. There was no response. I opened the door and peered inside. Empty. Some underclothes were scattered on the bed, a satin robe hung over the back of a chaise lounge. Otherwise the room was neat. The scent of her perfume made me lightheaded with longing, but it passed as I closed the door. As if magnetically drawn, I walked toward the other end of the hall to the room I had not been shown. As I stood there, undecided, the door suddenly opened, and in the doorway stood Mademoiselle Valentère, swaying slightly, glassy-eyed. She closed the door and walked past me as though I were not even standing there. She gave no sign of recognition.

Beyond the door I could hear low voices like those at a gambling casino. Then I heard Chris laugh. I opened the door, but remained on the threshold. There were four people in the room in addition to Chris. Two women were seated at a round teakwood table in the center of the room. Before each of them was a small square mirror with a tiny pyramid of white powder piled in the center. The women, holding silver straws, looked up at me wide-eyed. Two men were lounging on a blue velvet sofa, their jackets off, their shirt sleeves rolled up above their elbows. Chris had her back to the door. She never turned around. I backed away from this tableau and closed the door, more disappointed than surprised that my suspicions had been confirmed.

I went downstairs and found the leaning tower propped against a foppish character dressed in a mauve jacket and tight white linen slacks. The handkerchief that flopped out of the breast pocket of his jacket matched his yellow hair perfectly. He was shaking marijuana from a small pill box into a piece of cigarette paper. The leaning tower was gazing off into space over his head. He never even noticed when I drew her away.

We went out to the garden, over near the stone balustrade where Nanette and I had stood earlier in the evening. The Valentère was indeed a stunning creature, too thin for my personal taste but a tall, strikingly graceful figure who knew exactly how to move her body. She could have been a prima ballerina. She could also have been Paula Borghesi, Napoleon's sister, who posed for Canova's statue in the Borghesi Gallery in Rome, reclining on a couch, her thighs lightly pressing down the cushion as though it were a soft fabric instead of Carrara marble. Except this Paula moved and breathed and lived, and her equally beautiful body was warm and soft to the touch.

But I had not maneuvered her outside to study her topography. I had to find out what Chris's role was in this unbridled drug scene. I had seen too much of the damage drugs had done ever to feel comfortable around them. I told myself that it would not—could not—affect my feelings for Chris, but my friend with the shiny bald head kept asking me, Whom are you kidding? I knew he was right for a change. A lifetime in New York, plying my trade, had exposed me to the cracks and seams in society, high and low. I never tried to be a self-righteous reformer, but drugs were part of a solar system of values totally different from mine. I had pity, even contempt, for the weaknesses that made drug users. On the

other hand, I had come to hate the people who pandered to
other people's weaknesses, the suppliers, the distributors, the
purveyors of death.

Yet here was Chris, apparently a dispensing pharmacist in
her château-cum-drugstore.

I tried to cast out the interlopers spoiling my fantasy picture
of Chris, but I couldn't. I had seen what I had seen, and nothing
could erase those pictures. Closing my eyes to reality had not
been my style, ever. All an ostrich achieves by sticking its head
in the sand is to get grit in its beak.

The Valentère pried my fingers loose from her upper arm
and giggled. "Mon cher avocat, mon petit ami, we have been
observing each other all evening, non? You follow me with
your eyes, and I seek for you also. N'est-ce pas? We are close
apart, non? I think maybe we have queek love. How you Ameri-
cans say, where there is flame, there is fire."

I gazed at her, unblinking as a basilisk, waiting for her to
land. It took a good three minutes of my most baleful staring
to make her comprehend that she had not swept me off my
feet. I finally got her sobered attention.

"Mademoiselle Valentère . . ."

"Non, non, non, cheri, pas de Mademoiselle or Madame, s'il
tu plaît. Claudine. Claudine Gregory Mihailovitch Valentère.
My papa, he was Russian from Moscow. His father was a
Prince Royal until the Bolsheviks came. Then . . ." She
passed a flat palm across her throat. "My mother, she was born
Turkish. A Turkey. From Uskudar, on the Bosporus. Ver-r-r-y
riche and ver-r-r-y beautiful. Moi? I am born in Paris during a
shopping trip, a trip of shopping. I am Parisienne, but I have
many nationalities under my skin." She lightly touched her
lower body, leaving me confused over the meaning of her
last remark. I waited hopefully for her to reach the end of
her genealogy.

"I am now Valentère because I was married to a French
designer, a designer of dresses. He was French." Did she
always talk in echoes? "He was good. He was very good. But
in the bed . . ." She looked at me salaciously and waggled her
flat, outstretched left hand. " . . . comme si, comme ça. One
afternoon I come home and I find Raoul in bed playing. With
a jeune garçon, a young boy, maybe eighteen, maybe nineteen.
They play the game soixante-neuf. You understand, no? Then

I know why he is bad in bed with me. Ugh! Alors, fin de marriage." She washed her hands expressively. "Over. Finish. Fini. It is best. Now I rent a house in Angers, and Chris and I become good friends, very good friends, and I visit her much. I have been her model souvent, often. Not so often now, but we have nice friendship forever. Forever. Eternellement!" She took a deep breath, brushed her hair back, and nodded firmly. It was my turn.

"Forever, meaning as long as she supplies you with pot and coke and all the bonbons that keep you flying around zee room. Ness par?" I was becoming adept at the language of the house. "Or do you all come with your own drugs?"

"Not at all, not at all, mon chou, not the reasons we are friends. I love her, do you not understand? I love her. When I was a jeune fille, I had no sister, no brother, nothing. Rien de rien. It was lonely. Very lonely. Now I have a sister. It is very important to me. Très important." As she spoke she placed her arms over my shoulders and closed in on me like an iron maiden so that we were very close apart. The lights on the flagstone patio outside the living room doors caught her face, emphasizing her prominent cheekbones, and softening the shadowed hollows of her cheeks. There was nobody near us. Under different circumstances I might have been drawn by more than her beauty. She had a magnetism, but I was heading in a different direction at the moment.

"I asked you whether you brought the stuff with you, or does Chris supply you from her drugstore?"

"Drugstore? You mean pharmacie? Chris? Mais why? Porquoi? Chris? . . ." Asked with wide, dissimulating eyes and raised eyebrows. I pushed her back a step or two.

"My dear, I am not dumb. No? You know exactly what I mean. Answer me, please. I wish some truth. It won't hurt. Do you all bring the drugs with you?"

Claudine paused, evidently weighing the benefits of truth against falsehood. Her highest moral qualities triumphed. She shook her head.

"So Christine sells them to you, is that it?"

"Sometimes. Sometimes, like tonight, we are her guests. There is no money. She is a generous person, she loves us. So—" She gestured with palms up, letting me finish the thought for myself.

"Where does she get it?" I asked.

"That is her secret, mon choufleur. You ask me to be indiscreet, non? But ce n'est pas important—that is not of importance, really. She is with many friends. She paints for them. They love her. She loves them. They help her, she helps them. Here we are a big, happy family. Content. Très contente. And Christine now does her best painting. She is très formidable, une prèmiere artiste. She will be famous, very famous. Some day. You will see. And we all have a great love and respect for her. Do you not also? I think you do! Mais maintenant, now, we speak of us, seulement. Non? Our queek love? Oui?"

Claudine circled her arms around my neck as she finished speaking. My heart felt like a rock in my chest. All my self-discipline fled and I began to fill with anger and disgust and bewilderment. Most of all, I began to be afraid, the way I hadn't in a long time. The way I had felt when I learned that I had lost Lorna to Felix, and had lost Terry to death.

All the while, as I was struggling to grasp the significance of the facts I had learned, fighting against a desire to reject them, shred them so they no longer existed, Claudine continued to speak to me in French in whispered tones, her mouth close to my ear. She pressed her pelvis against my groin and rolled it as she began to moan softly. Then she bit my earlobe gently, and placed my hand inside her dress, against an engorged nipple. I withdrew my hand and lifted up her dress and put my hands on her buttocks, which were bare. She spread her legs and leaned back against the stone balustrade. I felt her wetness and I opened my trousers and I jammed myself into her standing up, like a rutting ram. She whimpered softly at the mixture of pain and pleasure as I raged into her, raged against all womankind, until I spent myself in a furious jolt. Then, without a word, I withdrew, adjusted my clothes and walked away.

53

I woke up in bed at about five o'clock in the morning. The only thing lying next to me was an unopened bottle of Jack Daniel's. I recognized it from its shape. Feeling around in the dark on the other, undented pillow I found a card. I switched on the lamp next to the bed, waited until my pupils adjusted to the brightness and, squinting, read Chris's note. It was written in lavender ink on the back of a shopping bag from a store in Angers called Les Chosettes.

Poor Darling—

Do not be too angry with me. Dina told me you saw us upstairs. It was naughty of her to tell you things that were untrue, and it wasn't nice anyhow for you to be playing house detective.

There! Now that I've spanked you, let me tell you I adore you. And of course I shall explain everything.

I must go to Nice, just for a few days. Be comfortable and we'll talk when I get back. And keep loving me, my love! Je t'adore.

C.

P.S. Stay away from Dina. She's a whore, you know. She really is! C.

There was no sleep left in me. My mind was heaving with indigestible thoughts. I began to find myself already forgiving Chris for unforgivable faults. So I got up and dressed and decided to see whether the truth would really make me free. Leaving my shoes off so that Marie-Louise would not hear me moving about, I padded silently into the master bedroom and pressed the light switch. There were no ceiling fixtures. The room was gently suffused with a soft pink glow from lamps around the room. The shades were decorated with reproductions of Van Gogh paintings done while he was in Arles. Two of them were brightly colored garden scenes in yellow, green and bronze tones; the others I recognized as portraits of the Ginoux family. And there was one more, a rectangular shade, with a self-portrait, repeated on front and back.

All the windows were closed and the air still offered up the sultry admixture of Chris's body scent and her perfume. I picked up an undergarment she had flung on the bed, and buried my face in it. Instantly she was back in my arms, her golden hair in a tangle around my neck and shoulders. Reluctantly, I replaced the garment on her bed. In a corner next to the window was a marvelously preserved black lacquer French Empire writing desk with its original flowered decorations in bright oils intact. Its slender legs were sheathed in gold leaf.

I opened the beveled cover, which became a writing surface. There were several cubby holes, and a shallow drawer in the center beneath them. The cubby holes held note paper and envelopes and some unpaid bills from stores with addresses in Angers, and from one in Nice for a bikini and "une paire sandales." I looked at the closed drawer and hesitated, feeling anticipatory shame over what I was about to do. I shelved the shame and opened the drawer. An envelope lay in the center, face down. I had come this far—I turned it over. It was addressed to Mlle. Christine Ward. The postmark showed it had been mailed from Palm Beach, Florida, two weeks earlier. I flipped the envelope over; no return address.

Again I hesitated. Remember Pandora's box, the bald man said. You can stop now.

But I couldn't. The note, somewhat cryptic, was just clear enough to leave me with a faint outline of a Chris I did not know and did not want to know.

Dear Christine—

Well, as you know, of course, it's all over here and thank God for that! Even though I suppose it will never be over for your parents, and for him for that matter. Such a terrible tragedy, dear, but one simply must get on with one's life, isn't that so? And your painting is too important to neglect. Harry and I do hope you are working at it. He says it will help you so much to forget, or at least to cope better with everything. For once I agree with him!

If you speak to your friend, tell him his man is taking care of everything. But you must get back soon, Chris dear, because there are things we must do. So try your best to hurry back just for a little while. And then you can also visit with your parents for a bit. I don't speak to them, but they must be very lonely for you at this point.

We had *Pegasus* . . .

That was it! *Pegasus*. That was the name of the yacht that I had boarded. But what the hell was Pegasus? I asked myself. The name was familiar but I could not remember more than having encountered it in college, perhaps when we were reading Bullfinch. I turned back to the letter.

We had *Pegasus* painted and your cabin redone. You're going to be very pleased, I'm sure. So cable the date, and we'll pick you up at the airport!

All our love,
R.

I thought I got a glimpse of something behind the fluttering leaves of the words, but then I wondered whether I wasn't seeing more than was actually there. More important, was I looking for answers that no longer mattered to me? For during the endless hours of that night, as I lay wide-eyed in bed, there had crept over me like warm, sudsy water in a tub the soothing feeling that what Chris did was no longer important. I had to know, but it would not alter my feelings for her. I wanted her, whatever she did, whatever she was. There was no escaping it: I was crazy about her. And if that was senseless, so be it. It was about time, I told myself, that I did *something* senseless.

There was nothing else in the drawer except a few yellow cards with a silhouette of a horse with wings. I pocketed a couple of the cards, shut the drawer and closed the cover of the writing desk. Then I went over to a bombe satinwood bureau against the wall and began rifling aimlessly through its drawers.

Tucked in the most intimate of her undergarments, there nestled a wicked-looking gun, an Army Colt from all appearances. Not a woman's weapon, I thought, as I hefted it in the palm of my hand. Too big and unwieldy for a sensitive hand used to the slender weightlessness of a paint brush. Not Chris's weapon, I was sure. But whose, then? And why in her house, in her room? I released the magazine in the butt to inspect it. It was filled. Little lead soldiers all lined up in a double row. Snapping the magazine back in place, I checked to be sure the safety was on, and dropped it, too, into my pocket. It didn't seem to belong wrapped in a pair of scented panties.

I had seen enough. Although I had originally intended to go into the third guest room, my mind refused to order my legs down the hall in that direction. Back in my room, I glanced out the open window and noticed that it was getting light.

Marie-Louise, wearing a blue denim work shirt and ridiculously oversized dungarees bunched together at her ample waist with a piece of twisted red fabric, was busy clipping and snipping at the rose bushes, a spray can at her feet. She was singing some French ditty softly to herself, in a pleasant voice. It occurred to me that she was completely happy in her small world, secure in the love and loyalty of Chris. I heaved a sigh of envy, and closed the window to keep out the insects.

Suddenly I felt an irresistible urge sweep over me. I had to find Chris. There was no waiting for her to return. I had to tell her that I didn't care about what I had seen, it made no difference in my feelings, as long as she kept on loving me. I knew I was acting as precipitously as a school boy, but I whistled away my embarrassment to the tune of *Sempre libera* from *La Traviata*.

I threw a few beach clothes and a pair of slippers into my bag, and took out a suit, hanger and all. Such was my haste that I almost forgot to take my toothbrush and razor from the bathroom. As I tumbled downstairs, I said to myself that Marie-Louise had to know where Chris was staying. I left my valise in the foyer and walked through the living room toward the French doors. The room was immaculate. Marie-Louise must have been tidying up while I played house detective. I came up to her in the garden from behind and startled her with a cheery bonjour. She spun around, but immediately broke into a broad smile that wreathed her face in a network of tiny wrinkles and seams.

Suddenly, her face turned dour as though a cloud had settled on it. I knew what it was. Chris had told me that Marie-Louise took great pride in always being ready. If she worshipped any deity, it was the God of Readiness. When Chris expected to use the car, Marie-Louise liked to have it in front of the door as she stepped outside. When Chris wanted a dress repaired, Marie-Louise had to have needle and the right color thread directly at hand. Dining hours varied, depending upon when Chris left her atelier next to the living room, and the length of our cocktail break. But Marie-Louise prided herself on having the meal ready to serve as soon as we sat down at the table. The beef had to be pink, the chicken moist, the eggs not overdone. It took a kind of wizardry to anticipate all this, but as long as I had been there Marie-Louise had not been caught napping.

Until now. As the sun began to paint the tops of the trees and the gold began to drip down through the leaves, I could read her mind as she stood there, clutching clippers in one hand and her dungarees at the waist with the other. Breakfast was not ready. The table probably had not even been set yet. We had become quite adept at signing to each other. I pointed to my mouth and waggled a finger to indicate I did not intend to eat. Then I handed her the note from Chris and pointed to the word Nice. She read it and looked up inquiringly. I took a pencil from my pocket and scribbled on the back of the note: "Hotel?" I was in luck. The word evidently matched its French counterpart. She took the pencil, and even though it was a gold encased beauty, a gift from a grateful client, she licked it before using it as if it were a stubby old lead pencil. In strong, square letters she printed her answer below my question: HOTEL NEGRESCO. TOUJOURS! ELLE L'AIME.

I kissed her leather cheek to her pleased astonishment, and took my rented fire engine red Peugot out of the garage, telling myself that life could be beautiful. After all, I was off to see Chris, to surprise her, to tell her that I forgave her the foolish faults I loathed in others. I absolutely, positively refused to allow my little friend with the big, shiny, bald head so much as to perch on my shoulder as I drove off, hunched over the steering wheel, determined to reach Nice that night.

54

It was dark when I reached Nice. Apart from a couple of pit stops, I had driven without rest. I went from Angers over to Lyon, where I entered the Autoroute, and sped south at a steady 160 kilometers an hour until I reached Aix-en-Provence. From there, narrow roads and an endless procession of ponderous trucks, laboring along at a snail's pace, built up the acids in my stomach.

Eventually I reached Nice and, although it was dark, I found my way easily to the Promenade des Anglais, a broad and beautiful avenue that skirts the beaches of the Mediterranean. Its waters lay under a glossy coverlet that reflected the lights along the shore and those decorating the occasional cruise ship at close anchor. Now I had to locate Chris's hotel.

When I had made my last stop, at Aix-en-Provence, a young service station attendant told me half in French and half in broad gestured English that I could not miss the Hotel Negresco. He called it "le grande pearl de Nice," which gave a glimpse of his possibilities above and beyond pumping petrol. He drew a hemisphere in the air with cupped, grease-covered hands, communicating that I should look for a building with a dome. He said there was a large sign over the entrance and that there was a doorman who wore a uniform that made him look like a dressed up "singe," which he finally made me understand by walking around with his knees bent and his arms dangling meant a "monkee." His envy for that job was showing.

Driving east on the promenade, the sea on my right, I saw a whole string of the most beautiful pearls, a glittering array of mansions and hotels across the avenue on my left. The service station attendant was right, there was no way I could miss the Negresco. Its vaulted roof and dome were placed in sharp relief by strategically located floodlights; and as I whizzed past it on the wrong side of the Promenade, I caught sight of the "monkee" opening the door of an attenuated limousine. I turned left at the first opportunity. But instead of being able to make a U-turn, I had to enter the streets off the avenue, which were filled with strollers and shoppers and revelers who overflowed the narrow sidewalks, heedless of cars, and were choking the way. It was like driving through a pedestrian mall.

I stopped a well-dressed man and asked him, Ooh is Hotel Negresco. Recognizing my fluency in his native tongue, he responded with a torrent of words accompanied by hand and arm gestures indicating a series of rights, lefts and straight aheads to the hotel. Had I been a crow, I could have reached it in two wing flaps and a short glide. Absent wings, it took fifteen long minutes before I drove up to the entrance.

The doorman approached me wearing a grin as wide as a welcome mat. I received it as I would have had he been waving a checkered flag at the end of the last lap of the Indianapolis 500.

I was graciously welcomed by a reception clerk in formal dress whose English pronunciation put mine to shame. He apologized that he could not accommodate me in a choice room but without an advance reservation—he offered me a helpless shrug and a quivering chin. The room he did have available turned out to be fine; small but beautifully appointed and overlooking the promenade and the dark sea at rest beyond it. I was tired but happy, and very anxious to find Chris.

As I drove to Nice I had asked myself how Ben Abbott would go about surprising Chris at the hotel, and he helped me work out the details. I unpacked my few things and hung them up so they could stretch and breathe, and then took a sheet of stationery from the desk set on a flat table in the corner. I folded the sheet and placed it in a Hotel Negresco envelope, which I sealed and addressed simply to Mlle. Christine Ward. Then I took the elevator downstairs, noting with amusement that in French it was called *ascenseur,* a lift. Anyway, it let me down.

I walked over to the concierge's station and got the attention of one of the multilingual, encyclopedic geniuses there who not only man the room boxes and keys, but also know everything about restaurants, museums, trains, planes, and weather.

I asked him to place my note in Chris's mail box. Without a moment's hesitation he picked up a pen and wrote "Chambre 608" below her name and placed it in the proper aperture. Either he had a photographic memory or Chris was well-known to the staff. I told myself Ben could not have handled that phase better. I saw that the large room key, which showed in many other boxes, was missing from hers. That probably meant that Chris was in residence. But I noticed a second key, without the large metal tag, lying in the box.

Then, realizing that I had not eaten since the night before, and then largely hors d'oeuvre, I found my way into the main dining room. An hour later, slightly tipsy from wine and fatigue, I walked from the dining room and staked out the concierge desk. The note was still in the box and so was the reserve key.

The lobby was buzzing with activity. A German-speaking group had just returned from a night tour of the city, which had probably ended at a bistro or club. There was much loud talking and laughter. The man I had spoken to at the desk was answering the questions of at least three guests at the same time, occasionally stretching back to reach for the room key of another guest. A young assistant was similarly besieged. I slipped around two women who had a small map of the city spread out on the desk and, catching the young man's eye, I asked for 608. Without interrupting his conversation with another couple, he extracted the key and gave it to me with the note. I melted away, commenting to myself that Chris might be well advised to speak to the management about the security of their guests. As I went up to the sixth floor, I asked myself, what if I had not been a friend bent on a prank?

Before I opened the door, I put my ear to it, listening for silence, hoping that Chris was in bed. She had surprised me a week ago, and I planned to return the compliment. Somewhere inside, a radio was playing. I heard the faint strains of a Mozart sonata. The door opened inward as I turned the key, and I found myself in a dark sitting room, the furniture outlined by the reflected lights from the Promenade below. Beyond it was another door. The music was coming from that room, and so was a glimmer of light. I undressed quickly in the dark.

I opened the door. In the dim light of a small bedside lamp with a scarlet shade, his naked torso throwing off a phosphorescent glow from the sweat that beaded it, Felix was astride

Christine. Her slender legs were around his waist, locked in the crooks of his elbows. Christine's eyes were closed, her arms outflung, her blond hair spread upon the white pillow like the mane of a celestial horse.

On the edge of the bed, a golden robe trailed to the floor. Embroidered on its back was a black monogram. It was easy to make out even in the dim light and despite the rocking of the bed. Probably because it was not unfamiliar to me. I had seen it on a deserted piece of God's earth called Round Key in the Gulf of Mexico. On the tongue of a sneaker that Ben and I had dug out of the moldy sand, packed underneath a weather-stained tarpaulin.

Greek beta over Greek pi. P for Pegasus, of course! The myth came back to me at last in a jarring jolt of memory. The winged horse. Pegasus lying there on the bed with her eyes closed, moaning ecstatically. And as a bolt of lightning throws unseen objects into momentary sharp relief, I saw on the retina of my mind a picture of Pegasus, the winged horse sprung from the body of Medusa, soaring through the heavens. And on his back was Bellerophon, a lonely figure in search of the monster Chimera, whom in time he would destroy. Bellerophon mounted on the body of Pegasus. There in bed in front of me, neither with any awareness of my presence. From the radio came the *andante* movement, the bed sounds providing a discordant counterpoint.

Felix and Christine. Felix and Lorna. Everything changes but nothing is different. I shut down hard on the scream in my throat. Backing out of the room, I closed the door, and put on my clothes. As I heard the sounds of the occupants in the bedroom rise to a crescendo, my heart once again began to beat its way out of my chest, and when the sounds of the lovers stopped altogether, so did my heart.

Heedlessly—heartlessly—I threw the room key on the glass coffee table. It clattered. I was walking out the door when the bedroom door opened. I turned. Felix stood there looking at me, his jaw slack with astonishment. I closed the door behind me and walked slowly to my room, my small sanctuary overlooking the Promenade and the beach.

I took the telephone off the hook and sat down in the chair in front of the window, trying to erase the picture of them from my mind. Hopeless. It might as well have been etched in acid on a copper plate. I pulled the Colt out of my pocket and pressed the coolness of its stock to my temple as I tried to figure out my next step.

The coolness went from my head to my heart, and a cold anger began to erode my self-pity and heal my pain. It was time to put aside giddy illusions and immature dreams; to stop playing in a make-believe world filled with fantasies and lies and deceptions and hypocrisy and fairy godmothers with magic wands. I had committed the same unpardonable sin that had cost Orpheus the love of his life. I had looked backward. Through Felix to a place I was meant to leave utterly behind. As though anyone ever could go back to his youth.

A good part of my anger was at myself. For it was one thing to be strong-willed, and an entirely different matter to be stubborn. I had refused to heed the warnings of Amos Stern. He had tried to tell me in half a dozen ways why I should steer clear of this case. He sensed the storm signals before the wind even started to blow. He had tried to make me see the ethical problems in becoming entangled in the defense of a man whose past was intertwined with mine. Not only that, but a man who had left me bereft and angry and hurt. A friend who was no friend. Someone, in short, I had every reason to hate and no reason still to love.

Amos had tried to make me understand that, during our long morning's meeting in New York, when he had marched into my office and we had tossed these issues around the room. He, like Ben, who had spoken about the same topic at breakfast near the end of the trial, had told me that it didn't matter that I had seemed to have gotten over the loss of Lorna. It was Felix's betrayal of me, his best friend—his only friend—that Amos wanted me to consider carefully. For, he insisted, I was going to represent a hostile client; and if I lost, it would be said that I deliberately threw him to the dogs, thereby breaching my professional integrity.

And I had damn nearly done exactly that in my summation to the jury. I had simply refused to recognize that the fury that had boiled up in me was caused by yet another betrayal. When I had walked out of the Sunday meeting with Felix and Ben, after Felix had lied about the clothes, I had not only violated the canons of my profession by concealing vital evidence—for which I could lose my license—but I had committed a crime. I had obstructed justice. And I had done all this for no better reason than because I had wanted to believe I was still merely protecting Felix from his enemies in school. Playing big brother, so he could look up to me and respect me. And love me, and most of all, need me. But, for God's sake, those were childhood years, and they *were* gone forever. I wasn't anyone's big brother any more. And Felix was no longer my responsibility, even as my client. The case was closed. He was on his own.

And so was I. On my own. And alone.

And how, after all I learned about Felix and me during the trial, had I allowed myself to be caught in the web spun by Christine? And worst of all, to become so besotted with her that I was willing to overlook the unforgivable sin of drug dealing. I had walked into *that* trap blinded by her sexuality into thinking that she somehow was the embodiment of her dead sister, and that through her I could recapture some semblance of the past part of me I had never been able to get behind me. It couldn't work, it never would have worked. It was mere fantasy and self-delusion. I had walked through Alice's looking glass. I had seen familiar sights and never realized they were distorted images that mocked reality. I had watched myself become an unrecognizable figure in the undulating mirrors of a make-believe world. Here I was in a strange city, in a lousy hotel room, light-years away from my real world and work, licking my wounds like a stray who has been kicked out of a place he had no business exploring in the first place.

I decided to clean up the mess.

Whatever it took. Even if it killed me.

I put the pistol on the dresser, and I dialed Room 608, and I heard Christine answer in a voice that betrayed tears. My message was short. I told her I wanted to see Felix and her in the morning in their suite; this time, I said, in their sitting room. No absences excused. Ten o'clock sharp. I hung up.

Suddenly I felt dog tired. The trip and the horseback lesson had drawn out all my reserves.

It was only after I had crawled into bed that I realized I was something else besides exhausted. I was relaxed. Thinking through—facing—my less than salutary part in all that had happened, I felt at peace now. Because facing the truth turned out to be a lot less stressful than hiding from it.

If, looking back over recent events, there was much to regret, there *was* tomorrow. A surpisingly consoling thought.

I slept on it.

55

Felix answered the door. His eyes were dark-ringed; they no longer looked soft and liquid. I wondered for the first time why I had never noticed that the disproportion between the size of his head and the size of his torso gave him a misshapen appearance, not very attractive at that. He was dressed in a cotton shirt and slacks, and woven leather sandals. Chris came in a minute later wearing a pure white burnoose that, ironically enough, made her look like Snow White. The hood was folded down along her back. Her hair was tied up with a piece of red woolen yarn. She was smiling at me with her mouth but her eyes told of her fright. They both sat down on the couch, hands folded in their laps like school children.

Christine spoke first. Too quickly. "Tommy, darling, however did you get here, and how in the world did you find me? Was it Marie-Louise, did she tell you?" She dabbed at the corner of her mouth with a pink tissue, her eyes seeking to catch my frame of mind. I did not keep her in suspense.

"You may not believe it, Christine, but I drove one thousand kilometers practically nonstop to tell you that I thought about your drug dealings, and didn't give a damn. It made no difference in my feelings for you. To me, the law-and-order man! Because I still saw something good in you: your God-given talents, which might make you a fine artist. If you didn't go down the drain first in some roach-ridden cell of a French jail. Now isn't that funny? Isn't that a scream?"

I wanted to tell her I had loved her, and that had been the reason I had raced down to Nice; but I couldn't say it with Felix sitting there. Whether I really loved her or not no longer mattered. Felix had made all that insignificant.

"Christine, tell me, did you ever see a bigger damn fool?"

Her head drooped and tears trickled over the soft down of her cheeks. Reaching into my pocket, I drew out the Colt pistol and placed it in my lap. Christine stared at it as the sun, streaming through the window behind me, spotlighted its outlines. Felix, who had not yet uttered a word, masked whatever were his feelings with his supercilious sneer. But the way he licked his lips told me that his mouth was very dry.

"Where did you get—that?" Christine spoke in a very small voice.

"The same place I got these." I threw the yellow Pegasus cards on the coffee table. "What does one buy me, a trip on a yacht? Access to some club so exclusive that its name and address are omitted? A drug party? A pass into your sacred drugstore in the third guest room? Tell me. Quench my burning curiosity, damn it." I realized I was fingering the gun, and tried to reclaim the self-control I prided myself on so rarely losing.

It was Felix who broke the silence that followed my tirade.

"Tommy, you're getting into something too heavy even for you. Why not throw your hand in and be done with it." He wrapped the fingers of one hand around Christine's arm. She didn't move it away. That still hurt me.

"Tommy," Christine said, "I do love you. That was no lie. But I love Felix, too. We all grew up together, Tommy. Even when I was years younger, when it was Lorna and Felix and you, I was always there. I told you I loved you then in a crazy, childish way. I did, Tommy, I really did."

"And now you would like our lives to go on, how? As a ménage à trois? A little love from each of us on a schedule to be worked out in advance? No collisions, if you please. And what about your business—not your career as an artist, your serious business, Christine. Does Felix know about it? Well, does he?"

They exchanged looks. Felix shrugged as if to say that the ball was in her court.

Christine's face flushed with anger. When she began to speak, her voice had a brittle quality I had not heard in it before. It was almost like listening to a look-alike stranger. "Who told you about it in the first place? Little Miss Innocence? That bitch Nanette? She's the one, isn't she? That meddling, prying—"

I interrupted her in mid-flight. "Hold on, Christine, it wasn't Nanette at all. She was totally loyal, if you can still understand the meaning of that word. She told me nothing. Nothing at all. It was Claudine who—"

"Dina! It couldn't have been. She wouldn't—"

"She would and she did. Claudine Gregory somethingovich Valentère."

Instantaneously, Christine was transformed into an alley cat. "She could tell you nothing! She knows nothing! She's a fucking whore from Marseilles. All she's trying to do is horn in. She can smell money and she wants to be a part of the act. She's never earned an honest franc in her life except by rolling around a bed. That piece of shit is being kept by an idiot revenue collector in Angers."

I stared impassively at her. I was suprised how much it hurt to hear her talk so brutishly. I reached into my pocket, still balancing the gun in my lap, and brought out the letter from Rose Crystal. "Let's use this for openers," I said, handing it to her.

Felix evidently had not seen it, and tried to read it over her shoulder. She glanced at the letter and expelled a very deep breath.

The dam had broken. "All right, Tommy, I guess I have to trust you. You've probably guessed most of it anyhow."

I didn't blink an eye. I know precious little, baby, I said to her silently.

Getting up as if moving took more energy than she had, Christine walked over to a small club refrigerator and opened a bottle of Perrier. I waved off an invitation to share it, as did Felix, who was delicately paring his nails with a penknife. When she sat down again and started talking, he dug harder. But never once as she spoke did he glance at her or at me.

No matter what I thought, Chris began, painting had always been her primary passion. "It's the very core of my being," she said, in a low, tremulous voice. "Without it, my life would have no meaning. But you have to understand. To go on painting, I must have total freedom. That means no financial worries." She said they sapped her energies and diluted her creative powers. Oh yes, she added, she knew all about the great artists and composers and writers who had lived close to starvation in garrets and still had produced masterpieces. But that, she said, would not have worked for her. She needed a comfortable environment and no money worries. To live *sans souci*. Without care.

"Felix loaned me the money, Tommy, to buy my house and to fix it up and furnish it. My parents, who don't know what to do with the wealth they've amassed, refused to help me. They told me they would help me only if I agreed to live near them. But not in France, not here in Angers. I understood why they took that position, but it was selfish of them anyhow, and I wouldn't—I couldn't—give in. That's the real reason we haven't been close since then. I wanted terribly to come to France—no, not just France, but this part of France. And so I asked Felix to help me out, and he did."

Christine smiled at Felix. It was lost on his downcast profile; and she seemed to shrink back into her corner of the sofa. I put the Colt back in the pocket of my jacket and moved to a more comfortable club chair on the other side of the coffee table. Having finished his impromptu manicure, Felix got himself a glass of white wine. Rather early in the day, I thought, to start working on grapes.

Christine took hold of herself, sat up straighter. "It took a lot of money to buy my house and then fix it up properly," she said in a businesslike voice. "I suppose I should have set my sights lower, but once I saw it I just knew I'd never be able to settle for anything else. Then came the matter of figuring out how I was going to repay Felix the millions of francs he was giving me—lending, of course."

She threw him a grateful smile, but avoided looking to see if he caught it this time. Then she excused herself for a minute. Felix and I sat staring uncomfortably into space. His time would come, soon enough. My Felix, my chum. When she came back, she sat in the chair between the couch and mine opposite it, where she could look to the right at him and to the left at me.

"As I was saying, I had to find a way to repay Felix. That's where Rose came into the picture. She had a super gallery in Miami and liked my work. She hung a few paintings, and they sold quickly. We worked out a deal so that she became my exclusive gallery in the United States against a minimum guarantee of annual sales, if I delivered to her not less than so many paintings a year. Not too many, but enough to keep me hard at work. She also had the *Pegasus*, darling."

Always trying to play the femme fatale, I said to myself. But it still worked on me. I winced at the loving word, and noticed that she had put lipstick on when she went inside.

"I don't really understand why I'm telling you all this except maybe I want you to understand why I got into the jam I'm in. It's sure going to spoil your day."

I laughed aloud. "My day was quite thoroughly spoiled last night, thank you. Nothing you say is likely to spoil it more." I took off my jacket and placed it, pistol pocket up, on the carpet to my left.

Christine shrugged, as if to say she had wished me only well. "An old friend of mine had an idea how I could make money through Rose. He knew of a second-hand car auction center on the outskirts of Miami, which was up for grabs. He had the idea of using it to sell a little pot and coke now and then by stuffing it under the trunk floors of cars—you know, where the spare tires are tucked away. Just some of the cars. The successful bidders for those cars would be arranged in advance. That's where the yellow cards came in. They furnished the introduction for safe visitors." She picked up one of the cards and fingered it. "My friend told me that if I could use the boat to carry some pot and coke from a source my friend had in Colombia, I would be paid a commission over and above the price to be settled with Rose."

"And," I said, interrupting her, "you knew that Rose would be receptive to the idea because she had dabbled in dope before."

"How did you know that?" she asked.

"I know. Go on."

"We set it up just like that. I began to make a trip every three months with Rose and Harry. The day we met on the boat we were heading back from—well, heading back. The other couple—they were just playing the part of fishing guests." She giggled. "When we took you aboard, they nearly collapsed with terror. I never dreamed you'd smell anything. I guess we were so used to it we never noticed."

"I noticed," I replied grimly. "Their names were Bannock. Fred and Ellen Bannock."

"That's right, Tommy, how clever of you. Anyway, my friend bought the car auction place, I began to pay off my debt, and Rose began to make more money than she ever had."

"Anyway, now Felix is about paid off," she said. "Right, Felix?"

But Felix continued to keep his own counsel, head thrust forward, lips compressed. His hands were busy cleaning his glasses.

She turned back to me, hiding whatever she felt about Felix's refusal to respond. "And once he's paid off, I'll quit the trips and—"

"Live happily ever after. Sure. And your old friend will let you walk away and leave him with empty cars. Just like that." I shook my head in astonishment at her utter naiveté as to the ways of the underworld.

Christine stood up to signal that she was concluding her chapter of True Confessions. "Anyway—" She kept pronouncing the word so that it sounded like "ennaway." It was getting on my nerves. "Anyway, about the party I threw last night— for you, Tom-Tom." She really knew how to hurt.

"The stuff I had there was just a little overflow that my old friend brought over on his way back from Marseilles. He loves bouillabaisse and flies over to enjoy it at the port restaurants there. He says it's the best in the world."

I decided to call the parade to a halt. "Sit down, Christine, and listen to a little dose of truth for a change. Read Rose's letter. It tells it much better than you did. For example. Your friend's nom de plume is Bellerophon. B for Bellerophon. The horseback rider. Remember your Greek mythology? Of course you do. And Bellerophon, your old friend, isn't eating bouil-labaisse in Marseille, he's slouched over there on the couch, occasionally sipping white wine."

I pointed my index finger into Felix's face. "Right, dear boy? Right, Bellerophon?"

Christine collapsed into the chair, her lovely features contorted by fear as she turned desperately to Felix. He looked at her with undisguised disgust. "That tears it, Chris. There goes a million dollar business." And then, as though reminding himself. "Never trust a woman." As he made that profound observation, he placed the empty wine glass on the table in front of him, and stood up.

I pushed him down again. "It's your turn now, old buddy. You're the main attraction, you know. Christine may have

blown the whistle on your South American triangle, but as
Captain Henry used to say—you remember 'Show Boat,' don't
you?—'stick around folks, it's only the beginning.' "

I turned back to Christine, who was sitting hunched in her
lime housecoat, feet together, hands limp in her lap. The red
yarn had come untied and her hair was hanging loosely around
her shoulders. Like the rest of her, it seemed suddenly to have
lost all luster.

"Now let's talk about Lorna. Do you remember her,
Christine? You mustn't forget your sister. Tell me, you
don't really think you heard the true story about that from
Felix, do you?"

She looked at me through bleary eyes. "Tommy, show a
little compassion. Felix has told me exactly how it happened,
just the same as it came out in court. I can't handle any more
pain. Not today. Please."

"You seem to be handling yourself pretty well these days,
from all I can see. Painting, pot and coke parties, and at least
two bed companions on an alternate-week basis."

Christine shook her head but said nothing. Maybe for this
one moment she was wringing her hands and screwing up her
face because I had reminded her of the loss of her sister rather
than over the threatened loss of a thriving drug business. Or
maybe, I thought, because she understood that it lay in my
hands to blow the whistle on them both and see them both
deposited in jail for a good long stay.

"Now it's my turn to spoil some lives. You two have done
such a thorough job on mine." I listened to my own voice as
though it had been prerecorded.

Standing, I faced Felix and took on his cross-examination.

56

"Let's start at the beginning, Felix, so Christine can enjoy the full flavor of your story. Did Lorna know that you and Christine were lovers?"

"I doubt it, but I don't think it would have mattered to her." He spoke, even now, in an offhand way that would have persuaded any casual eavesdropper that he hadn't a worry in the world.

"Why not?" I asked him coldly.

"Our marriage was heading down a dead-end street. We lived like a couple of strangers sharing an apartment." Felix suddenly got that glassy look in his eyes that signaled a monologue coming on, a kind of verbalizing self-indulgence he had favored even as a boy.

"She floated along with no interests other than gossip and taking care of her body. And clothes. Oh yes, always clothes. Lots of clothes. Closets full of dresses and shoes and sweaters and God knows what else. She took one of the bedrooms and filled it with clothes racks." He got up and began pacing back and forth before the open window. For the first time, I became aware of the sound of the traffic below.

"She was the most selfish, vain person I ever knew. The Lorna you used to know became an altogether different woman. Her sweetness and consideration disappeared. She thought of only one thing: herself."

"And whose fault was that, Felix? You probably gave her damn little attention. What happened to her ambitions? Did you stifle them, too?"

He looked at me as if I were a fool. "The world had to beat a path to her door. She had a manicure twice a week, but the girl had to come to our house. She had pedicures, facials, leg waxing, massages, hair treatments—our house was a stomping ground for the performing body arts. And for what reason? She never showed her body to me, and I'm sure she didn't let anybody else mess it up." He stopped in front of Christine and looked down at her.

"*You* know how she spent money on clothes, even after I refused to pay for them. So tell him."

It all seemed pointless, but I let them play out their little scenario. Christine picked at the ruffs on her robe, and said, "She milked Daddy dry, Tommy. That was another reason I didn't try too hard to get him to lend me money."

"See?" he said, as though Christine's confirmation were all the proof any reasonable man might require. "Anyhow, I don't think she knew about Chris and me, but she wouldn't have interfered even if she had."

So much for that as the missing motive, I thought. I girded myself to plunge into deeper waters.

Felix must have read my mind. He walked over to Christine. "Why don't you go down to the beach and reserve a couple of chairs? Tommy and I have to talk some more, but there's no reason for you to stay." As he spoke to her he stroked the back of her head until I ached.

When he turned back to me, his eyes had a beseeching look. I stopped thinking of my pain, and did something to accelerate his.

"You have it all wrong, Felix. She stays. Christine says she knows the whole story about Lorna. But you know that isn't true, don't you? You know that she hasn't heard the whole story, don't you? Because you knew that if you told her the whole truth she would probably kill you. Wouldn't she? Even Christine, your partner, your lover, would go for her gun, the one I have in my pocket, if she knew the truth. The woman who gave herself to you behind my back the same way her sister did! Your wife's sister, whom you befriended, by lending her money, and then with your benighted sense of generosity arranged for her to repay you by showing her how easy it was to become a drug dealer."

It was the pounding in my head that made me realize I had been screaming at Felix. Through the merciless trip-hammers at work on each of my temples, I managed to reach Tom Attleboro, the old pro, and warn him not to forget Courtroom Lesson Number Five. Remember that real anger destroys reason and renders you vulnerable. Taking a deep breath, I sat down and motioned Felix to the couch between Christine and me. Christine seemed to be shrinking before my eyes, looking smaller and smaller as she squeezed her limbs together in her chair, her blond hair hiding her face. However disinclined she was to serve, Christine was my jury of one. She had to hear this out. Maybe the truth would even set *her* free.

Suddenly she got up and went into the bedroom, rushing as if afraid I would stop her. In a moment, she came back, clutching a small, white stuffed bear. It was very old; one glass eye was gone and both ears were badly chewed. The toy creature had clearly suffered through a frightful childhood, but had survived. Clutching the bear to her chest, she folded herself up again in her chair.

For the slightest moment I wanted to reach over and comfort her, but the impulse passed quickly as I recalled the night before. I moved my chair a foot further away from hers and went back to work. "You told the Sheriff's Office after you were picked up at Round Key by Professor Melville that your engine came loose near Marker 13 and then you drifted out into the Gulf. Isn't that right?"

"Not right. It's a fact. It did."

"Wrong. You picked the wrong number, from an obsolete map. Did you tell Christine, when you were relating the trial events to her, that Ben Abbott and I made a test run through the channel?"

Christine's eyes were locked on Felix, who, feeling their fix, turned slightly to his right, legs crossed, as though to allow me to take a quarter-face photograph. He did not answer my question, gazing instead over my head seemingly at something outside the window behind me.

"Did you tell her that even without a northeast wind blowing in our faces we found it impossible to *drift* out into the Gulf? And just as impossible to *drift* one mile northeast against the current to the place the boat was found? Well, did you tell her that or not?"

Felix refused to look at me and shrugged Christine's hand off his arm as she sought a response from him too. I turned to her.

"You and your parents left court the day the boat was inspected by the jurors. You also missed the testimony of

Dr. Scott the same day. Did Felix bring you up to date that evening in bed? Did he tell you what the doctor found?"

She shook her head as she looked at Felix.

"You missed summations, too. Why? Afraid to hear some things that might destroy your image of Bellerophon? You weren't even there when the verdict came in, were you?"

"Yes I was!" she replied with weak defiance. "I came back in right after the jury went out, and stayed with Mother and Daddy."

"Maybe so, maybe so. But let's get back to Lorna. Let me fill you in on the pathologist's findings."

Christine raised a hand, trying to stop me. "Don't. Please!"

I ignored her plea, pushing her hand back into her lap. "Did your business partner and lover tell you that the boat contained a broken fingernail with red polish and a human wrist bone? Did he?"

Again she shook her head.

"Did he tell you that there were bloodstains in the boat and that they tested positive as human blood?"

Her shoulders shook as her crying racked her body.

"Well what in hell *did* he tell you anyway? Or didn't you want to hear anything?"

Christine leaned forward. She looked as though she was about to become sick. "Felix," she said in a soft, pleading voice. "What is happening here? Felix, look at me, please." She might as well have been begging a stone idol to talk.

So I responded to her plea, my tone cold, my words measured.

"Felix did not tell you the truth, Christine. He didn't tell me the whole truth either. But you're going to hear it now. I want to burrow into your brain. I want it to fester there. Your lover is not only your partner in drug dealing, he's also a killer, my dear. A wife killer. Your sister's killer. You may not have liked her too much—after all you betrayed your loyalty to her, too—but don't you ever forget, *she was your sister.*"

She tried to cover her ears, but I grabbed her wrists and pulled her hands away and placed them in her lap again.

"I'm going to tell you how Felix stole her life from her, just as he stole her love from me, and now has stolen you from me as well." I leaned over the glass table until our faces were only inches apart. And I told her what she did not want to know, watching the artificial, indulgent world in which she lived crumble before her eyes.

"Somewhere between the dock of the Seaboard Motel at Everglades City and the open waters of the Gulf, Felix hit Lorna over the head. He may have used the small shovel. He probably used the ax. He must have had to hit her many times because her blood splattered in the boat. You can take it to be an absolute fact that the bloodstains in the boat were from her head and body. Your sister's blood, carrying her life away in its flow. Think about that."

I stopped for a moment to let that image make its mark, so it would be etched in her mind forever.

"Then he drove the boat into one of the hundreds of bylanes that branch out from the main channel. He may have dragged it some distance because the water becomes very shallow outside the markers. And somewhere in that slimy, stinking swamp sand he dug a trench, and dragged your sister's body from the boat and dropped her in that trench like garbage. Bloody refuse. That's when his shirt became covered with her blood. I'll tell you about his clothes in a minute."

Christine had turned as white as the couch next to which she was sitting. She began to slump precariously. I slapped her face; my fingers left an echo mark on her right cheek. I pushed her head down into her lap until she forced herself up again into a sitting position. Her color had returned, but tears continued to flow down her cheeks.

Then, as my anger and hate rose like phlegm in my throat, thickening my speech, I continued.

"He may have used the ax to cut off her limbs so that she could fit in his hand-dug grave, until the crabs could do the rest of the job. Quickly. Real quickly. Think about *that!* I'll let you ask Felix about it later. Eh? Your lover, your partner. Think about it. Anyway, then he got the boat back into the channel—probably having buried the ax near Lorna's grave—and managed to get it into the open waters of the Gulf. Not easy to do because a sand bar blocked most of the gateway when easterly winds drove the channel water back. And then, as the weather worsened, he headed north and west to a small land mass. A boat captain—you remember Captain Turner, don't you, the skipper of the fishing boat?"

Slowly Christine nodded her head, the tears still streaming down her cheeks.

"Captain Turner saw Felix motoring in that direction. Alone. There was no one else in the boat, she said. She told the truth, of course, even though I succeeded in shaking her story up a bit with a clever cross-examination it was hard to be proud of.

"After that Felix somehow pried the outboard engine plate loose from the backboard of the boat. Maybe he used the shovel, maybe he kept the ax to use as a chisel or lever. But one way or the other, you can be sure he got the engine loose by unscrewing the plate from the backboard. He probably dropped it into the Gulf, and then paddled the rest of the way to the islet and let the oar float away. Or maybe he buried it. After all, he was surrounded by sand. And then he pulled the boat up and left it there. With the fingernail and the wrist bone and the bloodstains."

The sun began to slant into the room, catching Christine in the eyes. I adjusted the blinds to keep us in semidarkness. Light from outside wasn't the kind needed.

"Then Felix swam or floated to Round Key. He probably tied his sneakers around his neck. He was smart enough by then to realize that shells and debris littered all the keys, as they had on the isle where he left the boat. When he reached Round Key, he put on his shoes and walked inland. That's why he had no scratches on his feet, which seemed so surprising to the Melvilles, and rightly so. He slept that night wrapped in a tarpaulin that he lucked into, and early in the morning he took off his shirt and pants and shoes, and he buried them in the sand. Ben found them under the tarpaulin. Did he tell you about that? Then he waved for help. Pitiful, desperate, bereaved Felix. His wife, the darling of his life, lying below the waters, drowned in the Gulf, never to be seen again. That's what he told the sheriff. And me. Did he tell you how he looked back at her as he swam away for help? How the last thing he saw were her eyes? Only twelve hours before he first told those lies, he had been squeezing her mutilated corpse into green slime and crab infested sand."

I was nearly through. My throat felt hot and raw, but I didn't want to stop. It was like lancing a boil for me to get the whole poisonous story out in the open, late as it was. Too late for justice to take its course. In a court of law. Nobody, not even

Felix, could stand trial twice for the same crime.

"I'll be right back," I said, and went into the bedroom. The bed linens had been adjusted decorously, as if the two of them expected me to do an inspection. I found what I wanted in the closet. I took out Felix's robe and headed back to the sitting room. As I did so, my eye caught something glittering on the top of the glass-covered dresser. I found some keys, a man's wristwatch and a pendant strung on a thin gold chain. Picking up the pendant, I had a funny feeling it was familiar, that I'd seen another one just like it recently. But where the hell had it been?

And then it came to me. The same gold figurine had nestled each day of the trial between the breasts of the dark-skinned woman who had sat with her husband directly behind the Wards. The woman whose husband had skinned me with his eyes every time I looked at her.

With no feelings of guilt or shame, I decided to do a quick search of her bureau drawers. And there, nestled in her undergarments, was the twin brother to the Colt lying in my jacket in the other room. I left it there untouched.

When I returned to the sitting room, I dropped the robe on the floor next to Christine and I spread out the gold pendant and chain on the coffee table. The two of them gazed at it, Felix with disdain, Christine with growing horror as she realized what it told me.

"Well, we dug under the tarpaulin, Christine, and what do you suppose Ben and I found? Did Felix tell you that we found his bloodstained shirt, and his slacks? And his shoes? We found something else that puzzled us at the time. Inside the tongue of one of the sneakers was a strange monogram, a kind of symbol. We showed it to Felix, and he told us he was as puzzled over it as we were. He also told us that the clothes were not his, that he had taken his off in the boat before Lorna and he jumped off the unsinkable boat to swim to safety. Lorna, scared stiff of deep water, a non-swimmer, jumped in bravely—*he* said—clinging only to a skimpy flotation cushion!"

I picked up the robe and folded it carefully, placing the monogram up.

"Would you like me to describe the symbol we found on the shoes? The shoes that Ben and I dug up out of the sand on that natural excrescence called Round Key, where Felix had struggled to safety. *He* says. The shoes in the sand under the tarpaulin buried with a bloodstained white shirt and white slacks. Well, I don't have to describe that symbol. Here it is on Felix's robe. And—" I dangled the pendant on the chain before them—"here it is again, expressed imaginatively and so beautifully. It must have cost a pretty penny to have a bunch of these made up. Eh, Felix?"

It was the carved figure of Pegasus, the winged horse, its forelegs gracefully sweeping back as though the mythical creature were in flight through the skies. And on its back sat heroic Bellerophon, one of the master race of Greek mythology, urging the steed to seek out the monster Chimera so he could destroy it. Beta on Pi.

Pointing to Felix but looking at Christine, I no longer even tried to keep the bitterness out of my voice.

"Your old friend who had the brilliant idea how to raise money so you could repay Felix. The dear friend who bought the Miami car auction lot and introduced you to the drug game, is Felix, of course. Your Bellerophon, who knows how to bridle you. And ride you."

I stopped. There was no point in saying more. I stood over Christine, a whimpering mass huddled in the chair, clutching a tattered white fur toy animal, her hair hanging like a limp curtain around her face.

Felix slowly rose and walked around the table. For a moment, he only looked up at me, his eyes blazing. Then he punched me in the jaw. I did not return the blow, which had me reeling back more from having been caught off balance than from being hurt. His face was mottled, and a curious tic had developed in his left eyelid that made it twitch like a heartbeat.

Finally, through curled lips and clenched teeth, he told us both. "I killed her. Yes, I killed her. Do you want to know why? Do you really have to have the reason? I killed her because she found out about Chris and me. Not about our affair, you stupid bastard. She found out about the car exchange. I don't know how, but I think it was Maria, Manuel's bitch wife, who had some idiotic idea that if she could break up my marriage, I might run away with her! They sat in the courtroom, by the way, every God damn day. They pretended to be worried about me, but they didn't fool me for one minute. They were worrying about themselves."

Then, as quickly as he had flown into a rage, Felix became still again. He tried to straighten out my shirt, which was pulled askew, but I brushed his hands away and took two steps back from him, not because I was frightened, but because I was repelled by his touch. My thralldom to Felix was over.

Felix continued: "Lorna came to me a week before we left on the trip. She marched into my office, past my secretary, and announced that unless I closed the Auto Center immediately, she would tell her Daddy and turn me in to the police. How about that for a loyal and faithful wife!"

"And you such a loyal and faithful husband," I said stonily.

He went on as if I had not even spoken. "She had sucked me as dry as an empty lobster claw with her buying and her buying. And the one business that gave me all the money I'd ever need to pay her damn bills she wanted to stop!"

I studied him in total amazement as he spoke. He showed no awareness that he was discussing a vicious, criminal act as though it had been a normal undertaking. He evidently had lost the ability to make any moral distinctions. He actually blamed Lorna for her own death.

"I told her that she'd have to do it over my dead body!"

"No, Felix," I said quietly, "over *her* dead body."

Again he paid no attention to my words. "But I lost that battle as I lost all the others I had with her." He sighed. "The threat was too real to risk," he went on, blandly. "I finally told her that I would do what she wished, I would sell the Center to Manuel. Even that she wouldn't accept. She was dead set against my taking a single penny more out of the business or for the business. So I told her that when Manuel came back—he and Chris were on a trip aboard the *Pegasus*—I'd just give him the keys and walk away. Well, when I told her that, she beamed. It was like my mother had won again. She always knew what I liked, what was best for me. I almost expected Lorna to run into the kitchen and bring me a cookie as a reward."

He sat down on the couch, a faraway look in his eyes. With evident effort, he focused them on me and sighed. "Tommy, Tommy," he said, shaking his head. "I flew over here the day the trial ended. I couldn't face anybody at that time. Least of all, you," he added softly, looking straight into my face. "I decided to take a few weeks off, to relax here in Nice. The rest you know."

If he expected my understanding, he was wrong. I would never really fathom him. And he was far beyond my forgiving him. I took the pistol from my jacket and stormed over to the couch and stood over him while he sat quietly, studying his hands, palms up. I tried to keep my voice even, but the rage within me exploded.

"You're trash, Felix. You're worse than that; you're an evil force. You have no loyalty to a single soul, and have brought grief to everyone who touched your life. And you will never change. You can't.

"Maybe this has opened Christine's eyes. She may have been able to live with your drug dealings, but I doubt that she can accept your killing Lorna. I hope she sees you now as I do: not a Bellerophon crossing the heavens on Pegasus, but a puny, crawling creature. A cipher. A nothing."

I waved the gun in front of his face, and he looked at me, terror in his eyes. "I'd like to kill you . . . but I can't. You're not worth it to me."

I pocketed the gun and turned away. It sickened me to realize that even if he shouted his guilt from the rooftops, he was immune from prosecution. And Felix knew that. He was untouchable.

But not for his drug racket. Nor was Christine unaccountable for her involvement. There, their lives were in my hands. All I had to do was drop a word at the French Sureté about Christine, or at the Federal Bureau of Investigaton or the Drug Enforcement Agency about Felix, and both of them would be gray before they breathed free air again.

I told them both that I wanted some time to think over what they had told me, and to decide whether I would turn them in for their drug trafficking. I told them that I would meet Felix on the beach at seven o'clock sharp that evening, a short distance west of the hotel, and that he had better be there, or else. I told Christine I wanted her to wait in her suite, that I would "look in on her" after I had seen Felix. I felt like the Jehovah of the Old Testament, full of power and wrath and vengefulness in the face of wrongdoing.

I put on my jacket and returned to my gilded cage, where I sat at the window all day as shining ribbons of cars passed below my unseeing eyes.

Betrayed in friendship, befooled in love.

I thought about Felix. And Lorna. And Christine. Once in a while I even thought about myself.

He looked back on the years that were gone, never to return; on experiences that had ravaged his feelings and left him anguished and vexed in spirit. He saw himself victimized by false friendships, betrayed by misplaced loyalties, and demeaned by counterfeit love. He was brimming with suffering and self-pity and anger.

His mind remorselessly blocked out recollections of the goodness and joys and successes that were also a part of the fabric of his life, forcing him to dwell on his disillusionments and defeats.

He fell asleep in the chair next to the window above the ribbons of cars and beyond the sounds of the crowds of pleasure seekers on the promenade below.

When he awakened, he saw a figure carrying a beach chair advancing across the sand toward the edge of the sea. He focused his attention on that figure.

57

An old-fashioned biplane droned noisily across the darkening sky toward the east, towing a banner which advertised in red and orange a new casino in nearby Monte Carlo. The Hotel Negresco, its gilt Byzantine dome shining like a beacon in the sun's slanting rays, faced the immaculate lines of the Promenade des Anglais with its endless glistening metal ribbons of Mercedes and Rolls-Royces.

On the deserted sands beyond, a figure in a beach chair stared at the darkening Mediterranean, watching the sun make a path across the sea.

A figure dressed in a white hooded robe descended the wooden plank steps from the street level. As it reached the beach, a mongrel lying at the foot of the chair twisted its head and observed the hooded figure approach the chair from the back. Only its sharp ears, pricked up to attention, heard the slippers whispering across the sand. The dog sat up and growled deep in its throat, but the occupant of the chair was lost in thought.

The folds of the garment parted and an arm, hand clutching a pistol, stretched out on a line with the center of the body silhouetted against the back of the beach chair. One shot was fired as the dog barked. Only one was needed.

The mongrel slunk away, belly close to the ground. The robed figure, sweeping up the hem of the garment from the ground in one hand, quickly climbed back to the street.

A distant church bell slowly tolled the passing of the day.

Epilogue

Milton once wrote that the mind can make a heaven of hell and a hell of heaven. He had it wrong. There is no heaven.

The door to my darkened room opened, and someone switched on the lights. I had been sitting—it seemed like hours—next to the window looking down at the quiet sea and the passing cars. I wondered for a fleeting moment whether I had left the key in the lock outside the door. And then I saw a bellhop, and behind him Christine. A man with a thin mustache pushed the bellhop aside and walked into the room. Behind him came Christine and two uniformed gendarmes, each holding one of her arms. Her face was tearstained and deathly white.

I wanted to introduce all of them to my lifelong friend, the little man with the big, shiny bald head, who, having seen what I had seen, was once again perched on my shoulder, and was telling me that life is only a short vacation from death. But I decided to stay silent.

The man with the thin mustache walked over to me and flashed a gold badge in my face, and then spoke a few short sentences to me in French which I could not understand. But I knew. And I knew that Christine was aware that I knew.

The gendarmes allowed Christine to walk over to me. In spite of everything, I wanted to reach out and comfort her. She steadied herself on the back of my chair, her golden hair falling around her face and over her white robe. I stood up and put my arms around her and drew her body against mine so tightly that I could feel her heart beating.

"I'm so sorry, darling. I'm sorry for you and for my parents, and most of all for Lorna. I blinded myself, refused to see him as he really was. Until last night. And then this morning, when he said those things, what he had done, I knew what I had to—"

I kissed her to stop her words. Chastely, as though somehow she had passed into a state of grace.

The two gendarmes walked over and gently separated us. When the group reached the door, she stopped and looked back at me. Her lips moved silently. I think she said, "I love you." Then the door closed.

A little later, I walked over to the telephone and asked to be connected with the concierge. I told him to put me in touch with the best damn *avocat* in Nice. Immediately.

The telephone rang fifteen minutes later. I was ready for it. As I picked up the receiver, my little friend, the bald-headed man on my shoulder, said that the end can be the beginning. For once I agreed with him.

405

391